Books by J. D. Evans

MAGES OF THE WHEEL SERIES

Reign & Ruin
Storm & Shield (February 2020)
Siren & Scion (May 2020)
Ice & Ivy (August 2020)

MAGES OF THE WHEEL BOOK TWO

Storm & Shield

J. D. EVANS

Tero
CORSAN REPUBLIC
Corsyra
Marceo
Aklion
EANNEA
Isla Sora
Rieta
Haenna
Tyrus
SUN SEA
Nasiye
MENEI

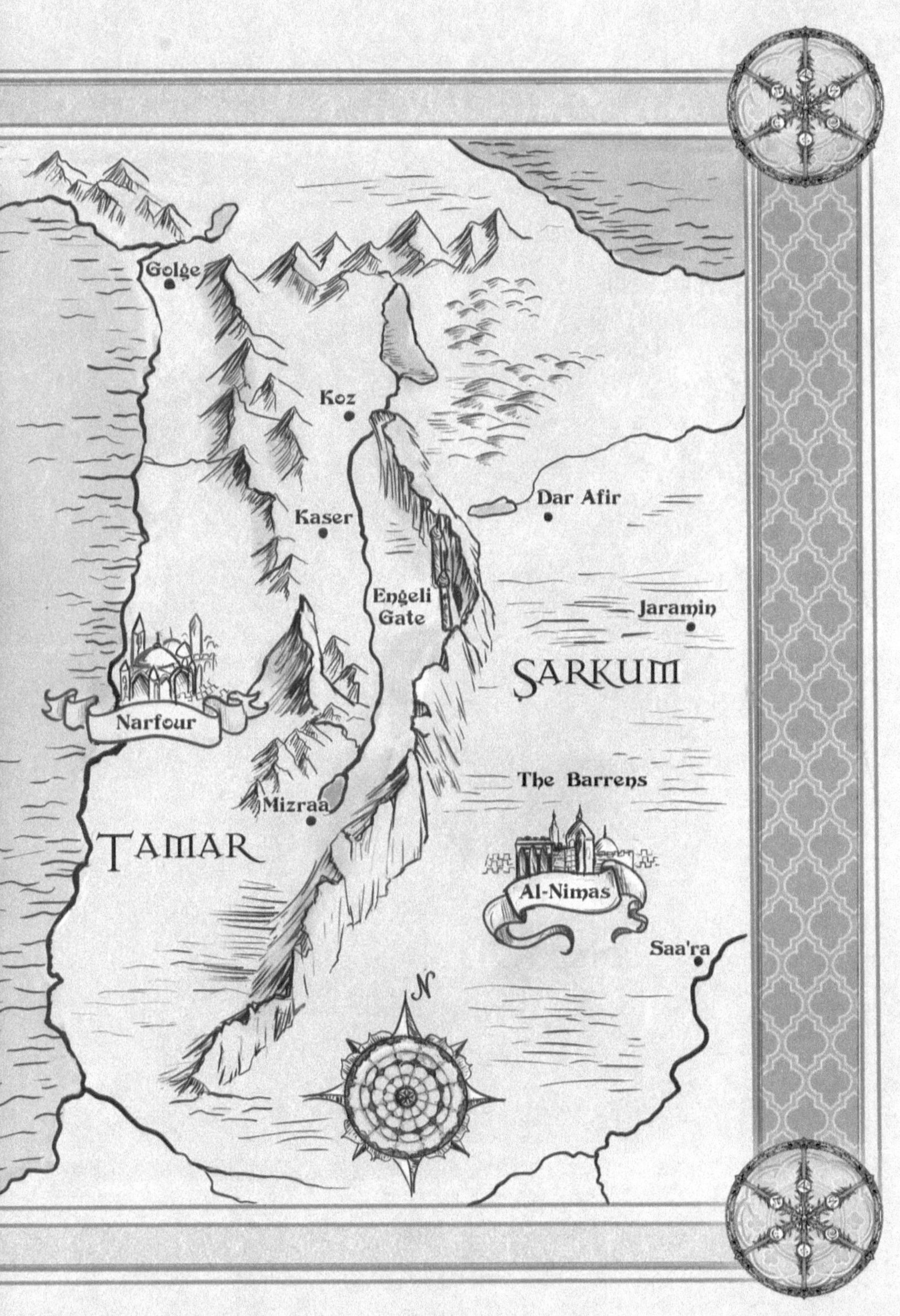

Golge
Koz
Kaser
Engeli Gate
Narfour
Mizraa
TAMAR
Dar Afir
Jaramin
SARKUM
The Barrens
Al-Nimas
Saa'ra
N

Poem of the Wheel
2nd

In harmony and opposition
Blank is forged to blade
Struggle the impression
Within which we are made
Hammer on anvil
Steel into fire
Conflict which does not kill
Shapes soul into spire

One

AYSEL GLANCED TO THE back of the formation where her family's confiscated horses were being led. Her brother Mathei had fallen back nearly a mark ago. He remained in conversation with one of the mounted guards on their perimeter, attempting to talk him into returning one of the horses. Aysel hitched the boy she carried higher up her back and reached to pull his slack arms more tightly over her shoulders. He was half asleep and was of little help bearing his own weight.

The muscles between her shoulder blades had seized and now a steady burn radiated down her back. She and Mat had been carrying the boy, Erkin, since the top of the mountain pass a few days ago, when he'd hit a patch of ice covered in powdery snow and taken a tumble that twisted his ankle badly.

They had been herded out of the snowy mountains and into the muddied city like a gaggle of errant goats. Mounted Tamar guards dressed in sand-colored caftans and salvar, knee-high leather boots, and fur-lined ferace had met them at the Engeli Gate, confiscating weapons and mounts, and had accompanied them for the small turn since, surrounding them and shouting orders if someone drifted even the tiniest bit from the group.

"I can take him, Mistress," Adem, her father's steward, said. The boy was his son, and he'd taken turns carrying him, but the mountains' brutal cold had inflamed Adem's arthritis. He was limping, his shoulders hunched, his hands curled against the pain.

Aysel shook her head. "We are close. See? I saw the palace from up on the slope. This road leads to it, and that's where the guards said we're going." She indicated the palace with a thrust of her chin. It dominated the city, a sentinel of shining domes and towering minarets, perched on cliffs overlooking Narfour and the sea. Aysel might have marveled at its obscene, sprawling size, if her stomach wasn't so empty, her muscles so sore, or her clothes so wet and cold.

"He's almost as big as you," Adem admonished. Aysel started to shrug, but the muscles of her neck cramped and locked. The boy wasn't into his tenth Turn yet, but his feet hung well past her knees. He was a tall boy and she a short woman, so it was to be expected. She was small, not weak.

"Just a bit farther, I think. Will you check in on Mother?" Aysel nodded to indicate where her parents walked, her father's arm hooked through her mother's. Adem frowned but obeyed, weaving his way through the people who separated Aysel from her parents. They were not old, yet, just past their middle Turns, but neither were they accustomed to walking leagues through winter landscape. The journey had been long, slow, and hard on everyone, for all different reasons.

A family trod next to Aysel, a farmer and his wife and their two young daughters. Aysel had given them most of the food she'd managed to snatch the night her father had roused her from a hard sleep and shoved a handful of plain servant's clothes into her arms. They, like the rest of the Sarkum refugees they had joined at the Engeli Gate, had never met before.

They had gravitated together into a swarm, forced into proximity by the single path to their shared destination. Unless they were masquerading, as her family was, most of them appeared to be farmers, likely fleeing the Blight and starvation. The winter crops had been decimated by a strange disease that appeared out of nowhere at the start of late winter. Nothing seemed immune to it, and no one had ever seen anything like it.

If the winter was any indication, the coming spring and summer harvests were in great peril. Already many families had succumbed to starvation. Camps of refugees surrounded Al-Nimas seeking aid. With neighbors turning against neighbors as the country sided with one brother or the other, little relief existed outside of what Al-Nimas' coffers could offer. It wasn't much, since the Mirza was deploying most of his money into outfitting an army to fight his brother. Desperation had driven some brave souls to cross the pass and the Engeli into Tamar, hoping Makram would have influence enough in Tamar to provide them aid.

But starvation was not the threat that drove her family. It was annihilation.

They had fled in the middle of the night, without any warning, when the Mirza's soldiers had tried to burn them alive in their home. Aysel knew they were not the only family from the council of Elders who had been rewarded for their loyalty to the younger prince with swords and fire-wielding mages. She did not know if any others had fled to Tamar, and none were among this group.

"Give him to me," the farmer said, his gaze following Adem's path through the crowd.

Aysel glanced sidelong at him. His entire family was gaunt, and they collapsed in mute exhaustion at the end of every day, sleeping so hard she had struggled to wake them some mornings. Aysel gave him a short nod—though she loathed to, she also didn't wish to insult his pride. He had little left besides pride. Mathei would return from his attempt at diplomacy soon and could take the boy. Even in this, the upheaval from their entire life and an arduous journey, her brother maintained his boundless energy, weathering it all with a ready smile and a quip. Though there had been fewer quips than usual, the only indication he wasn't completely at ease.

"You're noble," the farmer said, as Aysel arranged the boy on his back.

"No," Aysel replied. It wasn't a complete lie. They had been a noble family, her father a high-ranking Elder in the council. But he had believed Makram should be Mirza, and those who had spent a lifetime silent in their belief were now being exposed by looming war and the necessity of choosing sides. Whatever her family had been before the attack, they were something different now.

"You aren't farmers," he persisted, appraising her from head to toe.

"No," Aysel agreed. They would never pass for farmers.

Mathei's return saved her from more questions.

"Here now, I think it's about time I took a turn," he said, giving the man no chance to argue as he unslung the boy from his back.

"I'm a'right," the man said. Mathei gave his frail shoulder a rough pat.

"Of course you are. But I'd rather carry the boy than you so let's save your strength, shall we? Up you go, Erkin." The boy roused at Mathei's voice and slung his arms around his neck.

"Are we almost there?" Erkin asked.

"We should be," Mathei said.

Aysel assessed the cobbled street they'd been guided onto, into the shadow of buildings to either side. Residents stopped to watch the passing of the herd of refugees, women on balconies pausing as they hung laundry in the break between spells of drizzling rain, errand girls with baskets atop their heads stopping mid-stride to stare, stall vendors ambling to their neighbors' stalls to whisper and point. A group of men, sitting in a circle around a nargile and nursing cups of tea, stared as the refugees shuffled past.

They differed little from the people of her home city of Al-Nimas. If it weren't for the changed landscape and much brighter-colored clothing she would hardly have noticed the change. Most faces lacked the touch of the Odokan plainsmen in their shape, but Tamar was more a melting pot than Sarkum had ever been.

Aysel's homeland of Sarkum was mountainous in the east but flatland around Al-Nimas and the Barrens, where she had grown up. Tamar was the opposite, a north-south-running belt of valley sandwiched between the Engeli and the mountains of the Kalspire that butted up against the coast. The whole of Narfour was built along the slope of the mountains that flowed to the sea.

The buildings here were tall, to take advantage of breezes that swept up from the water. The weather in the city was mild, for deep winter, a benefit of its proximity to the warm coast. Even some flowers bloomed, vines trailing from the balconies they passed beneath. It was a nice change from the bitter wind and whipping snow that had slowed them at the pass. The street they traveled along was wide, and the horses' hooves clopped loudly on the cobbled stones. It also angled upward and north, toward the shimmering white palace she had seen from the higher vantage point up the mountain.

Aysel rolled her shoulders to unlock strained muscles. Even if they were destined for a refugee camp, it would be a welcome respite from the endless walking. It would not be all lounging about in a freezing hide tent in a muddy camp though. They had been followed from Sarkum, and while the Tamar guardsmen had not seemed to notice, Aysel and her family had. She could not fault the guards for their lack of awareness—they were focused on their jobs, the tasks they'd been assigned. There were not so many guards that it was an easy thing to keep two score of starving, frightened, and displaced people together and moving in the same direction.

Aysel had been the first to notice. There weren't many, perhaps three. Four at most. Their horses had startled in the night, when the camp was settled and the Tamar guards dismounted. They were an escort, not expecting an attack on their own soil. They were not listening for anything outside their charges. But Aysel was. Mathei was. And their mother and father. They were trained to listen.

Her father, Thoman, had been a spy for the Elder Rahal before his death when Aysel was five. An assassin trained at the knee of the current blademaster since he was a boy, Thoman had trained his children to do the same, though their allegiance had never lain with the Mirza, but his younger brother and Thoman's successor as Agassi—Makram, who now resided in Narfour.

After the first time she'd detected their followers, Aysel and her family had kept to the middle of the group and slept in shifts, with her and Mathei taking the longest because their youth and relative fitness could carry them farther than their parents.

As the hill steepened the street became narrower, and onlookers gathered as news of the refugees' arrival moved through the city. Whispers shifted through the group, and the guards at their perimeter altered positions, forcing everyone closer together. Aysel had to time her steps to Mathei's and the farmer next to her or risk tripping and being trampled by a score of shuffling feet.

Pushed closer together, she could make out the expressions of those around her, all travel-weary and ragged, their faces downcast and gazes turned from the sometimes hostile stares and shouts directed at them as they passed. They were afraid, but that seemed perfectly sensible to Aysel. She wasn't afraid, exactly, but she was aware that starving refugees from Sarkum were unlikely to be welcomed into the land of their enemy with open arms. Even though Makram had managed to negotiate a tenuous alliance.

"I can see the palace." Erkin pointed, his dark eyes round and his mouth gaping a bit. Mathei hitched him higher on his back. If Erkin was impressed, a steward's child who had spent as much time in the palace in Al-Nimas as he had at their estate, then the Tamar palace must be grand indeed. Aysel was far too short to see over the heads of those around her. If things had been a bit less grim, she might have taken her turn on Mathei's shoulders to catch a glimpse. As it was, she would not be at all surprised if a guard took advantage of her convenient new height to lop off her head. They had not been brutish or abusive, which had impressed her and spoke a great deal to their discipline, but they had also made no secret of the fact they would rather have left the group of them to freeze in the mountains than guide them all the way from the Engeli.

They emerged from between the buildings, and the cobbled road dropped off sharply to the west side, granting Aysel an open view all the way to the sea. The hill a tapestry of estates and houses, markets and streets, and the steel-grey sea beyond was made choppy by a winter wind that cut straight at them through the open space. Pale gulls circled in opposing loops overhead, their shrill, repetitious cries like laughter or ridicule.

The guards pushed the refugees up the hill and toward the great stone wall that surrounded the palace. The hill was brutally steep, and people stumbled and staggered with weariness. Someone bumped Aysel from behind, knocking her into Mathei, who bumped her again to steady her. The farmer reached out to grip her arm until she had her pace again, and she nodded to him in thanks. They trod through an arched gate flanked by looming, pointed towers. The large cobbles turned to small gravel, pinching at the bottoms of Aysel's feet through shoes worn perilously thin by travel they were not made for.

They were not allowed to spread out once they had arrived in the sprawling, pristine courtyard, but were driven to the right, toward what looked like the entrance to a stable.

"Do they mean to imprison us?" the farmer's wife asked Aysel, clutching her daughters to either side of her. Aysel did not want to tell the woman it was more sensible for the guards to execute them all than deal with the expense and risk of housing them.

"Doubtful. They wouldn't have troubled themselves and spent the manpower to bring us here," Aysel said, as the guards dismounted to usher them through the courtyard toward the low-built, sprawling stable complex. "I imagine they're reporting in and deciding how to sort us into the camp."

Her words seemed to soothe the woman somewhat, and she turned her attention to her daughters, who had begun to ask questions.

They emerged from a series of arches into an arena on the eastern side of the palace grounds. The arena floor was sand, a sprawling oval surrounded by empty stone bleachers and domed with a gloomy grey sky. What sports did they enjoy in Tamar that necessitated an arena of such vast size?

"Maybe they could be troubled to spare medical supplies." Mathei hitched Erkin up higher on his back.

Aysel kept her attention on the guards as they grouped together and picked four of their number to guard the only two exits to the arena. The rest left the way they had come in, carrying the sacks of items they had confiscated at the Engeli Gate.

The refugees began to chatter and spread apart, breaking into smaller groups. Most collapsed to the sand, grateful for ground not wet with mud and snow to rest upon. Mathei went about settling Erkin into the sand, and Adem and their parents joined them. Adem sat next to Erkin and removed his son's shoe before shoving his salvar up to take a look at his ankle. The joint was swollen, with a dark crescent of bruising below the bone.

"What have you seen?" Thoman asked Aysel, softly, doing a fine job of appearing as if he were not speaking at all, just standing idle. His sharp gaze was directed at the entrance, and she saw him occasionally sweep it over the high wall that surrounded them.

"Two paced us through that small market at the base of the hill," Aysel murmured. Mathei moved to stand on their father's other side.

"A rider on the trail above the eastern edge of the city," Mathei reported, reaching behind his head to dig his fingers against his back, the same muscles that had troubled Aysel after carrying Erkin.

They had silently agreed to split their focus when they had noted the followers. Mathei had taken the rider on the hill, she the two who managed to skirt the market at just the right distance that she could not take note of anything useful to identify them later. The pressure of the daggers she kept strapped to her wrists was comforting to her as she thought about the men she'd seen, but she had to find them to kill them. If that was necessary.

She wanted her family safe. If the Narfour authorities could handle it, that was fine. If not…Aysel rolled her head from side to side. Assassin she was not; but killing was not out of the question if all other avenues failed her. First she needed more than fleeting glimpses and paranoia. She'd feel better about everything if the guards hadn't stripped her of her swords when they took control of the refugees. Mathei was missing his sword as well.

"That's the commander," Thoman announced in a low voice. Aysel and Mathei followed their father's gaze to the arched entrance from the palace courtyard to the arena. The remaining four guards now gathered in a half circle around a new man. Aysel had become familiar with the dozen men who had been present for the two small turns of travel from the wall, though she hadn't worked out all their names. There hadn't been much conversation. This new guard was dressed immaculately, his clothes perfectly in order and unadorned with the mud and stains of winter travel that the rest of them wore. Tall and broad-shouldered, he wore unannounced authority, the kind that made even strangers fall easily under his command.

"See the gold braids at his shoulders?" Thoman said, though he did not point. He was dressed in the same sand-colored attire as the other men, but as her father had stated, three gold braids were sewn between the collar of his caftan and his sleeves. "Be on guard," he cautioned, then strode toward the group.

"That one's a damn sight easier to look at than his subordinates," Mathei said casually. Aysel took her attention from her father as he crossed the sand toward the guards and looked to the commander once more. His tawny hair was shorn short and his face clean-shaven. He was all squared jaw and wide cheekbones, as arresting to look at as a mountain vista.

"Fourth House," Aysel warned her brother. She could feel the weight of his earth magic despite the distance that separated them. It likely had a great deal to do with the sand that connected them, channeling it, but still suggested he was powerful. Possibly even a Sival.

"Your problem, not mine," Mathei teased. "I saw him first."

"How do you know you're his type?" Aysel huffed.

"I'm certainly more his type than a litter runt." Her brother was only half serious, and the banter helped them maintain a facade of unimportance while they watched their father and readied to move to his aid if it was required. Thoman had walked free of the rest of the refugees by then, and the guards had taken note and turned to face him, hands to the swords belted at their hips.

He held his hands open in front of him and slowed his pace. Aysel kept her attention on the guard commander as he assessed her father, pondered what he saw, then stepped between his men. Aysel tensed, leaning forward to run to him if he needed her.

"How may I be of service?" the man asked, his voice carrying in the stadium. It was not the reaction she had expected, but it eased some of her tension and she relaxed her weight from the balls of her feet into her heels.

"Deliciously serious." Mathei grinned when she shot him a look of censure.

"My name is Thoman Attiyeh. I seek an audience with Attaraya Agassi."

"Attiyeh Bey," the commander said, hesitating only slightly when assigning the title after giving her father an appraising look that saw a great deal more than Thoman's simple clothes. "I am afraid the prince and Sultana are unable to accept audiences with refugees at this time. He has been visiting the camp as often as he can. Perhaps you can speak with him then."

Aysel glanced to Mathei, a frantic weight pressing in her chest. They did not have days to wait. Whoever pursued them could make an attempt on their lives at any moment, now that they would be stationary. Mathei frowned, folding his arms over his chest.

"I and my family served him in Al-Nimas," Thoman said. "If you would only mention my name to him, I believe he would agree to see me."

The commander regarded her father for another long moment, then said something quietly to one of his men. It was too quiet for Aysel to hear, but the guard he'd addressed scanned the huddled refugees then pointed at her, Mathei, and their mother. Mathei took a quick step sideways, blocking her from view just as the commander's attention turned to them. It was habit. Aysel had been taught to fade back, go unnoticed, be perfectly unremarkable. Beyond being a spy, her survival depended on not standing out in any way. At least it had in Sarkum.

She did not know what Tamar had in store for her, but it would be best to keep to their habits, for now.

"I will pass along your name, Attiyeh Bey," the commander said. They bowed to each other, and her father returned to them.

Aysel watched the guard commander through the gap between her father and Mathei's shoulders as he continued to regard them for a moment that stretched painfully. He turned and strode back toward the courtyard.

"We wait," Thoman said.

Two

THE REFUGEE CAMP HAD been situated just outside the northern part of the city, well past the populated area. It squatted on a jutting cliff that overlooked the ocean and an arm of the city that curved below them and continued on up the shore. The clifftop was relatively flat, though the soil was hard clay and rocky, making it difficult to place tents and drive stakes.

The location was an inspired choice. Fully half the perimeter of the camp was inaccessible as an entrance or exit, meaning the guards only needed a small force to watch the eastern perimeter, where the mountain served to stymie entrance or exit except for paths leading back to the city and up the mountain to a spring that served as water source.

The logistics of it aside, the camp was heartbreaking. One could tell who had been in the camp the longest, both by the fact they occupied well-constructed hide tents on a tidy grid, and the empty-eyed look each of them wore. The later-comers were resigned to lean-tos constructed against the original tents, or scraps of blankets, burlap, and whatever else they could manage stitched together and supported by spindly branches scavenged from the mountainside to the east of the camp.

"I like it," Mathei said, as he and Aysel stood at the edge of the camp, overlooking the sheer drop to the city below and the ocean far in the distance. "You cannot deny it's the best view we've ever had."

Aysel leaned into him, tipping her head against his arm. She did not want to admit to her sadness, afraid she would then forget the important matter. Protecting her family. They did not come all this way to be cut down by some amateur assassin sent by the Mirza. Her family would not share the fate of the others who stood with Makram. She had silently vowed that to them, and herself, while running from Kinus' mages, watching her home burning behind them, like a great torch that lit the night.

"We'll be all right," Aysel said, quietly. Mathei slid his arm around her shoulders and squeezed her.

"Of course. And you will feel much better once you've retrieved our weapons." He grinned toward the ocean and the sun that had just begun to set, its pale colors deepening as it descended from the gloomy late-winter sky.

"Ugh. Why do I have to?" Aysel's whine was feigned. In truth, she would be glad for the task, something to put her mind to besides their misery and the misery of those around them.

"Because you are small and dull and I am tall and dashing. They certainly won't remember you." Mat smiled apologetically. Aysel rolled her eyes. "And handsome. I forgot to say."

While he was being playful with her, it was not entirely untrue. Where Mathei was swarthy and striking, Aysel was plain and forgettable. Aysel and her mother were both small, short, and delicate-boned. Mathei and their father were not exceptionally tall, but a bit more so than average. Thoman was slim, some of his strength waning as he aged and turned his more secretive duties over to his children. Mathei was similarly built, though his strength was surprising for a wiry frame. Aysel was the same in that way. Delicate, but not fragile.

None of these things bothered her. There were many reasons she needed to go unnoticed, and her stature and plainness had only served as aids to that.

"Did you see where they took them?"

"More or less," Mathei said, then released his grip on her and squatted, beginning to draw a diagram in the muddied earth at their feet. She recognized the general outlay of the arena; he added the outer wall of the palace to the extent it mattered to her, the stables, and the guard towers to either side of the Morning Gate. "Here." He pointed to the area where she had seen the guards take the sacks of confiscated goods. Likely the barracks, part of the stable converted to house guards. The sooner she went to retrieve the weapons the less likely the guards would be to notice their absence.

Mathei wiped the mud off on his already dirt-stained salvar, and cocked his head one way then the other as he studied the diagram. Aysel swiped her hand through it and stood. Mathei scuffed the remainder out with his boot.

"I'll go tonight," she said, "but I'm not certain I'll try for them, not until I'm sure of my path back out." She did not care for the idea of leaving her family with one fewer pair of eyes watching for their pursuers, but it couldn't be helped.

"And I will distract *Anne*." Mathei glanced over his shoulder and frowned. Aysel followed his glance where their mother, Dilara, picked her way through the camp toward them. Aysel suppressed a grin. Of the two jobs, she almost preferred to be the one risking prison.

Dilara stopped a few paces from them, eyeing the cliff edge where they stood with a look as though it had caused some personal affront.

"Whatever you're out here plotting will have to wait. They've brought rations, and I want you to eat," she said as if they were still grubby-fingered toddlers clinging to the sides of her brocade. She was dressed as they were, in plain, undyed salvar and thigh-length caftan, a cloth of similar color wrapped around her neck and over her hair. But she stood with her back straight as a sword, her chin tilted up, and the same expectation of obeisance as always.

No one would mistake Dilara for a farm wife. Aysel found a great deal of comfort in that. As long as their mother was not broken, neither would she be.

Dilara had not been born into a life of subterfuge. She was the daughter of a wealthy landowner, a minor noble. Her marriage to Thoman had been arranged. For the first few Turns he had hidden his occupation from her, but she was no empty-headed courtier easily distracted by shiny baubles and the chaos of her new life at court. When she had discerned what Thoman did, the story went that he slept in the barn for a small turn in the deep of winter, until he promised never to keep anything from her again. He had kept his promise, and while Dilara was not trained to it, as her husband and children were, she was sharp and observant enough to be useful in her own right.

"I do so hope it's lentils," Mathei said cheerfully. Dilara frowned at him. The steward, Adem, had possessed the wherewithal in the midst of the chaos of their hasty departure to bring a burlap bag of lentils. They had eaten nothing but since their departure. Aysel admitted inwardly that she wouldn't mind eating straw if it meant something different, but was reminded they were lucky to have even that by the gaunt faces and hungry eyes that surrounded them as they followed Dilara back to their new home.

Adem had managed to bully, cajole, or bargain his soul for one of the proper tents, possibly citing the fact there were two families that would be living in it. Aysel did not care to know what had happened to the previous occupants, who had left signs of their residence. There were empty crates arranged as seats, and a tattered woven rug in the center of the dirt floor. A small firepit just outside the entrance of the tent had ash and half-burnt logs in it when they had arrived, now it held a glowing pile of embers and a ceramic pot situated over them, full of a bubbling substance that emitted the distinctive, earthy aroma of lentils.

Erkin sat on a piece of folded burlap, his ankle wrapped thickly in fragments of torn cloth, tending to the coals with a section of cedar branch. The low voices of her father and Adem carried from inside the tent. She glanced behind her, where the setting sun approached the darkening sea. If the palace here was anything like her homeland's, the guard force would be at its lowest in deep night. She'd tried to sleep a little beforehand, to keep her wits about her. The journey had taken its toll on all of them, though none would admit that to the others. Little sleep and less food had sapped them of energy.

"I'm not that hungry," Mathei said, dishing himself a heaping portion of the lentils. He turned abruptly and left. Aysel suspected he was taking the bowl to the young family with the two daughters, and the farmer who had helped to carry Erkin.

Dilara gave a tired sigh and bent over the little pot, spooning some into a wooden bowl, which she held out to Aysel. Aysel took it and sat in the mud beside Erkin. She was already wet and filthy, more mud on her backside wouldn't hurt.

"Did you eat?" Aysel asked the boy. He shook his head, his chin-length brown hair, muddy and tangled, brushed back and forth over his eyes. Aysel tucked some of it behind his ear. "I know it's tiresome, but you need your energy. Just a little, all right?"

"I could give it away like Master—"

"Just Mathei here," Aysel corrected him. Erkin screwed his face up and nodded. "You can give it away tomorrow, if you like. But tonight, eat some."

Aysel handed him her bowl and took another one from the pile. They were all chipped and cracked, shallow, and roughly hollowed out. She served herself a small portion and watched her mother carry several bowls into the tent. There were no utensils save the serving spoon, so she and Erkin slurped the stewed lentils from the bowls in companionable silence.

Mathei eventually returned, looking sour.

"They made me eat with them." He sat on the far side of the little fire and took Erkin's stick to poke at the coals, sending a rush of sparks into the darkening night.

"The unbelievable gall," Aysel said.

"What is the point of giving them food if they insist on giving it back? I should have eaten it all."

"That would have proven your point," she agreed.

Mathei made a low sound of agreement, clearly out of humor for the moment. All of it wore on him too, he was just better about concealing it. They'd been filthy, wet, and cold for innumerable days, stripped to the bone with exhaustion, and now so far from where they started it was impossible to think about it all at once or be utterly overwhelmed.

Mathei stood. "I'm going to sleep. You too, Erkin, when you've finished." His voice was uncharacteristically gruff, and Erkin noticed as well. They both watched Mathei as he entered the tent, and Erkin looked down at his feet, picking at the thick wrap on his ankle.

"Is he angry?"

"Why?" Aysel asked, taking Erkin's bowl and stacking it with her own. Her stomach complained it was still half empty, but there was little to be done for that.

Erkin shrugged one slim shoulder. "It's so different here, from the estate. His clothes are muddy. I know he likes to be clean."

Aysel smiled and rubbed her hand between Erkin's shoulder blades. "He's all right. Just like you, right?"

He nodded resolutely. They watched the sun fade completely into the water then joined the others in the tent.

SOME TIME LATER, WITH a small amount of restless, cold sleep to ward her, Aysel slipped from her place between Mathei and Erkin on the rug and picked her way carefully to the front of the tent. She stood just inside the door for some time, her eyes closed, listening. Some kind of animal chirped up the mountainside, calling to its compatriots. The low voices of two of the nearest guards were unintelligible, and interrupted occasionally by snoring, and quiet crying.

Aysel opened her eyes. Dilara stood in front of her, her mouth set in a thin line, her dark eyes luminous in the pale moonlight that filtered in through the flap that didn't quite close. Dilara held up a length of threadbare cloth.

Aysel tipped her head, and Dilara moved to stand at her back, where she coaxed Aysel's thick, curly hair out of its tangled braid and gently rebound it, then wrapped the cloth around Aysel's neck and across her head, tucking it into itself. She hugged her arms around Aysel's shoulders from behind and whispered, "If you do not return to us, no power on the Wheel will keep you safe from me."

Aysel smiled grimly and turned to face her, kissing her cheek. "The wind is with me tonight, I think."

Dilara frowned, but said nothing, and Aysel slipped outside.

THREE

HE TEMPTATION TO GO seeking the men she'd seen following them from Sarkum was great, but she could do little with the knives at her wrists. Those were used for distraction, to harry someone, or occasionally pick an easy lock. They were no match for men with full-sized yataghans or bows.

The camp was quiet. Nearby a steady splashing indicated someone relieving themselves. At the far side of camp, occasional flickers of movement identified the guards. There had been eight at the eastern perimeter when they'd entered the camp. The steward had informed her he had seen three returning to the city while he cooked lentils.

Aysel released a thread of power, wrapping it around herself and allowing it to spread, so the air around her shimmered and distorted. *Fade.* She repeated the thought as she slunk through the camp, sticking close to the untidiest of the dwellings, so the visual chaos made her harder to detect.

Her whole life she had hidden her magic. Unable to use it outwardly, she had perfected the use of it on herself, adding to her anonymity and her ability to fade from notice and memory with careful manipulation of the air around her. She could not turn herself invisible, that was impossible. But she could lighten her step, appear to the peripheral glance as a simple rustle of wind, change the air around herself so whoever looked at her did so through rippling air that appeared distorted by heat.

When she neared the edge of camp on the southernmost side, she paused, well hidden in the shadow of a tent and hunkered down in a stack of crates and discarded burlap. A guard strode past her, about a hundred paces away. He was gone from her sight for a count of ten, then reappeared, heading in the opposite direction. He curved around the edge of the camp, across a path worn against the hillside, until he reached the drop-off of the cliff, then turned and headed back. Past him the hill dropped steeply, a gully sandwiched between the rise of the cliff and the carved-out stretch of road, studded with broken rock and scrub. There was nothing large enough to hide her if she made her way past him, and the moon was bright enough through the clouds above to outline her.

Aysel chewed the inside of her bottom lip, contemplating her options. Just as she'd decided on throwing something farther into the camp to try and attract his attention, a man walked out from between the tents and called to the guard. Mathei.

Aysel took the chance he offered. When the guard crossed in front of her and toward Mathei, who stood nearer the cliffs, Aysel darted from her hiding place and for the hillside, grabbing an empty burlap sack from the pile on top of the crates. She could hear Mathei's cheerful voice as he asked the guard something, then there was only the hum of her power as she ran down the hillside, leaping over rocks and brush, grinning.

It was like flying when she used her magic. She was already small and light, but more so as she ran, nearly untouchable, more agile, and far faster. No one had ever caught her when she ran.

When the hill blocked her from view of the camp, Aysel slowed. She continued to pick her way down the hill, within sight of the path to the city but not on it. She rolled the burlap up and tucked it into the cloth twisted around her waist. The going was slow, but better that than be caught by a guard on his way up or down the hill. It took her the better part of a candlemark to reach the edge of Narfour. The northern section of the city seemed dominated by smaller houses than those near the center and the palace. These were the families that kept the city going. Merchants, tradesmen, and day servants.

Aysel wove through alleys and main streets until she found a smaller side street running north to south that she liked. Traveling in alleys was suspicious, traveling on main thoroughfares too bold. Those that worked at night traveled the side streets. There were only a few souls she encountered, a man pulling a cart of refuse, a woman with a satchel full of her master's laundry, and a four-count pack of street urchins who looked far too sinister for their apparent ages. They observed her and deemed her unworthy of pickpocketing, or whatever their game was, and she was glad of it. She had caught sight of only one person who had the look of a city guard, dressed differently than those at the palace, but with the same purposeful gait and watching gaze. She didn't want to draw his attention by schooling a pack of child thieves.

When she judged herself roughly in line with the main street that led up the hill to the palace, Aysel found a side street that ran west, up the slope. The hill was extreme, and her legs were tired from the long days of walking during their exodus. Under normal circumstances she would not have needed to rest, but she was malnourished and spent, and so she stopped twice on the slope and leaned against the nearest wall to catch her breath.

The palace shimmered above her, lit by silver moonlight peeking through the winter clouds, its white plaster and pale sandstone making it appear to gleam. It was at least twice the size of the palace in Al-Nimas, but it was also far older, the seat of the Old Sultanate before the Sundering War. That meant it was better fortified as well.

Aysel had taken note of the evenly spaced guard towers along its perimeter wall, and the alcoves to either side of the Morning Gate where more guards could be stationed. During the day she might have slipped in alongside other traffic, but there was none at this deep period of the night. East of the gate and its towers was a spot where the wall met an outcrop of the mountain, stopped, then took up again several hundred paces later.

That was her best chance.

Aysel finished climbing the hill, the backs of her legs and calves screaming for rest, and crossed the main road that led to the palace. Her climbing was not finished yet. She scrambled, halfway to hands and knees, up the steep, crumbling rock of the hillside until she was roughly at level with the top of the wall, then traversed the mountain face in slow increments. Every few moments she stopped and held her breath, listening and looking for signs of notice.

When she had made it approximately halfway from where she had climbed onto the slope, it became a cliff face, and her trek more perilous. A fall would not kill her from this height, in fact she could protect herself from falls of triple the height she hung now, but it would certainly make her presence known. As well, she was completely exposed as she hugged the rock and made careful progress sideways, toward the break in the wall.

Voices carried from the road, and Aysel stilled, cursing her luck. She was in her most precarious position so far, the toes of her shoes barely caught on a sliver-thin ledge, her fingers gripping one of little more depth. Her arms shook, and she couldn't draw a full breath or push herself too far back and lose her grip.

Boots scuffed on the cobbles below, and a man laughed at something his companion said. Aysel pressed her forehead against the rock, closing her eyes and daring to lend another thread of power to her aversion spell. *Not here. Nothing here.*

Her left calf began to shake, her leg bouncing up and down because her muscles were so tired. A chip of stone broke from beneath her foot and bounced down the rock face and onto the cobbles. Aysel didn't see where it landed, but each time it struck and bounced sounded as loud as thunder to her.

The boots stopped.

"Did someone throw that?" a voice barked up toward her. *Not here. Nothing here.*

Aysel squeezed her eyes more tightly shut, her back crawling with the sensation of being observed, her instincts screaming to whirl around and look. They would not shoot her down. They would not shoot her in the back and make her fall. They would not.

"Hello?"

Aysel let her breath out in a thin stream and drew another. Sweat beaded on her brow, and her forearms cramped, the fine muscles in her palms doing the same, and her clammy fingers began to slip against the stone. She would fall, roll, and run. That was the new plan.

"Come on. I don't want to be late to report," a second voice said. The first made a sound of agreement, then came the tapping of their steps. Only when they had faded did she move.

Aysel blinked the sweat out of her eyes and dared to lift her head. The two men passed through the broad arch of the Morning Gate. She shifted her weight and reached for a larger hand hold, and after a few more adjustments, attained a place on the cliff that was roomy enough for her to catch her breath. She did not linger long, even winter nights did not last forever. The rest of the cliff was more forgiving, allowing her to walk on a thin ledge with only one hand against the rock for balance.

The rock face hit the palace wall abruptly and Aysel crouched down, sitting on the place where the wall ended against the cliff as she surveyed the courtyard below. She lowered herself carefully, the wall was almost five times her height, and landed soundlessly in the gravel courtyard. The rugged stone bulged outward where it pierced the wall, and she crouched in the shadows with her back wedged between the wall and the rock as she watched and listened.

Gravel crunched off to the left, toward the gate, and voices carried in low tones. To the right, where the stables, the arena, and the barracks were, she could hear nothing. There was a spell to amplify hearing, but it was easily detectable and sapped energy at a high rate. Aysel needed all the energy she could muster, because she suspected she would be running when, and if, she retrieved the weapons.

Keeping to a crouch, she shimmied along the outcropping of rock, her back to it, her focus on the courtyard that spread into view as she moved into the open. Several guards lingered just inside the gate, one of them calling up to a comrade in the towers above them. That was a good opportunity to sprint across the remainder of the jutting rock, which she did, taking up another crouch on the far side, where the wall began once again. The stables grew from the outer wall, stretching toward the palace and serving as the wall to the southeast section of the arena. They were entered the same way the refugees had been brought that morning, an archway that led beneath the seats of the stadium and branched off to the stables and the ground-level aisle that circled the entire sandpit.

It was too visible an entrance to use, and Aysel eyed one of the stable's windows, one of three whose wooden panels were not shut tight. It was a risk, she would be banking on the assumption that the stables in Al-Nimas were modeled after these. If they were, then once she had shimmied through the little open square in the plaster-covered wall, she would be in a stall that was open to the interior of the stables. If they were constructed otherwise, she might find herself trapped in a stall. And she could only hope she did not pick one with a particularly unfriendly horse.

At this point in her journey quickness and boldness were the better tactic. It was not unlikely she would be seen, but if someone just glanced at her and she wasn't sneaking, they might look past.

So she waited until those guards she could see were occupied with each other or looking away, and took up a quick stride toward the stable wall. When she reached it, she pretended to have business with the wooden panels that were swung open, while glancing behind her once more. Aysel had to jump to catch the lower edge of the window frame, and hauled herself up, using her feet against the wall to speed herself up. She didn't have time to be careful. She launched herself headfirst through the portal, but kept her grip on the sill, executing a folded roll through the window so she ended up hanging from it on the other side, her back against the wall.

A horse threw its head up, ears flicking toward her, but did not shy or squeal. It had funny-shaped blaze. Instead of a solid stripe of white it was broken into three round dollops of white from its forehead to its nose.

Aysel clucked her tongue at it in hopes of keeping it calm, and let herself drop to the sand of its stall. One ear flipped back, the other remained trained in her direction. Its nostrils flared.

"Steady, friend," Aysel soothed, skirting the edge of the stall farthest from it toward the stable aisle. She was in luck, the stalls were low-walled plaster and open-fronted, gated with lengths of rope. An industrious horse could easily escape, but it would have nowhere to go.

Aysel crept to the rope and peered into the aisle. The stable was dark, filled with the sounds of horses breathing, their occasional stamped hoof or shifting in their sleep. When she neither saw nor heard anyone, she hoisted herself onto the low wall between this stall and the empty one next to it, then used the wooden support beam between them to pull herself into the loft above. She took a moment to orient herself once more.

If she followed the hay loft to the left, she'd reach the main entrance. To the right she suspected she would find the soldiers' entrance to the stables from their barracks. That's what she wanted.

Aysel touched her back, checking to see if the burlap bag was still in place. She tucked it more securely into the fabric at her waist and adjusted the cloth her mother had arranged around her head. She pulled it over her forehead and tucked it up over her mouth and chin. Finally, she checked her knives, shaking her sleeves to make certain they weren't caught on themselves and that she could reach inside to retrieve the only weapons that remained to her.

She walked the length of the hayloft, between the edge and where the hay was shoved back, placing her feet carefully and pausing each time a board creaked. It gave her view to see if anyone entered the stables and freedom from entangling in the hay or kicking it down and disturbing the horses. The loft ended against the far wall, and Aysel crouched there, examining a doorway across the aisle and below her. It stood open, and faint light bled out of it.

There were occasions when she thought having been born a water mage would not have been so bad. To be capable of dousing mage orbs whenever she needed darkness would have been a very handy skill.

A narrow beam ran from the side of the loft where she crouched to the wall above the door. Aysel rose and stepped onto it, crossing the width of the barn then lowering herself so she crouched on the balls of her feet once more and gripped the beam in her hands.

Closing her eyes, she listened, counting a score of her own heartbeats to mark the time. There was not a sound that indicated movement beyond the door below. She sat on the beam, hooking the backs of her knees against it, then let herself fall backwards with enough force that she flipped, landing softly on the sand of the aisle. Perhaps the sand made sense from a maintenance view—easy to clean, good drainage. But from the standpoint of security, it was a sneak's best friend. She slipped to stand beside the door, her back to the wall, and took a quick peek around the frame. A hallway greeted her, empty and lit with a single hovering mage orb. Doors lined either side, six on the left, seven on the right.

Aysel grimaced as she drew back, tipping her head against the wall to think. The odd number of doors on one side indicated something different in at least one room. She guessed it was either the armory or the commander's quarters.

She pulled a knife free of its sheath on her wrist and cut a square of fabric from the length wrapped around her waist. As she considered her options, she laid it on the sand and smoothed it out, then put two fistfuls of sand into it and gathered it closed in her hand. Closing her eyes, she brought back every detail she had noted as they walked through the courtyard upon arrival. They had passed the barracks and the stables. She could remember the long white wall, broken by windows, just like the one she had used to enter the stable. She'd have to wager that each room had one, a way for her to escape. And she was going to take the chance the extra room was an armory. The commander of the palace guard was surely housed in the palace, with an office to conduct business from and accessible to his ruler without trekking through the palace and courtyard to get to him.

Her last educated guess was to assume the armory would be located closest to the exit they used to go to their posts. She had seen them using the far end of the building as entrance and exit, not the stable.

Aysel mentally walked herself through her plan. Down the hall on quiet feet. Open the last door on the right, take the weapons, exit through the window, run like the wind, hide in the city until she could fall in with a group going to the refugee camp or night fell.

Backup plan...she'd make it up as she went.

She took another quick look down the hall. After a deep inhale she turned and strode into the light.

The mage orb pulsed in slow rhythm, casting her shadow in wavering changes as Aysel moved toward, under, and past the light. She picked up her pace, breaking into a quick trot, and stopped outside the last door. The walls were, like the rest she had encountered, brick covered with plaster and painted white, and the doors were paneled wood, with large iron rings fastened as pulls. She hated iron, it never failed to creak and squeal.

Aysel took an extra moment to listen with her ear against the door, just to ensure her guesses had not been completely off course.

She slipped her fingers around the ring and lifted it in a quick, sure movement, as that had proved a better method than slowly torturing them open in the past. The door, perhaps the first time in her life, opened smoothly and quietly on well-oiled hinges. Aysel grinned and stepped into the doorway.

There was a bed on the opposite wall, and on the floor in front of it a pile of weapons. She recognized Mathei's yataghan on top of the pile. Her swords, unfortunately, were clasped in the hands of a man sitting on the bed. He looked up in surprise when Aysel shoved his door open. Her gaze locked with his.

Earth mage. Not the armory. The commander's quarters. Her hand tightened on her cloth-bound bundle of sand.

Aysel cursed and swung.

Four

ASHIR SANK ONTO THE edge of his bed, staring at the pile of confiscated weapons. He reached for the set of swords on top, frowning. They were buckled into sheaths sewn to a harness that he thought was meant to be worn over the shoulders. He turned the mess around in his hands and drew one of the swords. They were yataghans, but in half size. He'd never seen their like and it puzzled him. His men who had returned with the refugees couldn't tell him anything about the people they'd taken weapons from. It was not unusual to carry weapons, but the uniqueness of the set of shorter swords troubled him. They would have been specially forged, and not only would that be expensive, it seemed an elaborate vanity outside a few professions he could think of. None of which gave him peace of mind. He shoved the sword back into its sheath.

He rubbed a hand over his face and when he dropped it his door was open and someone stood silhouetted by the faint light from the hallway. For an instant he thought it was a child, but it was just an exceptionally short adult. Bashir's muscles bunched to stand, but the figure moved, faster than he had ever seen anyone move, and swung at his face. Bashir jerked to block the strike, but something exploded against his temple, and sand showered everywhere, into his eyes and mouth, nose and ears, and he felt the swords ripped from his grasp. He clawed at his face and his attacker slammed their body against his, knocking him backwards onto his bed, snatched something else from the pile of weapons, then dashed for the hallway. He tangled in the pile of weapons the thief had shoved into his path and cursed as he regained his feet and caught himself against the frame of the door.

"On your feet!" Bashir roared to his sleeping men, and the building rumbled with his push of power. He commanded the sand out of his eyes with a thread of magic, as he lunged into the hall. The thief had just made the stable door and paused only long enough to shrug into the harness that held the swords, then darted inside.

Bashir sprinted after. Doors slammed open behind him, but he couldn't afford to take his attention off the fleeing figure. Wheel and spokes the bastard was fast. He had only just made the stable when the thief was nearly to the far end, then turned toward the arena. Bashir smiled grimly. No one could outrun him there.

He barreled down the stable aisle, sending the horses into a frenzy, and charged out the other side, barely able to round into the archway that led into the arena. He vaulted over the low wall that separated the ground-level seats from the pit and landed in a crouch. The thief was halfway across the sand toward the other side. There was nowhere for him to go in that direction, unless he could fly.

Bashir shoved his hands forward through the sand and the earth shattered, shoving up from beneath the sand like a boat running aground, a long fissure racing across the arena. It was lightning fast, the travel from his hand to the thief running from him, but the bastard dodged it. Not only dodged, but launched himself into the air, flipped a complete circle, and landed running on the other side of the quake.

Bashir jumped to his feet, but kept his focus on the ground, and commanded the magic within him to churn, calling to the sand of the arena. *Sink.*

One moment the thief was sprinting, the next the earth swirled open beneath him. He tried to leap but landed on the edge and the sand sucked him in, up to his arms.

"Stay," Bashir ordered as several of his guards caught up to him. He didn't want to have to worry about them on the sand when he was casting. They hovered at the entrance, half-dressed and disoriented.

Bashir drew his sword and stalked across the arena. In his gut, the vortex of his magic bucked, swelling as if being pushed, then broke open like an egg. Sand twisted up from his trap and burst outward, and the thief was free. An air mage, Wheel damn him.

Bashir lunged, swinging his sword. The thief scrambled back through the sand like a crab and was on his feet before Bashir recovered and swung again. This time his sword met steel. One of the short blades.

They held together for a moment that lasted only long enough for Bashir to realize the man he fought only barely reached his chest in height, and to see the tail end of a braid that had fought loose of the head covering. Not only an air mage. A woman.

Bashir faltered, and the woman swung both swords at him, parallel to each other, one at neck level, the other at hip. He managed to parry, and she spun, dropping low and trying to sweep his legs out from under him with a kick, followed by one of her swords. Bashir jumped over her strike and landed with his power in it. The impact of his boots on the sand was amplified by his magic and the earth shuddered, knocking her off-balance. Now was his chance. She was far too slight in comparison to him to win in a contest of strength, and the earth at her feet was his. He grabbed for her.

But instead of recovering from the unbalance caused by his mini quake, the Wheel-cursed mage toppled sideways into a roll and laughed as she danced out of his reach. When he turned toward her, she dodged behind him, laying one blade against his throat and the other over his belly. He felt the upper one nick his skin.

"If you want to catch me, you'll have to be faster than that, Ox." She sounded breathless and not in the least concerned, as if it were all some funny game.

Bashir exhaled, prepared to drop them both into another sinkhole, but she clucked her tongue in admonishment. She slapped the flat of her blade against his belly then she was gone, running, again. Grudging admiration flitted through his stunned annoyance. In one move she sheathed the swords against her back, crossed over each other, and pommel down.

He blinked once and she was twice as far as she had been. Was that a trick of magic? If she wanted tricks…he kicked the sand in front of him and a wave of it chased her all the way to the far side of the arena. But she outpaced it, launching herself up in a leap a man twice her height couldn't have made, catching the edge of the stone bricks that formed the roof over the outer aisle. The sand wave exploded against the low arena wall, spraying up into the bleachers beyond. Missed her again? Unbelievable.

She took one swing for momentum and curled up, catching her feet against the edge between her hands, and stood. She turned to look over her shoulder and touched her cloth-wrapped brow in mock salute. Cheeky little…he gathered his power but held it at the last moment.

Bashir did not want to bring the stone of the arena down just to capture someone who had stolen three swords, because he did not wish to explain the expense of the repair to the Sultana. So he let the thief go. She ran across the narrow roof, leapt into the stone bleachers, and bounded her way up them with no apparent effort at all, then took a suicidal leap off the upper wall of the arena. Bashir's pulse hammered, a shout billowed in his throat, but logic saved him from his emotion. She would not have leapt to her death over three swords. He hoped.

"What in the Wheel's name was that?" His lieutenant, Erol Terzi, joined him in the center of the arena.

"A thief," Bashir ground out. Assuming she survived her jump there was only one place she was going, if she came specifically to take weapons his men had collected from refugees. "Search the camp. You're looking for a short woman with dark hair. An air mage. And someone can explain to me how she managed to sneak in here in the first place." Was that anger burning in his chest, or something else? He had not lost to anyone as Commander, and it was exhilarating and infuriating.

Erol cleared his throat. "I'll ask the soldier whose room she stole those swords from what he was doing."

When Bashir threw him a dark glare, Erol tapped his fist against his chest and departed.

Bashir shoved his hand through his hair and grimaced as sand collected between his fingers. He swept his hands together to dislodge the sand, and looked again to the arena wall, where she had disappeared. The Sultana would wish to know, and he would see if he could speak with Makram. A mage talented at such specialized skills was rare. It was not impossible that Makram knew of her, if she was a refugee from Sarkum. As if his guards weren't stretched thin enough, now he had to send them on a hunt for a thief.

The mark of her blade burned on his skin as he swiped his finger across it and grit scratched the wound. He wiped the blood on his fingers off on his caftan with a mumble of disbelief, then strode back toward the stables.

It was still several sun marks until morning, perhaps he should not wake the Sultana. The incident wasn't so important it could not wait. Once Bashir reached his room he arranged his clothes back into order, using more filaments of magic to chase the sand from his skin and hair. He cleaned the blood from his throat with a damp rag, glaring at the wound in the mirror.

The entire episode was absurd, and he loathed having to inform the Sultana. He could already picture the look on her face. Disappointment. He tipped his head back and groaned.

First, he'd go with the men to search the camp. If he could present the thief, it would go a long way toward redeeming himself and his men.

When he stepped into the hall Erol was standing there, his arms folded, overseeing a handful of the men as they put their things together in their rooms. He looked up at Bashir and frowned, his dark eyes disapproving. "You haven't slept."

"That is a recurring problem lately. I'll sleep after we catch the girl. Are they ready?" He knew Erol was only trying to look after him, but he couldn't make himself take more than his men did. Of sleep, of anything.

"Just," Erol said as the three men stumbled into the hall and gave halfhearted salutes.

They'd been stretched as thin as filament, each man forced to pull almost twice as much standing time as Bashir would normally deem effective. There was the palace itself to man, then the refugee camp, which required day and night guard, and now runs to the Engeli Gate to escort the refugees, by the Sultana's order. She would offer them refuge as long as she could, but she didn't want them settling wherever they wished in the city. It was too disruptive, carried too much risk of disease or fights between the refugees and citizens.

And now this thief. She was only a harbinger of things to come, as more refugees grew bold and went into the city. He needed more men, but the Sultana and prince were building an army, and there were no fighting-age men to spare for the palace guard force.

He couldn't tell her he was falling short, that he couldn't do what she required with what he was given. His ability to make do with what he was given was exactly the reason she had promoted him so quickly through the ranks. Telling her he couldn't do the very thing she paid him to do was unacceptable.

Erol grabbed the collar of one of the men and gave it a tug to the side so his caftan wasn't twisted and wrinkled, then clapped him on the shoulder and headed down the hall.

In the stables, another guard was just finishing saddling horses. Though the woman was on foot, at the speed she could move she would easily beat them to the camp, even if they were on horseback.

Bashir gave his irritated horse, Huzur, a pat, stroking his hand over the three white spots on its nose. "Steady, friend," he cajoled as he swung up. Steady tempered, but also a glutton for attention, the gelding was the first purchase Bashir had ever made with his own money that wasn't food or clothing.

A last thought occurred to him and he reached to the back of his belt to retrieve the small leather pouch he carried money in. No need to offer temptation in a camp full of hungry people. His hand closed where the pouch usually hung, but nothing met his grasp. Bashir swiped his hand across the entire length of the belt.

It was gone.

He clinched his eyes and exhaled, his slow temper building in his belly like the heat of a volcano.

"What is it?" Erol asked, as Bashir sat dumbfounded.

"She stole my coins."

Erol was not so brazen as to burst into laughter, but a harsh rush of air escaped him and he guided his horse around Bashir's, toward the exit, grinning like a damned fool.

FIVE

YSEL TOSSED THE BAG of coins to Adem as she stopped outside their tent. "For the farmer and his girls."

He looked at her in wide-eyed surprise, opened his mouth as if to question her, then shut it again and ducked his head back to tending the cookfire.

Mathei burst from the tent. "What took so long?" He snatched the burlap bag from her as she held it out. His anger was only because he'd been worried. Aysel squatted across the cookfire from Adem and held her hands out to the warmth. All the exertion had made her sweat, and her slow walk up the hill with a returning group of night dock workers had been cold torture.

"I miscalculated. You'd better get those hidden, because I think we can expect some company shortly."

Mathei pulled the bag open and looked inside. He frowned. "Father's?"

Aysel shook her head. "Didn't have time."

Mathei muttered a curse and ducked inside the tent.

Dilara stepped out a moment later, her gaze turned toward the path that led to the city. "Come inside," she said.

Aysel rose, grimacing. The sword swipe she'd parried from the commander had jarred her to her bones, and her muscles were protesting by cramping. She was not built for fighting men of that size. She'd been extraordinarily lucky, but she would be keeping the details to herself. Her family would not be pleased that she had so openly used her power, but if she hadn't broken free of his sinkhole she'd be in a prison cell now, or worse. Who knew what the punishment for stealing was in Tamar? Though technically, the guards had stolen first.

Mathei was already digging a shallow hole in the dirt floor, using a broken board as a shovel to break up the packed, half-frozen earth. Aysel wrapped the swords more securely in their burlap bag and laid them in the hole. Mathei pushed the dirt back over them, then pulled a frayed woven rug on top of that.

"Filiz," Dilara said as Adem's wife carried an armful of rags into the tent. Filiz bent forward in a quick bow. "Change clothes with Aysel."

Filiz set her pile of rags on top of a crate without questioning and she and Aysel stepped behind a partition sewn of more burlap, where they exchanged clothes. These types of strange requests were a normal occurrence for Filiz and Adem, and the couple seldom questioned.

Filiz's clothes were dyed a pale grey, the typical clothes for high-level servants in a noble's household. Aysel's clothes were undyed, heavy cotton, and did not necessarily set her apart in the camp, but the guards had seen her in them, even if it was dark.

Filiz toed out of her shoes, which were in only slightly better condition than Aysel's, and traded them. Aysel grimaced as Filiz put the wet, tattered shoes she took on her feet. When she hesitated, Filiz crouched, helping Aysel into the shoes as though she were a child incapable of doing so on her own. Filiz rose, and kissed Aysel's cheek, then stepped from behind the curtain.

When Aysel followed, Dilara motioned for her to sit. She untangled Aysel's braids and combed her hair with her fingers until it was manageable enough to twist into a coil at the back of Aysel's head, which she secured with several of the pins that remained in her own salt-and-pepper hair.

Then Dilara pulled the cloth free of her own hair, one of the only bits of finery she had brought, a cherished gift from Thoman. It was grey silk, with flowers embroidered around the edges in pale pink and cream. She wound it around Aysel's neck and over her hair.

"Do not give them a reason to notice you." They were the same words Dilara had said countless times before, throughout Aysel's twenty-three Turns of the Wheel. In Sarkum, Aysel's powers were a curse, but that didn't matter as long as no one cared enough about her to realize what she was.

Aysel kissed her mother's cheek in reassurance. She could tell from Dilara's tired face that she had stayed up after Aysel left. She always stayed up.

The sun was just rising over the Kalspire and shedding enough cold light on the camp to see by when a group of mounted guards ran their horses into camp at high speed. Aysel heard the sounds of the hooves and poked her head outside to check. Mathei tugged her back and flicked her forehead with his finger, glowering at her.

"Where is *Baba*?" Aysel asked.

"He took Erkin to the guard house to ask for a healer to look at his ankle."

"Alone?" Aysel demanded. Dilara nodded, her expression drawn with worry. It was just like her father to do something foolhardy like that, with possible assassins lurking in the hills around them. They could pick him off with a crossbow bolt with the smallest of efforts and be gone before anyone could make it up the slope to look for them. Or they could easily blend in to the camp and knife him in the back.

Aysel shuddered. "Maybe I should look for him?"

"Have you lost the one wit you have?" Mathei snapped. "Why don't you blow the guards a kiss while you're out there?"

Aysel glared at him.

"We need water." Dilara held out a wooden bucket that had seen better days. Aysel doubted it would hold water at all. She frowned. Dilara had a particular expression that Aysel and Mathei had learned at a young age meant she had taken up a position as immutable as rock. She wore it now.

Aysel snatched the bucket and stalked from the tent, then dodged sideways behind it when she saw how close the guards were. They were dismounting their horses, and the commander was with them. Aysel closed her eyes, wrapping her power as tightly as she could inside, into the mental barrier she had used from a young age to disguise herself from detection.

It was the Wheel's twisted humor that had put her directly against an earth mage. He had to be a Sival. She'd never seen a Fourth House mage do what he had done, as if it were effortless to command the very earth at her feet. Sinking into the sand had been the most terrifying experience of her life, feeling it crushing closed on her ribs, its weight squeezing the breath from her, and fearing the sand would pour down her throat.

She lifted a hand to her throat and gasped for air, the memory so vivid she was certain she was being crushed at this moment too. Her mother was right, she needed to stay as far away from him as possible.

Aysel skirted the tent, keeping it between her and the men. She could faintly make out their voices as they explained the situation to the men guarding the camp perimeter. She slipped deeper into the camp. It was the long route to the path that led up the hill and to the spring, but the direct path would take her straight through the guards' midst.

The early time and hand-numbing cold meant most of the refugees were still huddled together in their shelters, though a few were tending cookfires, as Adem had been. The shoes Filiz traded to her had been dry and in slightly better repair than her own, but now the chill mud of the camp had soaked through them and her feet ached with the cold.

Aysel walked with her face down, not casting exactly, but adopting a facade that others found uninteresting. She was small-framed, with dull brown hair that was just a little too curly and wild, a step beyond appealing and into disheveled. Her face was neither beautiful nor ugly, her eyes mid-hazel with a ring of steel grey encircling the iris. She was unremarkable, and people barely looked up as she passed.

When she reached the edge of the camp nearest the footpath up to the spring she chanced a look back toward the heart of the camp, where her family was. She could not see through the jumble of tents and detritus, but she could make out the horses the guards had ridden up. They were tethered at the head of the road that led back to the city. What had become of her family's horses? Likely absorbed into the string for the guards. Aysel turned her back on the scene once more and strode up the path, resuming her mental deconstruction, convincing herself she wasn't noticeable, so others would think so too.

Her thoughts kept interrupting themselves though, as flashes of her encounter with the guard commander replayed in her head. No one had ever caught her. She should not count it, since he was a Fourth House mage, and she a First. Houses in opposition bore magic in opposition. Earth and air canceled each other. But still, her pride stung. And now it would be all the harder to protect her father from whoever was following him because she must also be alert to the palace guardsmen. She'd brought it all on herself. She should have observed longer before charging into the barracks, making baseless assumptions. Something Mathei was always reprimanding her for.

She'd never been any good at wielding a full-sized yataghan. It had been Tareck, then-Captain of the janissaries under her father's command, who had proposed the idea of the shorter blades. He said her speed was her advantage. Though she would never be able to hold herself against a stronger opponent for long, wielding two short, light swords would allow her to distract and confuse them long enough to get away. But being the only wielder of weapons like that meant she now couldn't carry them openly.

The path curved abruptly to the left, across the steep hillside, then dipped again before Aysel arrived at the spring. It was no more than an upwelling of water through the rock, but it had been dug out, a section of wood driven in to create a long spout sticking out of the earth and spilling into a narrow gully.

Aysel picked her way into the gully and slung the bucket underneath the spout. She crouched, propping her elbow on her knee and resting her chin in her hand as she watched the water trickle in. "Stupid, ox-breathed mud mage," Aysel grumbled.

Behind her, on the path, a stone was dislodged and cracked against another, then tumbled down the hillside. Her first instinct was to roll, to dodge in case a blow was coming her way, and she reached reflexively for the knife hidden beneath her sleeve. But that would give away a great deal of her skill, if the person behind her was a guard searching for an escaped sword thief. Aysel lowered her hands and plastered her best wide-eyed, vapid-daughter-of-a-noble expression on her face before she turned with a little gasp of surprise.

Her gaze met his, the same jasper gold she had seen only a short while before when she burst into his room in the barracks. She barely maintained her composure. A sigh of irritation rose and died in her throat.

"You surprised me." Aysel stood to bow to him. "My bucket is almost full then I'll be on my way."

His gaze traced her movements, his mouth set in a thin, hard line of temper. Aysel suppressed a smile. Weren't Fourth House mages known for their slow tempers? Whatever could have vexed him so? She was pleased to see she had also irritated *him*.

"I'm looking for a thief," he said. When he wasn't bellowing at his men like an angry ox his matter-of-fact voice, with just its hint of earthy gravel, was quite…nice.

"Oh dear. I'm sorry…Guardsman, is it?" She pretended to search his uniform for rank of some kind. "Well I'm the only one here." Aysel retrieved her bucket and held its handle with both hands so it hung in front of her legs.

"Commander," he corrected, and relaxed. Aysel relaxed in turn. He picked his way down the little drop to where she stood, and because it was a dug-out gully they were forced close together, so the only thing keeping him away from her was the bucket. This would be a tricky escape.

"Or Ox, if you prefer," he said under his breath. Aysel had to tip her head back to meet his gaze. She despised that aspect of being so short, it made her feel too vulnerable, baring her throat, conceding that she was too short to meet people at eye level.

"Did your mother name you that? What a terrible name to inflict on a child." Aysel shook her head. Her father had drilled the lesson into her. Never remove your mask. Even when you are certain they know, maintain the lie. They rarely know as much as you think they do.

Her heart thundered, the rhythm to which her magic pulsed, fighting to be free of her hold, antagonized by the proximity of his. Aysel resisted every impulse, every instinct—they were betrayers, children of pride. A smile, a bite of the lip, a twitch of the finger, all of them were allies of the enemy, truth.

What would she do if she had never seen him before, never fought him? She'd think he was insane. She was a poor, frightened refugee woman confronted with a bulwark of a guard. Terrified. That's what she would be.

His mouth twitched, one corner lifting up. "No. Only one person has ever called me that, and they will only do so once."

"You're frightening me," Aysel whispered, affecting her best lip quiver and lowering her gaze. "I haven't done anything and I don't know where your thief is. Please let me go." Make him doubt what he believes. She needed tears, something she could normally produce whenever needed, but for some reason could not, now, in front of him.

"The problem with lying to an earth mage once you've stepped foot on his ground..." The commander lowered his voice to a near whisper, and Aysel lifted her gaze to his again. He had leaned down a little, so their eyes were closer to level. The pale jasper color of his eyes was cut with dark striations, just like the stone.

But what had drawn her gaze and held it now was the swirling movement of the dark against the light, like the shifting of earth in a quake. He held his hand palm up, just below her chin. There was an odd tug across her skin, the movement of tiny grains of sand as they slipped free of her skin and hair, where they had lodged when he'd trapped her in the arena. They settled in his palm.

"…I can always find my earth." He straightened and let the sand stream from his palm into her bucket of water.

Aysel despised the glint of arrogant triumph in his gaze.

She bent and slammed the bucket down, then straightened, and regarded him slowly, with disdain.

"What am I supposed to have stolen?" She swept her fingers across his palm, gathering a few of the remaining grains and rubbing them away between her fingers. "Sand?"

"You stole weapons. And my money."

"*I* did?" She gestured at herself, moving her hands up and down to emphasize her height. "From all you big, strapping guards?"

"Don't play games with me." He practically shook with restraint. The fact he was restraining himself at all told her a great deal about him. He was certain of her, but wouldn't touch her unless he was sure he could make everyone else certain as well.

"How did you explain that to your Sultana, I wonder?" She tapped a finger against her lips. "Efendim, a woman half my size managed to sneak through the palace grounds, the stables, and the barracks where my guards *live* and steal weapons," she said in a deepened voice. "Right. Out. Of. My. Hands." She gave him a wide-eyed look of sympathy.

That simmering temper hardened the lines of his face.

"You're coming with me, and you can try your taunting on your fellow prisoners." He pointed down the hill. Aysel cocked her head. Not accustomed to being thwarted, this one.

"Mmm. No." Aysel smiled. "They were in fact my weapons, and your men stole them from me. And I will explain that to your court, along with a few other details I'm afraid you will find very embarrassing."

"There is no court for citizens of Sarkum. You can rot in prison just on my say-so." He sounded far too pleased by the prospect.

"Prove I stole them," Aysel challenged, banking on her earlier assessment.

"You are covered in arena sand."

"You take the refugees to the arena for documenting. And I'm covered in a great many other unpleasant substances." She raised her eyebrows.

His nostrils flared. "You're short."

"And you're ugly." Lie. He was an earth mage. They were not all beautiful, but they were strong and magnetic at the least. He was both, broad and tall, his caftan pulled just tight enough to suggest expanses of muscle she would take great pleasure in exploring. She noted again his stubbled cheeks, angled between a square jaw and high cheekbones. A straight, broad nose and lips that, when not pressed into a frown, invited slow nibbles, were almost enough to make her forget the fact he was very likely going to imprison her. "But that doesn't make either of us criminals," she said.

"You're an air mage." He was beginning to look a bit flustered.

"Prove it." Aysel rocked onto her tiptoes, baring her teeth at him in a snide grin as she clasped her hands behind her back. She lowered herself to her heels once more and waited. He frowned, his tawny eyebrows drawing down over his eyes. He tapped at her with a thread of power—the equivalent of tossing a magical stone looking for an invisible barrier.

Aysel gave another sigh, casting her gaze down the hill as if in boredom, but was looking for her family to make certain they weren't being harassed by his guards. This was her greatest talent, one honed through a lifetime of necessity. Other mages learned to use their powers, casting spell after spell to perfect their skill. She had learned to hide hers, to bury it so deeply it ceased to exist to anyone looking for it.

His magic pushed and prodded, sending tremors through her muscles and a shifting in her balance. When he withdrew, she looked at him and raised an eyebrow. "Finished?"

"That is remarkable," he said, staring at her as if she were a fascinating curio.

"Not as remarkable as the amount of time you're wasting blaming the wrong person for this egregious crime." Aysel dropped her gaze to her feet. She'd never been complimented by a stranger. And even in these odd circumstances it knocked her off guard.

"Let me make something clear. This isn't over. You are at best, a thief, and at worst"—he gave the entirety of her a long, appraising sweep of his gaze that made her aware of how dirty and unkempt she was—"a gifted First House mage with intent to take life in the place I have sworn to protect."

He reached between them and grabbed her arm, twisting it up in front of him and shoving her sleeve down. Aysel squawked in surprise, and the commander pried the knife on her wrist free of its strap against her forearm. "Weapons are forbidden in the camp, little girl." He pointed the tip of the knife at her nose.

"Call me that again, and I'll turn you into one."

The one corner of his mouth quirked up again. The damned bastard was distractingly attractive. Her brother would be in fits. She'd be as well, if he wasn't bruising her arm and stealing her knife.

"I'd like to see that," he said.

Aysel flicked her other wrist, a combination of technique and placement that had taken seasons to perfect, and the other knife slid into her free hand. She pressed it to his groin, hard enough he began to jerk away and stopped, anger flaring in his face then fading to disbelief. She pressed harder, narrowing her eyes as she glared at him.

"Hard to get to, down there, isn't it? But so terribly vulnerable," Aysel murmured. "There are advantages to being so short. Would you like to throw that knife on the ground, please?"

"Or I could jam it into your neck." He flipped his grip on it, and a quick downward thrust would fulfill his suggestion.

"Not before I make you a eunuch. Didn't you find out last night I'm faster than you? Are your boys a reasonable price to pay for my murder?" It was wrong that she found perverse pleasure in their taunting.

"I have never wanted to commit murder as much as I do now," he admitted, but the anger was gone, and Aysel was almost certain she saw a kind of amused admiration in his stony gaze. She could not help grinning.

"I have been told I have that effect on people."

"That amuses you?"

"If I am not amused by the worst of things, then there would be no humor in my life," she said. He might have replied, but someone else spoke, from behind and above him on the path.

"Doesn't this look cozy." Mathei's voice was always full of amusement, but it was even more of a lie than her mocking. "All right there, Aysel?"

Aysel peeked around the commander's broad shoulders. Mathei stood above them, where the path dropped into the gully—Tareck, Makram's steward, at his side. Relief swept through her so suddenly that she wavered, her knees nearly giving beneath her.

There hadn't been a shred of doubt in her that she was going back to the palace in shackles. When she rocked in place, the commander released his bruising grip on her wrist and took up a gentler one on her arm to steady her.

"Just having a chat. Someone stole this man's toys," Aysel said as she retracted her knife from its place between his legs, and he lowered her other away from her neck. Mathei executed a standing slide down the gully path, plucking Aysel's other knife from the commander's hand.

Mathei regarded him with a baited smile. "Aren't you pretty? Almost worth the dreadful hike up here. Keeping him all to yourself, little sister?" Mathei circled them, and put one hand on the commander's forearm where he still gripped Aysel, and the other on Aysel, pushing them apart. "No one ever taught you to keep your hands off a lady? Tsk."

"You mean a thief. A whole pack of you, are there?" The commander looked up the gully slope to where Tareck stood. Tareck nodded a greeting to him, then turned his attention to Aysel.

"Hello, Kit." Tareck smiled down at Aysel. She wanted to run up and hug him. "Making friends, are we?"

"I'm afraid I've upset him." Aysel tucked the knife she held back into her sleeve. Mathei was tapping the other against his lips as he gave the commander a long, appreciative look from head to toe. Aysel suppressed her smile when she noted the commander's discomfort, and plucked the knife from Mathei's grip.

"Bashir. You'll have to stand down on this one. The prince has need of her," Tareck said in his steady, imperturbable way of speaking. As if there were not a thing in the world that could ever affect him enough to change his mood.

"He has need of a criminal?" Bashir scoffed.

"What did she steal?" Tareck squinted up at the sky as the sun swung slowly overhead, bringing a bit of warmth to the morning.

"Weapons."

"My weapons," Aysel added.

"That's not really stealing, is it?" Tareck suggested. Bashir exhaled slowly, turning from Tareck to look at Aysel with frustration.

She patted his arm and frowned, then stood on tiptoe again so she could speak quietly. She whispered, "I win."

"Not yet." Bashir shook her off. "Where is the prince?" He lunged up the gully side, and Mathei hummed, tipping his head to one side as he watched Bashir's backside at work. Aysel slapped his arm.

"Stop it." She grinned. She could not blame him for enjoying the view.

He looked at her from the corners of his eyes. "You're all right?" He dropped the exaggerated facade. Aysel nodded.

"I've been sent in his place, he is still at the palace," Tareck answered Bashir, and offered a hand down as Aysel climbed up the gully side. She took it and he pulled her up. Aysel threw her arms around Tareck's neck and he chuckled, swinging her in a circle and setting her down.

Bashir gave a nearly soundless curse of disbelief and started away from them down the path. Mathei grabbed the bucket of water and followed. Ahead of them, Bashir shoved a hand through his hair, the set of his shoulders indicating he was furious. Aysel skipped ahead of Mathei and Tareck and paced her stride to Bashir's, which was not an easy feat. His legs were long, his stride paced for eating ground.

"I'm Aysel," she offered in truce. "Since we'll be allies of a sort, I thought introductions were in order."

He slowed his pace, turning his head just enough to fix her with a disapproving gaze.

"No."

"I suppose I'll just have to call you Ox, then."

"Not if you don't want me to bury you in this mountain you won't," he said.

Aysel looked up at him, wide-eyed. If he were jesting, she couldn't tell.

"Oxen are very noble creatures. It's a compliment." She clasped her hands behind her back.

"They are beasts of burden. They pull carts and plows. And I've had quite enough of your mocking."

"Well, you *are* very strong." Aysel meant it, but she couldn't help that she teased him a little. She wasn't certain she'd ever met anyone quite so uptight.

"Is there a point to you speaking with me?" he asked without looking at her.

"It was a little fun, wasn't it?" She glanced over her shoulder at Tareck and Mathei, who were chatting quietly, both with serious expressions. Keeping Bashir engaged in conversation prevented him from trying to listen in to whatever they were discussing. That Tareck had said Makram had need of her had not been idle words, and a bead of concern had been sitting in her belly ever since.

"What?"

"Losing," Aysel said.

Bashir turned a gaze on her that could have melted stone. "I did not lose."

"You did. Look at me." She held her hands up between them. "Shackle free. You wanted to put me in prison."

Bashir shook his head, one hand at the hilt of his sheathed yataghan. "Your prince is not the ruler here, and whatever you are to him, I can guarantee the Sultana trusts me more than he trusts you."

SIX

ASHIR STOOD NEAR THE windows, as far from the group in the center of the room as he could get. The room the Sultana had chosen to receive them in was on the far west side of the palace, removed from the bustle of the main palace and away from curious stares and wagging tongues. They stood speaking quietly amongst themselves—the family and Tareck. If they spared him a glance at all, Bashir did not notice. He'd stopped looking at any of them when he realized the woman wasn't going to stop smirking at him in triumph.

His suspicion of her had only grown when he'd realized her father was the man who had approached him to speak with Makram. Now the Sultana would find out how spectacularly he had failed, and it would be all the more humiliating because they would be hiding behind Makram. Criminals were criminals in Bashir's mind, whether they were the lowliest of pickpockets or the most sophisticated of court spies.

His gaze strayed from the wall of arched windows overlooking the ocean far below, and to the family once again. To her.

She'd wasted no time in outfitting herself with the blades she had stolen, and the other was now hanging from a belt at her brother's waist. Bashir had orders to return another, which apparently belonged to the father, when their audience was over. She wore the contraption of harness, crossed sheaths, and swords with as much ease and comfort as other women wore silk. She was a puzzle, and Bashir hated puzzles. He'd rather cut something in half or smash it to pieces than fiddle with bits to make a whole.

How could she possibly move as she did without being an air mage? She'd escaped a sand trap. It was impossible without earth magic strong enough to beat his or an air mage's opposition. But he'd felt nothing, not even the tiniest stirring when he'd probed her. What kind of mage hid their power?

As if he'd asked the question out loud, her gaze snapped to his. Bashir continued watching her as she excused herself from the others and crossed the room to him. She moved with the grace of a dancer and arrogant surety of a cat. It was…disturbingly pleasant to observe.

She stopped beside him, her back to the room, her hands clasped behind her, and her gaze on the ocean. Silent.

Bashir's temper smoldered. Why had she come to him if she didn't have anything to say? The woman was like a buzzing fly that wouldn't be thwarted no matter how it was swatted away.

She made a humming sound in the back of her throat, tilting her head one way then the other.

"Do you like the sea?" She looked up at him in that odd way she had of raising her eyes but not her chin. There was plenty of light in the room, which was open on three sides to the garden and the sea view, enough for him to take note, again, of the curious composition of her eye color, hazel and steel. Earth and sky. He'd had plenty of time to study it on the mountainside, when they were standing so close they might as well have been embracing.

Bashir grit his teeth. He'd sooner embrace an angry alley cat. This one would probably put one of her knives in a soft spot and laugh while he bled to death.

"I don't dislike it."

"Earth mages sink, don't they? Like stone." She gave him a mock pout that drew his attention to the fact she had a small, perfectly bow-shaped mouth. He pulled his thoughts, which had started down a disturbing track involving her mouth, up like a bolting horse. Criminal. Most likely a spy. Possibly also an assassin. Not someone whose mouth he should be looking at.

"I can swim." Bashir managed not to follow it with a curse of frustration. He sounded like a simpleton. She smiled, slowly, her gaze taking a leisurely tour of his body. Heat rose up his chest and neck and into his face. "What do you want?" he said, too sharply, making her effect on him obvious.

"I gave your money to a starving family. A farmer with two little girls." She held her hand at her rib level, indicating their height. "In case you were missing it overly much, I thought it might please you to know it went to a good cause. But, I can point them out if you would like to demand it back. They're living underneath a hide shelter that leaks at the seams." Her eyes narrowed a fraction. "I would offer to pay you back, but we find ourselves suddenly humbled by the Wheel."

She smiled at him, tossing her head so that her two chestnut braids fell to her back instead of forward over her shoulders.

Bashir lifted a hand to his face and pressed his fingers to his eyes. His head was pounding. "Leave it alone," he conceded. He gave all his money to his mother anyway, and she was doing fine. They could both survive without a few turns' pay. She was always saying how she wished she could help more in the camp, she'd be pleased. If he left out the part where it had been *appropriated* by someone.

He lowered his hand. "I'm supposed to believe you were ever anything but a thief?"

"What you believe about me has no bearing at all on the truth. So believe as you like."

Bashir stared at her for a moment, trying to decide if he was marveling at her or perplexed as he had never been by a woman. Especially not a noblewoman, if that's what she was. "Are there many women like you in Sarkum? Who wield blades and bear not a wit of humility?"

She made a soft, bitter sound that he thought was a laugh and turned to face the windows, putting her side toward him. "No."

From his peripheral Bashir saw her brother glance at them, then break away from his parents and Tareck to join them. "You two do spend a great deal of time flirting." He slid an arm around his sister's shoulders.

"He doesn't know how to flirt," Aysel said. "I was apologizing for stealing his money."

"I do know how to—" Bashir snapped his teeth together to cut off the rest of the ridiculous sentence and faced the center of the room. Where on the Wheel was the Sultana? Every moment with these people was torture. "And you didn't apologize. You told me you gave it away."

"To a good cause." She folded her arms.

"Yes," Bashir conceded. She smiled. It was a real smile this time. Her eyes crinkled at the corners, and her lips parted to reveal her teeth. It was hard to take his eyes off her when she was looking at him like that.

"Tsk," her brother said, drawing Bashir's attention to him. Mathei raised a dark eyebrow, and Bashir got a glimpse in his nearly black eyes of the real man beneath the show he put on. Dangerous. Protective.

Mathei smiled, showing the same even, white teeth of his sister, but his smile was all threat. Bashir's magic rumbled in response, and some of his confusion settled away. Threat was something he knew how to handle. He was rock and stone and they were fleeting moments that would pass. He just needed to stand his ground and keep them from doing any harm. Then a time would come when they would be gone, and he would remain. Like earth.

The movement of the carved wooden doors of the entrance caught his attention, and everyone in the room turned to face them.

The Sultana swept into the room, Makram only a step behind. Samira, the Sultana's lead handmaiden, followed with two other attendants in tow. She was, as always, perfectly composed, moving with efficiency and quiet authority that sat easily on her slim shoulders. Bashir, Erol, and Samira had gone through the University together, and were friends, though it was hard to maintain such a relationship when their duties kept them to such different places.

Bashir let his gaze slip sideways to Aysel's face. He enjoyed watching people when they saw the Sultana for the first time.

Aysel frowned a little, and chewed on her lower lip. Bashir suppressed a knowing smile. The Sultana was beautiful, one of the most beautiful women Bashir had ever seen. But beauty was, especially to an earth mage, fleeting and mutable. There were so many other traits that mattered, traits that remained when beauty was only a memory.

Others did not see those traits when they looked at the Sultana, they saw the way she moved, as if she barely touched the ground, but not the exacting control of one of the finest air mages in Tamar. They saw her flawless honey skin and hair the color of black coffee. They saw her perfectly arched eyebrows and wide, warm dark eyes. But they rarely noticed the razor-sharp intelligence in them, only that her lashes were thick and dark and her mouth full and often smiling.

They did not know that the smile covered the fact they were being taken apart and put back together without a word.

Bashir had seen all those quieter traits when he was brought into the guard force. He had also seen that she was honorable, and loyal, and cared for her people. All the reasons he would do anything for her.

"Well"—Mathei leaned forward to whisper to Aysel—"she's a cow. I cannot imagine what Makram sees in her."

Bashir exhaled sharply in disbelief. Aysel glanced over her shoulder at her brother, and Bashir saw silent laughter in the set of her mouth and her eyes just before she grabbed her brother's hand and dragged him toward the others. She joined her parents and Tareck in their deference to the Sultana.

Bashir bowed, but did not approach. He always waited for the Sultana's invitation before inserting himself into affairs.

"Thoman." Makram clasped the older man's shoulders as he rose from his bow. "I only just received word you were here. We have much to discuss, not the least of which is that I will not have you living in the refugee camp." He dropped his hands and looked to the Sultana.

"I believe the least of the things we need to discuss is that one of your offspring broke into my palace grounds and stole weapons." The Sultana looked from the Elder Attiyeh to his two children, who were managing to look obedient and innocent. The Sultana's gaze raked the brother and dismissed him, then landed on Aysel. Bashir had been subjected to that look before and had felt stripped to the core by it. He enjoyed the idea that the woman would have to endure such, as a bit of penance for her crime.

"Forgive her methods, Sultana," Makram said. "They are often… frustrating. But she has never done anything without good reason."

Aysel bowed to the Sultana, then dropped to her knees in front of Makram. She crossed her hands behind her back and drew the swords, and Bashir jerked, ready to lunge closer. The Sultana lifted a finger to signal him to hold. He did not relax, his own hand resting on his yataghan's hilt.

Aysel set the swords at Makram's feet, and did the same with the two knives she had sheathed against her forearms. Then she prostrated herself. Her brother followed suit, laying his blade beside his sister's weapons.

"Your brother sent his Firestormers to the estate. They destroyed it all, and we barely escaped." Her voice was matter of fact, her words quick, like a soldier reporting. "There have been at least three men trailing us from Sarkum, who we believe are *katil*. Our weapons were confiscated at the Engeli Gate, and I feared for our family's safety."

This was news to Bashir, his men had not mentioned being followed. Firestormers? Were these people criminals in Sarkum? Or just criminal for being allied with Makram, instead of his brother? Bashir gripped his hilt harder to prevent himself rubbing his eyes. Politics were an impenetrable web to him.

"Thoman has the loyalty of many of the nobles and the fighting forces under their command," Makram said to the Sultana. "It would not surprise me if Kinus had sent assassins after him, especially if his Firestormers failed."

Aysel sat back on her heels, her palms flat against her thighs, and her brother did the same. Bashir realized why her surname sounded so familiar. He'd heard the Sultana mention Elder Attiyeh. He had been instrumental in convincing Makram to move against his brother. Bashir closed his eyes, briefly. The entire situation was becoming more and more tangled.

"Given your esteem for Elder Attiyeh, it surprises me that he would choose to steal from the palace rather than approach us in a more suitable fashion." The Sultana looked from Makram to the Elder. "Why did you not send word to us that you had arrived?"

"We attempted to, Efendim," Elder Attiyeh said, bowing slightly at the waist as if in apology. Bashir frowned. The Sultana frowned. Makram frowned.

"He means that he approached the guard commander to request an audience and was told Makram would be informed," Mathei said, flatly. Sinking nausea filled Bashir's belly. He'd forgotten. In his exhaustion and the confusion of the initial arrival, then his obsession with catching Aysel, he had forgotten.

"Your tone, Mathei," the mother said, firmly but softly. Mathei lowered his head but managed to cast a scathing look at Bashir before he did. Bashir breathed a curse.

"You requested an audience and the same night conducted a raid?" the Sultana asked. "That suggests a disturbing lack of interest in alliance, and a bias toward acting only in your own interest and as free agents in my city."

"Sultana," Makram said, but she cut him off with a raised hand.

"Commander Ayan," she ordered. Bashir crossed from the window and dropped to a knee in front of her. "Explain."

"Forgive me, Sultana," Bashir said, miserably. "I became consumed with catching a thief and failed to relay the message to you."

"Tell me about this thief."

He glanced sideways, without turning his head, to look at Aysel. She still knelt, her hands on her thighs, her head bowed. She was dirty, disheveled, and he had to assume exhausted and hungry. The entire episode of her theft was burned into his memory, from the moment he lifted his head and met her gaze in his room to their battle of wills at the spring above the camp. Not once had she appeared afraid. But when he looked at her now, just her profile, he saw panic. His brow furrowed, something inside him rolling over like a stone overturned.

And when he spoke, he did something he'd never done once since entering the palace as a novice guard.

"The weapons were unguarded, and as I understand it, she climbed the cliff on the southeastern wall, entered the barracks through the stables, and retrieved the weapons." He lied to her. Wheel break him, he lied to her.

"There was a fight," the Sultana said, revealing she had already heard of the encounter. Bashir was certain she knew. There was no way in the Fourth House she didn't know. The Sultana could sense a lie from halfway across Tamar, and that was for anyone. He was an earth mage lying to a mage in opposition. He could feel her gaze piercing straight to his heart.

"I chased her, Sultana. Forgive me, I was still encumbered by sleep and I was too slow." He looked at Aysel again from the corners of his eyes. She remained as she had been, head bowed, silent. Her expression was impassive, and Wheel bless her, she did not look at him or move.

"*You* were too slow," the Sultana repeated, as if she could not understand. Bashir's breath stilled in his lungs. "And if I ask your guardsmen I will receive the same version of events?"

"You will, Efendim," Bashir managed to say without sounding as strangled as he felt. Her silence stretched until he felt he would shatter under her scrutiny. All he could hear was the scrape of boots as Makram shifted his position beside the Sultana and they both stared at Bashir.

"Elder Attiyeh," the Sultana said, with the end of a sigh in her words. "We will move you from the camp and into our guest quarters. Unfortunately, your family has broken my trust. Until I feel that has been resolved, I will require that you give up your weapons and have a guard escort, for your protection and my comfort."

Bashir drew in a breath when the crushing weight of her focus was off him. He barely resisted the urge to look at Aysel to gauge her reaction.

"You are most generous, Sultana Efendim." The Elder bowed. His wife did the same. His children bowed forward to prostrate on the floor again.

"Commander Ayan," the Sultana said, "at least two men. Day and night."

Bashir allowed his muscles to relax. He gave a sharp nod. There were no guards to spare for such a duty, but if he had to do it himself, he would, as payment for his lie. He wouldn't fail her any more than he already had.

"I would like to remain in the camp," Aysel said, quietly. "With my weapons."

"No." The Sultana turned to go. Bashir got to his feet.

"Sultana," Makram said, in a firm tone that Bashir rarely heard from him. He habitually deferred to her, as he should, and rarely, if ever, contradicted her in public. The Sultana's shoulders stiffened, and she turned her head to bestow an unforgiving, ice-cold stare on her betrothed. Makram looked at Bashir, his hooded eyes seeing more than Bashir cared for him to, and said, "I will take responsibility for Aysel."

"Fine. But if Commander Ayan reports to me that she has done so much as upset a trash cart, not only will she and her family be in the Cliffs, you and I will have a reckoning."

The corners of Makram's mouth twitched as he bowed to her. The Sultana turned completely around and stepped in front of Aysel, who proved she had more common sense than she let on by remaining prostrate.

"I do not know what turns of the Wheel conspired to gift you luck enough to escape Commander Ayan the first time, but do not make the mistake of thinking it will happen again." The Sultana looked at Bashir for the last words, and he nodded agreement.

"No, Sultana." Aysel's voice was muffled against the sandstone tiles.

"Commander, attend me." The Sultana spun and strode up the stairs. Bashir obeyed, trotting after her.

SEVEN

AYSEL SCRATCHED AT THE stones with one fingernail, listening to the stampede of soft steps as the Sultana and her entourage exited the room.

"You can stand up now, you little liar," Mathei said. Aysel straightened and rolled to the balls of her feet, standing.

Makram bent to retrieve her swords, looking at her for a long time as he swung one in slow circles. He wore the finery of Tamar now, not armor. He looked like a prince as he never had in Al-Nimas, stifled by his brother. Tiraz circled his upper arms, bands of cloth that displayed for all the world his magic and its power. Four black sigils embroidered into charcoal cloth. A twinge of jealousy pinched in her gut. What would that be like? To not have to hide?

"Do not take the Sultana's words lightly. Commander Ayan is a formidable mage and as determined as any hound I've ever seen." He eyed the edge of her blade as he spoke.

"I am aware." Aysel wanted to look for Bashir's retreating back but did not care for the suggestion that might give the others and kept her gaze on Makram. He reached up and tapped his ear with one hand, to indicate they were not safe to speak freely.

Tareck shifted, looking up toward the doors. "I could give you around a tenth of a mark," he said, referring to his ability to counter the Sultana's magic. Tareck was not a powerful mage. His talents lay in soldiering, but he was still earth, and it would counter even the most powerful of air mages, at least for a small time.

"First." Makram looked from Aysel to Thoman. "Elder, I have need of Aysel."

"Not for murder?" Dilara demanded. "We cannot build a life here if the Sultana believes us criminals."

"To observe," Makram said. "May I have your consent?"

"My family is yours to death, Agassi." Thoman caught himself and smiled. "I mean, Rahal Charah." He looked at Aysel then back. "I hope you know her actions were necessary, or I would not have sanctioned them and risked your reputation."

Aysel let her gaze slip to the doors, chewing the inside of her lip. She'd been so certain everything was about to be revealed. Even Makram did not know about her magic. To have it all exposed while she sat there defending herself for taking a sword was likely to send her to the hangman and endanger her family for keeping the secret. If given the choice, she would die before she'd let them do anything to her family.

"Tareck." Makram's order interrupted Aysel's stormy thoughts. "Let us direct the Elder and his family to the guest quarters, then you, Aysel, and I will have a chat."

"This way." Tareck led off into the hall. Makram gave Aysel's blade one more spin, then crossed behind her and sheathed each one.

"You have so many titles now, what are we to call you?" Mathei asked Makram, grinning and wiggling his eyebrows. "Agassi? Charah? Prince Consort?"

"I am not consort yet. You may take your pick of the others." Makram frowned. As always, grand titles did not fit him right. Though of any Aysel had heard, she liked Charah best, to know he was acknowledging his power. And he'd dropped his mother's name and taken his father's, an act that spoke more of his resolve than almost anything else.

Melancholy shadowed her mood. Acknowledging power seemed something that would be forever out of her reach.

"You have a story to tell me," Makram said, quietly, in the silence that descended over their group. Aysel grinned up at him, but inside she shrank. How could she tell him without giving everything away?

"What's to tell?" Mathei appeared beside them, always ready to rescue her. "He's a bumbling simpleton and she's quick as a fox."

"He is nothing of the sort. You know better than to play your games with me." Makram gave Mathei a look of reproach. Mathei spread his open hands and gave a little grin.

"Tell me how the refugees fare," Makram said as they followed behind Tareck, Thoman, and Dilara. Aysel let Mathei do most of the talking. She didn't feel like it. All she could think of was Bashir. Had he lied to prevent himself the humiliation of admitting she'd taken the swords right out of his hands? That had to be the reason.

When Tareck had led them through several turns and hallways and they finally arrived at the suites they would be using, Aysel almost retracted her statement about staying in the camp. The beds looked sinfully comfortable, and she felt even grubbier for standing in such a bright, polished room. But she would not be able to track down hunting katil if she was trapped in the palace under guard. And that was far more important than… She looked at the plush rugs layered over the stone floors, and the velvet-covered, deeply cushioned couches and chairs. Assassins, she reminded herself, when the desire to stay and enjoy them plucked a little too hard.

"I'd like to bring Adem and his family as well, is that possible?" Thoman asked. Dilara patted an overstuffed pillow on one of the chairs with a thoughtful smile on her face. Aysel wondered if she would warn someone that if her mother were left unsupervised for too long they would find this room redone to her tastes, specifically dark. And wood. A great deal of unnecessary wood.

"Tareck will arrange it." Makram looked from Thoman to Aysel then Tareck, giving his head a quick tilt toward the garden door. "Join me outside."

"Why Aysel?" Dilara whispered to Thoman as Aysel stepped through the arched glass door Tareck held open for her. Aysel suspected it was because whoever Makram wanted information on was especially wily. Mathei was a very good spy, but only for certain situations. He was particularly gifted at making people open up to him and reveal secrets without realizing they had. If someone needed to sneak into places, Aysel was the better choice. She wasn't charming enough to do what Mathei did, and she was small enough to fit through windows.

Makram tipped his head back to face the grey sky. He looked tired, and worried. She was accustomed to the humorous facade he usually kept. Like Mathei.

This was different, burdened by looming war with his brother. Aysel could not imagine what it would feel like to forsake Mathei for the greater good. She didn't even believe in the greater good. But she could always count on Mathei. And Makram.

Makram had never had that, not in Kinus anyway.

"When you are ready, Tareck," Makram said. Tareck was a Deval, which meant to cast he had to either utter a spell or draw its sigil. Sigils had more staying power, so he crouched to draw the symbol for *dampen* in the earth at his feet. When he completed it he breathed it to life with a spoken word. The sigil glowed and silence assaulted Aysel's perception.

Chirping sparrows, fighting over seed scraps and bouncing about the bushes outside Tareck's spell were muted inside it. The ambient noises of the palace, splashing water in fountains, the hum of voices in conversation, were now absent. Even the distant rustle of the sea, which was constant, was gone. Aysel's talent had never lain in the ubiquitous spells of sound and hearing that most First House mages could cast. Yet, the absence of all sound made her skin crawl. Or perhaps being corralled by an earth spell did. They were not separable occurrences so that she could identify the cause of her discomfort. Her magic coiled inside her, prodded to life by the touch of Tareck's.

"I have been blind since I came here. I need you to be my eyes," Makram said when Tareck gave a stiff nod.

"Of course. And Mathei?"

"I will engage him separately, for what he can hear. I have a specific person in mind for you." Makram glanced at Tareck, who was still crouched, eyes closed, sweat beading on his forehead. Aysel wondered at the effort. She had never formally trained, not like Mathei and her parents, it had been impossible to send her to the Academy. All her ability was instinct, and while she had practiced some, rarely used it in such a way that it drained her as it did Tareck. She would also not be able to use a sigil if her life depended on it. She'd never studied them.

"Ask and I am commanded," Aysel said, formally, eliciting a smile from Makram. He had rarely been formal with her and Mathei, more like an elder brother. When Mathei was younger and just beginning to realize he would never desire women, he had thought he'd loved Makram. In honesty, there had been a time Aysel had thought the same, but she had been a girl and Makram undeniably handsome and charming. And lonely. Aysel had simply ridden out her crush until it changed to what it was now, admiration and loyalty. Mathei had confessed his feelings to Makram, who had been kind and understanding in his rebuff. Aysel would do anything for him because of that, because he was not cruel when so many in Sarkum could be, and had been, to Mathei.

"I need you to spy on the Sultana's Grand Vizier, Behram Kadir," Makram said. Aysel raised her eyebrows. That would certainly be the highest-ranking person she had ever spied on, with Makram's sanction anyway. She had always kept an eye on Kinus. "And no one, absolutely no one is to know. Not Mathei, not your father, not anyone. You understand?"

Aysel hesitated. Her family did not keep secrets from each other. But Makram had demanded it. "What do you need to know?"

"Everything. But listen to me, Aysel. He is dangerous, and he is intelligent. Be more careful than you have ever been. Do not take unnecessary risks, do you understand me?"

"Yes," Aysel said, her skin prickling in response to the dire tone of his voice.

"Only a moment more," Tareck warned, in a voice strained as though he were holding the heaviest weight in the world.

"And do not, under any circumstances, let Bashir Ayan know what I've set you on. I guarantee the Sultana has given him instructions to prevent you from moving freely, and that man does not acknowledge grey areas."

Aysel's entire life was a grey area. Poor Bashir. She bared her teeth at Makram in a feral grin. "As you wish."

Tareck's dampening spell gave with a pop. Aysel tugged on her earlobes to settle the piercing sensation inside her head. The influx of sound momentarily bewildered her. A harrier called above them.

"This"—Makram handed Aysel a piece of paper folded so small she wasn't certain she'd be able to unfold it—"are the names and locations of his estates. Do you require anything? I'll have Tareck take you back to the camp, and he can retrieve your father's steward then." In answer, Tareck sat on the cold ground, wiping the sweat from his face.

"I'd like a bath," Aysel said. Bashir had tracked her once. She'd be certain to stay clean enough that he could not do it again.

As she started for the door, Makram spoke. "How did you get away from Bashir?"

Aysel glanced at him over her shoulder and gave him a half smile. "I ran like the wind."

EIGHT

AYSEL COMMISSIONED TARECK AND Adem to help her move the farmer and his family into the large tent her family had taken, and she took their smaller, lean-to shelter. It was a patchwork of oiled hides, secured between the edge of one of the large tents and two wobbly poles. The floor was a mud puddle, as it sat in a low spot in the camp. Aysel thought again of the beds in the palace, of how her brother was probably fast asleep at this very moment, drooling into silk sheets. But this was their lot. He was glamorous and made for life among fine things and the rich and wealthy, she was unglamorous and perfectly suited to sneaking about in the dark and sleeping in cold, dirty lean-tos.

"I'll see about sending you up some oiled canvas for these sides." Tareck didn't say, "so the katil can't sneak up on you while you're asleep," which is exactly what she had been thinking, that more than the cold, she didn't wish to sleep where she was perfectly visible to anyone out on a stroll.

"Thank you."

"I don't like you up here alone, Kit." He eyed the darkening sky with irritation.

"Well then hurry up and see about getting me some canvas. And perhaps some throw pillows while you're at it. Then it will really feel like home." Aysel smiled, but Tareck didn't buy her sale, glowering at her.

"I'll send it up with someone." He gave her shoulder a squeeze, then strode in the direction of the larger tent, where Adem and his family were preparing to follow Tareck to the palace. Aysel watched them leave on horseback, Erkin sitting in front of his father in the saddle.

Only when they had disappeared from her view did loneliness settle on her. The gloomy day, with its threatening dark clouds, did not help things. It did help that she was clean, and that she had new clothes, a gift from Makram. He said he had more, but it would take time to have them made. The set she wore now were the type she'd seen servants wearing about the palace. Heavy cotton salvar dyed dark brown to hide the mud, with oiled leather boots that reached her mid-calf. The caftan was the same material as the pants, long, but not floor-length like the formal kind the nobility wore. It hit her knees and was split up the sides to her hips for freedom of movement. All of it was loose, like everyone else wore, so she would fit in. As much as she could. The people of Sarkum carried much more of the Odokan blood than most people in Tamar. Her skin was a shade duskier, her hair a bit coarser, even without its curl, her eyes narrower and deeper.

"Miss Aysel?" a little voice said from behind her.

Aysel turned. The farmer's daughters were twins, she had learned, and so she had trouble telling them apart. "Ceren?" she guessed. The little girl smiled and shook her head. "Lale, then. I'll get it right one day."

The girl shrugged. They were perhaps five or six Turns, too thin and wiry.

"Mama wants you to eat with us." Lale took Aysel by the hand and led her back to the tent she had relinquished. She was greeted warmly and fed from the food they had bought with Bashir's stolen money. Aysel lingered for some time, watching the girls play a muddy game of touch and go. The sky darkened with each passing sun mark, and the temperature dipped. Aysel was glad for the company, even if the farmer said perhaps three words, and the wife could only speak about returning to Sarkum. Aysel was secretly relieved when both girls begged her in high-pitched unison to join their game.

"Be careful!" their mother warned as Aysel dashed into the fray— by unanimous, giggling decision she'd been nominated as the chaser. The girls scattered in opposite directions, and Aysel went after Ceren, or whichever one had darted in between the nearest two shelters. It was a maze of cloth walls and stacked crates, and Aysel only just kept sight of Ceren as she ran, laughing.

Unfortunately, the mud was as slick as ice in some places, kept nearly so by the shadows of the shelters. Ceren took an impressive tumble. Before Aysel could reach her Bashir strode into view from beyond one of the shelters. He crouched down in the path and slipped his big hands beneath Ceren's arms so he could hoist her to her feet.

"All to rights?" he asked with a warm smile. Aysel's eyebrows lifted, but she said nothing to give herself away.

"I scraped my knee," Ceren said, though she looked a bit intimidated. They had not experienced any of the guards beyond the orders they shouted and the armor they wore. Aysel could see the girl's salvar had been ripped across the knee.

"May I look?" Bashir asked. Ceren nodded. He set a bundle he carried on the ground and rolled up the leg of her salvar. He made a show of examining her knee, complete with gruff rumbles of concern. Aysel sucked her lips between her teeth to stifle a smile.

"Well"—he draped his forearms over his bent knees and gave Ceren a serious look—"I think you'll be all right. But if you wake up in the morning and the whole leg has fallen off, you should definitely go see a guard and ask for a healer."

"It won't fall off!" Ceren squealed, giggling.

"Probably not. Why were you running?"

Ceren pointed to Aysel, who stood only a few paces away from them, tucked between two of the smaller tents. Aysel wiggled her fingers in a wave when he saw her watching him. Bashir tipped his head back and sighed, closing his eyes briefly. Ceren looked up at him as he straightened, grabbed his bundle, and rose. "Want to play touch and go with us?"

"No. She cheats," he said. Aysel let herself smile. Ceren slumped and returned to Aysel, with Bashir only a step or two behind.

"Back to your tent, Ceren. And tell your mother I said thank you for dinner." Aysel patted her head and Ceren groaned in disappointment. Aysel clasped her hands behind her back, facing Bashir. "Was that a soft underbelly I just witnessed?"

"No." He took the bundle from beneath his arm and shoved it at her. Aysel had to take a step back to keep her balance and wrapped her arms around what appeared to be the canvas Tareck had promised.

"I am honored to have the commander himself delivering my household goods." Aysel turned and strode toward her new home. "Whatever have I done to deserve such a thing?"

Aysel dropped the roll of canvases on the wooden pallet that served to raise her meager pile of blankets out of the mud and began unrolling them. Bashir stood just outside the shelter of the hides that masqueraded as her roof, frowning at the measly structure.

"You could step inside," she suggested, when rain began to pelt down in cold, fat drops. Bashir frowned at her. "I won't accost you." She shook out one of the canvases. "Unless you want me to, of course." She tossed him a grin just before she turned her back to him and began securing the canvas to the lowest side of the shelter, at the corner where the hides were lashed to the poles.

"I volunteered to bring them so I could see what you were doing up here." Bashir ducked beneath the shelter roof as he spoke in suspicious tones. Another benefit of being short, she didn't have to duck when she was inside.

"The usual," Aysel grunted as she stretched on tiptoe to fasten the canvas to the higher portion of the roof frame, "freezing, dining on lentils." She made a thoughtful noise when she knotted the tie in place and relaxed back to her feet. She blew on her fingers and tucked them under her armpits to warm them before attempting the next tie. She could pull the pallet over and use it as a step, otherwise she wouldn't be able to reach the rest. "There will be a camp ball later"—she tried to pull the canvas tight and secure it an arm span from the last tie but couldn't reach—"but I won't be able to attend because I don't have anything to wear."

"You're funny," he said at her back, reaching his arms around and past hers, making quick work of the tie she couldn't even reach.

Wheel and spokes he was warm. She wanted to snuggle into him like she used to the feather-stuffed comforter that had burned with her home.

"Yes I am. But I haven't seen you laugh once. I don't think you have a sense of humor." Aysel wove quickly out from under his arm before she did something utterly foolish. "Thank you." She gestured at the canvas as he tied the last one in place.

"I do," he said, turning to grab another canvas and affixing it to the other side of the shelter. "I do have a sense of humor, I mean."

"No," Aysel gasped, stepping onto the pallet and pulling the last canvas into place as the final wall. She'd move the pallet into the center of the room, both to get it away from the leaking sides and so no one could stab her through the walls while she slept. She glanced over her shoulder at him to goad him, and he met her gaze, and somehow they silently agreed to race to the corner where their two walls would meet.

Aysel beat him by two ties. "Your fingers are too big and clumsy for this kind of detailed work." She grinned.

"I bet my ties hold better than your dainty girly ones," he said. She caught the tiniest, fleeting flash of laughter in his eyes and the upturned corners of his mouth.

"Dainty? That is a word no one has ever used to describe me." Aysel hopped off the pallets and sat, patting the place beside her. Bashir looked at her as if she had offered him a place in a snake-filled pit. "Oh, yes. If you sit here my criminal tendencies will rub off on you." Aysel leaned back on her elbows and stretched her legs out, crossing them at the ankles. "You'll be stealing silver from the Sultana's rooms in no time. Best not sit, far better to stand half bent over like that with the rain leaking down the back of your neck. Cold, is it?"

The muscles in his jaw went taut as he grit his teeth, and Aysel admired the intensity of him when he was irritated. What kind of expression might be coaxed from him if she were to run her nails up his back?

He gave in and sat, though on the far end of the pallet.

"I didn't mean you were dainty. Just your knots," he said, grumpily. "You're strong enough." He said it as though it were the most precious of compliments, and Aysel laughed. Only an ox of an earth mage would think that.

"Strong enough for what?" Aysel sat up. Lying back like that with him sitting so close made her feel vulnerable, exposed. Not that she was entirely opposed to being vulnerable or exposed to the man, but perhaps after they had agreed upon some kind of truce.

"Just, strong enough. I've never met a noblewoman who could handle herself as you do. Who would volunteer to stay in a refugee camp in the mud and the snow, or help anyone in it, for that matter."

He was leaning forward, his arms propped on his knees. There was still enough light for her to see the large swaths of muscle across his back and broad shoulders beneath his caftan. It wasn't fair how maddeningly attractive the man was.

"I see. You're one of those who thinks all nobles are self-important and self-serving. How boring," Aysel said.

He rubbed his hands over his face, and it occurred to her how tired he looked. She almost gave in to the urge to invite him to take a nap. Perhaps he was being pushed too hard, or his men were. They were a force meant to man a palace, not run refugee trains from the border, guard their camps, as well as families of political asylum. And also personally account for a spy.

She wished she could take it easy on him, she didn't have anything personal against him, and she did owe him for the lie he'd told on her behalf. But she couldn't, not when her family was in danger, or when Makram gave her orders. "If it makes you feel better, I did use your money to help them. Not my own. Does that fit your ideas better?"

"I didn't need it," he said, softly. "And I don't think all nobles are like that. Just most."

"Why did you lie to the Sultana?" Aysel asked, just as softly. *Please.* She pleaded. *Say it was to protect yourself.* She didn't know what she would do if he had lied to keep her secret, without even knowing what it was.

"I don't know." He dropped his hands, glaring at the mud that surrounded his boots.

"You cannot make me beholden to you by such acts." Well, he could, but she did not know how she could repay him and still follow her orders.

"Why were you afraid?" He turned his head to look at her. A shaft of light through the gaps in the canvas sliced across his eyes, lightening the gold and emphasizing the dark streaks. She had not thought she'd worn her emotions on her face, but apparently, she had enough for him to see when she had believed her secrets were about to be revealed.

"If I am in prison, or at the hangman's mercy, then I cannot protect my family, can I?" It was not a lie, but it was not the truth either.

"Is that really what you're doing? Protecting your family? I can do that. My men will keep them safe," he said with a hint of sympathy. Ugh. Selfless nobility. Mathei would call Bashir adorable.

"You are stretched thin. Even I can see that. And look at you. I almost offered to let you nap a moment ago when you looked like you might collapse sideways from exhaustion," Aysel accused. He stood too quickly, as if the bench were hot, and she did too, facing him, her arms folded, frowning.

"The Sultana wishes for me to relay a message to you." His eyes narrowed, his voice hard and filled with authority and command as it had not been moments before. "You are to contain yourself to the camp and the palace as it pertains to visiting your family. You are not to hunt assassins in her city, or harass any citizen of Tamar."

"Define harass."

"No spying, no stealing, no entering places that are not open to the public. And I have been given license to broaden the definition as I see fit," he said with menace that did not suit him.

"And you're going to stop me from doing any of that?" Aysel twisted her mouth in disbelief.

"I or my men." Such confidence.

"Tsk. You're the only person who has even come close to catching me. Your men don't stand a chance." She did not miss the quick flash of pleasure in his expression, and she liked it. "And I bet you can't do it again."

"No?" Confidence leant humor to his tone. Aysel squeaked when a surge of power rippled through the earth around them and it shifted alarmingly. She stumbled, catching herself against Bashir, her hands pressed to the flat, muscled plane of his stomach.

He caught her arms in his hands and gave her a slow, half-sided smile that almost buckled her knees. "Caught you," he murmured.

"Cheater," Aysel said, a bit breathless, her gaze locked on his mouth.

"A little," he admitted, a distracted tone in his voice. She wanted to climb him, lock her arms around his neck and her legs around his hips and kiss him until the neediness he inspired in her went away. "And I don't like the thought of you sleeping in a swamp," he added as his hands tightened a fraction around her arms, coaxing her an increment closer. She realized at his words that what he had done was command the earth under her entire shelter up, so it was no longer sunken in comparison to the land around it.

"Thank you." She was shy as she had never been, and that was all that stopped her from trying to kiss him. She had never been so furiously attracted to someone she shouldn't be.

"You're welcome." His voice was filled with gravel, his eyes with a lingering glint of magic, his hands were warm and commanding on her arms. She was lost. Oh, Wheel help her. Her fingers flexed against his belly, and he inhaled sharply, pulling her against him and up, to her tiptoes as he bent down.

"Commander?" a man's voice called from outside, but nearby. Cold sense exploded in Aysel's body and she took a jerky step away from him. Bashir gave a slow blink, staring at the canvas at her back in confusion, in the direction the voice had originated.

"Do you want him to find you in here?" Aysel asked. The sense that had returned to her found its way to him, and he shoved a hand through his tawny hair as he shook his head. "That can't happen again," she said, flatly, and pointed to the back wall of the shelter, in the opposite direction of the voice.

"No," he agreed, turning from her.

"Back to the palace with you. And get your rest, Ox." Aysel faked a smile. "You're going to need it."

He stood with his back to her for a moment, one hand at the back of his neck, the other gripping a handful of canvas.

"Commander Ayan!" the voice came again, this time louder, and closer. Bashir breathed a curse and shoved the canvas aside then hunched into the rain.

Aysel flopped on her back on the pallet and laid her arm over her eyes. Mathei was going to laugh her right out of the palace for being a witless simpleton. And she would deserve it. Wanting to kiss the man who was ordered to prevent her from everything she needed to do. Aysel groaned. It would not happen again.

NINE

AYSEL CRAWLED OUT OF the slightly less cold cocoon of her moth-eaten blankets a few marks before the sun came up. She sat on the edge of the pallet, groggy, thirsty, and irritable. As she gave herself a few moments to wake, she entertained herself by imagining waking up next to the inferno of warmth that Bashir had been. It was best that he was not with her, or she doubted anything could have coaxed her from his side and his heat.

She combed her fingers through her tangled curls and managed them into a messy braid. Her mother had all the secrets to taming Aysel's hair, though in Sarkum she had worn it down more often. She'd noticed many women in Narfour wore their hair down. Perhaps when she went looking for the Grand Vizier's estates she'd give her poor abused curls a break from the braids.

She pulled on her boots then shrugged into her harness, checking that her blades were secured in their sheaths. It was time to hunt, and no imagined bedmate was going to save her from that.

Aysel pushed herself to her feet and out of the shelter in one surge of effort. The blast of cold, wet air helped sharpen her senses, bringing her fully out of the grogginess of sleep. The guard standing outside her shelter appeared irritated by her sudden appearance. Aysel cursed Bashir in her head.

"It's late for you to be up and about," the guard sneered. If he was going to be unpleasant, then she would return the favor. Aysel pressed her hands over her low belly and bent forward a little.

"I'm bleeding like a stuck pig," she wailed. "I just need—"

He shook his head violently and pointed toward the pit toilets that had been dug on the far end of the camp. He didn't follow her as she started toward them, and as soon as she could safely veer off the path she did. It might be fun to see the conversation between Bashir and his guard when he reported losing her because she had needed to treat her menses and he couldn't stomach it.

Aysel grinned as she cut through the dark, quiet camp and up the hill toward the spring. The lingering clouds from the winter rain served her well, keeping the moonlight from highlighting her movements. She planned to hike to the rise of the hill and walk the ridge, or at least near it, to gain a better viewpoint downward. In that, the lack of light would hinder her.

The climb was interminable, her calves and hamstrings aching and useless by the time she reached a point she thought was suitable to cut across. Aysel sat to catch her breath, looking down the hill and over the city. Mage orbs floated all through the streets, fading as daylight neared. They'd be renewed the next evening by whatever Lightbringers maintained them. Some windows were lit, so the city was hundreds upon hundreds of points of lights, like a strange map of pulse points, flickering flames and pulsing orbs. It was beautiful, and beyond it, in contrast, the black expanse of the sea, burnished by the dim moonlight that filtered through the clouds.

Some people had the luxury of sitting to observe things like this view without a care in the world. Would she ever be able to? Perhaps when she was older, and people like the Sultana and Makram had reshaped the world. It might be a warmer place for mages like her and people like Mathei. Maybe they would finally fit.

She rose to her feet and picked her way across the face of the hill, far enough down the slope that she would not be silhouetted against the sky, but high enough that most of the hill was below her. At one point a fox darted past, down the hill, making his way to the city for a hunt through the garbage, or simply moving out of her way.

Every few hundred paces she paused and crouched, listening and watching. The ground at this altitude was frozen solid, and frost had settled on the plants and stones, so her footing was poor, and it slowed her progress.

A quarter mark of the moon later she knew she was being followed. The night air carried sound well, and her first hint had been the faint clack of rocks knocking together. She didn't look, there was no need to let them know she was aware of them. Aysel puzzled over their identity as she began to weave threads of her power around her like a cloak, stretching them thinly, like layers of the most ephemeral silk, one by one across herself. *Fade.*

She stepped off the path when a thick bank of clouds dimmed the moonlight even more. Aysel took two steps and dropped to her belly in the dead grass. The wetness of winter had bent it all to the ground, so there was nowhere to hide on the slope. That also meant her chosen spot was no worse than any other. It would have been rather obvious if she'd hidden in the only crop of bushes on the hillside. She dared not run too far from the path, or risk catching her pursuer's attention at the change in direction. Her magic hid her well, when she worked within its limitations.

Time passed in slow beats of her heart, and she concentrated on her breathing, keeping it slow, measured and silent, her hands pressed to the frozen ground to either side of her so she could push herself up quickly if need be. A lifetime passed before she heard a footfall, a scrape of boot on grass, and she carefully turned her head toward the sound. The light did not favor her. There was only the dark silhouette of a man as he moved, placing his feet with care. He was a few hundred paces away, and Aysel watched his progress while renewing her spell, imagining herself fading into the grass, so if he looked at her it would be like looking through a pane of glass.

There was no spell to slow the beat of her heart or wet her dry mouth as he drew near. At least not for her. He'd become aware he'd lost sight of her now, every few steps he stopped and surveyed the slope with a calculated turn of his head, listening. Whoever he was, he'd done this sort of thing before. He neither panicked nor changed his pace. He knew she was likely hiding or following him in turn.

Aysel's hands flexed, ready, itching, to draw her blades. This must be one of the assassins, perhaps one they'd left behind to deal with her when the rest of the family moved to the palace. That he was alone suggested his companions had followed her family to the palace. Urgency made her muscles jump. She shouldn't be on this hillside hiding from a single man when there could be a whole pack of them after her family. But she schooled herself to stillness. Leaving this man now would be a mistake.

Aysel's hands were cold against the frozen ground, beginning to ache. She moved with deliberate slowness, pressing her arms against the ground and carefully retracting her hands into her sleeves. Then she shifted, rocking back and forth to get them under her chest. If they were cold and numb, she'd struggle to handle her swords. And if the man was one of the Mirza's katil, then shoddy bladework would be a problem.

He stopped just a few body lengths from her. Aysel tightened her magic, mentally chanting her desire more quickly. *Fade. Fade.* She turned her face toward the ground, the moonlight less likely to highlight her dark hair than it was her face. He was big. That was a descriptor that could be used, at least in her case, for most men. While he was not as tall and broad as Bashir, he was big enough and tall enough to be a great deal stronger than Aysel. If she had to fight him, she would need to end it quickly or she would not outlast his strength.

Energy surged through her with the rapid beat of her heart, and she tried to steady herself.

He took a few more steps and stopped, putting him nearly at level with her on the path above. Aysel took the tiniest sips of air, holding as still as she was able. Her magic had gotten her through closer calls, but she had not been lying prone in the moonlight.

The man crouched, and Aysel almost cursed out loud. He whispered a sharp word and her hopes died on its blade.

Pale, pulsing light burst forth above her, and Aysel closed her eyes. Wheel-cursed fire mages and their damned orbs.

"Well, well, well."

Aysel lifted her head to look at him and released her grip on her fade spell. The real problem was that she did not know if he was only an Aval, a Lightbringer, the least powerful of all fire mages, who had to use spoken words to cast their small arsenal of weak spells, or something more powerful, like a Firestormer, a Sival. Aysel had always hoped she would not be cast off the Wheel by a fireball.

When she looked at him she knew he was a katil. He wore all-black caftan and salvar, and his boots were dyed-black leather as well. No one wore black, it was considered unlucky because of its association with the Sixth House. Except of course if your profession circled around murder. Then black was entirely appropriate.

More telling was the sword at his hip. The katil employed by the palace in Al-Nimas all carried a yataghan with a stamped gold medallion on the hilt. His light made that stamp glint, casting the Rahal crest in relief. Aysel pushed up to a crouch.

"The littlest Attiyeh." He grinned as if he'd made the cleverest of jokes.

Aysel rolled her eyes. "If your friends chose you to hunt me, it must be because you're the littlest katil?" she said. His grin dissolved to a frown. Aysel rose.

"I heard they called you Little Fox at the palace."

That rumor had been started when someone overheard Tareck call her Kit, his affectionate nickname for the girl he had mentored for long Turns. Aysel did not mind either moniker, foxes were small and clever, and she liked to think she shared some of their traits. Right now she could use a healthy dose of clever.

"I did not realize they brought Lightbringers into the Mirza's katil," Aysel said, casually. If he were anything but an Aval, fire mage pride would not allow the mistake to go uncorrected. He smiled. Aysel was not completely confident that had answered her question.

"Everyone needs light."

"So, how would you like to do this?" she asked in resignation. He chuckled, rising from his crouch. Not only was he tall, but he was uphill from her, and that advantage displeased her.

"I'm only out for an evening stroll. I simply thought I heard a snake in the grass. Or a fox."

"I see." So, he was not out to kill her, only to follow her. But katil were not spies. Possibly he had drawn the short stick and been put on observation duty. Someone was marked to die, and if she were to guess, it was her father. Perhaps her brother as well, who would inherit her father's estate and possibly take over the reins of her father's hold in Makram's rebellion.

"And if that fox decided to go on its way?" she asked.

"By all means." He held a hand out as though inviting her to stroll. But he couldn't afford to let her go and warn her father about meeting one of the katil. She knew that, just as she could not afford to let him go and warn his companions that she was aware of them. Even if she did fight him and win, she didn't exactly wish to leave a body lying around that would anger the Sultana and cause hardship for her father and mother. Or Bashir.

Thinking of Bashir brought a half-formed plan into her mind…

"Well then, goodnight." Aysel turned down the hill. She made toward the camp, the skin along her back and arms crawling with the sensation of his gaze and her body hyper aware he was still plenty close enough to launch an attack on her before she could turn. But he did not.

He did follow her though, at a distance. The sensation of being stalked by someone she was absolutely sure was going to try and kill her, and who wasn't necessarily trying to hide it, was a new, nauseating feeling. He'd given her enough lead that she could outrun him, especially on a rocky, uneven slope, where her magic would give her speed and agility he could not match. But she didn't want to outrun him. She wanted to keep him far enough away to have warning if he decided to attack, but close enough she could lure him into her trap. At least she hoped it would be a trap. It was hard to set a trap when the party that was supposed to be the trap was unaware of their role.

Aysel crossed the broad road that led from the camp to the city. That route was too long; certainly, he would lose patience and attack long before she reached her destination. She had traversed the hillside far enough that she crossed the road outside view of the perimeter guard on the camp. The slope on the other side would deliver her very close to the palace, beyond a few alleys and up the hill. Aysel pondered the best way to keep her katil's focus without it escalating into a fight. He would about-face and run the moment he saw the palace gates, and even if she could get him that far she didn't think the two guards at the entrance would be enough to catch him. So. She would have to try a spell she was only barely capable of. Aysel had managed it twice before, but she had been safe, able to concentrate, and she could see the subject.

Well, it was worth a try. Aysel glanced around and spotted a winter-deadened shrub down the hill and to her left. She made her way to it, then made a show of lifting up her caftan and wiggling as she pushed her salvar down to her boot tops. She squatted. She could just make out the katil's dark shape on the hillside. He had stopped.

Aysel snorted. If she were an assassin…well. If it were someone she was trying to kill, she'd have no qualms doing it while they had their salvar around their ankles. She shimmied hers up at the thought, though she remained squatting. If he did attack her, she wanted her clothes on.

Aysel closed her eyes and released her grip on her power, but only enough to let it sink into her bones—and her voice, which was the most important part. She could not see Bashir, but she could picture him, the faded wash of freckles over his brow and nose, the exact golden hue of his eyes, their dark striations…the feel of his body against hers, strong, and warm. His hands on her arms, the smoldering way he could smile with only one side of his mouth, the shape of his broad shoulders and back beneath his caftan.

"Ox"—she tried to conjure him further with her whisper of her name for him—"there's a katil chasing me. I can get him to the first rise in the palace road. Fire mage."

If the spell worked, he heard her as though she were speaking directly in front of him. If he didn't, or he ignored her, that road to the palace was going to be very lonely. And if he ignored her she hoped he was the one to stumble on her crispy remains the next day.

"Talking to yourself?"

Aysel opened her eyes and frowned. The katil now stood just uphill from where she crouched, chewing lazily on a long blade of dead grass he'd retrieved from the hill. She'd been concentrating so hard on the spell she hadn't heard the man approach. She rose, then almost tumbled backward down the hill when vertigo assaulted her, making the world spin.

Too much. She'd used too much power. Stupid girl.

"It makes it less boring to take a piss."

"Do you always piss with your pants on?" He bared his teeth, clenched around the grass blade. His hand moved to his sword hilt. He was close enough, and she off-balance enough, that all he had to do was unsheathe his sword in an arc and it would slice her open across her chest.

Aysel glared at him, and he tensed, yanking on the sword. Aysel leapt, cutting sideways and down the hill. She let herself roll, tumbling once to get her feet under her, and popped up into a sprint. Her instinct was to put all her power into speed, but she didn't want to lose him. And her instincts laughed at her. She had to fight them all the way down the hill, forcing herself to pull up, to allow him to keep her in his sight lines.

Fire exploded on the hill next to her and Aysel looked back at him in shock. First, he was obviously not just an Aval, and second, what kind of imbecile would throw fire on a hill overlooking a palace full of guards? She almost shouted a thank-you to him for helping her cause but thought better of it. Fire mage pride. Always their greatest weakness. Or maybe he just hated running and hoped to finish things quickly.

The hill ended abruptly in a broken-off bluff, and Aysel launched herself off the edge, flipping once and landing on the road at its base. Her magic kept her light, so she barely felt her landings. There were two rows of houses and a smaller street to cross before she reached the palace road. She jogged into an alley, glancing back once she was in the protective shadow of a home. Her katil had run to the right of the bluff, where it became less steep, and was taking the slope sideways, sliding down the slick mud. He jumped, landing somewhat gracefully for someone without her talents, and broke back into a run. Aysel took off, dodging to the right when she broke out of the alley, and ran up the side road until he emerged from between buildings and caught sight of her again.

She cut through another alley and tripped over a pile of lumber, barking her shin and falling flat on her belly, skinning her hands and her chin on the stones. "Damnit." She staggered to her feet and took off in a painful run just as he appeared in the alley mouth behind her. Too close. She didn't want him that close. Fire exploded against the wall by her head.

"Are you missing on purpose?" she called over her shoulder. He replied with a foul curse referring to recreational activities and Aysel clicked her tongue in admonishment, to herself of course. Her mother always told her that people who resorted to ugly name-calling were ugly people. Dilara was usually right about things.

Aysel's feet almost slid out from under her again when she emerged from the alley and turned onto the palace road, hitting a slick spot on the cobbles where water had dripped from the roof of the building above. She caught herself on her hands and scrambled back into a run.

The katil hit the same spot and fell, landing hard on his side and letting out another curse. Aysel laughed, both to provoke him and to release some of her growing tension. It never served to be too wound up. If her spell had failed and there was no one to meet her, she didn't have a backup plan. Except run faster. Unfortunately, attempting to cast a spell she barely knew at a person she couldn't see had cost her a good portion of her reserve, and a mage's reserves were not infinite. Not even hers.

The hill was steeper than she remembered. Her pace slowed, and the katil gained, because he had longer legs and a body not drained by a spell he shouldn't have cast. She could feel the heat of his unleashed power growing stronger against her back and she pushed harder, her lungs burning like he'd set them on fire, her shin aching where she'd caught it against the lumber in the alley. He reached for her just as the hill leveled out, and Aysel dodged, spinning from his grasp, but her legs failed her, and she fell flat on her back, her swords cracking against her spine and her breath rushing away from her.

Aysel lay stunned and breathless, like she'd been struck by a cart and left in the road.

"I hate running," he snarled as he stalked toward her. He drew his hand back and fire blazed over his skin as if his entire arm were a torch. Aysel rolled and tried to kick to her feet, reaching for one of her blades. Every inch of her burned with exhaustion, but she fought through it, drawing the sword and swinging it clumsily at him. He barely needed to sway to avoid it, and Aysel faced him, breathing hard as she drew the other one.

She'd heard stories. They said Chara'a could draw magic from other mages. Mathei had told her they could do so from mages of their own House. Perhaps there was a slim chance she could draw power from the katil, even if he was Fifth House and she First.

She had no idea how to do it, but now seemed a good enough time to give it a try. Aysel lunged at him, swiping her sword at the side of him armed with fire and he dodged again, drawing his blade with his free hand. She took that brief pause to reach out with her magic, and called his to her the way she called air to encircle her. A sluggish thread of hot, burning magic wove through hers, bucking and whipping. Aysel grit her teeth against the pain. It wasn't supposed to hurt, was it?

The flame on his arm snuffed out, and he looked at it as though it were someone else's arm. Aysel pulled harder on his magic, thinking she'd drain him of his power then use what she'd stolen to speed her getaway. It proved another mistake, because his power, and its heat, came at her with the same force of his fireballs. Lights and fire exploded in her mind and against her own power.

Aysel reeled, staggering back, momentarily blinded by the pain. She saw only the fuzzy shape of him and managed to twist out of the way of a broad swipe of his sword, losing her balance and falling backwards in the process. The tip of his blade opened a slash across her shoulder and collarbone. Almost her throat. She fell hard enough it knocked the sword out of her right hand. Aysel flipped onto her belly, grabbing for it, but it skittered down the hill and out of reach.

The katil kicked her in the ribs so hard it flipped her over. Aysel curled into a ball, coughing, gasping for air.

"Hold still, you little bitch."

"Go jump off the Wheel," Aysel replied with venom, because being polite was not going to save her life. She managed to get to her hands and knees, though she kept one arm wrapped around her ribs, certain at least one was broken. Lights still burst in her vision, and she felt as if she were burned all over. Every breath she drew was molten heat.

"You first." He lifted the sword in one hand to plunge into her back. Then came a whip of air and a *thunk*.

Aysel looked up. Twin images of him, one more solid and one like a ghost of him, lowered the sword slowly. Aysel blinked and her vision cleared enough so the two images became one, with a mystified look on his face. Then he choked on a cough and dropped to a knee in front of her. His sword clattered to the stone and Aysel grabbed it, kicking to get away from him. Had she killed him by trying to pull his power? For some reason that horrified her.

His hands dropped to his sides, then he fell face first onto the stone. Aysel sat on her haunches, staring at him.

He didn't move. She collapsed onto her back and closed her eyes, still holding his sword in one hand and her own in the other. Aysel's head throbbed, her throat dry. She started to laugh, but then clutched at her ribs, yielding to a fit of shallow coughs of pain. She opened her eyes.

Bashir stood over her, crossbow in hand, his head tipped so his face was above hers. A long way above hers. Aysel started to giggle again, and the angry look he already wore took on the threatening heat of magma. Aysel couldn't think straight, like she'd been drinking arak all night, her body filled with buzzing energy and fizzing terror, and she could only stare up at him mutely when the giggling stopped.

"What is funny about this?" he rumbled, and Aysel was certain she felt the earth beneath her shift.

"I bet you wish you had a crossbow when I stole my swords. You could have shot me right off the arena roof," she babbled, then started giggling again, then tears streamed from her eyes from the pain in her ribs and she arched away from it, rolling to her side and drawing a breath that sounded a bit too much like a sob. The high was gone, and Aysel started to shake as if she'd just emerged from an ice bath.

"Take him out of here," Bashir said over his shoulder. "And get me a blanket." He crouched beside her, handing the crossbow up to one of his men that passed behind Aysel on their way to collect the katil's body. "Can you sit up?" He took the katil's yataghan from her and handed it to another man who joined the first. She didn't look as they tugged the dead man away from her and lifted him up, dragging him up the road to the palace.

"I'm just going to stay here." Aysel felt half frozen to the ground anyway. "I'll walk it off in another moment." She swiped the tear tracks from her cheek.

"Mmhmm." Bashir tucked two fingers into the tear in her caftan where the katil had sliced her with his blade.

She slapped at his hand when he prodded the wound, pinching at the torn flesh. Her body sizzled with the pain. "Stop it." She sat up and gripped her head as ache thrummed through it.

He paused his assessment for a moment, then put his big hand on her ribcage and dug his thumb into her ribs. Aysel grunted in pain, shoving at his chest with both hands and having no impact whatsoever. "Just bruised." He sounded relieved. He looked up the hill to where his men dragged the katil, his hand still resting against her ribs.

Aysel forced his hand away because she was still not in her right mind and him touching her made her want to collapse into him. "*Stop poking me, Ox.*"

He glared, dropping his hand.

A guard strode up to them, giving the blanket he held to Bashir.

"Send Lieutenant Terzi to check on Elder Attiyeh and his family," Bashir ordered. The guard clapped a fist against his heart and trotted up the hill. Bashir rocked forward, dropping a knee to the stones, and swung the blanket around Aysel. She lifted her gaze to his face, and met his stern stare.

"You told me I was the only one who had ever come so close to catching you. That katil looked damn close."

"I had it under control," Aysel said. Not because she believed it or thought he would, but because she was so grateful for his intervention that she knew if she thanked him out loud she'd sob. Her hands shook as she hugged the blanket around herself. Whether it was her spectacularly failed attempt at pulling the other man's magic, the expenditure of her own, or simple shock from almost dying, Aysel didn't know.

"I know." When he looked at her again she could see his magic quaking in his eyes, unleashed with his temper, or some other emotion. Righteous indignation, perhaps. Gold light painted jagged lines over his temples and cheeks, as though his power were breaking him into pieces, like a quake showing the molten earth beneath. She'd never seen someone's unleashed magic manifest like that. Aysel lifted a hand, compelled to touch him, but stopped, hugging the blanket more tightly around her and turning her gaze toward the palace.

He stood abruptly and retrieved her first sword from the road where she had left it when she sat up, then strode down the hill and found the other. He moved slowly, deliberately, and when he returned the light had faded from his skin and eyes.

"I cannot let you return to the camp tonight." The words were a gruff command.

"I want to see my family, but I'm returning to the camp tomorrow," Aysel countered. She wasn't going to be made a prisoner.

"We'll see." He crouched in front of her again. "Can you walk?"

"That depends. What happens if I can't?" Bashir lifted an eyebrow. "Ohhhh." She grinned. "Shall I pretend to faint and you can carry me, limp and helpless, to my father?" She raised one hand out of the blanket and drummed her fingers against her lips.

"Aysel," he rumbled as he stood. "Get up."

"Spoil sport," Aysel muttered, secretly pleased he had called her by name, and obeyed, albeit slowly. Bashir's hand curved under her arm when she swayed from dizziness. He left it there, steadying her uneven, limping steps as they walked up the hill to the palace.

He was silent beside her the entire way, stopping only to give orders to his men about the katil's body when they passed beneath the gate. Then he led her into the palace. Aysel followed him like a docile sheep, leaning harder into his grip with each passing moment as exhaustion sapped her. She'd had far too little sleep to begin with, and two nights of running and fighting with very little to eat was finally catching up to her. And almost dying. Mustn't forget almost dying.

"Could I possibly convince you to tell my mother that I was not even close to being skewered like a kebab? Perhaps something more along the lines of 'she fought bravely and valiantly and I vanquished her foe for her all before he was even within shouting distance'?"

Bashir grunted, which might have been a suppressed laugh. "Only if you would care to explain to the Sultana why I assisted you in defying her command that you not hunt assassins in her city."

"I went to the toilets and the man accosted me," Aysel said. "What was I to do but run to the nearest guards?"

"You bypassed every guard in camp, including Guardsman Macar, who has yet to report to me and explain why you are here and he isn't." The displeasure at his subordinate shaped his words into jabs. Oh he was not going to be pleased once he knew the entire story.

"If you're serious about this guarding business you're truly going to have to conscript some smarter guardsmen."

He raised an eyebrow and changed the subject. "You don't have the sense to be afraid of a fire mage, but you're afraid of your mother?" He turned them down another hall and Aysel stumbled against the rug and grabbed for his sleeve with both hands. Bashir's arm slipped around her waist, catching her against him for the briefest of instants, the front of her pressed against his side. Aysel was certain, for a moment, that he held her that way for more than just to allow her time to steady herself. But when she pulled away there was nothing in his impassive expression to suggest she was right. She wasn't in her right mind, that was obvious.

"You don't know my mother," Aysel said as she glanced around. This was the hall where her family's suite was, she remembered the carpet in patterns of pomegranates and peonies, and the arched alcoves that framed portraits of the generations of Sabris that had ruled in Narfour.

"And I was afraid." There was no shame in admitting it to him. People who pretended they weren't afraid of things it made perfect sense to be afraid of were laughable.

"Not afraid enough." He stopped in front of the doors to the suite, nodding to the two men who saluted him. One of them knocked on the doors, eyeing Aysel with alarm. Or curiosity. She couldn't quite tell. Adem opened the doors, and when he saw Aysel his expression, usually reserved and difficult to read, twisted with alarm. He stepped to the side and Bashir led her in. Adem moved first to her parents' rooms, knocking and giving them a brief summation, then did the same for the room where Mathei was apparently sleeping.

"Not on the couch! I'm bleeding," Aysel gasped when Bashir maneuvered her toward the furniture.

"Sit." He took her by the arms and plopped her onto the couch. Aysel curled her lip at him and he narrowed his eyes in response.

Mathei arrived first from Adem's summons, shirtless and groggy from being roused from deep sleep. He looked from Aysel to Bashir and back again, his gaze roving over the wound that had stained half her left side with blood, the tear of her salvar where she had run into the lumber in the alley, and her slumping posture. "Did you do that to her?" Mathei accused, albeit sleepily.

"Don't be absurd," Aysel snapped.

"Aysel!" Dilara gasped, rushing from the room she shared with Thoman, still shrugging into a quilted entari as she came.

"I'm all right." Aysel lifted her hands in placation.

"You're bleeding all over that lovely couch. Sit on the floor." Dilara pointed. Aysel obeyed, casting a glare at Bashir as she slid herself slowly from the seat to the floor.

Bashir folded his arms over his broad chest. "Your daughter is under arrest for defying the Sultana's orders. One of the katil she was hunting was killed just outside the palace tonight. As long as she commits no other crimes, I will consider staying here in the palace as her imprisonment. Otherwise, she will be held in the Cliffs until a trial can be arranged."

Thoman had exited his room and now stared mutely at Bashir, then looked at Aysel.

"A trial? He chased me!" Aysel cried, then flinched. "There are more of them, you know. At least two. And they're coming after Father and Mathei."

"Precautions will be taken. You should rest here and heal." His face was stone, a commander accustomed to being obeyed.

Aysel could not understand how the man standing in front of her and the one who had been in her tent holding her as if he meant to kiss her could possibly be the same person. Had the Sultana spelled him? Some air mages were capable of convoluted mind magic. He wasn't even looking at her.

"I will stop by in the morning to inform you of the guard plan and my requirements so we can be assured of your safety." He bowed to Thoman.

"Goodnight, Commander," her father replied, stiffly, looking bemused.

"I will see you in the morning," Bashir said as Adem opened the door for him.

"I wouldn't bet on it," Aysel shouted at his back, just before Adem closed the door.

"What is going on?" Dilara demanded.

Aysel cursed, realizing why she felt off-balance. "He has my swords!"

<h1 style="text-align:right">TEN</h1>

BASHIR PINCHED THE BRIDGE of his nose and bowed his head, his elbows propped on the table that served as his desk.

"She said she was…" The guardsman, Ali Macar, who Bashir had assigned to watch Aysel in the camp, fidgeted with his collar. "Well she said…" He scratched the back of his neck and his entire face had flushed when Bashir looked up at his pause.

Standing to Bashir's left, Erol sighed impatiently. "Spit it out, man."

"She said she was bleeding like a stuck pig and needed to go to the toilets." Ali appeared as if he might be sick. Bashir briefly contemplated leaping across the table and wrapping his hands around the younger man's neck. Erol burst into loud laughter. Ali flinched, staring at the sandstone tiles at his feet.

"The next time I give you orders to guard someone, they are to be in a room they cannot escape from, or they are not to leave your sight until you are relieved by my orders or another guard. Is that clear? I don't care what they tell you. Most especially if it is Aysel Attiyeh." Bashir let his breath out in a slow stream, something his mother had always done to control her temper when he was being difficult.

If he did not need to commit his seasoned men to the border runs to retrieve refugees, this would all be a great deal simpler. Instead he was forced to give his newest guards orders they could not possibly uphold. And if he hadn't had to rid the guard force of a quarter of its men because they were in the Grand Vizier's pocket, he wouldn't be stretched so thin.

"Yes, sir," Ali said.

"Stables," Erol said. Ali grimaced, but bowed slightly, pressing a fist to his heart. He left, and Erol chuckled again.

Bashir rubbed his hands over his face.

"I want to meet this woman," Erol said, eliciting a surge of temper in Bashir that he wanted to attribute to tiredness and fatigue of Aysel's endless testing, not to his growing admiration, not to a seed of possessiveness.

"Since when do you want to meet criminals?" Bashir asked. "Never mind. You can come with me now. I'm going to make certain she's still where I put her last night." He rose.

"Commander," a guard said as he jogged through Bashir's door and stopped, giving a hasty salute.

"Omar." Bashir's tension made his jaw pop. Omar was one of the men who would have been taking over the guard on the Attiyeh family. On Aysel. A muddy mix of disbelief, fury, and resignation puddled in his belly. "If you are about to tell me—"

"She's gone."

"Wheel take her." Bashir shouldered his way out of the office and out through the barracks into the courtyard. A handful of his men were gathered just outside the barracks near the stables, staring upward like a pack of sun-struck lunatics. His surge of temper became a flood. He never forgave idleness, but especially not now, when there was no time to spare in their too-small force for his men to be loitering aimlessly.

"I've got them," Erol said, when he arrived at Bashir's side. He knew when Bashir was on his last kernel of patience. Even in boyhood, he had always stepped in when Bashir might have lost his temper. They were an odd pairing, fire and earth mage. Not opposing on the Wheel, but counter, like oil and water. It had never poisoned their friendship though.

"You lot!" Erol barked. "Get to your posts or be prepared to polish tile for the rest of your miserable lives."

One of the men, a mid-ranked guardsman, pointed toward the barracks roof. Aysel was perched on the peak of the roof, facing them with her feet on the slope and her head propped in her hands. Guardsman Macar had managed to get himself onto the roof in some foolish bid to redeem himself, and Aysel turned her head slightly to look at him, her expression bored.

"The man's idiocy knows no bounds," Erol said as he squinted at the pair of them.

Bashir shoved aside the tangle of curiosity about what she would do, his anger that she wasn't resting to recover from her wounds, and his maddening exasperation. He'd been trying to untangle webs like these all morning in his mind, a pointless waste.

Ali had obviously reached the end point of his plan now that he was on the roof and tried crawling toward her but panicked when one of the ceramic tiles broke loose under his boot. He clung motionless and wide-eyed to the peak of the roof with both hands.

Wheel preserve him from fools and nuisances. "Down!" Bashir called to Aysel.

She lifted her head, looking from the struggling guard toward Bashir, and flashed a toothy grin at him. She stood, and his heart leapt because the roof was steep, but she might as well have been walking on flat ground for all it seemed to affect her. She took easy steps down the slope and stepped off the edge.

Erol jerked, reacting to the drop-off that was the height of two men, but she landed like a feather in the sand. Bashir felt the barest touch of the power she used to soften her fall, like the faintest of breezes. She recovered quickly, she'd been half mage-sick the night before, had expended too much of herself fleeing the katil. Not that it seemed to bother her this morning.

"This area is off-limits to anyone but guardsmen," Bashir said. He'd sworn to himself, when he realized he was so tired and overtaxed that he'd been utterly unable to control himself in her tent, that he'd stay away from her. And he'd sworn to himself, when he'd seen her nearly impaled and it had taken everything in him not to tear the road beneath that fire mage into cavernous ruin, that he would do nothing else to help her, that he would follow the Sultana's command to the letter.

Desire happened. It was not the first time he'd desired a woman, but not quite like he wanted her. He shouldn't have to remind himself that she was a criminal. A spy. He was going mad, and he wasn't going to allow himself to go any further.

She crossed the sand toward him and Erol, her hands clasped behind her back, her mouth set in a thin line, and a smoldering look of accusation in her steel-ringed eyes. Eyes that held the shape and reminder of her Sarkum heritage. Her hair was loose from its usual braids. It was pulled back from her face, but the rest hung to her shoulder blades in loose chestnut curls that begged for his hands to tangle in them—

"You have to my count of five to return to your rooms, or I will have you in the Cliffs." Bashir managed to keep his voice steady and his magic reined in. He hadn't realized how her twin braids had made her appear younger than she was, more innocent. She wore more formal caftan and salvar than he had seen her in, grey-green silk that matched her eyes and hugged her slim, lithe frame far more closely than her other clothes had. A noblewoman, at least in Sarkum, and today was the first time she had looked like one.

"Rough morning?" Aysel's voice sounded a bit more strained than he'd heard it before. Scratchy. She was not as recovered as she was pretending to be. "I won't trouble you for long. I came to take my blades back." She held out her hands. They were small and calloused, strong enough to wield blades and help her climb as easily as a spider. Her skin was dusky, like Makram's, her tiny frame a legacy from whatever of the steppes had been in her ancestry.

Bashir twisted his face into a scowl to banish the thought of how easy it would be to lift her up against him.

"No." His voice betrayed him, breaking the word in half. Aysel smiled sideways at Erol, letting her gaze roam obviously from his head to his toes.

"Then perhaps you can spare your"—she blinked, studying Erol's clothes—"lieutenant? To accompany me to the market. My family has need of some things before I return to the camp."

"I can—" Erol began.

"When the Wheel shatters," Bashir said without raising his voice. "I told you last night that you are confined to the palace grounds."

"Makram says otherwise. So, if not the lieutenant, then how about that fine gentleman?" Aysel jabbed her thumb over her shoulder, indicating the barracks. Bashir realized his guard was still trapped on the roof. Erol snickered, grinning at Aysel, who smiled back in a way that made her eyes spark and her mouth curve conspiratorially. It was not normal to want to kiss a woman he also wanted to strangle.

Bashir shoved one hand after the other through his hair. Wheel he was tired. She was exhausting.

"You're a little cruel," Erol said, as if he found that alluring. Bashir knew he did, he always chose women who treated him more like a pet than an equal.

"Lieutenant," Bashir said too sharply, "get Guardsman Macar a ladder."

Erol dipped his head to Aysel and strode toward the group of loitering guards.

"Ox. Wheel's mercy, would you go to sleep?" Aysel looked at him with genuine concern on her face.

"I cannot sleep, because you won't do what you're told," he grumbled. "Couldn't you just sit still for a day?"

"Couldn't you just not follow orders for a day?" she said in sing-song.

"Do you have the faintest idea what will happen to me if the Sultana finds out I lied to her about how you got away that first night? She'll strip me of my rank, at the very least." More likely she'd send him straight back to the slums.

Aysel's skin blanched, then her thick eyebrows drew together. "I'm not an enemy, you know. I don't understand why she wants to make me into one."

"The Sultana has many enemies that wear friendly faces. She cannot afford to trust anyone just on one person's say-so. And my job is to obey her, not question her."

Aysel looked away. "I just want to protect my family."

"Then I think you proved last night that job is best left to my men and their crossbows." He narrowed his eyes. A look of surprised betrayal stiffened her expression and her shoulders. They stood in stony silence, glaring again at each other, until a sinking feeling of regret anchored Bashir to the ground beneath him.

"I did not thank you, last night," she said in a tone like ice. "So, thank you for saving my life only to make your best efforts to ensure that the next time I am confronted with a katil I have neither freedom to run nor weapons to fight with. And I will be returning to the camp today, with my weapons, no matter how much you strut around like a puffed-up pigeon."

"A what?" he snapped.

"No no no." She somehow managed to make the *no* sound like the cooing of a bird.

Bashir almost laughed, but she stalked past him and toward the palace. He spun and shot a thread of power into the ground after her, just enough to trip her. She staggered forward as the ground rolled beneath her. When she recovered, she swung around and held her hand out toward him, palm up and canting it from side to side. *Unbalanced.*

It was a rude and foul gesture that no noblewoman he had ever met would dare use.

"Broken spokes," Bashir cursed under his breath.

A CANDLEMARK LATER, MAKRAM strode into the barn where Bashir was tending to Huzur. Bashir clenched his teeth, scrubbing the brush so hard across the gelding's back that the poor beast bowed away from it.

"I can guess what you're here for."

Makram watched him, mutely, as Bashir gentled his brushing, refusing to meet the other man's gaze.

"I think we respect each other…don't we?" he asked.

Bashir stopped, resting his arms against his horse's back. They'd had enough interactions over the season since Makram had come to Narfour for Bashir to judge him to be a man he liked. He'd even demanded Bashir call him by name, when it would not cause raised eyebrows. He did not act like a prince. He acted like a soldier, and he, Tareck, and his handful of men from Sarkum often joined in Bashir's drills and sparring bouts. Bashir's men were improving for it, and all of that made him easier for Bashir to trust. But, still.

"As much as a prince and a guard can, I suppose," Bashir said.

Makram folded his arms and leaned against the support for the hay loft above. "Do you trust me?"

Bashir considered, grazing the brush over his horse's back. The man had quickly earned a reputation for considered recklessness. People, both noble and lowborn, were still talking about his gamble with the Council, to take control of the palace with only seven men. He took risks Bashir never would. But he'd proven himself.

"As much as anyone from Tamar might trust a Charah of the Sixth House," Bashir said.

Makram grinned, showing that particular expression that made Bashir's skin prickle, when he could sense the breadth and power of the magic within the other.

"Do you think I would do anything to harm or undermine the Sultana?" His voice, always tinged with darkness, took on a dangerous tone.

"No." Bashir had seen the way he looked at her, knew he respected her and what she was trying to do. Bashir had been there the day he committed himself to war with a brother he cared about because he believed in her. "No," he repeated.

"I know it is asking a great deal, because I know how loyal you are to the Sultana. Bashir, you cannot control Aysel, but you *can* trust her. You can trust me."

"I will not defy the Sultana for you," Bashir said, quietly.

"Believe it or not, what I am doing is all for the Sultana. But she would not approve," he said, one corner of his mouth tilting up.

"Then I do not." There was no room in his duties for two masters. He would always choose the Sultana's will over anyone else's. Even his own.

Makram shook his head. "I know what she's done for you, and you don't want to betray her. But I also do not think you give her enough credit. She trusts you, and so you should trust you. If your instincts tell you something, you should listen to them. She will understand. On that same note, Wheel's sake man, tell her you need more guards. The lot of you are walking around like the dead risen."

Bashir cast him a horrified look at the phrase, and the other laughed, though it was not a pleasant laugh. "No, I cannot raise the dead." Makram shook his head.

"We're making do," Bashir said stiffly, taking another hard swipe with the brush then apologizing with a few pats.

"Fine." He pushed away from the column. "Thank you for assisting Aysel last night. I trust you took her warnings about more katil seriously?"

Bashir gave a short nod.

"I have spoken with the Sultana and she remains firm on her original command regarding Aysel and her family. However, she has allowed for Aysel to visit the market on behalf of her family today, along with her brother and a guard force of your choosing. She will also be allowed to return to the camp with her weapons."

"But…" Bashir let the thought and words die out. Fine. Let her get herself killed. What did he care?

"You should consider," Makram said, carefully, "that Aysel is experienced and capable. She knows when and how to take risks and can, for the most part, take care of herself. If you interfere with her, it could get her killed."

"If I hadn't interfered last night she would have been."

"Oh?" he said, expression neutral. "Helping her was your idea?" Before Bashir could answer, Makram continued, "Or, was she using all the tools at her disposal to be rid of a dangerous criminal?" He regarded Bashir with an assessing look. "Aysel knows her limits and works within them. Do not make the mistake of thinking her asking for help means she is incapable."

"That katil was about to drive a sword through her back," Bashir argued. Magic rolled out of him in ripples, and Huzur bucked sideways with a shriek. Bashir turned and threw the brush so hard into his bucket of supplies that the bucket tipped and sent things all over the stall floor.

"I see," Makram said, watching Bashir as he crouched to retrieve the brushes, combs, and cloth that had scattered. Embarrassment heated him from head to toe as if he'd been dunked into a pot of stew. "I think you need some rest. You're no good to anybody in this state. Consider it an order," Makram said, before he turned and left the stable.

Bashir set the bucket in the corner and sat with his back against the cold plaster wall, tipping his head back. Huzur turned, taking cautious steps toward him and lowering his head, blowing long puffs of air from his wide nostrils as he flicked his ears forward and back.

"Sorry old friend." Bashir patted the white-spotted face and Huzur laid his ears back as if accepting...grudgingly. Makram was right. He needed rest. All his men did. Tempers were short, their discipline was falling apart. They couldn't appear to be lacking in order, or the nobles would complain to the Sultana and his position would be in jeopardy.

How could he possibly do what Makram asked? Even if it wasn't directly defying the Sultana, if he let Aysel run around wreaking havoc his men would never take him seriously again.

"Are you in here?" Erol called from the entrance to the barracks. Bashir closed his eyes, his weariness growing heavier.

"Yes," he said.

Erol's boots scuffed down the aisle then he appeared in front of the stall, looking surprised to find Bashir sitting in the sand. "Hiding out?"

"Not very well, apparently." He got to his feet and slapped the sand off his clothes before retrieving the bucket of grooming supplies and handing them across the rope gate to Erol.

"You all right? I was home last night and my anne said Havva's been complaining that she hasn't see you lately."

Bashir rolled his eyes. "She says that even when I visit once a turn." It had been some time since he'd been home, though.

Erol gave him a sly grin. "They love you more when you're the only one, I'm sure of it. Mine could barely care if I came home once a Cycle. She's too busy with the littles." He meant his three younger siblings, who were not that little. Two were already apprenticed in the merchant district and the third would be going to the University soon.

"Always trying to make it about you. You're everyone's favorite down there and you know it." Even his own mother was always gushing about sweet, charming Erol.

"Oh no. Not me." Erol gripped Bashir's hand as Bashir stepped over the rope that served as gate to the stall. "I'm not the golden guard commander. Prodigal son."

Bashir grimaced. "Why are you out here anyway?"

"Aysel's back, with her brother," Erol said. Bashir saw the focused glance Erol gave him, and Bashir made certain he didn't see any of the turmoil inside him.

He rolled his shoulders. It would be best if he didn't go out to meet her. And while he didn't trust anybody else to keep her—and apparently her brother as well—under control in the market, he knew he was far too frayed to handle her.

"The prince gave orders to escort them. Pick two others and get them to the market. Don't let her, or him for that matter, wander out of your sight. And stick to the market, nowhere else."

Erol tapped his chest with two fingers in a lazy salute and started back toward the barracks.

"Erol." Bashir climbed over the rope and into the aisle. Erol turned back. "Find out something useful about what the prince has set her on. She isn't going to the market for oranges."

"My pleasure." Erol grinned.

Bashir watched his friend's back as he strode down the aisle and set the supply bucket into the first empty stall where they kept all their tack and supplies. He frowned, then shook it off. He needed to distance himself from her, and this was a good way to do it.

After a moment to collect his thoughts, Bashir returned to the barracks and his room. He pulled his caftan over his head and slung it at the wooden stool in one corner, then collapsed face down on his bed. Even a little bit of sleep would help clear his head.

After a moment of staring wide-eyed at the wall, he stood up, on the bed, and shoved the shutters of his window outward. Chill air wafted in, and Bashir cast his gaze toward the gate, where Erol was speaking to Aysel. Her brother stood at her side, all of them framed in the high, wide arch of the Morning Gate and its flanking towers. Aysel frowned, and Erol gestured at the barracks. Two guards trotted toward them, saluting Erol then bowing briefly to Aysel and her brother. Aysel linked her arm through her brother's and the group of them started down the road. Mathei said something that made everyone laugh.

After a couple of steps Aysel turned her head to look toward the barracks. Bashir almost dropped out of her view, but he was already being childish enough, so he stayed. They were not so far away he couldn't see her smile a secret, teasing smile that made him fiercely regret sending Erol in his place.

Wheel, he felt as if he were being quartered, pulled in every direction but forward. He dropped to his haunches on the bed then onto his back. He slapped his hand against the wall and willed a dampening spell into place, then let out a roar of frustration, letting the sound drain him of every infuriating, impossible thing that had wound itself around him these past days. When his voice failed, he released his spell and let his hand drop to the bed. He stared at the ceiling for long moments then sat up and retrieved his caftan from the chair.

He returned to the stables and saddled his gelding. When he rode him out of the courtyard and past the gate guards, he stopped.

"If Lieutenant Terzi returns before me, tell him I went to the city. He'll know where."

The two men saluted, and Bashir wheeled his horse and urged him to a trot. The travel from the palace to the old Earth District of the city took a candlemark at a leisurely pace. Today he rode faster, unable to sit alone with himself for too long. Huzur knew the route, and after the first two turns barely had to be directed. He knew there would be apples or carrots waiting for him.

When they stopped it was at a tiny, one-story home built of sandstone bricks that, like its neighbors, appeared to have been thrust directly out of the cliff behind it. Unlike the larger, two-story houses in the newer sections of the district, the door was wood, with no courtyard or porch to frame it. Bashir tied Huzur to a post he'd dug and set himself a few Turns ago. He rapped lightly against the door then entered. The smell of cumin and onion filled the house.

"Anne." He didn't yell, the house was a single, long room, though she had hung stretches of inexpensive fabric at the back and each side to partition off her bed and what had once been his. It was still his, when he chose to stay in the city.

Just inside the door, to his left, a cookfire's smoke wafted up to a purposeful hole in the arched ceiling, and to his right a square table set low to the ground with cushions scattered around it. He grimaced. He'd promised he'd fix one of the table legs this small turn and had forgotten. He peered into the tureen sitting on a grate over the coals. Kibbeh simmering in broth.

"I'm coming. Don't you touch that food," his mother scolded from behind the fabric hiding her bed. Bashir set down the spoon he'd picked up. Between where he stood and the curtains that stretched across the back of the house was a living space of sorts. There was enough room for a handful of large cushions she'd sewn to keep them off the cold stone in the winter, and a rug they'd had for as long as he could remember.

A long, narrow counter he'd built for her after he'd been offered a scholarship at the University served as her worktable in the kitchen, and he pulled a carrot out of the sand-filled bin she used to keep them over the winter. He dusted it off against his caftan and stepped back outside to offer it to Huzur. He took it, giving Bashir a baleful look, unhappy at being made to wait for the expected tribute. Ornery beast.

"Bashir?" His mother poked her head out of the door then held it open when he returned. "It's the middle of the day, what are you doing here?" She frowned at him. Bashir almost laughed at the admonishment in her tone. As though he were still a teenager in need of steering the right way around the Wheel.

He dropped onto one of the cushions that surrounded the square, low-set table. His mother looked at him for a moment more, then turned her back to tend to the kibbeh, nudging them around in their broth bath. "These will be done soon. What else do you want?"

"I'm not hungry," Bashir said. He wasn't even sure why he'd come. But she usually knew.

"You're always hungry." She wiped her hands on a cloth, which she folded and set on the worktable, studying him. "You look tired. Do you want to rest?"

He shook his head. She made a clucking noise and turned back to the meal, taking a chipped earthenware bowl from a stack in the single cabinet that hung on the wall across from him. She ladled two of the kibbeh into it and set the bowl on the workbench, then lifted another ceramic dish and took the lid off. She added a spoonful of its contents, lentils and rice, to the plate and set it in front of him with a spoon. Then she sat on the cushion and patted his thigh.

"Sometimes," she said, as he pushed one of the kibbeh patties around on the plate with his spoon, "we think we have finally reached the top of the hill we've been climbing, and we get comfortable, and we think we are done struggling." She tapped a nail against the tabletop. "It's never true."

What special magic did mothers hold that made them able to understand a problem without a word of explanation? "I think I'm failing."

"You always think you are failing." She smiled and shook her head. "Especially when you are excelling."

He stabbed the spoon into one of the kibbeh patties then set it down. "I can't do what they want me to do. It's impossible. One of them wants one thing, the other wants another, my men are exhausted, and still the list grows longer, the demands more ceaseless."

"Mmm," she hummed thoughtfully. "You will be well prepared for when you finally give me the grandbabies I keep asking for. If you think the Sultana is a demanding taskmaster, you should try a colicky baby boy who shakes the house when he doesn't get what he wants."

"Anne," he protested. But inwardly he was ashamed. He should not complain to his mother about how hard his work was, or his life, or any of his trials. Because hers had been harder. She had weathered storms and humiliations that would break him.

"Eat," she said, gently. "The Wheel will turn and your trials will be countered with joy."

"Have you been to the camp lately?" he asked around a mouthful of food. She frowned at him and he swallowed. Even as a grown man she corrected his manners.

"No. I am due again. All of us have been setting some aside, but every time I go there are more in need than I have food to give. It breaks my heart." She stood, walking back into the kitchen. She had always moved when she was troubled, pacing, cleaning, rearranging things. This time, she stirred the food again and lifted it from the fire, then returned to the table. The all-of-us she referred to was the short curve of road they lived on, the ten or so families that had lived there together, raised their children together, and remained now that those children were grown.

"Food is not the only thing they need, if it is easier to give something else. Clothes, more shelters."

"Elif told me someone from the camp was attacked by a fire mage. Some of them saw the bolts from the hill." She looked at him. Gossip was the fuel of friendships, feuds, and most conversations in his childhood neighborhood. She knew better than to ask him outright, but usually did at least once, because his indignation amused her.

"Someone was attacked," Bashir said. "But she is fine. And the mage has been dealt with."

Her sandy eyebrows rose in surprise. "A *woman* was attacked?"

Bashir gave a soft laugh as he tried to picture the poor, helpless woman his mother was visualizing next to Aysel. His mother looked at him more sharply, her expression relaxing, and a small, knowing smile curving her mouth. The two bites of food he'd eaten sat heavy in his belly.

"I see." She turned back to the workbench, putting the lids back on the ceramic pots and swiping at the wooden table with the rag in her hand. After a few moments of tidying, she said without looking at him, "This woman who was attacked, she's a refugee?"

"She was a noble in Sarkum," Bashir said, carefully.

"Ah." She cast him a sideways look of disapproval. "I am glad she's all right."

Bashir cut another section of the kibbeh off with his spoon but didn't eat it. He wanted to tell her about Aysel so she could tell him why a woman he barely knew was making him feel as though he was losing his mind. But he couldn't. His mother was a generous, gentle person. But in her mind there was no greater crime than being a noble. It didn't matter if that noble was from another country, had been chased out of her home by assassins, or was not blind to the need of others. He'd grown up believing the same. Working day and night at the palace had shown him plenty of examples to change his mind, including the Sultana, but he doubted he would ever change his mother's.

"I should go."

"You don't want to finish your food?" she asked, with a scandalized frown.

"I'm sorry. I need to get back to my men." They both knew the truth. He couldn't talk anymore, and if he stayed, she would poke and prod until they argued.

"Come back soon, yes?" She kissed his cheek. He nodded, and she watched him mount. He always rode at a walk while he was still in view of the house, because she always watched until she couldn't see him anymore.

The journey back to the palace took twice as long as the ride down, and when he arrived, he handed the care of the gelding off to Ali, who was still serving his penance for losing track of Aysel. He would probably never stop serving penance with his fellows for needing help to get down off the barracks roof.

Instead of returning to his office or room, Bashir went to the armory. It was the only windowless room in the barracks, the central room on the right. Her harness and swords were hanging next to the hook where he hung his sword, on the rare occasion he was without it. Bashir lifted all of it off its hook, the leather of the harness supple and soft in his hand. He retrieved an oiled whetstone from the end of one of the two benches in the room and sat. He pulled one of her swords free, laying it against his knee.

Bashir sat like that for a long time, staring at the shortened blade, tracing his thumb across the edge to feel its angle. Then he set the whetstone against it and swiped it across the blade's short, curved length.

His mother's oft-repeated words flickered in and out of his thoughts as he worked, because she had called them out to him as he rode away.

"Be careful, Bashir. They are never what they seem."

Eleven

AYSEL SET A WOODEN crate on the floor of her shelter and slung her satchel of supplies on the pallet. She stretched the cramps out of her back. The bruise along her ribs protested, and she touched her fingers to the place between her shoulder and the hollow of her throat where the katil's blade had left its mark. It was deep where it began near her shoulder and shallow as it neared her neck. The physician at the palace had stitched half of it and given her ointment to keep the skin supple and prevent tearing. He had recommended she rest. Aysel doubted his idea of rest and hers were the same.

She unwrapped the folded cloth of the satchel and withdrew the clothes she had brought. She'd been measured for them that morning when they went to the market and she had picked them up on her way to the city. The purchase had taken a bite out of the small amount of money her mother and father had been able to spirit away with them, but it was a necessary purchase. Sneaking about, climbing in and out of places, and occasional thieving required clothing that would not catch, flutter, billow, or otherwise give her away. There had been no time to collect a wardrobe when they had fled Sarkum, and so she'd made the purchase. She lamented the loss of her collection of tools as well, lockpicks, wires, lightweight ropes, and a pair of perfectly worn-in boots that fit like a second skin.

Aysel sat on the pallet and put her head in her hands, overwhelmed with the loss of her previous life. There had not been time to mourn. There had not been time to even think of it, because they were filled with the everyday tasks of survival and consumed by exhaustion. The single night with her family in the palace had stirred memories she'd been holding inside. Her mother was quiet and sad, moving about their lavish prison as though it were a stone cell. She reminded Aysel of a caged songbird the Mirza used to keep, that had begun as a flighty thing that would never sit still, singing its lovely song, and slowly grew listless, dull, and silent until one day she saw that its cage was empty.

Her father had a bit more faith that the Sultana did not mean for them to waste away as prisoners, that they would prove themselves to be allies in her eyes and somehow build themselves a life in Tamar. He'd held a similar hope for Kinus.

And Mathei. Aysel tapped her toe against the crate, watching it rock back and forth, until she finally kicked it over. She'd seen him in one of the chairs, reading and rereading the only book he'd brought with him. He took after their mother that way, always reading. It was one of the things that made him so capable of blending into a crowd. He could talk about anything at length. If she had been searching for him at home, she'd go to the library first, and find him sitting in their father's chair reading some dusty tome. Her favorite way to irritate him was to sprawl herself across his lap and ask him to read to her, then feign boredom with dramatic yawns and groans when he did.

Now they were trapped and miserable, someone wanted to kill them, and Aysel was stuck spending her time convincing that bonehead pack of useless ruffians that she should be allowed to do something about it. And their double-boneheaded, infuriating commander. Her mouth curved in a smile as she picked at the drying mud on the toe of her boot.

"Are you in there?" Bashir's gruff voice immediately set her on edge in the best and worst of ways. She got up and slapped one of the canvas pieces aside.

"I was just thinking about you," Aysel said. He raised an eyebrow and tossed a bundle of something at her. Aysel caught it, barely, and glared at him. It was her swords and harness.

"Should I be flattered?" he asked.

"Not at all. And I think you must have wanted to be an errand boy and fell into being a guard by accident," she said, shaking her swords at him. "This is the second delivery you've made for me, your most-wanted criminal."

"I'm the only person available to take this watch on you. Still sour?"

"I don't know why I would be." She arranged the harness and swords on another crate she'd set by the firepit. "The welcome here has been nothing but warm and lavish."

"Did you expect something different? Even if you weren't a criminal, you are a noble from Sarkum," he said.

Aysel crouched by the fire and began to poke at it with a stick that had been propped on the rocks that formed its edge.

"How am I a criminal? I took back my own belongings and rounded up a murderer for you. In Al-Nimas, my brother and I were the right and left hand of a prince," she said. "My father was an adviser to the Elder Sultan and then his sons, Commander of their armies. My mother was a respected and well-loved daughter of a family long known for their generosity and charity. I did not realize crossing an imaginary line in the rock would turn my entire family into dangerous villains."

Her vain hope that there might be a coal remaining to begin a new fire died a slow death as she poked and prodded through the ashes.

He watched her in expectant silence for so long she began to feel crushed by it.

"Do you know how to start a fire?" he finally asked.

Aysel pointed her stick at him. "Of course I do." She did not. Adem made all their fires, cooked their meals. It was a simple matter for a Fifth House Aval—he needed only to speak a word and fire obeyed his command.

"You can scale a cliff face to infiltrate a palace and fight off men three times your size—"

"Twice, maybe," Aysel corrected.

Bashir raised an eyebrow. "Three times your size, but you cannot start a cookfire." He felt about his belt as if searching for something, then tucked his hand into a small leather pouch tied to the thin leather sword belt that crossed over the fabric wound at his waist. "Only a noble," he sighed as he withdrew a stone of some kind, then drew a knife from a sheath at his hip.

Aysel silently mimicked his statement about nobles and stuck her tongue out at him. He nearly smiled as he rounded the firepit. "Hold these." He handed her the knife and stone as he crouched beside her.

Aysel watched as he dug about the pile of sticks and wood that Adem had scavenged for them. Bashir withdrew a handful of dead grass from the middle of the pile and set it in the center of the firepit, then fluffed it, reminding Aysel of watching her mother arrange flowers in a vase. She snorted, and he gave her a baleful, sideways look. "Do you want my help?"

"I'm not certain." She studied the knife he'd given her as he continued his work, building the grass into a little nest. "You're very brave, handing me a knife and then sitting right next to me." She danced the knife over the tops of her fingers and spun it into her grasp, leveling the point at his eye.

Bashir, without even flinching, reached up and took the knife from her hand, then the stone. "If you knife me in the eye, you can forget your fire." He held the stone over his pile of grass and began to strike the dull edge of his knife against it.

Aysel hugged her knees and set her chin against them, watching his short, quick strokes in fascination—she'd never seen someone start a fire without magic. A few times a spark landed and glowed, and Bashir blew carefully on them, but it took him four tries before the grass caught. He tended that for a few moments, as if it were the most fragile of infants, then began to feed it more grass and small bits of twigs, gradually building it up until it was steady and strong, and adding larger and larger pieces of wood until it was a proper fire.

He looked at her in irritation. "You probably can't cook, either. What are you doing out here? Go back to the palace and sleep in a dry bed and eat good food. Do you even have any food?"

"I'm not a child, Ox." She stood and ducked back into the shelter to sort through the rest of her things. She'd bought rice and lentils at the market, and two oranges. Only things she thought essential. Aysel fished the cookpot out from under the stack of pallets that was her bed and dumped some of the lentils into it, then placed an orange on top before carrying it back outside.

She handed it all to Bashir. "Do you know what one of your problems is?"

"You are my only problem." He settled the cookpot into a section of coals he'd pushed away from the main fire. He set the orange on the ground beside him, tugged her bucket of water over and dumped some into the pot, then put the lid on. Aysel touched her foot to his back and gave a little shove in reprimand for his sarcasm. He caught himself with one hand as he tipped forward and twisted to catch her ankle with the other.

Aysel grabbed his wrist in both of her hands and shoved her weight into her leg to break his hold, grazing his cheekbone with her knee as she threw her leg over his arm.

"No." She wrenched his arm up between her legs, putting her weight against the back of his elbow and torqueing his arm toward her chest. Bashir tried to yank out of her hold but only put more pressure against his arm and cursed. "The problem"—she gave his arm a little jerk that made him hiss—"is you keep underestimating me."

She released his arm with a shove and stepped over him like she might a little boulder in her path, swiping her orange as she moved to the other side of the fire. She sat in the dirt, folding her legs in front of her, and started peeling.

"I don't blame you really," she said, tossing a piece of orange peel into the fire as he glowered at her and worked his hand against his shoulder. "I've yet to meet a man who doesn't. And you think because I *asked* for your help once it means I need some kind of rescuer. But I don't. If you hadn't been around to use as a tool, I would have found another way."

Not entirely true, but mostly true. His comment about the crossbows that morning still made her temper simmer.

"You say the most flattering things." Bashir swung his arm in a slow circle, no doubt trying to work out the lingering pain from being twisted.

"Oh, did you come up here for flattery? I thought it was to prevent me from looking for the men who want to kill my family." She pried loose a wedge of orange then freed the rest of the fruit from its peel.

"And I thought it was to cook your dinner," he said.

Aysel nibbled on a piece of the citrus, meeting his gaze across the fire. She held the other half out to him. "I didn't ask you to do that. You're just trying to rescue me again."

Bashir finally took the fruit and sat down, folding his legs up toward his chest and shoving a piece of it in his mouth. He'd looked strung-out and exhausted when she had seen him that morning; now he appeared dead on his feet. There were dark circles beneath his eyes, and he moved with the same kind of slow determination as the exhausted refugees at the top of the pass.

The man was utterly spent. In fact she wouldn't be surprised if he fell asleep right in front of her.

"Where did you learn that?" he said after he had lifted the lid on the lentils to give them a stir.

"Well I'm not exactly going to win a fistfight, am I?" She ate her last piece of orange and brushed her fingers off on her salvar. She got to her feet and retrieved her harness and swords from where she'd set them. "My brother and I have been working through scenarios for Turns. We tried to find things I could use on someone if I were foolish enough to get caught." She sat down next to him and took another piece from the half she'd given.

"I doubt I underestimate you as often as you think," he said, quietly. "I've never met a woman like you."

Warm pleasure filled her belly at his praise, but she laughed softly. "I know you can't help it. You're so big, and you're the kind of man who can't help wanting to protect people, can you? And small animals too, probably, hmm?"

Red crept up his neck and she knew she was right.

"Well, rest easy, Ox. Cooking and fire-starting aside"—she drew one of her swords and looked at it—"I take care of myself very well."

She narrowed her eyes and brought the blade close to her face, then tapped her thumb against its edge. A thin line of blood bloomed across her skin. Aysel sighed, setting the blade in her lap and turning her gaze toward him. He busied himself with prying loose another wedge of orange.

"Who sharpened these?" She knew. She knew exactly who had sharpened them.

"I don't see a whetstone around this mudhole, do you?" he said around a mouthful of citrus. "You can't be running around with dull swords. And they were bouncing all over those cobbles last night. It'll chip your edge." Then he shoved the last piece in his mouth.

"What am I supposed to do with you? You insist I'm a criminal and I need to be guarded, but you came when that katil almost caught me. You should be sleeping, but you're here instead of sending your men. You don't want me hunting the katil, but you sharpened my blades…" She motioned to the soaking lentils. "…you cooked my dinner!" Aysel held his gaze.

And waited.

Bashir rubbed his palms over his face. "I don't know." He shoved both hands into his hair. "I don't know what I'm doing."

"You know what I think?" She slid her blade back into its sheath. "I think you want to trust me, but you don't trust yourself or your judgment because the Sultana says something different."

"You can't possibly understand what I owe her."

"Don't be insulting. Even a simpleton can understand feeling indebted to someone." Aysel sighed, and reached up, tugging his hand away from his hair. "Come on."

"What?" He looked up at her as she stood. Aysel pulled again, and Bashir clambered to his feet, his fingers slipping between hers and tightening in a way that made her pulse flutter. She stepped toward her lean-to and he balked. Aysel jerked him harder, smiling a little.

"Don't be afraid, little Ox, I won't hurt you," she teased, stepping closer and sliding her fingers into the cloth at his waist, then walking backwards and towing him with her. He looked bewildered, and hopeful, and like he was trying not to feel either.

When he had ducked inside, she let go of him and turned to clear her purchases off the bed, right the crate she'd been kicking, and place them on it. Then she maneuvered him so his back was to the pallets.

"Aysel," he said, the censure in his voice broken with interest. "I thought we agreed…" He shook his head, but his hands found her waist.

"For right now"—she unbuckled his sword belt and tugged it free of his hips—"just this moment. Trust me." She set the sword on the edge of the pallets. "Lie down," she ordered.

Bashir frowned. Aysel put her hands on his shoulders and pressed until he sat, then positioned her knee next to his hip and pushed, following him as he fell back because his hands tightened against her waist. She swung her other leg over him so she straddled him on all fours. Wheel but she wanted to do so much more than she was about to, especially when desire unleashed in his gaze. Even if her intent was not what he thought, she liked that he was willing to give over his control to her.

Aysel bent her face over his. His body shifted as he tensed to lift his head to hers. "Go to sleep," she murmured.

"Wheel and spokes." He dropped his head against the folded blanket she used as a pillow and grit his teeth as he glared at her. "Is this funny to you?"

Aysel pushed up on her knees and put her fingers together in a circle, the symbol for the Wheel. "I swear on the Wheel that I will be right here"—she pointed toward the cookfire on the other side of the canvas—"when you wake up."

"Get up," he ordered, though he did not move his hands from her hips. Aysel dropped her hands back to his shoulders as he started to sit up.

"Go to sleep. You have taken care of me, and now you're going to let me repay the favor. I will stand watch outside until you wake up."

"You're going to stand watch on yourself? Why on the Wheel would I believe you?"

"Because your instincts are right. You can trust me." Aysel placed one hand by his head, lifting the other toward his hair and hesitating.

"That's why you came to help me with the katil when I asked. And why you sharpened my swords, and why you haven't turned me into mincemeat for putting my grubby Sarkum hands all over you."

He frowned at her and shifted his head to butt it against her fingers. She smiled as she stroked them through his tawny hair.

"Bashir," she said, in the warm, unguarded way she would have always said his name if they could have started out under different circumstances. "You need sleep. How can you take care of your men if you won't take care of yourself?" She continued sliding her fingers through his hair, enjoying how it slipped through. It was softer than hers, softer than Mat's, lacking the coarseness that spoke of their mixed heritage. He closed his eyes.

"You're smart enough to know this is not making me want to sleep. Your hands aren't that grubby." His voice was a quaking rumble, his hands on her hips squeezing in reprimand.

"I'm afraid in your current state you wouldn't be much use to me," she suggested. "You'd fall asleep halfway through then I'd have to murder you."

He laughed, softly, his big body shifting under her as he opened his eyes, lit with pale streaks of warm earthen power. "Give me more credit than that." His hands on her hips pulled, and Aysel stretched out on top of him because her control felt no stronger than a thin, silken spider thread. He was broad and hot and solid beneath her, and she wasn't certain she'd be able to force herself to get back up. His hand slid up her back, big and warm, and the streaks in his eyes spread, drawing his power across his temples.

"I've never seen someone's magic do this," she breathed, touching her fingers against the light that traced his temples like gold veining. A mage's magic showed in their skin in some form or another when their emotions were strong and their focus elsewhere, depending on their own control. It expressed differently for everyone. She had never seen it manifest like Bashir's, light piercing through his skin like jagged fault lines.

Aysel had never seen her own. Her entire life had been about controlling it, keeping it hidden.

"Stay," Bashir coaxed, his hands cupping the backs of her thighs and pulling her up his body so her face was directly above his. "Stay so I can see yours too." His voice, deep and laced with power, did things to her body that some men couldn't even have done with their hands and an entire night to try. But the words splashed a bit of cold sense into her quickly fogging thoughts.

Aysel had been with men, enough to know she could control herself even in the throes of intimacy, but none of them had been earth mages. He was powerful, as was his effect on her, his ability to sense her magic stronger because of their opposition on the Wheel. Being with him posed a risk of her losing herself too much to desire to keep her power restrained.

"Sleep," she said. "I need you at your best to keep my family safe."

"Aysel." He put his hands on either side of her face. "They're safe."

Oh, he was a problem, this one. There were threads of sweetness within that rough exterior she didn't think she had defenses for.

"How can I trust you if you won't even trust me to keep this simple promise?" It would be so easy to turn her face into his palm and nibble his skin. She bit her bottom lip instead.

Bashir's hands fell to his sides. "I'm not sure I can remember my name right now, and you're doing logic leaps."

"I'm faster than you in every way." Aysel grinned. "You are just going to have to accept it."

"Slow isn't always a bad thing," he said. "Let me show you." He dragged his hands up her waist. Skeins of heat swirled through her, threading through her limbs and making her feel heavy and needy. Oh Wheel, she wanted that. She wanted to be slow with him, to take all the time she needed to acquaint herself with the intimacies of his body and that mouth, which was half-curved into a smile.

"Bad Ox," she whispered. "Bad." She put her hands over his face so she couldn't see the way his lips were parted and his eyes were half-closed with desire, and forced herself to stand.

Bashir chuckled, grabbing her wrists and pulling her hands away from his face. "If you aren't going to behave then I see no reason I should."

"Because you are an upstanding guard commander in the palace and I am just a deviant criminal." She freed her hands from his grip and tugged a blanket out from under him.

"You know I don't…" He frowned, and she suspected he was about to tell her he didn't believe that. Poor Ox. He was so mixed up.

"I know." As she laid the blanket over him she laughed a little, because it only covered about half of him no matter how she arranged it. "Which is why you're going to sleep like a baby."

Twelve

MATHEI SAUNTERED UP TO her fire while Aysel was eating the lentils Bashir had helped her make. She had just put one of her last handfuls of wood on the fire, and was contemplating where to hunt for more fuel, when he came from between the rows of tents in front of her. He had two guards in tow, who meandered in separate directions, one to the right, one to the left. Aysel held a finger to her lips as Mat selected a stump too big to burn as a seat and set it next to her. When he frowned in confusion, Aysel indicated the tent with a little jerk of her head.

He continued to frown and stepped behind her to pull the canvas aside with two fingers and tipped his head to look inside. He paused, looked at her, then looked inside again.

"Aysel…" Mathei let the canvas swing shut. "…why is there a mountain that looks a great deal like the guard commander sleeping in your bed?" He sat on his improvised seat and fixed her with a gleeful expression. "You naughty little fox."

Aysel slapped his shoulder with the back of her hand and set the pot of lentils aside. Without salt, spices, or other vegetables, they were a chore to eat. How did Filiz manage to turn such a humble thing into so many delicious dishes? These tasted like dirt. "I am building trust." Because they should be friends. They should be allies.

"No wonder you were so eager to leave that soft, comfortable bed in the palace and return to your little mudhole." Mathei lifted the lid on the pot of lentils and peered inside, then raised a dark eyebrow. "You cooked?" he said, looking as though he were ready to be impressed.

"No." Aysel snatched up the pot and moved it out of his reach. "What are you doing here? I'm supposed to be behaving while he's asleep and I don't think he'll believe me if he sees you out here."

"How long has he been like that?" Mathei handed her a little handful of something wrapped in a scrap of fabric.

Aysel peered up at the sun as she held the parcel in her hand and began unwrapping it. "About a quarter sun," she said. She doubted he'd sleep much longer, even though he needed about three times that amount. He couldn't even be disobedient when it meant his health.

The package Mathei had given her was a handful of dried apricots and figs. Aysel selected a fig and wrapped the fruit again, leaning to kiss her brother on the cheek. "Thank you," she said. He tugged one of her braids.

"Here." He produced a skin she suspected was wine, as well as two small wooden cups. He leaned forward to poke at her fire with the stick she'd left on the rocks, so the new log would catch from the old. Aysel tucked the bundle of fruit into the fabric around her waist and set the cups on the ground. She unstoppered the wine.

"I've been reading some of the books the Sultana has on Chara'a," Mathei said.

Her glee at his gift of wine evaporated and she fell back, throwing her arms out to her sides. Mathei scolded her with a click of his tongue as he filled the cups and set hers beside her on the ground. Aysel folded her hands over her belly as she contemplated the streaks of grey clouds above. It had been dry the last couple of days, so the ground was less muddy, but still cold.

"Just listen. Remember when Makram visited, just before Kinus declared him an enemy of the state?"

"Yes," Aysel said. When she'd heard Kinus had declared him a traitor, she had been afraid she would never see Makram again.

"The Sultana is standing a Circle of Chara'a, Aysel. Makram has already agreed to stand as Sixth." Mathei's eyes were lit with dark fire, fervor because the study of Chara'a had always been one of his most cherished subjects. Because of her.

Aysel let her breath out slowly. A ripple of magic that left the scent of loam and granite in the back of her throat spread across the dormant surface of hers. She smiled a little. Bashir was awake and checking for her. She wanted to bat at him with her magic, playing, but didn't. She did not know exactly which of her abilities would mark her as a Charah, so unless completely necessary, she had to keep her magic silent. As always. No matter what scholarly idea Mathei had in his head.

Bashir ducked out of the shelter a moment later, one side of his face creased from sleep, his tawny hair sticking up oddly on the same side, looking a bit like a grumpy bear woken too early from hibernation. She wanted to leap to her feet and kiss him while he was still disheveled and defenseless, because at just this moment all his seriousness and guardedness were stripped away.

He looked down at her, lying on the ground much the way she had been when they'd met on the street after fighting the katil, and he started to smile. Then he saw Mat, twisted around on his log seat and staring up at him, and his smile and all the softness evaporated.

"Why is he here?" he asked Aysel, as if she had conjured him as a trick. "And where are his guards?"

Aysel sat up. "I don't know, he's babbling about things I don't care about."

"Well thank you very much. You would care, if I'd had a chance to finish. My guards are off scratching their backsides, but I'm sure they'll snap to attention if I attempt to make a rabbit-like dash to a toilet." Mathei smiled, and whatever remained of the good mood Aysel had instilled in Bashir with her flirting and his nap disappeared. "More importantly, I am told the Sultana is attempting to stand a Circle of Chara'a. Is that true?" He eyed Bashir. "There hasn't been a full Circle since before the Sundering."

Bashir gave a single nod, watching Mathei darkly as he circled around them to the far side of the fire. Aysel wasn't certain she wanted to talk about the Circle of Chara'a in front of Bashir, or why her brother would share such a thing with her. She couldn't stand for the First House—her power was just another blade she hid, only she had far less precision with it than her swords and knives. She'd spent a lifetime hiding herself from a mad prince. All that time she'd lost to train her power. It was too late.

"Wine?" Aysel asked Bashir, holding her cup out to him. He frowned. "Let me guess, you don't drink."

"He drinks." Mathei tossed the wineskin to Bashir, who caught it, still looking offended at the entire situation. "You seem more of an arak man. But alone, in your room, to great excess when something hasn't gone your way."

Bashir blinked at him liked he'd just performed the greatest of Wheel-spun miracles.

Aysel laughed. "Have you met Mat yet?"

"Not formally." Bashir twisted the stopper out of the wineskin.

"Mathei Attiyeh, Commander Bashir Ayan." Aysel gestured from one to the other.

"Now that is an interesting name, isn't it?" Mathei said, sipping at his cup. "Ayan. It sounds a bit…Eastern for your coloring." Bashir did have unusually colored eyes, a hazel or brown diluted to gold, and Ayan was a name more likely to be heard in Sarkum than Tamar, where Odokan blood and names tended to belong to duskier complexions and eyes dark like basalt.

"I took it when the Sultana commissioned me into the guard after I left the University." Bashir took a large swig of the wine, and Aysel cast Mathei a wide-eyed look of surprise. He winked at her. She was especially good at sneaking into places, but Mat was a master of ferreting out people's personal secrets.

"I hear you are a talented Sival. But you must be, if you almost caught my little fox."

Bashir almost spit his wine out, and looked from Aysel to Mathei and back again. "Is that what he calls you?"

"Sometimes. Tareck started it. He calls me Kit," Aysel said. The look on Bashir's face was some cross between bewilderment and adoration. Aysel had seen that look before, and one man even told her what it was. Imagining her as a little fox with pettable ears. "I have knifed men for thinking what you're thinking right now," she said.

His face blanched. "It fits, I suppose." He cleared his throat and looked away.

"She didn't actually knife the man, but she did give him a good kick in his stones then almost pushed him off a balcony." Mathei looked between Bashir and Aysel with suspicion. "I'm still curious about this business of you taking a new surname. Is there a particular reason? Do all mages in Tamar do that after they leave their studies?"

"No." Bashir took another large swallow of wine and glared at the wineskin. When Mat drew breath to ask another question, Bashir cut him off. "They do it when their name is Whoreson." He looked at

Aysel in defiance as he said it. She almost dropped her cup into the fire, but managed to hold onto it and her neutral expression.

"I could see how that would not endear you to the nobles in the palace," Mathei said, his dark eyes bright with his triumph at uncovering a secret. "But not the worst thing you could be. Try explaining to your father, who is adviser to kings and noblemen, that you prefer men to women." Aysel made a sound of disapproval. Mat liked to pretend their father had spent more than a few marks in irritation at his son's proclamation. Thoman held nothing for Mathei but a father's pride. They were, by any standard, great friends.

Bashir took another swig of wine, looking at Mathei as if he'd just drawn a blade and challenged him to a duel. "I don't have a father," he countered.

"Obviously you have a father," Mathei said. "Unless your mother is the last remaining creation mage and put you together using moss and twigs she gathered from the mountains under a full moon."

"As far as I know, it was the usual way," Bashir said with a hint of bitter humor as he stoppered the wineskin again. "Some noble who swore he loved her then disappeared. I saw that name, Ayan, in a history book and I liked it."

Aysel reached over and touched Mathei's knee as a signal to stop prying. Mathei waved her off with his fingers. He knew when to stop without her prodding, but something in Bashir's expression made her want to protect him now.

"Are you permitted to speak about the Sultana's plans for the Circle? I fancy myself a bit of a scholar, and that is a momentous decision."

"I know very little. I know she made the declaration to her High Council, and that the prince serves as the Sixth." Bashir glanced up at the sky and rubbed a hand over his face, scratching at his jaw.

"Are there creation mages in Tamar? A Charah?" Mathei's words tumbled out, his face and eyes bright with excitement. He always became so when he was speaking about magic, or history.

Bashir shook his head. "We have not seen a Third House mage since before the Sundering. I assume it is the same in Sarkum. That is part of why she is doing this. She hopes if she can balance the Wheel, the Third House will regenerate."

Mathei's excitement melted. "And the other Houses?"

Aysel stared into her little cup of wine, then took a melancholy sip.

"The prince is the only Charah who has come forward. She knows of one other, Second House, but the refugee situation, and the Sarkum civil war, are more pressing." Bashir looked up at the sky again and frowned. "My relief will be here soon. Or better be, in any case."

He stood, tossing the wineskin back to Mathei. Then he stretched. The stretch pulled his clothing tight against his arms and shoulders and emphasized his height and strength in a way that made Aysel feel dizzy with desire. Mathei pressed his knuckles to his mouth, looking sideways at Aysel, who suppressed a smile.

"You can return with me to the palace," Bashir said to Mathei as he relaxed.

"Happily," Mathei said. "Perhaps you'd like to take a nap in my room as well?"

Bashir's skin flushed hard, and he turned an accusing look on Aysel. She met it over the rim of her wine cup, gulping at the tart liquid. Then he shrugged one shoulder, recovering quickly from his discomfiture.

"I tend to stick with one nap partner at a time." He came around the fire and stood over Aysel, taking her cup from her hands and turning it so when he drank from it he did so from the same spot she had. He held the cup down to her, his eyes slightly narrowed as she took it. "I'll give you a moment, come find me at the guardhouse when you're ready," he said to Mathei when Aysel took the cup.

He left.

Mat gave a soft, breathless whistle. "Did he just all but take a territorial piss on your tent, because—"

Aysel slapped him on the back of the head. "That is disgusting. And no he did not"—she was not entirely sure he hadn't, because there was an entire swarm of butterflies dancing in her stomach—"because we have agreed that anything more than napping between us would be a very poor decision."

"His mouth may have said he agreed to that, but I can tell you right now that not one other part of that man has agreed to any such thing."

"Mat," Aysel said. She didn't want to talk about it. She needed to move, to be doing something. There was no reason to talk about Bashir or think about him outside of his part in protecting her family and keeping her restricted. It shouldn't be so hard to shift her mind from him.

"I see we're playing innocent and virtuous. Fine, fine. Have it your way. I want you to think about something for me." He stood and pulled her with him, enveloping her in a hug. Aysel clung to him, burying her face against his chest. "Without you, the Circle cannot stand," he murmured into her hair. He pulled back and looked down at her. "We should tell the Sultana. You must stand for the First."

"Mat." Aysel pulled back. "I can barely be called a mage at all. I am a spy. It's the only thing I'm good at, and Makram has given me a task I have to complete. If I admit I am First House, then you will all be exposed as Sixth House, and I will not put you in more danger."

"I have been exposed as worse, by some people's estimation." He lifted an eyebrow. "Makram is here, and they haven't burned him alive yet."

"He is a Charah. The city would fall before they could harm him. You are a Deval. Baba and Anne are Aval. Your magic makes you targets without giving you power enough to protect yourselves. That is my job. Besides, how will it affect your lives if I reveal myself, beyond the danger? Anne will never find a place here, if the courtiers know she is Sixth House."

"This is about you, this time, not us. Just think about it." He pulled her into another hug. "Makram suggested to the Sultana that she employ me in her library, as a researcher. She is considering it, after I prove to her my skills. She's given me books to read and report on in a variety of subjects, such as fauna of Narfour and an architectural—"

"Go away." Aysel pushed him gently in the direction Bashir had gone.

"You'll think about it?"

"No," Aysel said, but she would. It would circle in her head as a dangerously distracting series of what-ifs and keep her from concentrating on the two things that actually mattered. The remaining katil, who would only lay low for so long before striking again, and the Grand Vizier.

Aysel looked down at her wooden cup and the single sip of wine left. She turned it, running her thumb around the edge, then sighed and drank it.

THIRTEEN

S IX DAYS. THAT WAS how long it took to find any trace of the remaining katil. Six days, a full small turn, sneaking from the camp, scaling the cliff down to the hill, sprinting across the palace road and into the city in the dead of night. Searching, asking, hunting, listening, skulking in the various district markets to pick up rumors. Her hands were cut, callouses ripped open, body scraped from numerous tumbles from rock that gave way as she was climbing down. Her temper had grown shorter with each futile attempt to find them.

Finally, on the sixth day she tracked men matching the description of katil to the Merchant Pier.

All goods coming into and leaving the city were moved through or stored at the Merchant Pier. It was, besides the Grand Market, the most diverse section of the city. She saw skin as pale as milk and dark as kohl and every shade in between, heard languages she could not put name to, saw clothing that left her baffled. For all those reasons, it was a very good place to blend in, both for her, and the katil she hunted.

Unlike the Grand Market, unease permeated the interactions at the pier. The palpable threat made her stick close to escape routes and think about exit points before she entered any buildings. Every dark corner and alleyway felt only moments removed from violence and she suspected none were virgin to it. Gazes followed her everywhere she went, in a way that left her shuddering and flighty afterward.

There was an inn, sandwiched into the middle of the warehouses, of sorts, run by an old woman who was not much taller than Aysel and missing three of her teeth. She had the confident, arrogant way of a fire mage, which Aysel suspected had a great deal to do with her ability to run an inn that appeared to be populated in majority by pirates, thugs for hire, and gamblers. Aysel stood at the bar, managing a conversation by snippets exchanged with the old woman as she moved back and forth from the kitchen to the main room.

Men sat around low tables and benches that lined the walls, drinking tea, and stronger things. Though most of them bore the honey-to-bronze coloring of Tamar and Sarkum, a single group of Meneians occupied a table in the far corner of the room. They were all possessed of skin in shades of deeper brown and the loose-fitting, billowy clothing of a people accustomed to oppressive heat.

Though they had trade routes through Sarkum, they preferred to trade via the Sun Sea. Sarkum was unkind to travelers. She looked but did not stare overly long. Three were sitting, one great behemoth of a man was standing, arms folded over his chest, pinning the others with a blood-chilling stare. The man who stood was shaved clean from jaw to pate, something Aysel had also never seen. When he turned from his comrades, his gaze found hers. It hung for a moment, assessing, then he left, flashing a grin that blazed white against skin like pitch.

"That's Djar," the old woman said when she noticed Aysel staring after him. "He likes 'em with more meat." She winked.

"No. That isn't why I…I've never seen a Meneian," Aysel corrected, taking her gaze from the door and back to the old woman.

"Mmm," the woman said, appearing skeptical.

"Anyway. My question," Aysel said impatiently, "about the men?"

"I had three in here at the start"—the woman set a tray on the bar—"then only two. They've gone now. Antsy sort." She gave Aysel a quick examination out of the corners of her eyes and found something that made her frown.

"Could I see the room they stayed in?"

The woman sniffed, squinted, and picked at the flaking paint that decorated the tea tray. Aysel cast her gaze skyward in irritation as she dug in her belt for the few coins she kept on her and handed two of them to the woman.

She looked at them, bit them to make certain they weren't wood or clay, then jerked her head toward the stairs as she squirreled them away. "Last room on the left."

The room was at the top of the inn, beneath the peak of the roof. Under normal circumstances, Aysel would have been disgusted by it, convinced there were fleas or bed bugs in the blankets. But staying in her cold, wet shelter with thin, half-rotted blankets made her appreciate the relative princeliness of the room. Heat from the fire downstairs warmed it to near summer temperatures. She lingered a bit longer than necessary as she searched. There was a single dresser with two empty drawers. A table with a washbasin and pitcher stood in a corner under a mirror, and the bed was missing all its blankets and pillows. Inns often required a deposit for blankets and pillows, returnable upon turn-in of the items, to prevent theft. She doubted there was anything of use in the used blankets. She searched the bed, running her hands over the straw-stuffed mattress and lifting it to look beneath.

With no help or clues to be found, she trekked back downstairs.

"Come have a glass with me sometime, girl," the old woman called to her as Aysel left, and promised to keep an eye out for her errant friends. Mathei always said it paid to have friends from all walks, so perhaps if she could sneak him from the palace she'd bring him along. He'd probably befriend every hulking, stained, and fierce-looking creature that populated the docks and inn.

Frustrated by yet another setback, Aysel made her way up the formidable slope of the roads leading to the heart of the city, the Grand Market and Fire District that surrounded it.

From what she could tell, the Houses of the Wheel each had a district within the city, though if there were destruction or creation sections, she had yet to find them. The Air District sat centrally, to the north. West of the palace and below the cliff it sat on was the Water District. The far south end of the city was Earth, and scattered in pockets throughout she found districts that the inhabitants referred to by direction. So, Air District North, or Air District East.

Where might her family live, if given the opportunity to settle in Narfour? She liked the feel of the Air Districts. There was more space between the buildings, and they were built taller. The buildings tended to be tidy, not swarmed by vines or crowded with balconies. And they had more windows.

Despite that night had settled and the city grew quieter, Aysel did not travel directly through the Grand Market. It was heavily patrolled by city guards day and night, sometimes accompanied by palace guards during the day if they had discovered her missing. It amused her that their assumption was that once she escaped, she would immediately go to shop. She doubted Bashir was responsible for that logic—he'd know she was hunting.

She frowned. But she hadn't seen Bashir since his nap in her shelter, and the small turn was almost complete. It surprised her how often she thought of him and wondered what he was up to. A little restless spark zipped about her consciousness, making her want to hunt him down.

Their separation was for the best, of course, which she assumed was one of the reasons for his absence in her rotation of guards. They were, it seemed, unable to keep their hands off each other. And as that would complicate both their lives immeasurably, she had to respect his efforts to prevent catastrophe. It didn't mean she wasn't a little mad at him for having the discipline and self-control to stay away. Because it meant she had to as well.

As her direction took her from the perimeter of the Grand Market to the Fire District, the buildings transitioned from small, squat shops with living quarters above to larger multi-family dwellings or estate houses. They were often decorated with red, orange, pink, and purple in some combination that always gave Aysel a headache. While the more modest houses might have a door painted a bright color, or the trim around the arched windows, the large ones proclaimed their magic House in every gory detail. The other Houses had one color associated with them and their magic. Fire mages co-opted the rest of the rainbow, it seemed.

The Grand Vizier's estate was the most egregious. It was a looming square building, with a door painted blood red and the trim of the windows to either side to match. A balcony above the entrance had a matching set of three arched windows, one of which was a door, and had a view of the market below. The lower half of the building had no windows on the lower floor besides those by the door. The top level had two more sets of triplicate portals, one on the back, and one on the side. She suspected those on the top floor opened to a living area, and its sister, on the side of the house, to a master bedroom. Both had narrow balconies, neither with more than two potted plants for her to trip over.

She had observed it every night on her way to and from the camp. Even at the Wheel-forsaken time that she moved about the city, the estate showed signs of activity. Servants working late, people moving about in lit rooms, sometimes there were even visitors leaving or arriving. The Grand Vizier was a busy man.

Aysel had already chosen the back of the house as her entrance point. It was never a good idea to enter a house through a bedroom in darkness, and the back of the house nearly butted up against a low retaining wall that supported the homes on the street above. It would give Aysel the height she needed to jump to the balcony.

Tonight, the house was the darkest it had ever been. Only the lower levels were lit, and voices raised in song and laughter filtered through windows thrown open to the chill night air. Aysel slipped into an alley across the street, nestling in among a jumble of discarded pots.

Watching and waiting were not her favorite activities. They were, however, a necessary part of her job. This was the first time getting inside and accomplishing anything seemed plausible. But she wouldn't break into a house on a whim. So she waited.

Aysel forced herself to remain in place until a lone city guard had sauntered by, north toward the Air District. The party inside began to quiet, and a few guests left. When the door had closed behind them and the voices picked up again, Aysel left her hiding place and crossed the street, slipping between two houses into the narrow path behind them, and picked her way to the back of the Vizier's estate. She hopped onto the retaining wall and looked up at the balcony. A running start and a lucky grab would allow her to catch the iron bars that surrounded it. She paced back on the narrow wall, then turned and dashed back, leaping as she unleashed enough of her magic to make her light and fast. She caught two of the bars, then, hand over hand, traversed them to put herself next to the wall so she could use it to climb up to the top rail. She pressed her feet to the wall and pushed her weight back, extending her arms and walking her feet and hands up until she grabbed the top rail and wedged a foot between the bars and on the balcony floor, then swung her other leg over and crouched inside the balcony rail.

Aysel peered into the window nearest her, holding as still as she could, breathing the same fading spell she had used on the katil on the hillside.

The moon offered little assistance, hiding behind thick dark clouds. Pale, fading light from a spent mage orb cast a melancholy glow inside. Aysel waited, watching, and listening, before quietly reaching up and trying the latch on the door. It moved only a bit, but it was locked. Aysel withdrew both her knives from the sheaths on her wrists. These style of doors were common even in Al-Nimas, and the locks flimsy. They were not meant to be unlocked with a key, but a latch on the inside. The lock itself would slip open if she put pressure on it, she didn't need anything as sophisticated as a pick. She used one knife to pry the door open a fraction, and the other to work at the fragile bolt. She didn't want to break it, because that would be evidence she had been there, so she took her time. Just when she began to grow impatient, it clicked open.

Aysel put her knives away and waited another moment before swinging the door open enough to slip inside.

She immediately slid away from the windows and door, so she would not be silhouetted by moonlight outside, then crouched, waiting for her eyes to adjust. The room was sparsely furnished. The dying ghost of the single lingering mage orb cast enough glow to highlight the looming shadows of furniture. A rug ran the length of the room, and there were two chairs and a table, making the large room feel hollow and empty. Three doors lined each side, and a staircase on the far end led to the lower level. Voices drifted from below, peals of a woman's laughter, at least two men talking.

The rooms on this level would be bedrooms, or offices. Downstairs there would be a kitchen, a dining room, and servant quarters. It was a common layout in Al-Nimas as well. Aysel's own home had been similar.

Some guests had already left—the party was winding down. She'd need to be quick or risk being caught by whoever was downstairs moving up to the bedrooms when it ended completely.

Aysel relocked the door she'd entered through, then moved to the first door on her left. It opened, and she put her back against it as she peeked inside. A bedroom, but it was small, with a bed barely big enough for two people. Likely guest quarters. She shut the door and crossed the main room to the one opposite.

As she had guessed, it was the master. There was a wardrobe and a bed. Aysel entered and searched the wardrobe, opening the cabinet and finding it empty, the two drawers as well. The room was tidy and the bed made, though in the dark there was no way to tell if it had been slept in recently or not. The rest of the room was empty. She took a quick look under the bed and saw nothing but deeper shadow.

The third door was locked. Aysel grinned. She dropped to her knees in front of it and reached into the back of her collar, where she had cut the lining of her caftan to create a deep pocket to hold picks she had bought on her foray into the market. She unfolded the leather case that held them, laying it out in front of her on the floor. She selected three picks and put the rest away, then bent and peered into the lock. Without any light in the room behind the door she couldn't see anything, so she'd need to do it all by feel.

Something tickled her senses, something that made her nose itch, like the barest hint of smoke. She frowned and lifted a finger to touch the lock. The metal of the plate felt oddly warm. Oddness usually hinted at bad things.

Aysel put her hands in her lap and listened, turning her attention to the far side of the room and the stairs down. Voices still hummed from below, but they were quiet. She doubted the gathering would last much later. Not enough time to try and pick the lock and go through whatever she found in the room beyond. She chewed her lip, then let out a small puff of breath.

It was a risk, but she lifted her fingers to hover near the door and let the faintest trail of her power course across the lock, just a trickle of air. It heated against her fingertips. *Burn.* She felt fire magic in the lock and frowned. Was it possible to spell objects? Mathei might know, or Makram, but she did not. There could only be one reason to spell a lock with fire magic, if it were possible.

Aysel had never encountered anything like it, but she suspected it was a trap. If she picked the lock, the magic would activate, and burn her hands, at the very least. And anyone who took the trouble to spell a lock wouldn't stop at something so benign. Makram had said the man was dangerous. This little trap seemed to indicate he was vicious and remorseless as well. Or hiding something very important.

That settled it, she needed inside.

Wrapping her power around her hand, and the lock, Aysel shifted to the side, pressing her torso and face against the wall adjacent to the door. She carefully aimed her pick at the lock, took a deep breath, and jammed it into the keyhole. Fire exploded from the lock, and Aysel clamped her power around it, guided by instinct only, barely holding what was likely meant to be a gout of flame inside a cage of her own magic. The sound was muffled by her power, but not silenced. It still sounded loud enough, in the quiet, to compete with a stampede of angry, bellowing oxen.

When it seemed to have burned itself out, she wiped sweat out of her eyes with her sleeve, taking a few gulps of cool air. Working magic by instinct was taxing, and the fire spell had been stronger than she imagined. Her pick was a sad, melted bit of metal, indicating the heat of the spell would easily have removed her hand, and if she took it directly in the face, could have killed her.

She shifted and put her back to the wall, her heart thundering in her chest, and took several calming breaths as she watched the central room and listened. The party went on, undisturbed. Someone was singing a bawdy song, accompanied by occasional titters of laughter.

The one beneficial tilt of the Wheel in the situation was that the spell also burned out the lock mechanism, so Aysel was able to push the door open with ease. She observed the darkened room beyond. Was that the only trap? Did he have half a dozen scattered around the room? Or would he count on the first to stop or discourage someone on a first pass? It rather depended on how labor-intense it was to create such traps, she wagered. And since magic traps were not commonplace enough for her to have heard of them or seen them, she had to assume it was no small feat.

Aysel stepped into the room and gave her eyes a moment to readjust as she closed the door quietly behind her, retrieving the remains of her lockpick as she did, and tucked it into the cloth at her waist.

The room came into just enough focus that she could move about, lit by a sliver of moonlight peeking through velvet curtains at the far end. It was expansive, twice the size of Makram's office in Al-Nimas. It would take all night to explore thoroughly, and she probably only had moments left. Once the burned-out lock was discovered, there would be guards on the house, meaning a second try was out of the question.

A single, high-backed chair and small table sat in the corner to the left of the door. The two walls encompassing it were filled with books, and she dismissed it. If she felt she had time after looking at everything else, she'd looked through the books. Some people tucked things in their pages, which was a good enough hiding spot, since it took ages to riffle them.

The desk near the wall of windows was clear but for a stack of papers. Aysel took them to the window and quickly thumbed through, then set them back as she had found them, going so far as to cant the top paper a bit off, as it had been when she picked it up. The desk had three drawers, all of them locked. She touched each with her magic but felt nothing of the fire she'd felt in the door. She used her second pick to open them, one after the other, then tucked that lockpick with the first in the cloth at her waist. The left drawer was completely empty. The center drawer held quills, paper, and ink on one side, and sealing wax sticks beside a medallion meant to be affixed to a stamp for sealing letters. Leave it to a fire mage to need a seal three times as big as anyone else. Aysel stared at it for a moment, wondering what bothered her about it besides the size. A loud crash from downstairs startled her back to her task.

The right-hand drawer was deeper than the other two. "What have you got for me, my dear?" she said on a breath. A tangle of braided cord she suspected was some mark of office. She set it on the desk. A pile of letters. She took them to the window. There were five. Two were ledgers of expenses. She scanned them briefly, but saw nothing that gave her pause. The third was a note of exchange, marking the purchase of several horses from a breeder in the eastern valley. Aysel frowned. The fourth was addressed to the Vizier in an awkward hand, not a noble's oft-practiced calligraphy. Personal things were always good. She pulled the single sheet of paper from the envelope and read it.

"Esteemed Kadir Pasha," the greeting read. An honorific, from someone whom the Vizier vastly outranked. "I am Temel Irmak Mizraa-ih, who saved your life at Mizraa. I would consider that life-debt repaid if you might see fit to arrange a marriage for my eldest daughter into a suitable household." The names and words blurred together as Aysel scanned the letter.

She folded the paper and returned it to its envelope without reading the rest. She doubted the marriage of a farm worker was of any import to Makram.

The fifth envelope was empty, but felt a bit crumpled, like it had held something bulky and oddly shaped instead of paper.

She laid them back where she had found them and felt around in the drawer. Something was strange, and she had to sit back and stare at the drawer, with her hand still in it, to realize what. The front made it appear deeper than it was. Or…she swept her hand around the edge of the wooden bottom and discovered a tack, stuck into the very back corner.

"Aren't you a tricky mink," she breathed, and removed the contents of the drawer, laying them out on the floor next to her in the same order and disposition she had found. Then she hooked her nail under the tack and worked the bottom panel loose, lifted it out, and laid it on the desk.

Jewelry. Aysel blew a puff of air at an errant strand of hair tickling her face, and glared. It wasn't even expensive jewelry, though it was displayed on a pad of velvet as if it were. She picked through it. A few simple chains with charms, three rings, a bracelet, and a set of gaudy, heavy-looking pearl earrings. Trinkets for lovers, perhaps? Payoffs for court gossips? Surely these pieces, which might barely fetch enough money to buy a swayback plow horse, were not the reason the man kept his door locked with fire and a false bottom in the drawer? It made no sense.

She picked up a ring and examined it. It was completely unremarkable, a gold filigree band with a dark stone set into it. Just as she moved to put it back, a trickle of malignant warmth stung her magic.

Aysel scowled, started to turn to examine it in a shaft of moonlight from the window, and the front door closed below.

Guests leaving. Out of time.

She moved to set the ring back with the rest of the jewelry and something gave a brighter glint. Amongst the tangle of baubles was a thin gold medallion. A second sealing stamp perhaps? Odd. Aysel grabbed it and shoved it into the cloth at her waist to be examined later, then slipped the drawer back inside its cubby. As quickly and quietly as possible, she returned the false bottom, then the items she had removed in order, and carefully slid the drawer closed.

The window behind her overlooked the alley and the building next door. She'd have to jump. There was no balcony, and the drop was significant. Aysel worked at the lever that swung down to lock the window closed and cursed silently when she discovered it was rusted in place. She drew a knife, working it around all the edges, and tried again. It popped open with a scraping of metal against metal and she hissed as she started to push the window, which gave an offensive screech. Aysel stopped.

"Curse it," she hissed.

"Indeed," a man said from behind her.

Cold shock exploded across her back and gripped her heart as it leapt to a gallop. She should have just jumped, but something made her spin back around. Something made her look, like a silken thread tugging at her power. The man snapped his fingers and an orb burst into life above him, flooding the room with pale light. Aysel blinked as her eyes adjusted.

Whoever he was, he couldn't possibly be a Grand Vizier, he was too young, though he was obviously a fire mage, and a Sival at that.

"Interesting," he said. "Are you going to throw yourself to your death because I've caught you? How gruesome. You may use the front door, if you like. If you can reach it before I roast you like a pheasant." He took a sip of wine from the goblet he held, examining her.

The window was only open a fraction. She'd have to throw herself against it, hope it opened enough to let her through, then manage to get her power around her before she splattered on the stones below. She tightened her grip on the casement. He raised an eyebrow. Her magic sizzled with a sense of danger, though the man looked more bored than threatening.

"I'd rather you jump than have to explain your smoking remains to the Grand Vizier. So be about it before I change my mind." He looked at her with dull interest. Aysel lifted a foot to the window frame, slowly, testing. He mimicked her by lifting his goblet in slow motion to take another sip. He smacked his lips and eyed the contents of the cup before looking at her again.

"Only a half-wit would try and steal from the Grand Vizier. Why don't you try the courtier next door, she has some rubies that would turn your head, I'm sure." Was he drunk? That might explain the strange behavior. There had been a party, after all. Could he be a steward? He was young to be such to a noble as highly ranked as a Grand Vizier.

"I've no need of rubies, but thank you for the tip," Aysel said. Why was she talking to him? Why was her magic whipping around inside her like the wind before a storm?

"A spy then." He took a long drink from the glass and came toward her, his gaze sweeping over the desk and the rest of the room. Her body tensed, her hands tightened on the casement, and she prepared to leap away from him. His movement closer felt as threatening as the lock. Had he designed the trap?

"Listen, Pigeon, he doesn't just leave things lying about. If you want to put dear Behram in the Cliffs you're going to have to do a lot more than survey a few desk drawers. Trust me." He looked at her over the rim of the goblet with raised eyebrows. The man was clearly Unbalanced. "You're certain it's death by impact and not the door?" He circled his glass in the direction of the stairs to the lower level.

"Who are you?" Aysel asked.

"Either a drunk, or your executioner. That depends on your speed." The goblet dropped, and fire took its place in his hand, filling his eyes and her vision. Aysel threw herself against the window, kicking against the sill to dive through. A ball of crackling fire shrieked past and above her as she tumbled through the air, the ground racing toward her as she scrambled mentally to wrap enough air around her to cushion her.

She hit the ground hard, her magic protecting her life and bones but not her breath. It rushed from her lungs at the impact and she lay stunned and gagging on the cobbles below the window when he leaned out to look down at her. He seemed amused she was alive, giving a grunt of interest before tugging the window closed. The lock gave a grinding shriek as he turned it.

Aysel stared up at the window, but he pulled the curtains closed, and a moment later she saw the light of the orb go out. The scent of burnt hair wafted to her as she staggered to her feet.

Madman. A madman who could easily describe her to Bashir or the City Watch. Hopefully he was as drunk as he seemed, and would forget the salient details when the time came to report them.

Aysel cursed as she began a limping jog back to the camp.

FOURTEEN

AYSEL SLIPPED BETWEEN THE tents, giving herself plenty of time to skirt the perimeter guards. She'd memorized the schedule of the guards assigned to her and liked to be in place during their handover so that if they checked on her, she was there. Most of them checked on her and maintained vigilance for between one and three candlemarks, the night guards less, before they began pacing to keep warm and losing interest in staring at her shelter.

When her current guard turned his back and paced a few steps away from the firepit, Aysel slipped in through the canvas side opposite him. She was exhausted. Too many nights spent awake, searching the city, and too many days as well. Today was for rest, and when she woke up, she'd be a good girl and ask for an escort to the palace to tell Makram what had happened.

She'd found a discarded scrap of rug on the way to the water source a few days before, and now she used it to keep her feet out of the dirt as she toed out of her boots. Aysel unbuckled the harness and tugged out of it, setting it on top of the crate that served as her table and wardrobe. She unbraided her hair, because she hated sleeping in braids, and fluffed it with her fingers, scratching her scalp and humming in pleasure. From the inside of the crate, which was turned on its side and propped on some rocks to keep it off the ground, she retrieved her more loose-fitting caftan and salvar and set them on the bed.

She removed the medallion she'd taken from the Grand Vizier's desk, as well as a small piece of candy set on a wooden skewer and wrapped in paper. The candy had been given to her as a thank-you from a stall vendor that morning, after she'd stopped a pickpocket from taking his purse while he was busy unloading his wares.

Stripping down to just the fabric around her chest and small clothes, she traded the tight-fitting caftan for the looser, and paused to fold up both the salvar and caftan she'd been wearing all night and stow them in the crate. She picked up the blank medallion and examined it. There was nothing stamped on it, so it wasn't a seal, and it was very lightweight, flimsy even. She was certain she'd seen a very similar one on the desk, but it had been engraved. Aysel closed her eyes to try and remember, to picture what she had seen on the other. But her body and mind were tired, and everything swirled together. She'd try again after some sleep. She folded her waist cloth, then tucked the medallion into it and put them both on the shelf.

Next she unwrapped the candy. It had been too long since she'd eaten, but she didn't want to spend the time to cook proper food. She stuck the candy in her mouth. It was hard, sweet, and flavored lightly like pomegranate. Aysel sucked idly on it as she lifted the clean salvar.

The canvas at her back, which would be on the side where her guard paced outside, snapped like someone had shoved it aside.

"You little slug—"

Aysel turned. None of them had been bold enough to walk into her tent without warning her first. She'd leave this one with at least a black eye for his audaciousness.

"Big slug," she corrected, when she saw Bashir framed in the light from outside. A little thrill zinged down her throat and through her belly to see him. Aysel pulled the candy stick from her mouth and gestured at him with it.

"Are you going to stand there holding that open so all the world can see me?" she said. "Your guard is staring." It was not an exaggeration, he was just behind Bashir, but she could see him attempting to peer around his commander.

Bashir turned, put his hand on the man's face, and pushed him backward. "Give your turnover to Guardsman Macar," Bashir ordered, then stepped inside and let the canvas fall closed behind him. Aysel could see the red creeping up his neck as he tried and failed to look anywhere but at her.

"Even your men"—Aysel stuck the candy back in her mouth—"have the decency to announce themselves." Bashir's gaze had settled on her bare legs. "Hello?" She didn't smile, though a grin was fighting her awfully hard. This was fun.

"Four times this turn," Bashir cleared his throat, "four times my men have reported you missing." He squinted at the far corner of the shelter.

"As in, missing entirely or, missing while I went to get water, or use the toilets, or chat with the farmer and his family?" Aysel removed the candy again because it was difficult to speak around it, and folded her arms, drawing in the air with it as she spoke. "I'm sorry to tell you, they get bored very quickly around here. I even came back from fetching water yesterday to find my guardsman nearly asleep on his feet. Poor man."

Aysel popped the sucker back in her mouth. His mouth twitched, his jaw tightening, then he lifted a hand and rubbed his fingers and thumb together across his eyes, pinching the bridge of his nose.

"I did eat my dinner with the farmer and his family last night. The girls want me to bring the big guard to play chase. I believe they mean you." She slid the sucker out again. "Perhaps your guardsman didn't realize where I'd gone? I could announce myself more frequently to them if you'd prefer."

This could have been her best distraction yet. Bashir looked ready to sprint from the shelter. Mathei would be very proud of her.

He lowered his hand just enough to cover his mouth, glaring at her. Aysel sucked the candy back in, hollowing out her cheeks.

"Please—" he said, sharply, dropping his hand, "*stop* playing with that Wheel-cursed candy."

"Tsk." She removed the sucker and bent to retrieve the paper to wrap it, revealing more of her legs as she did. Bashir's nostrils flared as he exhaled forcefully, and she faced him again, wrapping the sucker and setting it on the top of the crate. "Language. I am a noble's daughter after all. I'm not certain I can stomach such coarse—"

"Aysel," Bashir said, "put your clothes on."

"These?" Aysel shook out her salvar and held them in front of her legs, looking from them to Bashir and back again. It was all she could do not to burst into laughter and fling herself at him to wrap her arms around his neck and apologize for the tortured, exasperated expression she had caused on his face.

"Now, please," he said. She saw the barest flash and spark of warm golden power in his eyes. She turned her back to him and bent to fit her foot into one of the legs. "Aysel"—he slid his hand beneath her arm and spun her around and against him—"stop." He grit his teeth, his magic flaring and fading as he fought it.

"Stop what?" She tugged her salvar up, shimmying her hips a little against his to pull the salvar up to her waist.

"I know you're doing this on purpose, and I am not made of stone."

Aysel hummed in the back of her throat, leaning her body against his. "Are you certain? You feel like you are." She decided not to rub her hands up his chest and over his broad shoulders. Though she wanted to. She was glad for his closeness, it had been cold standing in only her caftan, but the growing heat in her body was almost entirely internal.

"Aysel," he sighed.

"You're getting mud on my new rug." She pointed down between them.

"Wheel, you drive me mad." He lifted her, standing her up on the edge of the lower stack of pallets, so her face was level with his. The little thrill zinged her again and left a swirl of anticipation and heat in its wake. Aysel slid her arms around his neck and smiled at him. His hands on her waist held her tightly against him, and power crackled in his eyes and fissured across his temples.

"It balances you right, for barging into my house," she said, softly.

"House?" he murmured, his gaze locked on her mouth. Aysel touched the tip of her nose to his. She wanted him to kiss her, and she didn't care that they shouldn't. She was too tired, and her common sense was fast asleep.

"I've missed you," she breathed.

"Good." His voice was torn open by the quaking threat of his unleashed magic. "Because I can't stop thinking about you."

"You like that I drive you mad." She let her lips touch his, just the barest brush as she spoke. His breath stopped, his hands tightened on her, pulling her harder against him as he stepped as close as he could. The jagged lines of gold magic shot down his neck, disappearing into his clothes. Aysel's fingers twitched to tear them off and see his magic all over his skin.

"I do," he said. "I like the way you talk, and the way you move… I can't think for the wanting of you."

"Tell me more." A warm, deep heat pulsed in the cradle of her hips.

He kissed her. She was prepared for it to be the kind of hard, desperate kiss their flirtations had demanded. But his mouth was soft and warm. He only gently captured her at first, her upper lip caressed between his, then her bottom lip, his breath mingling with hers. Her

Ox was too sweet, it made it all the harder to resist him. After he allowed her a quick sip of air, she tasted coffee lingering on his tongue as he invited her to a deeper kiss. Her body responded with eager agreement, storm and lightning heat filling her core and threatening to whip free of her mental control.

Just another moment, she begged herself as she opened her mouth in invitation.

The softness of his kiss vanished. He slid a hand up the back of her neck and into her hair, winding it around his hand and gripping it in his fist. He demanded then, as she had expected of him, hard and unrelenting, like his morals and his magic. His other hand skated down her back, settling in the curve above her hips, and molded her to him.

Aysel sucked his lower lip into her mouth and hopped up, slinging her legs around his hips. He caught her, his arm under her backside, and groaned.

He turned his face away from hers and used his hand in her hair to tip her head back and to the side. He kissed her jaw, her chin, then her throat, working his way around to the slope of her neck in soft, sucking kisses that drained the strength from her limbs and the will from her mind. Her thighs clenched around him, and she whimpered. Bashir lifted a knee to the pallets, then the other, so he knelt, and laid her down, settling himself over her exactly as she had done to him not so long ago, on all fours. His sword banged against the pallets.

Aysel slid her fingers into his belt and pulled the buckle open as Bashir continued his languid, mind-numbing kisses along her neck and collarbones. She tugged the belt free and let it drop on the ground. A brief, weak knowledge that she had let things go much too far entered her thoughts then burned to little pieces of ash when his mouth found hers again.

"You taste like pomegranate," he said when he released her.

"The candy." She caressed his chest, slowly, fixing into her memory the exact feel of the bulky muscles there, and his shoulders. She slid her nails up the back of his neck. Bashir's eyes closed and he tucked his chin. "You taste like coffee." She propped herself on her elbows and pressed her mouth to the swell in his throat, then nipped along his jaw.

"I've been drinking it," he huffed an exhale when she kissed a spot just below his ear, "a lot of it, these days. There is no other way to stay awake."

"You are always welcome to sleep here. It gets very cold at night," she whispered against his ear, then nipped and kissed his earlobe.

"I would say don't tempt me"—he tugged up her caftan to reveal her belly and let out an appreciative rumble—"but it's too late."

He flattened his hand against her stomach, curving it around to her waist, and Aysel arched under his touch, damp heat spreading between her thighs. He buried his face against her neck and bit her skin, his teeth sending skeins of lightning through her body. She said his name, her hands clenching in his caftan. Even if her common sense had been of any use at all, she knew she wasn't going to be the one to stop them.

A breeze slipped through the shelter, touched with magic, and Aysel stiffened, lifting her head to glance around. Bashir went still, then dropped his head. "Broken Wheel," he cursed.

"Commander. Attend me."

Aysel recognized the Sultana's voice, and it was as clear as if the woman were standing right next to her. She looked around again, dazed. Surely the Sultana was not there, outside the shelter? Bashir climbed off her and snatched his sword from the ground. It must be a spell. The same spell she had used.

Aysel sat up, kneeling on the blankets. "Is that what happens when I do it?"

Bashir looked at her with a raised eyebrow, yanking the buckle closed on his sword belt. He shook his head, slowly, and leaned over her, his hand laid against the slope of her neck.

"Not exactly. You"—he kissed the opposite side, sending more heat and longing through her—"woke me out of a dead sleep by murmuring in my ear about fire mages. Next time murmur something else."

Aysel grabbed his head in her hands, shoving her fingers into his hair, and pulled his mouth to hers. "How about"—she turned his head and nuzzled his ear, then kissed it, and he shuddered violently—"come back soon."

"Yes. Something exactly like that." He sighed, which became a plaintive sound, as he straightened. "Be good, Aysel."

"Even when we're alone?"

Bashir grinned, and shook his head, then turned to leave. "I'm going to be a mumbling simpleton in front of the Sultana. So, thank you for that."

He grabbed the canvas to shove it aside, but then let go and turned back to her. Aysel rose up on her knees as he returned. When he dipped to kiss her again, she nipped his bottom lip. He breathed a laugh and wrapped her in arms that made her feel completely enveloped, lifting her halfway off the pallets, and kissed her, hard, and a little frantically.

"Stay," he whispered, and after a lingering look that left her boneless, he left.

Aysel tipped her head back and glared at the top of her shelter.

"Imbecile." She stretched out on her belly. "You were supposed to distract him, not seduce him." Aysel rolled onto her back. It wasn't completely a failed attempt, she *had* distracted him. He hadn't even asked where she'd been. And so she hadn't had to skirt around her break-in at the Grand Vizier's.

Cold replaced the warmth in her limbs, extinguishing her lust and sharpening her wits. She sat up. Why had the Sultana summoned him with magic instead of sending someone to retrieve him? What matter could be that pressing?

Aysel pulled at her fingers, cracking the knuckles. It was very likely that either the Grand Vizier had discovered the burned-out lock in his house, or whoever had caught her had informed him, and he in turn informed the Sultana. She was summoning her guard commander to hunt down the thief. Bashir would know immediately it was Aysel, or at least suspect her.

She jumped off the pallet and pulled her boots on, grabbed her swords and put the harness on. Then she bundled her clothes up into the smaller of her two blankets and tied the corners around her shoulders like a pack. Time to run. She hesitated, observing the pallets, the warmth of Bashir's hand on her belly still present on her skin, the memory of the taste and feel of his mouth threatening to torture her indefinitely.

Maybe if she explained to him, he would listen. Maybe he would understand.

This was wrong, running with no explanation at all. But, Makram had sworn her to secrecy, and Bashir did not see grey. Not even for her.

FIFTEEN

Bashir left Huzur at the gate with Erol and moved as quickly as he could without running toward the palace. There were any number of reasons the Sultana would have summoned him so suddenly, and all of them made his jaw clench. It was impossible to keep rumors circling through his guard force from eventually reaching the Sultana's ears. Especially considering she was capable of listening to any part of the palace she wished, no matter where she was. She might have heard about his inability to contain Aysel, or be dissatisfied with the guard rotation, or wonder about the situation with the katil, who Aysel claimed were still at large.

The very worst case was that she somehow knew about him and Aysel. He would not put it past her to know about something like that long before the people involved even realized it was happening.

He shoved a hand through his hair, then swept both hands across his temples and back to make certain he didn't look too much like someone who had just been soundly and wildly kissed. Aysel's fingers in his hair and on his body had sent his good sense spinning off into the void, and it was just barely coming back. The memory of her, half-naked and with that damned candy in her mouth, was going to haunt him for many small turns. He'd never been so aroused in his life. Her little body had been torture enough covered in loose fabric and only hinted at in movement. Now he knew every inch of her was muscle. Not unfeminine, but her shape was drawn by lithe, graceful strength, and he wanted days and nights to memorize it.

Bashir tried to bury the thought beneath more mundane subjects, but they wormed their way back to the surface. What was he thinking? He couldn't do this with her. He couldn't go any further. It wasn't in him to be casual the way others were, like Erol. Aysel might even be someone like that. But he was not. And she wasn't for him. She bent rules, and danced around right and wrong, she hid things from him. She was infuriating, exasperating, and funny. He'd never known a woman who could fight like her, like a man, like she could hold her own beside him, even best him. She challenged him. She was amazing, a bundle of chaos and storm that he had never known he wanted.

Bashir slapped a hand to his face and dragged it down, then worked his jaw to loosen it. He'd been lost to thoughts of her the entire walk between the gate and the receiving hall, and he wrestled himself under control just as he arrived at the receiving hall doors. Samira stood, calm and serene as no other fire mage he knew could be, and smiled at him, though her smooth brow had a tiny furrow down the middle.

"They've been waiting." She opened the doors as Bashir approached. "The Grand Vizier is in fine form."

"Thank you for the warning," Bashir said. Samira bowed, which always made him wince. Samira was noble born and shouldn't be bowing to the likes of him.

Bashir slipped past her and down the aisle to where the Sultana sat. The Grand Vizier sat nearby, on a bench against the wall. They were both glaring, but not at each other. Makram stood just behind the Sultana, and Samira joined him as Bashir dropped to a knee in front of them, pressing his fist to his heart. The Grand Vizier was attended by his steward and his son, Cemil. Just the sight of Cemil made Bashir's temper roll over and warm.

"Commander," the Sultana said. When he glanced at her face he saw nothing unusual in her expression beyond what she allowed to show of her distaste for Kadir. "The Grand Vizier has troubling news."

Bashir felt a thread of relief and his muscles relaxed, though he had not realized how tensely he'd been holding himself. This had nothing to do with Aysel at all.

He turned to the Grand Vizier and rose to his feet, then bowed. "How may I serve you, Kadir Pasha?" He remained bowed until the Grand Vizier rose and spoke, leaning very slightly on his staff to support his weight off his injured leg. Cemil folded his arms and looked at the floor, as though he were listening. Bashir expected it was simply to hide his bored expression.

"This morning I returned to my estate in the Fire District, only to find the lock on an interior door had been tampered with."

A moment of silence stretched in the wake of Kadir's words, as Bashir's brain slowly sorted the information and bits of it clicked into place. The coolness of his relief turned to ice, a block of it in his belly. He held his voice, and his immediate suspicions, enough to say, "May I ask you some questions, Kadir Pasha, to gather information?"

"If you believe it will help." He waved a dismissive hand, his expression pinched in irritation. As though Bashir were a bothersome insect instead of someone capable of solving Kadir's trouble.

"Was there any other indication someone entered forcefully? Broken windows, or—"

"I know what entering forcefully means, Commander," Kadir snapped. "And no. The doors were locked, the windows, everything. I cannot find anything missing, I just know that someone was there, because the lock on the door to my office had been…forced." His eyebrows twitched inward but the expression quickly left.

Cemil reached up, brushing his fingers under his nose, and gave a little cough.

Bashir frowned. "May I have your permission to examine the lock?"

"No. What I want is for you to find whatever thieves are running rampant in the streets while you devote all your guard force to meaningless endeavors," Kadir demanded.

"He does so by my orders, Grand Vizier," the Sultana said, as steady-voiced as she would be if ordering coffee, instead of reining in the most trying man in the whole of Tamar. "Let us continue with the subject at hand. How do you propose Commander Ayan capture this supposed thief if he is not allowed to examine evidence pertaining to the crime?" A facade of cool patience carried in her voice.

Behind the Sultana, Makram was not giving the same effort to hide his irritation. Dark eyes fixed on Kadir as if he were vermin.

"What could he ascertain by tramping around my house and poking at locks and desk drawers? He need only stake out my houses until the criminal is caught."

"Grand Vizier"—the Sultana seemed to hold in a sigh—"I'm afraid I cannot commit my palace guard force to petty thievery. If nothing was stolen, and you are not comfortable allowing Commander Ayan and his men to look for evidence, then we simply have to alert the City Watch and hope no one else is victimized before the thief strikes again."

Kadir tapped his staff against the floor. "It is an unacceptable farce that the dregs of Sarkum society warrant more regard by the palace than its own officers of the Council." He turned to his steward and Cemil, the latter somehow managing to make his abject boredom look arrogant, and gestured them to follow him. "I will be sharing my concerns with the Council," he announced as the three of them left the room. The steward shut the doors behind them.

"Of course you will," the Sultana ground out. "Bashir." She flicked her fingers in wordless command for a dampening. It took him a moment to gather his magic, separating it from his rising temper. A lie. The entire thing, the teasing, the torture, the touches, the kisses. Lies to keep him from the truth. How far was she willing to take it to lead him off course? How foolish could he be?

His mother had been right. Nobles were never what they seemed and had no qualms using people toward their own ends.

"Commander Ayan," the Sultana said, sharply. He flinched, forcing back his thoughts of Aysel, and cast the spell.

"Forgive me, Sultana." He ripped his gaze away from Samira; the worried and surprised look in her eyes felt like salt dumped on a wound. He was failing, noticeably now, because of Aysel. He'd allowed himself to step further into it, because he thought she felt the same. He had trusted her. She had asked him to trust her and he had.

"He is keeping something from us." The Sultana rose, pacing across the room. "There is more to this than just a break-in. But I cannot ignore the situation just because he is lying. Bashir." The Sultana spoke to him, but her gaze was on her betrothed, whose eyes were tight at the corners. "Bring me Mistress Attiyeh."

"Yes, Sultana," Bashir said, holding onto his anger, and his magic, by what felt like only his fingernails. He had to get away before either slipped loose.

"And you," the Sultana said to the prince, quietly, but with all the fierceness of a winter storm, "will explain to me what you hope to accomplish by counteracting my orders as it pertains to the Grand Vizier."

"I have sworn my loyalty, and more, to you. Do you doubt me?" Makram said, with forced blandness that was not reflected in the near-black depth of his eyes.

"If my Council believes I condone the act of spying on them, I will never gain their loyalty."

Bashir felt fractured, his temper quaking harder. What had made him believe Aysel? He had never been so manipulated.

"But if you are ever going to unseat that man, you need physical evidence," Makram said. "Physical evidence you will never obtain through the means you have employed. Aysel will find it. Give her time."

"Have you forgotten how dangerous—how brutal he is? You have put her at a risk I will not accept." She rarely revealed when she was angry, and her quick, sharp words and fierce glare proved she was now.

"Aysel is not what she appears to be, Naime. She is a woman very capable of handling herself," Makram said, with confidence Bashir shared, except for Kadir. Bashir had seen the scars on the Sehzade's body. Had witnessed the mindless fear of fire in an otherwise steady, controlled, and intelligent man. He could not bear the thought of Aysel anywhere near Kadir, and he could not hold himself under control a moment longer.

"I have to go," Bashir croaked. The Sultana and the prince looked at him as if he had sprouted another head. He drew a breath and straightened. He caged his magic in the last bit of control he had. "She was present when you summoned me, and she will run. If you wish for me to bring her to you, I must go now."

"Very well," the Sultana said. Bashir bowed to both of them, then spun for the exit. If he could just get to his room, or the arena and be alone for a moment, he could get himself under control enough to look for her. The Sultana did not permit her servants or her guardsmen to run in the palace—outside of catastrophe, she considered it indecorous and a sign that things were out of control. He walked at long strides, but he wanted to sprint, and keep going until his legs gave out.

He didn't want to believe it was Aysel, he almost couldn't, because he wanted to believe her so badly. He wanted to believe the way her teasing and her flirting made him feel. He wanted to believe her when she said he could trust her. But how could it be anyone else? She had snuck into a fully occupied barracks. She could certainly sneak into an unguarded house. Yet, he struggled to believe she'd leave any evidence, especially evidence like a tampered lock.

He trotted down the stairs from the palace entrance and started for the barracks. If she was still in the camp…maybe she could explain. His anger cooled slightly.

"Ah, Commander." Cemil's voice calling to him made all his muscles bunch and his teeth clench. Bashir stopped, took a steadying breath, and turned as the Vizier's son crossed toward him.

"You look a bit less…unflappable than you usually do. Things not going your way?" He smiled, all teeth and taunt, and the ground at Bashir's feet cracked open, shifting and scraping beneath Cemil. To his credit, Cemil only continued smiling.

"If you wish me to catch your thief, then I suggest you let me get on with it." Earth rolled in Bashir's voice, its heavy strength unleashed in his body by his broken threads of control. He flexed his hands open then closed them into fists. He could crush Cemil, and the only person in the world who would care was Samira. It might be worth hanging just to see that arrogant smile wiped off his face.

"Ah ah ah. I've seen that look before." Cemil lowered his voice, and fire flashed in his eyes. "One day, I think, you and I will have our differences out. But"—the glimpse of magic disappeared and Cemil shrugged, resuming his bored look—"not today."

Deep breaths slowed his temper. "What do you want?"

"A rather odd little pigeon perched on my window last night," Cemil said.

Bashir's power was silenced by a bloom of frosty fear. Cemil knew. He'd seen Aysel.

"It flew away with something shiny that I think my father will miss. I suggest you retrieve it before he realizes it's gone." When Cemil smiled it reminded Bashir of street dogs that appeared to grin right before they attacked.

"I will return your items as soon as I am able."

Cemil's expression flattened. "Let us hope so." He turned his focus over Bashir's shoulder, gaze darting. He was looking for Samira.

Bashir frowned. Cemil did not deserve her care. Her devotion. Bashir had never understood it.

Cemil gave Bashir one final glance, then sauntered back toward his horse, which was held by one of the young men the Sultana employed to care for her horses. Bashir watched him, seething, until he'd ridden through the Morning Gate.

He could not decide which of the pair of them was worse, the Grand Vizier with his plotting and violence, or the son, who was complicit in it by bored disinterest. Everything else was a game to Cemil.

"Lieutenant Terzi!" The courtyard rumbled with the veins of power that shivered through Bashir's body and into the earth as he walked toward the stable. Erol appeared in the barracks entrance. "Prepare any men not currently on a guard shift for a city sweep."

"Sir." Erol looked confused, but also quite aware that now was not the time to ask him questions. Under the influence of his unleashed power, Bashir's attempts at denial were turned to rubble.

Aysel would not be at the camp, waiting for him. She had run the moment he left. He'd bet money on that. "Even if they are sleeping. The Sultana wants Aysel. She's running."

"Sir." Erol stepped back inside. Bashir closed his eyes and squeezed his fists, indulging in a full breath. Easy in. Slower out. He opened his eyes, and his hands.

"Run fast, Little Fox," he whispered to the air. "You don't want me to catch you this time."

Sixteen

AYSEL STASHED HER THINGS in an alley a few blocks away from the inn. She didn't want to go in looking like someone running. She also didn't want them to be right outside the place where she was hiding if someone who was looking for her found them. She'd retrieve them later.

"I knew you'd be back," the old fire mage said. It was early in the day, and since most of her patrons preferred the cover and privacy of night, the large central room was empty. She was busy wiping down the low-set tables with hands beginning to curl from arthritis. "Still haven't heard about your friends though."

"I thought I might hole up here in case they come back," Aysel said.

The woman stopped and straightened, folding her rag between her hands and giving Aysel a once-over. "You don't belong here, and I'm not the only one who will see it."

Her hair had been black once, Aysel decided. There were still streaks of it, black shocks through hair mostly the color of ash. She had it pulled back into a tidy bun, which looked prim and strange against the woman's threadbare clothing.

"I belong more than you think," Aysel said, but she knew the woman meant she was small and female in a place mostly populated by men—men who might take that as invitation. "And I can take care of myself."

"Three quarter silvers a night." She raised an eyebrow. Aysel grimaced, and the woman made a sound like she had known Aysel didn't have any money. "No money, no room, *tatlim*." She went back to wiping the tables.

"You could use help around here. I can work. I don't even need a real room. Just a corner somewhere." Just a place where a certain mountainous guard commander would not think to look for her.

"Oh? What kind of work can you do?" Her voice held a permanent scratch, from decades of trying to be heard over the din of the place, perhaps. Now it also held incredulous amusement.

"Anything you want me to."

The woman shook her head, squinting at her. "Girl, you're barely tall enough to see over my bar. I can't send you out with drinks, you'll be trampled or hauled off to some alley corner." She stood, her knees popping as she did.

"Dishes?" Aysel suggested, losing hope. There might be places on the pier she could hole up in. But they would be just that…holes, and she didn't want to spend her nights sleeping in a rat-infested hollow under a warehouse roof.

"Fine. I'll try you out today. If you can't keep up, you're out. And I'll let the Watch know you were here."

"That seems unnecessary," Aysel said.

The woman shrugged. "It doesn't do me well to draw that kind of attention. But you seem like someone who can keep her head down. So, grab a rag." She pointed to her bucket.

Aysel obeyed, and while she had never worked, or been responsible for cleaning anything, it wasn't such a hard thing to mimic what the woman was doing.

After a while, the old fire mage said, "You know how to use those?" She waved her rag in the direction of Aysel's back and her swords, spraying dirty water in her direction with a flip of the cloth.

"Reasonably well." Aysel dodged the foul-smelling water. The tables were set each over its own carpet. They were sticky with spilled wine and whatever else the woman served.

Aysel had never been particularly fastidious, but she suspected this place might make her so. She wiped her hand against her salvar when she encountered a wet, spongy mess of crumbs or some other substance that overwhelmed her rag and smudged over her hand.

"My name's Ela," the woman said.

"Aysel," she replied, and Ela smiled, showing the gaps in her teeth.

"All right Aysel, I'll show you the kitchen."

"Faster, girl," Ela demanded, as she dropped another load of plates and cups. "The glasses first." She called the last as she disappeared again.

The kitchen was divided from the central hall by a latticed door carved in a geometric pattern. Ela had three other people working for her, two women who served the drinks, and her son, Harun, a thin, tall man who bore an unfortunate resemblance to a serpent with his sinewy frame and small, dark eyes. He seemed nice enough. He gave her encouraging smiles whenever he brought a load of dishes, though he hadn't said a word.

Aysel's hair was falling loose from its braid, scuffed from the repeated times she had swiped her sleeve over her face to wipe away soap or splashed water. Ela tended to just dump dishes into the tub, so Aysel was soaked from head to toe.

Thankfully the kitchen was warm. Aysel was trying to count it as a bath, but the water smelled of coffee, wine, and arak, and the rag she was using stunk of mildew. She didn't think her own smell would improve by the end of the night.

She had not felt Bashir's tracking spell yet. She suspected he would start his search around the camp, then work his way through the city. It would take them several days, if they were being thorough. There was no way to know how many other earth mages in his force were capable of the same tracking spell. Even an Aval of the Fourth House could cast a tracking, which rippled through the earth and could locate a person by either their magical or personal signature. But the distance, sensitivity, and duration of the spell would depend on the mage's power, control, and knowledge of the person they were trying to find.

Aysel stood on a crate, just to add a measure of protection from their searching.

The worst part of washing dishes was that it did not keep her mind engaged, and so her thoughts were flaying her over and over with Bashir. Under normal circumstances she might have been dreamy-eyed about the—by a wide margin—best kisses she had ever received. Aysel had kept her relationships casual, not always by choice, but, like her brother, knew that her family had too many secrets already. There was no reason to bring another person into the mix, one who had the potential to cause pain, or worse.

Kissing had reflected that necessity, a means to an end, a step on the way to the bigger act. But Bashir had kissed her like he meant it, like it was a reward all by itself, like he intended to keep doing it with no end goal in mind.

Aysel's legs felt weak just thinking about it. But she couldn't. Even if he ever forgave her after today, they couldn't. Their worlds were different in too many ways. There were too many secrets. Never mind how she cared about him, the dumb ox, or how she craved more glimpses of his sweetness, had started to want them for her own.

She slapped a plate through the murky dishwater and set it in the pile to dry. The washing was not particularly difficult—dump the uneaten food, swipe the rag over anything sticky, move on to the next. It was the speed that was challenging. Aysel had found her rhythm halfway through the night, dump, rinse, scrub, and stack. Then, when the stack was big enough and the tub empty enough to be ignored for a bit, she would dry the dishes with a linen towel that did not smell much better than the dish rag. Aysel doubted she'd ever eat off the dishware in this inn.

Ela's son, Harun, entered through the lattice door and set a stack of plates down, loading them one by one into the water.

"If Ela catches you going that slow…" Aysel said, shaking her head.

"I know." He nodded sagely. "The risk is worth it for the break. It's rowdy out there. I guess the palace guards have been in the city all day, looking for some thief that stole from the Grand Vizier. Nobody likes it when they're around. They take themselves more seriously than the Watch."

Aysel puffed at the hair hanging in her face. News traveled fast in this city. Thieves were so commonplace in Al-Nimas it would have taken her break-in an entire small turn to make the gossip streams.

"Did you see them?" She kept her exact pace, the same tone of voice and eye contact. Even the smallest change could alert someone, especially with the intent way Harun was looking at her, of her involvement.

"Not yet. But they'll be by. The Watch always sends the palace thugs down here when they're looking for anybody."

"Hmm," Aysel said. "I'll make certain their plates are especially clean." She winked at him. Harun scratched the back of his neck and looked thoughtfully at the ceiling.

He gave her a shrewd look. "Whoever it is has stones of solid steel, I'd say."

"Oh?" Aysel said, trying to sound disinterested.

"Man's a menace. There's a new ex-housemaid of his down every quarter turn or so that's either quit after he beat her or nursing burns from a temper tantrum. Rumor is"—he leaned an elbow on the edge of the washbasin and picked at his teeth with a thumbnail—"when that son of his was ten Turns or so, and the wife had enough of the Grand Vizier's temper, she tried to leave him."

Aysel's eyebrows shot up. "Tamar allows that?" In Sarkum there was almost no greater shame. A broken marriage was a broken Wheel, the saying went, and people who chose to null their vows became pariahs for their trouble. That was why so few actually entered into marriage, outside those arranged in the upper classes.

Harun shook his head. "No, especially not the nobility. She might just have been taking the boy home to the valley." The valley that ran north to south between the Kalspire range and the Engeli that bordered Sarkum. "But we'll never know. No one has seen her in Turns."

"He murdered her?" Aysel asked in a savage whisper. How was the man still in office and not hanging from the gallows? And why did Makram want to keep her spying a secret from the Sultana if Kadir was such a terror?

He shook his head and pressed a finger to his lips, indicating the dining room with a tilt of his head. As if anyone could hear anything they were saying over the din of voices and dishes. "I don't know anything. Just pissin' gossip." He grinned. "Anyway." He straightened and dug his fists against his back. "Hate to see what he'd do if he caught a thief in his house."

"Mmn." Aysel set the last clean plate on a stack, then returned to the washbasin as he left. She reflected on the midden heap she'd gotten stuck in the middle of as she tackled a precarious stack of glasses. Ela served coffee, tea, arak, and wine. That meant there were coffee mugs, small arak glasses, and larger goblets for the wine. They didn't stack, so they took up the most room on the table next to the washbasin. Aysel's small hands served her well in this circumstance—it was not such a hard thing to get her fingers and the rag into the glasses. Bashir would be less useful here.

She had to blink at the sting of tears. Wheel damn her, she'd let herself get attached to him, to the way it felt to be around him. She knew better.

Aysel pushed the sadness away and continued washing dishes. After a time she was able to lose herself to it, the rhythm of the task.

The night passed her in cadence, wash, stack, dry, repeat. When Ela came to her and announced she was done when she finished the last stack she'd set on the table, Aysel had to stop and listen to realize the central room had grown quiet.

"Not too bad," Ela said, as Aysel and Harun hauled the washbasin back from the alley where they'd dumped the water. "You can stay here in the kitchen. I serve breakfast for workers and tenants early. You'll miss it if you sleep late, but it will be hard to sleep in once I start on the food." She laughed.

Aysel tried to smile but was too exhausted and emotionally stripped to manage it.

"I'll bring down some blankets. The pallet's over there in the corner." Ela pointed to a pallet in the corner of the room on the other side of the smoldering cookfire. At least she'd be warm, something that hadn't been true for sleeping since she'd arrived. Except her one night in the palace.

"Thank you." Aysel hung the towel on the side of the basin. Ela left and Harun turned from where he was lifting large stacks of plates onto shelves bolted to the stone walls.

"Drink?" he suggested. "I know where she keeps the good stuff."

"Not tonight, but thank you. I'm so tired I might fall asleep in my cup."

He chuckled. "Another night then?"

"Yes." Being unfriendly was a quick way to get oneself turned over to guards. She'd have to come up with a plan for her next moves, she couldn't stay at the inn indefinitely. The katil were still out there, and now her freedom of movement was severely restricted.

"Are you here every night?" she asked as Harun stacked the last plates onto the shelf.

"Most. I'll be back in the morning." He lifted a hand in farewell as he left.

Ela returned as he slipped out the door, carrying blankets. Aysel sighed. She'd probably trade a limb for a pillow. Her pillow in Al-Nimas had been perfectly stuffed, her favorite part of ending the day.

"Thank you," she said as Ela put the blankets in her arms. When she left, Aysel took the blankets to the bed and shook them out, then crawled underneath the top one. It was wool and itched where it touched her skin. She flopped onto her back to stare at the stones of the ceiling. Then she sat up, wrapping the blankets around her shoulders and staring at the floor.

It was too quiet. The stillness in the absence of the din from the central room and the splash of the dishwater and the ring of the plates as she stacked them was unbearable. All she could think of was the kiss, and how foolish she had been to do it, to let it start to mean something. It needed to be play, between them. That's what she'd meant for it to be, nothing more. A kiss shouldn't have made her feel like she owed him, or that she couldn't bear the thought of him despising her.

Aysel touched her fingers to the stone floor. If he was still searching, she couldn't feel him, the rippling touch of his spell. Without thinking, or realizing she had decided, Aysel closed her eyes. She did not have to expend effort to visualize him in her mind, he was already there, the feeling of him etching deeper.

"It wasn't a trick," she whispered, the thread of magic she'd released swirling around her. It had started that way, but not the kiss. That had been real down to her breath and heart. She needed him to know.

"Please believe me." She breathed the last across a swell of tears in her throat and cut the spell off with a brutal jerk of control.

What was she doing? Aysel lay on her side and allowed herself one large, angry tear. She swiped it away and closed her eyes. It did not occur to her until she woke the next morning that the spell that had cost her so much the first time she cast it had hardly cost her at all this time.

She staggered out of the kitchen and Ela's way and sat on the floor at one of the tables in the central hall. When she shifted to put her elbows on the table, the lingering stench of dirty dishwater and her own body wafted up to her. Aysel wrinkled her nose. Her other clothes were still tucked away behind crates and midden in an alley. She'd have to retrieve them. The clothes she wore now were stiff and itchy from being wet the night before.

Aysel propped her head in her hands. She needed to get word to Makram, both that she was safe, so he could tell her family, and about what she had found at Kadir's. Perhaps she could try her voice-casting again tonight. Makram was almost as familiar to her as Mat, surely she could picture him well enough to cast her voice to him. Or she could to Mat, but Makram had forbidden her speaking about her spying to anyone but him.

She still could not understand the power of the spell on that lock. What had been so important in that room that the Grand Vizier had concocted such a thing? Had Mat ever spoken to her about enchanted objects? Aysel pressed her fingers to her temple.

"Good morning. How are you feeling today?" Harun said as he folded himself awkwardly beside her at the table. There were so many reasons Aysel was glad she was short, one of them being not having to manage long legs around the low tables.

"A bit sore, if I'm being honest." Aysel couldn't believe washing dishes could make her sore, but her neck and shoulders were tight.

"It's the standing. It gets better." He set his things between them and folded his arms on the table. Aysel glanced at his belongings, a large, baggy caftan he'd been wearing last night, likely to protect his other clothes from spills. A belt and a small, hard leather purse embellished with a bright medallion. Aysel raised her eyebrows.

This did not seem like an area to be carrying something so valuable in plain sight. It was silver, a flower stamped on its surface.

"Harun!" Ela demanded from the kitchen. He unslung a larger bag from his shoulders and dumped it on the floor before he jumped to his feet and walked away. Aysel peeked over her shoulder when she heard the wooden lattice to the kitchen swing shut. When she didn't see him, she reached for the purse. Aysel flipped it open and looked inside. It contained a pile of little clay disks. Odd.

She eyed the bigger bag, then the door to the kitchen. Ela and Harun were discussing something, the particulars of which were muffled. Aysel slid the bigger bag close and opened it.

Rolled letters. Perhaps he was a messenger during the day. It would be a way to make extra coin when he wasn't working the inn. In Al-Nimas at least, those who lived in the poorer areas of the city often worked many small jobs to survive. Though as the son of an innkeeper Harun was practically noble in comparison to some of the patrons. She pushed the big bag away and looked at the smaller one again.

The valuable Tamar coins were gold, but she'd seen smaller denominations in silver. Why would he carry something valuable openly, for any thief or pickpocket to see? He didn't strike her as a fool.

Unless he meant for people to notice it. A decoy bag perhaps? That would explain why it was empty. So thieves stole the purse, instead of the bag of messages and letters. The delivery fee for all of them would certainly be worth more than a stamped silver medallion.

The medallion was thin and light. It might not even be silver, making it worth less than a half coin, and the engraving was stamped onto it to make it look official. Aysel brushed her thumb across the embossed surface.

A clever fake, even stamped to look important. The clay tokens inside only to give it heft so it didn't feel empty and worthless.

Fake, indeed. Her thoughts stilled then tumbled, and a memory she couldn't quite filter from them demanded attention. Aysel put her elbows on the table and her face in her hands as she concentrated. The memory came in pieces. Medallions. Silver…but no, that wasn't it.

Gold.

A glint of gold in a shaft of moonlight. A medallion she saw and thought was something else. The memory bloomed full in her mind and Aysel lifted her head, one hand sliding to cover her mouth as she stared, unseeing, at the wall. She gripped the little purse in her other hand, squeezing.

The gold medallion in the Grand Vizier's desk. It had been too big for a sealing stamp. And there had been something wrong with it, but she'd been distracted. Now she could remember. It had been embossed with the Rahal seal. The royal crest of Sarkum. Flames on a crown and spear.

She dropped a hand to her waist, over the cloth that concealed the blank medallion she'd stolen. The same size as the embossed one she'd left behind. Aysel's breath left her in a huff of disbelief.

Of course. That was why. That's why he'd shot at her on the hill, something a katil would never do. That's why he'd been following her, not stalking, just keeping an eye on her movements. That's why there hadn't been an attack yet. Because the men who had followed them from Sarkum, the men she still hunted, weren't katil after all.

That gold medallion she'd seen on the man's sword was a fake, just like the one in Kadir's desk. Why would they pretend to be Sarkum royal assassins?

She dug her nails against her scalp. To hide who they truly worked for. To hide who they were after.

"*Broken spokes.*" They weren't after her family. They were after someone else.

"What are you doing?" Harun snatched the purse out of her hand, looming over her with a glare of suspicion.

Aysel leapt up, smacking her knee against the table edge as she did. Harun staggered back.

"Sorry," Aysel gasped. Ela came out of the kitchen as Aysel limped toward it, carrying a tray with plates of food.

"Breakfast," Ela said as Aysel limped past her.

"I'll be back tonight," Aysel replied, regaining her step as the ache in her knee faded. She darted to the pallet she'd slept on to retrieve her swords from beneath it. Then she left at a run.

She had a blank medallion, she needed to see the katil's sword to verify her suspicions. That meant the palace and getting through a city crawling with Bashir's men. Her first stop was her hiding place, and she changed her clothes, in full view of anyone who might pass the alley, into the set she used for spying. She tucked the blank medallion she had stolen from the desk drawer into the cloth at her waist. Perhaps it and its stamped brother had arrived in that battered envelope, proofs for approval from the Grand Vizier.

Getting into the palace would not be the challenge. As most of its guards were in the city, according to Harun, it was her path to the palace that would be a struggle. Aysel checked the buckles on her sword harness and surveyed the back of the alley, where one of the buildings abutted a tall stone retaining wall. This city, with its hills, cliffs, and walls, was much easier to traverse out of sight than Al-Nimas, which was flat and full of squat buildings. She ran at the corner between the building and wall, using her momentum to run upward a few steps, one foot on the building, the other on the wall, until she could grab the top of the wall, which she then used to vault to the roof of the building.

She made progress out of the Merchant Pier on the roofs of the buildings, and only had to avoid two patrols of the City Watch. She'd need to make it around the Grand Market and through the Fire District to get to the palace. Briefly she considered stopping at Kadir's house to retrieve the stamped medallion, but it would be best if Bashir and his men found it and subsequently presented it as evidence. His word was beyond reproach, and she was just a refugee and a spy from Sarkum. She doubted her word about where she had found it would hold much weight, even if Makram stepped in on her behalf.

And the house would likely be under guard, which would make it too great a risk to take now, in broad daylight. Proving there was a fake medallion on the sword was more important. She could use that to make Bashir listen to her.

The first of Bashir's men made an appearance when she reached the Fire District. One was an earth mage—his uniform bore the gold-embroidered tiraz that represented the Fourth House. He was casting a tracking, squatting in the street and drawing the sigil for it, and his companion stood beside him, making certain no one disturbed him as he cast. If he had to use a sigil then he was unlikely more than a Deval. The spell worked by vibration, and the stronger the mage, the more distance they could control their spell. It also meant they might feel fainter vibrations, like those from someone who was not in direct contact with the ground, but she doubted a Deval would be able to feel her with the entire height of a building between him and her.

Aysel surveyed the streets from her perch on top of the final building in the Merchant Pier before a long, broad open space where the three main roads through the Grand Market converged on the main road from the warehouses. There was no other way but to descend. She wouldn't take the main road, but a capillary road she'd discovered on her treks through the city. It was almost empty this time of day.

Aysel jumped from the roof to a balcony, then hung from the balcony railing and dropped to the ground. From there she wove her way between carriages and carts, along retaining walls and stalls, until she had cleared the most open section of road. At the same time, she worked on drawing her magic closer, silencing it except for the thread she needed to weave her fading spell, and a bit she put to use lightening her footfalls to make it harder for the earth mage to track her. *Silent. Fade.*

She fed her will to her magic and it obeyed, and people did not even look at her as they passed.

When she reached the road she wanted, which ran two streets behind the Vizier's house, she concentrated on her spell to maintain it. A loss of focus meant the spell might slip off her in the worst of times. At points she turned into alleys or between houses to look behind her and forward. And when she was nearly to the end of the street, she felt a ripple of magic, followed by another, pass beneath her feet. It was not Bashir, that familiar aftertaste of granite and loam was missing, perhaps the other earth mage she had seen.

Aysel risked using more of her magic to give herself speed. The magic made her more visible to the tracking spell, but she could outrun them, if she didn't encounter any other problems. She ran up the street, dodging around a mother with three children of perfectly descending heights as they turned around a corner from the market. If they saw her, they gave no notice, but she was moving fast enough that the speed of her passing stirred the woman's caftan.

When she reached the palace road she released her speed spell and maintained the others, lightness, and fading, and inserted herself into a group of day servants heading from their homes to the palace. Aysel was careful not to touch anyone. They could see her, they simply didn't notice her, she faded from their awareness the way the shadows of everyday objects did. But if she bumped into someone, the spell would break.

There were seven of them, four women, two men, and one boy who looked of age to be a messenger or stable boy. All were dressed in the plainclothes of servants, such a drab contrast to the bright and garish colors of the nobility. They did wear tiraz sewn into the sleeves at their upper arms, proclaiming their magic Houses and power.

"I don't know," the woman to Aysel's right said, in answer to a question Aysel hadn't heard. "They seem nice enough. I just clean the rooms."

"But they don't wear tiraz. If they were anything but death mages why wouldn't they?" one of the men said, impatiently. Aysel grit her teeth. Her family.

"I heard one's escaped. What if they are death mages? I don't want some murderer sneaking around at night," the woman at the front of the group said, adding a forced shudder for emphasis.

It was difficult to believe that such old superstition still existed, especially after what she'd seen of Tamar and how it fully embraced magic and powerful mages. Not the way everyone was forced to tiptoe around it in Sarkum. Most mages didn't practice openly, though they didn't hide their powers, and no one whispered about death mages being soulless killers.

"The guards are everywhere in the city. Have you seen Commander Ayan lately? He looks madder than a stuck ox," the other, older, man said.

Aysel grinned, which quickly turned to a frown. That did not bode well for her convincing him to listen to her or forgive her. And she was the only one allowed to call him an ox.

"I haven't seen him lately. More's the pity," the woman to Aysel's right responded, winking as the woman in front tossed her a knowing look. Aysel considered giving her hair a good solid tug, just to see the look on her face when she realized Aysel was there.

It was a foolish, childish thought spurred by a flash of jealousy that surprised Aysel. She knew she was fond of him, and certainly knew she wanted him, but she had not realized it was beginning to grow into something that might spawn possessiveness or jealousy. That was troubling.

They passed through the Morning Gate, surrounded by other groups of servants arriving for the day. Aysel didn't look at the guards to either side as they walked by. It wouldn't break the spell if she looked at someone, but she didn't want to risk meeting their eyes, which would.

The group of men and women broke slightly to the left, and Aysel prepared to slip right, out of their midst. She'd run behind the barracks, then either through a window or over the roof and into the stables to get to the armory and hopefully, the dead katil's sword.

The scent of Bashir's magic hit her before the spell did. First, loam and granite, then a rumble of earth beneath her feet. Her magic dissipated, and her weight came hard into her feet. "Fire and water," she mumbled, and the group of servants turned collectively to stare at her, then around them in confusion.

"Step aside," Bashir ordered, appearing out of the barracks and striding toward them as he made a swiping gesture with his hand. They obeyed, and Aysel stood alone and exposed as Bashir, his lieutenant Erol, and two guardsmen came toward her. She didn't need more than a glance at his face to know there would be no talking him into listening.

She shoved her hand into the fabric at her waist, withdrew the medallion, and threw it at him, guided by a thin stream of air. He reached up and caught it, and his steps faltered.

"That is what I found," Aysel said. "Check the katil's sword."

"Arrest her," Bashir said, dark lines of magic in his eyes visible even at this distance. "She's admitting to theft and break-in."

"Please!" Aysel said, as the servants she'd hidden with chattered excitedly and moved quickly out of the way, and Erol and the two soldiers broke away from Bashir and toward her.

Aysel gave a wordless cry of exasperation and kicked her foot sideways into the mix of sand and gravel at her feet, shoving a push of air into it to send it into the faces of the men coming toward her. Midway through its arc it showered straight to the ground as if it had hit a wall. Bashir lowered a hand, his eyes narrowing.

"Listen to me," Aysel pleaded. He shook his head, slowly, and Aysel broke into a run, darting toward the arena. It was not ideal, because he controlled its sand so well, but if she could get up and over the wall they would be trapped, unable to pursue her without backtracking. That would give her enough time to hide.

The ground rolled underneath her, and two of the women shrieked in surprise, then the entire group of them ran for the stairs to the palace, out of her sight. Aysel rode the wave of earth with bent knees and spread hands for balance and leapt off when she felt its trajectory change. She landed running.

As she neared the arena sand whipped up into her face and she pushed the air away from her in all directions, driving it away.

Her pace slowed when she made it through the arches and walkways, her steps mired in the sand, but she recast her spell to lighten herself and dashed across the arena floor.

"Coward." His voice shook the arena.

Aysel slowed to a jog, then stopped, and turned.

Bashir stood just inside the arena, in the sand. "Cowards run and hide and steal and lie," he said this time without his magic, but his voice carried easily inside the arena, bounced about by the stone that surrounded it.

It stung, more than she would have liked, to hear him say it.

"And what are men who do not trust their own judgment and instinct, and only follow orders, so that if things go wrong they cannot be held accountable?"

She despised herself for saying it as soon as the words had left her mouth. She did not want to hurt him, she never had. His expression blackened, and a shift of his right foot and a tingle along the edge of her power was the only warning she had of his spell.

The earth opened up between them, pouring sand into a fissure deep enough to swallow her. Aysel leapt sideways, and the earth rolled beneath her feet, knocking her to her back. Bashir stalked across the sand toward her and she jumped to her feet. Distance was not her friend when it came to him. She ran at him, and the look of surprise on his face only lasted a moment.

He reached for his sword. Aysel kicked herself into a leap, somersaulting once through the air, landing, and leaping again, this time with power pushed into it to send her over his head. The benefit to flipping was that it confused people, both because it confounded their sense of where she would land, and how long she would stay in the air. It also tended to shock them into giving her an extra breath of reaction time, which it did in this instance, when he watched her spin through the air instead of continuing the movement of drawing his blade.

Aysel landed behind him and slammed the heel of her fist against his sword hilt, shoving it back into its sheath. She leapt on his back, locking her legs around his waist, and catching his throat in the crook of her arm. She used her other hand against her wrist, cinching her arm tight around his neck and cutting off the flow of blood.

"We're on the same side," she grunted. "I am not your enemy."

"You're choking me," he gasped as he pulled at her arms. It only took a few heartbeats, Aysel reminded herself, closing her eyes. She just had to hold on.

"They aren't katil. They're not here for my family." She squeezed her legs tighter and grit her teeth as his hands slapped and grabbed and yanked at her arms, her head, and her hair. "You have to listen to me."

He was so much stronger than Mat, who was the only one she had ever practiced on. He gave up trying to pull her off and simply fell backwards, letting his weight hammer her into the sand. Aysel coughed, lights dancing across her vision, and Bashir rolled loose of her broken grip, flipping to his hands and knees and pinning her arms against the sand.

For a beat their gazes met. His brow furrowed, as though thinking just as she was, that it had not even been a full day since he had done the same thing on her bed, with kinder intentions.

"Bashir," she said.

"I'm never listening to you again." He got his feet under him, tensing to yank her up. Aysel took advantage of the gap between them to drive both her boots into his chest. He stumbled back and she jumped to her feet, swinging immediately around with a high kick. He ducked, but a tall opponent had to drop a long way to get out of range. Another advantage she enjoyed. Aysel's heel connected with his jaw and he swung halfway around with a curse.

"You are smarter than this," Aysel said. "That man is plotting something and I can help stop him!" She shoved him with both hands, a useless move born of pure frustration that did nothing more than rock him a bit.

"If I were smarter, I would have put you in the Cliffs the moment I laid eyes on you." He straightened, and raised his hand in signal to someone behind her. Aysel glanced back to see Erol and the others coming across the sand.

She glared at Bashir. "I'm sorry I ran from you, but I knew you'd never listen to me, and I can't let you stop me." She backed away from him. "You sit in your room and pretend I'm the enemy here, if that's really the best you can do. I respected you because I thought you were smart enough to keep up with me. But you really are just a dumb ox."

She kicked sand at him and he swiped it out of the air with one hand while drawing his sword with the other.

Aysel fed her magic more than she ever had in front of anyone but her family, drawing a circle of wind and anger around her, whipping the sand in a tornado that obscured him from her view and forced him back. She felt his magic against her own, trying to command the sand away—she even saw the strike of it as gold flashes at the edge of her vision. But he wasn't a match for her. Not when she couldn't let him be. She was the only one who knew the katil were after someone else, and her guess was Makram or the Sultana.

If Bashir wouldn't listen to her, then she had to find and stop them.

Aysel thrust the wind and sand outward, forcing away Bashir and his men, and when she had a clear path, she ran.

SEVENTEEN

"**W**ELL?" EROL TURNED TO him, his expression painted with the same bewilderment that left Bashir standing like a simpleton in the middle of the arena. He'd known she was powerful, it would take a mage of uncommon power and control to completely hide their magic as she had done. But this was power that rivaled the Sultana's. It might even be…

No. She couldn't possibly hide a Charah's power.

"We have the Water District and the Merchant Pier to search. Wherever she's been hiding, she'll move now. Put Fourth House mages on every main intersection between those districts and the rest."

"Yes." Erol saluted, then motioned to the guardsmen to follow him out of the arena.

Bashir followed them from the arena but cut through the courtyard and into the palace. He fought himself the entire way, how desperately he wanted to believe her, to listen to what she had said. The look on her face when she had pleaded with him. The time that had passed between their kiss and her appearance in the courtyard had allowed him to shape her into much more of a villain than she had appeared a moment ago. That had just been Aysel, the woman who had proved herself his equal in every way, laughing and teasing as she had done it, and made him laugh too. The woman who touched him like she meant it, with desire in her earth and storm eyes, not deception. How could she do that?

Still he wanted her, wanted to believe her. He wanted her to be telling the truth about everything, so he could feel what was in his heart without revealing himself an utter fool.

The guards in front of the doors to the Attiyeh suite came to attention when he approached, and one of them knocked on the door when he nodded. "Anything to report?" he asked.

Ali Macar shook his head. "It has been quiet. The son goes to the library once a day and stays for marks"—a tortured look passed across his face—"but he's back now."

The door opened and the steward bowed when he saw Bashir. "Commander, please." He stepped to the side and Bashir entered. Mathei was the only person immediately visible as Bashir entered the room. The steward closed the door.

"If Elder Attiyeh and his wife are here, I would like to speak with them," Bashir said. The steward bowed again, turning away and entering the master end of the suite.

Mathei lounged on the couch nearest the door and set the book he was reading open across his chest when Bashir faced him.

"I was wondering when you were going to show up," he sighed, looking curiously at Bashir. "She does have you in a bother, doesn't she?" Mathei clicked his tongue, draping an arm over the back of the couch. "You might consider leashing your power before you speak to my parents." He wiggled a finger in Bashir's direction.

Bashir looked down at his hands. Broken streaks of his power glowed through his skin. Wheel help him, he hadn't even realized.

"We don't know where she is, if that will save us from the tedium of your questioning," Mathei said as Bashir forced his power back under control. He couldn't believe he was so lost in his internal fight he hadn't even felt his magic bleeding from him. She was tearing him to pieces and she wasn't even here.

Bashir swept a hand through his hair.

"Why should I believe the family of a liar?" he asked.

Mathei huffed a laugh, and the smile he gave Bashir was a twin for his sister's when she was teasing him. It made his throat ache.

"Is Aysel a liar, or is she clever and you can't bear it? You wouldn't be the first man who couldn't handle my sister, so don't be too hard on yourself. I find most men need to find a reason to make her into something she isn't when she hurts their tender pride."

"This is not about pride."

Mathei rolled his eyes and sat up, tossing the book on the table. "Then let us discuss what it is about." Mathei stood. "Do you believe the prince and the Sultana are allies?"

"I came here to question you—"

"It's a simple question."

"They are," Bashir said.

"Then puzzle over this arithmetic, will you? If the woman who holds your reins and the man who holds Aysel's are on the same side"—he held out his fist and unfolded his thumb and his pointer finger—"then what does that make you and my sister?" He held up his other hand and did the same. "I'll give you some time." He gave Bashir a disdainful look then turned to leave as the steward appeared, with the Elder and his wife.

"I'm not finished with you," Bashir ordered.

Mathei stopped and turned, folding his hands behind his back. "The good commander has come to torture us for the whereabouts of your other child."

"Is she in trouble?" Aysel's mother asked, stepping around her husband as she did. The woman shared the same petite frame and thick, wildly curly chestnut hair as her daughter. Hers was tamed into a single braid and twisted at the nape of her neck, layered under a midnight-blue silk scarf that wrapped around her neck and over her head. But she was delicate, fragile. Aysel's mother looked small, though she carried herself just as proudly.

Aysel was small, so short that when she stood against him the top of her head barely reached his shoulder. But he didn't think of her like that, fragile. She felt barely contained, fierce and stormy.

"The Sultana wants her questioned in relation to a break-in."

"Is Rahal Charah aware of this?" the Elder said. His tone was polite, his temper contained in the set of his jaw and his narrowed eyes.

"He is."

"Whatever she's done, it is at his behest. She isn't a criminal, she—"

"Dilara," the Elder said sharply. The woman pressed her lips together and glanced over her shoulder at him and when she turned back, Bashir felt the slightest stir against his magic. A trace of shadow he had only ever felt from one other mage. A death mage. Charah Rahal.

"What House are you?" Bashir asked, his thought from earlier resurfacing.

"Is that relevant?" the Elder asked, and Bashir barely caught an edge of fear that coasted through Dilara's gaze before she dropped it.

"I will decide. What House are you?" If they were destruction, as the touch of Dilara's magic against his had suggested, that would mean Aysel was the Air Charah. Chara'a were born to the previous House on the Wheel. Air was born of destruction, order from chaos.

"First House, Commander," Mathei said, just as the Elder opened his mouth to reply. "You know that, since you've seen Aysel use her magic."

Bashir observed the look the Elder gave his son. Surprise.

He turned to Mathei. "Prove it."

The younger Attiyeh folded his arms. "Is Tamar still in the business of inquisition? Rooting out unsavory magic through torture and interrogation? And here I thought the worst a tyrannical ruler could do was burn your home and drive you from your homeland." Mathei's near-black eyes fixed on Bashir in accusation.

Bashir's frustration and anger drained away, leaving shame and confusion in their wake. "Do you know where your daughter is?" Bashir asked the Elder.

"No. And if your plan is to arrest her—"

"My plan is to bring her before the Sultana. If she turns herself in to me, I'm certain the Sultana will be more lenient than if I have to continue to search the city for her."

"If we see her, which we won't, we will tell her," Mathei said. Bashir narrowed his eyes. Mathei widened his, and smiled. Again, Bashir saw Aysel, the look on her face when she hassled him.

He turned and strode through the door when the steward opened it. He considered briefly speaking with Makram but knew he would get nowhere. There was nothing for him to do but ride back into the city.

It wasn't in him to sit. He could barely concentrate, fighting the war in his mind. He wanted to hate her and he wanted to trust her. He wanted to rip her clothes from her and make her his, and he never wanted to lay eyes on her again. When he'd felt the touch of her on his power when she entered the palace grounds he had badly wanted to walk out of the barracks and see her standing there, alone, coming back to him. But she'd been hiding. She'd been continuing to do everything to thwart him and what the Sultana demanded of him.

Huzur was already saddled and tethered to a hitching post outside the barracks. They'd been preparing to depart when Aysel had come through the gate. Erol would already be out in the city, directing their men in the search. Thank the Wheel Erol at least had his wits about him. Bashir mounted and headed for the Merchant Pier. He'd question the people he knew there, people who would answer him truthfully because of his mother and her history of helping the poor of the city. There were only a handful, but they had proved invaluable on several occasions.

The first stop was one of two inns at the pier. One served as overnight accommodations for sailors on the merchant vessels and was only useful when he was looking for information pertaining to ship traffic and passengers. The other was a gathering spot for the locals of the district and some unsavory characters, and was owned and run by a woman who had known his mother since before he was born.

"Ela," Bashir greeted her as he entered the main room of the inn. She looked over her shoulder at him and raised a silver eyebrow, straightening from where she had bent to set a tray of tea on a table. The three men she had served it to looked up only long enough to recognize him as a guard, then did their best not to look at him again. Bashir ignored them. They were the City Watch's problem, not his.

"I'm looking for someone," he said as Ela set her empty tray on the counter behind which she kept her bottles of wine and arak. She wiped a rag over the tray as she looked at him.

"Let me guess." Ela lifted a hand, holding it a fraction above her head. "About this tall and made of trouble head to toe."

Fondness swept through him, seizing his mind for a brief instance. "Yes," he said. Nothing but trouble.

"I haven't seen her." Ela slid the tray beneath the counter and glanced around the room. Certainly everyone, including the three men drinking tea and two others by the fireplace on the far end of the room, was listening. But none were watching. Ela nodded toward the kitchen. Bashir pushed through the latticework wooden doors and Ela followed.

"Harun might know something." Ela named her son as Bashir walked through the room to the pallet in the corner. If Aysel had been there she hadn't left evidence. He lifted one of the blankets then tossed it back into place.

"Is he here?"

"Will be in a moment or two, went to run a message."

"She can't stay here anymore," Bashir said.

Ela snorted. "You don't tell me who to put up, and I won't remind you there was a time no one would put up your anne, either."

Bashir ground his teeth together. "Different," he said.

"Not my place to judge why someone is hiding. That's your job. She washed dishes, I let her stay. The way she ran this morning, I doubt I'll see her again."

"Why did she run?"

Ela shook her head. "Ask Harun." She led him back into the main room. "I've seen your men all over the city, looking wrung-out and too tired. That's not like you."

"I haven't a choice right now." Bashir looked at the door impatiently. He didn't have time to stand around waiting for Harun.

Ela made a sound, reaching beneath the counter for a bottle of arak, and set it on the top. "You've always got a choice. Perhaps you're just making the wrong one."

Before he could reply, the door to the street swung open and Harun walked in. He frowned when he saw Bashir, moving to stand beside him at the counter.

"Bashir is looking for someone to wash dishes," Ela said. Harun frowned harder and shook his head. Bashir had never known why Harun didn't like him, they'd practically grown up together. But he was always uncooperative, sometimes even hostile. "Did she say anything to you this morning? Do you know why she left like that?"

"No. One moment she was looking at that decoy purse I carry, the next she was up and gone." He only looked at Ela, the muscles in his narrow jaw tight.

"Can I see it?" Bashir doubted it had anything to do with Aysel running to the palace, but he needed clues.

"Someone stole it this morning," Harun said. Bashir wasn't certain he believed the other man, but he wasn't going to force him to give it up or search him for it. It wasn't worth the goodwill it would cost him.

"Fine. If you see her again, tell me."

"Why?" Harun glared. Bashir ignored him, and looked at Ela, who ducked her chin as she nudged the bottle toward him.

"No."

"For your men, then. Wheel can see they need it."

Bashir snatched the bottle from the counter and stalked out. He put it in his saddle bags and spent the rest of the afternoon checking in with his men, only to be told by every single one that they had seen, heard, and felt nothing of Aysel. It was so unbelievable as to be absurd. No one had ever evaded him so effortlessly, with all his resources turned against them.

When he returned to the palace near nightfall Samira was waiting for him in his office in the barracks. Exhaustion and a kind of frustrated hysteria descended on him, so that he felt like laughing.

"What does she want now?" He collapsed in the chair behind his desk and set the bottle of arak Ela had given him on the floor. Samira's eyebrows rose, her lips parting in prim shock. Bashir leaned his arms on the desk, lacking the energy to give Samira an explanation as to why he was acting completely unlike himself.

"The Viziers have informed the Sultana that there is a great deal of unrest in the city. Discontent over her choice in betrothed goes unanswered, and the people are concerned the camp may be harboring death mages. Rumors are spreading that there are some loose in the city."

"I cannot imagine who might have started such rumors," Bashir said in weary sarcasm. Why did she let the Vizier lead her around by the nose like she did? She knew he was a murderer and a liar, yet she still had not moved against him because she feared the repercussions in the Council. If she would just...

Bashir hung his head and laughed softly. If she would do what Makram had done, and employ a spy.

"Are you all right?" Samira moved around the desk to put her hand on his shoulder. "Bashir, I'm worried about you."

"What did you come to tell me?" He looked up at her. Samira withdrew her hand, frowning.

"Tomorrow the Sultana and prince will ride procession through the Grand Market and finish with a visit to the refugee camp in an effort to dispel rumors that the city is unsafe, or that the prince is somehow controlling the Sultana. I believe she plans to bring the Elder Attiyeh and his family with them. She leaves the number of men up to you."

"When?" Could he possibly pull enough men together for a procession detail? It would leave the camp with almost no men, and reduce those inside the palace as well.

"Mid-morning, during market." She examined his face as she spoke, looking for answers to his mood.

"Fine." He stood and went to the door, holding it wide for her. Samira hesitated, her brow furrowing.

"You can talk to me, you know. I think...I think you need to talk to someone."

"No. What I need is a dozen fewer tasks to complete. Goodnight." Perhaps in the morning he'd have the sense to be embarrassed at his rudeness. But for now, he just needed her, and the reminder she served of his inability to do everything he needed to do, gone.

"If you change your mind," she said gently, and left.

Bashir swung the door shut and returned to his desk. There were guard rosters to read, men to choose for the procession, and logs to update. He reached down and lifted the bottle he'd set on the floor, placing it in front of him and staring at it.

Aysel wasn't here, in fact she was probably all the way on the other side of Narfour. But when there was nothing to distract him, she took up all the space inside him. Impressive, for someone so small.

Bashir thumbed the cork out of the bottle and paused when he realized he didn't have a glass. He cast about the surface of his desk like one might materialize. Instead he found the thin medallion she had thrown at him in the courtyard.

She'd tried to tell him something about it. He hadn't been listening to her, he'd been too angry. Bashir turned the worthless piece of metal over in his hands. There was nothing on it, it wasn't a coin, or a true medallion, just a thin disk, some metal alloyed with gold.

He wasn't a smith and knew little about such things. Whatever she wanted him to do with it, whatever it meant to her, it was lost on him. He closed his fist around the neck of the bottle and shut his eyes.

Maybe if he were drunk he wouldn't dream of her tonight. In his dreams she was playful and wild and smiling. And in his dreams, he didn't care about any of the things he cared about when he was awake. She was his, he was hers, and that was that.

"To us, Little Fox." He took a swig directly from the bottle.

EIGHTEEN

WHEN HE WOKE, IT was to the sound of Erol's voice, followed swiftly by a feeling like a dagger jammed between his eyes. He was still at his desk, the empty bottle of arak on its side at his elbow. Had he finished the entire thing himself? Bashir put his face in his hands and propped his elbows on the desk.

"Now I've seen everything on the Wheel," Erol said, wryly. "Did you hear me? Tareck is outside, wants to know where the Sultana's escort is."

Bashir cursed, jumping to his feet but staggering and catching himself on the desk.

"Wheel's spokes. Are you drunk?" Erol said, then gave a sharp, incredulous laugh.

"Not anymore," Bashir groaned.

"At least you're dressed. Who do you want?"

"Whoever isn't assigned. Pull the rotation about to go up to the camp, and send a runner to tell the men there they have to pull a double shift. And a runner to tell the City Watch to man the route through the market and to the camp." That would earn him a great deal of ill will from both his men and the Watch. Everything Bashir did lately earned him ill will. He was growing quite accustomed to it. "Tell Tareck I'm on my way."

"You're all right?" Erol sounded truly concerned. Bashir waved him away, and Erol obeyed.

Bashir went to his room and washed his face and ran wet hands through his hair, squinting against the throbbing pain in his temples. He tugged at his caftan and adjusted his sword belt and the fabric that bound his waist, trying to hide evidence he had slept slumped over on his desk. There was nothing to do about the smell of stale alcohol emanating from him, except to stay at a distance from anyone who would care. Which would be approximately everyone, since he had never done something so pathetic in all his time at the palace. Twice he'd done it during University, when Erol had been visiting family in the valley and wasn't there to talk him down or distract him. Those had earned him the ire of Samira and his mother, who had teamed up on their harsh lectures about his self-pity.

When he left the barracks the pale winter sun personally assaulted him, sending more blinding pain through his skull.

"Get on your horse and try to look like yourself," Erol said beneath his breath, shoving Bashir's reins into his hands. Bashir did, grateful he'd need to do little but look like a guard for the duration of the event. Anything more complicated would likely be beyond him. And when they returned, he was going straight to beg pain-relief herbs from his mother.

His eyes and his pounding head were beginning to adjust to the torture of the insipid sunlight when the Sultana and Makram rode from the stables, their horses outfitted in their most elaborate saddles and headdresses, the entire ensemble of both adorned with dozens of tiny bells. Their incessant jingling promised to make Bashir crawl out of his skin.

Erol sat his horse beside him, barely suppressing laughter at the miserable expression that Bashir was not succeeding in hiding. "You've done it to yourself, you know," he said sagely when Bashir glared at him.

"Ride point," Bashir said, "take Tareck with you. I'll take the rear with three, and the rest can ride the flanks."

Erol nodded, urging his horse to the front of their procession.

It had been some time since the Sultan or his daughter had ridden a procession through the city. The Sultan had been too ill, his mind slowly warping, his identity disappearing. The Sultana believed the chaos of a procession would upset him. She had not ridden one herself because it posed the risk of giving the impression she had prematurely taken power from her father. Even though he had declared she would, to appear to be hurrying into his seat, when he was still alive, posed the risk of casting her in unfavorable light. And securing her position as a ruler the people and Council trusted was the painstaking work of details, not the kind of heavy-handed maneuvering Bashir enjoyed in his position as Commander. He had to remind himself of that now, more than ever. She knew what she was doing, each move carefully calculated in a plan only she knew.

Bashir tried to ignore the stabbing pain caused by the sun and looked around the courtyard as the procession organized. The Attiyehs mounted their horses when the Sultana and Makram had taken up positions behind Tareck and Erol, then Samira and two more of the Sultana's handmaidens, then the Elder Attiyeh and his wife, followed by Mathei and their steward.

Mathei appraised Bashir as he positioned his horse behind theirs, and Bashir was certain Mathei missed nothing about his condition. He ignored the other man's raised eyebrow and derisive smile. He was appalled at himself as it was, the last thing he needed was to be heckled by Aysel's brother.

Erol directed the rear guards he'd selected to ride some distance behind Bashir, and when the Sultana looked at Bashir in question, he saluted with a fist to his chest to indicate they were ready. Barely, and thanks due only to Erol.

Whenever the Sultan or his family entered the city the people followed. This time, as it usually did, it began as a trickle, near the palace, and by the time they made the Grand Market it was a flood. On a normal day it would have been a simple matter for Bashir to maintain a spell perimeter around their procession, a ripple of earth that warned people back. Today it took everything he had, his mind and control sluggish and slippery under the aftereffects of the arak. By the time they were halfway through the market Bashir felt nauseated and weak. He dropped his spell while the Sultana and Makram took a break to chat with some of the market vendors and the delegates the district had chosen to meet with them.

One of those delegates was Amara Mutar, whom everyone in the city knew, if only by reputation. His mother knew her better than he did. Amara chatted amicably with the Sultana and Makram, and her ever-present companion and bodyguard, Djar, stood within arm's length, with his unwieldy-looking scimitar hanging low against his legs. Bashir tipped his head to him when Djar caught his eye. Djar tapped a finger against his brow. They had never spoken, not once, in all the Turns Bashir had known of him. Instead they circled each other at a polite distance, some unspoken territorial boundary they both obeyed keeping them apart.

Erol caught his eye, and Bashir pointed to the four corners of the market in answer to his silent question. While Erol and a squad of fire mages encircled the meeting, Bashir took a short break to gulp water. He bought an orange to help settle his stomach. As he sat on his horse, peeling the fruit and scanning the crowd for signs of tension, he thought of Aysel. He was too tired and sick to fight it this time. Thoughts of her seemed to be his fate, one way or another. He'd watched her peel an orange the day he'd taken a nap in her tent. She'd tricked him then too, but only to convince him to do something he'd badly needed to do. Sleep. She'd been trying to take care of him. She'd made him a promise and kept it, to be there when he woke up. He liked the way she'd looked at him when he'd come out of her shelter, like she was completely at ease with him even though he was supposed to be holding her prisoner.

The orange did settle his stomach, and the scent lingered, holding her in his thoughts.

When the sun was well on its way to reaching the midday mark the Sultana and prince finished their discussions with the district delegates and mounted their horses once more. Erol and Tareck led the procession out of the market and up the hill, toward the refugee camp. Bashir was able to hold his spell a bit more easily with food in his belly, but the truth was he needed real sleep not poisoned by drunkenness. In the light of day it seemed like one of the more senseless things he'd done in some time. But he hadn't been thinking clearly.

Now, with fresh air, a bit of food, and some time, his sharpness was returning, albeit slowly. People lined the path to the refugee camp, and they were in a far less celebratory mood than those in the Grand Market. People in the Grand Market had thrown handfuls of colored paper scraps and ribbons. The crowds lining the road up the hill threw insults and derogatory comments at Makram. Chants of *"death to death mages"*, *"death to the Sixth"*, and *"send them back"* accompanied their slow progress up the hill.

Makram seemed undisturbed, relaxed in his saddle, face as impassive as the Sultana's, for once. That was enough to tell Bashir he was unsettled. He rarely hid his emotion, the way the Sultana did. He had little to fear from any of the protestors. Though Bashir had never seen the man's magic unleashed, he was the most powerful destruction mage alive. If he was worried about anything, it was the Sultana. He rode with a hand pressed to his leg, the other curled around the hilt of his yataghan, his face turned forward, but his gaze darting ceaselessly across the lines of yelling, angry people.

It was impossible for Bashir to forget the man was more soldier than prince, since he regularly attended sparring sessions with Bashir's men and more often than not left them in soundly beaten heaps. But now he had shed his prince's mantle and appeared only a moment away from drawing his sword on the angry, jeering citizens. Bashir suspected some of that control was due to the Sultana reaching between their mounts to lay her hand over his in warning, or solidarity.

The noise lessened as they reached the top of the hill and entered the camp. Everyone within its confines was subdued by hunger and cold, as harsh as it was to think of in those terms. They did not have the luxury of protests. Makram was also known to them, and Bashir doubted they would waste their energy yelling at the man responsible for them having a place to go at all. Logistically the camp posed far less threat than the Grand Market. There were a great many people, but they were scattered through the camp and were not surrounded by buildings and endless hiding places.

When they crested the hill and rode between the guards stationed at the camp entrance, the chanters turned their focus from the prince to the camp, screaming for the refugees to go home, that they weren't welcome, they were trash. Bashir ordered the guards at the entrance to the camp to prevent any of the protestors from entering. The Sultana and Makram continued farther into the camp, away from the road.

"Go around to the perimeter guards and draw them in closer around the Sultana and prince," Bashir ordered the men behind him. They nodded. The people in the camp milled toward the entrance, trying to see what all the yelling and screaming was about. Children began to cry, and desperate faces took on expressions of fear and anger. The Sultana's procession had been a poorly conceived idea, it seemed. If it had meant to ease tensions, it had only served to worsen them.

"I've sent two around to the others to draw the perimeter in. This road is to remain blocked, and I want two on the path to the spring, watching the hill," Bashir said to the Watch commander who held Huzur's reins while he dismounted. The man saluted and left to obey.

Bashir joined Erol, where he stood directing guards as they moved in from the perimeter.

Beyond him, the Sultana and prince had dismounted where a large section was cleared as a gathering place for the refugees and now served as a receiving area. Elder Attiyeh and his family had dismounted and were speaking with another family, a husband and wife and two little girls. Bashir recognized the twins from their game of chase with Aysel. One of them waved shyly at him, but when her mother saw she clutched the girl to her side and shuffled to stand on the far side of her husband. Bashir frowned.

"All around the center there." Erol pointed for the benefit of the four guards nearest him. He glanced at Bashir as he came up beside him. "Better?"

"Well enough." Bashir's malaise had been replaced with tension, and he glanced toward the road, where the protestors had clustered. Bashir thought he saw a flash like fire, but after staring for long moments didn't see it again.

"I don't think we should stay here long," he said. "I'll tell the Sultana when I have a chance."

Erol nodded grimly. Bashir glanced back to the central gathering. Aysel's mother leaned into the woman she was talking to, placing a small purse in her hands. The woman shook her head, but Aysel's mother closed both her hands over the other woman's and spoke urgently to her. If her family was generous, if they cared about people who did not matter to them at all, then why couldn't he let go of his resentment of Aysel's activities? She was doing it by the order of her prince. Doing exactly what he would do.

"You're the only man I know who can go from never drinking to finishing an entire bottle by himself and still get up in relative working order the next day," Erol said, distracting Bashir from the scene.

"A benefit of the Fourth House," Bashir said. Earth mages were notoriously good at holding their alcohol, though Bashir wondered what it felt like to be bad at it, if his splitting headache and reduced ability to cast were considered good.

"No, I think it's a benefit of being built like a mountain." Erol grinned. "Remember that time we skipped lessons and stole that bottle of barley wine?"

"I remember it was off." Bashir nearly gagged at the memory of what it had done to his stomach. That experience was the primary reason Bashir rarely drank. Erol chuckled.

Bashir looked to the road at the same moment the guards blocking the camp entrance shouted and flames erupted from within the mob. A scream pierced the relative quiet of the gathering inside the camp, and fire engulfed several of the shelters nearest the road. The mob at the front broke into chaos. More fire shot from someone in its midst, lighting more shelters.

The damned oiled canvases, meant to keep the wet out, lit and burned like dry grass. The first leapt from shelter to shelter, lighting the detritus in between, as people scattered, screaming.

"Go," Bashir ordered, and Erol darted toward the road. Someone ran past Bashir in Erol's wake, and Bashir recognized Samira's bright red entari. He turned to the center of camp to wave his men toward the fire. "Someone find me that mage! You two get some water on that fire," he called to the two water mages he had with him.

Makram stepped away from the Sultana, calm as could be, toward the camp entrance. As Erol and Samira fought the flames for control, and the two water mages struggled to put the fire out faster than it spread, Makram reached a hand toward the nearest shelter. Black smoke swept up his arm and engulfed him in shadowy whips, and the shelter collapsed into dust. The fire flickered out.

He continued, swiveling his focus from one side to the other, tents and shelters reduced to smoking piles of scrap under the touch of his magic.

Bashir's men turned their focus to herding the refugees away from the fire. Bashir tore his eyes away from the hypnotic sight of the magic and looked for the Sultana.

Her attention fixed to a smaller fire, near her, which diminished as she held the air away from it. Refugees clustered at her back, but Elder Attiyeh and his wife stood to either side of her. Mathei stood nearby, sword drawn, acting the part of personal guard. They were not even her people and they stood for her. A deep, mental tension released. Bashir did trust Makram and those of his people he had met. He would not invite a family into the palace that was a danger to the Sultana, and he would not employ a spy who was anything but loyal.

Aysel's family were not enemy spies or criminals, and neither was she.

The realization felt like letting go of a boulder three times his size.

"It's out," Erol called to Bashir.

"Did you find the mage who started it?" Bashir asked. Erol shook his head.

The guards trudged back, most of them skirting widely around Makram, whose freed magic made swirling ink tattoos across his face. The Attiyeh family moved away from the Sultana and toward Makram.

And in that brief moment, when there was no one near her, the distinctive, sickening click and snap of a crossbow firing echoed in the camp.

A streak like lightning shot across the center of the camp—Bashir had never seen anything like it, magic or otherwise. It took him another heartbeat to realize what he saw. Aysel had thrown herself on the Sultana. For one half of a heartbeat he was certain she was dead.

"Aysel!" her mother shrieked, waking Bashir from the tortured paralysis that held him.

"Close ranks!" Bashir bellowed over the eruption of shouts and melee. Refugees ran in every direction. Aysel got up when Makram reached her and the Sultana, and Bashir saw her snatch a crossbow from one of his guards as they converged on the Sultana.

Aysel sprinted for the base of the hill on the east side of the camp.

He looked up, and saw a figure running toward a wash that would conceal him. Bashir ran after Aysel and gathered his power as he did. When he reached the road at the base of the hill, he sent his power up through the slope, leading the running archer by a few paces, so that the quake hit him just before he reached the draw. He fell, and Aysel cursed as she missed.

"You aren't helping. Go find the other one!" Aysel ordered as she braced the bow against her hip and fumbled the lever into place to draw again. The archer got to his feet and leveled his bow again. The man aimed at Bashir.

Something crashed into his chest, sending him tumbling two full rotations onto his back. He coughed and lifted his head to look at the weight on his chest.

"You're all right?" He wrapped an arm around her, and she arched with a whimper of pain. Bashir released her and his arm came away wet with blood. He sat up, panic shrinking his breath and holding it tightly, and she slid off him, landing on all fours before staggering to her feet.

Bashir exhaled. She was moving, that meant she was all right. There was a trail across her back, just below her swords, where her caftan was torn and blood stained it. Magic whipped along her skin and through her hair, lightning that left blue and white and the scent of ozone in its wake. Her eyes, when she looked at him, held storms.

"Aysel."

"Get off your ass, Ox. There's another one somewhere in the camp. I almost had him before I saw this one." Then she was gone, after the archer, presumably, but he couldn't see her. He didn't understand what had happened, and he didn't have time to think about it.

He turned and shoved his way back through a huddle of refugees to the center of camp.

He came up behind Erol at the edge of the circle and put a hand on his shoulder. Erol was stiff, his jaw set. Bashir looked past him where Makram stood at the center of the circle of gathering refugees, whips of smoke and ink trailing around him and bleeding across the ground at his feet, his eyes black oblivion as he stared down at a man who was very clearly dead.

Silence festered. The air was still and heavy. Erol had traveled with the Sultana and Makram when they went to Sarkum for negotiations, and described the first time he saw Makram's power. But this was the first time Bashir had seen it firsthand. Makram kept his power to himself, or risk worsening tensions. Whatever he had done had left the man dead but unwounded. But a dead man was a dead man, whether by magic or sword, and Bashir didn't think it was much different than being torched by a Firestormer.

"Lieutenant, get these people back and settled. The rest of you sweep the camp for anything suspicious," Bashir said as he approached and crouched at the man's side. His orders broke whatever shock had silenced the entire camp, and everyone moved at once, though a curious few lingered as close as they dared.

"That was foolish," the Sultana hissed at the back of Makram's head. "I could have handled him, and now…" She pressed her fingers to the spot between her eyebrows. Makram's power dissipated as he threaded it back under his control.

"Wheel damn me if I'm just going to stand around and pretend I'm not what I am when someone is threatening your life," he replied, and when he lowered his voice Bashir stopped listening. The dead man looked a great deal like his companion who Bashir had shot the night he chased Aysel. Black clothes, a sword stamped with the gold seal Makram had informed Bashir marked him as katil. His memory finally recovered something Aysel had said to him.

Check the sword.

Bashir pried what was left of it out of the man's hand. It was eroded down to the hilt, just a broken, rusted, and pitted bit of the blade left. The seal on the sword was damaged too, the gold melting away, the stamp on it unrecognizable. Bashir looked up at the hill.

Aysel was wounded and chasing a killer by herself. Concern for her supplanted everything else in his mind, so he rose with urgency, ready to charge to his horse and hunt her down.

"Commander." The prince turned to look at Bashir. It was a look Bashir hoped to never see again, threat and anger only thinly disguised as disappointment, and made all the more blood-chilling by the fact the man's eyes were imbued by the endless black of destruction magic. He rarely referred to Bashir by title. "When we return to the palace you will explain your failure to protect the Sultana to my satisfaction, or there will be a sudden and painful end to your tenure as Commander."

Bashir let his breath out slowly, his gaze drifting to the hill once more. He could not explain his failure. There was nothing to be said. He should have listened to Aysel and he had not. He should have listened to his gut instead of his head and now everything was falling apart.

None of it mattered, not the way it mattered that he didn't know where she was. He couldn't bear her out there alone and injured, no matter how powerful she was.

He said, "Yes, Efendim."

NINETEEN

Aysel collapsed against a wall as the sun set against the ocean. She should have been able to catch the bastard, but her magic and her legs weren't obeying her anymore. A suspicion had been worming its way into her consciousness despite her vehement denials, and she pushed it away once more. She was overextended, that was the problem, simple as that. To save the Sultana, and Bashir, she'd done something she'd never done before, moved faster than even she had known she was capable of. Aysel could not have told anyone how she did it, she'd simply willed it to happen and it had. She'd puzzle through it later, but for now, she was drained more completely than she ever had been. Sleep was what she needed, then she could see to her wound and go hunting for the remaining assassin.

It wasn't too much farther to Ela's inn, if she could just stay on her feet. And if no one decided she was an easy target and tried to rob her. Aysel grimaced. She was an easy target. Wheel the wound hurt. She'd thought the bolt had grazed her, and when she felt the wound, it was shallow, but it was bleeding more than it should, and she felt weak and addled. The fear that kept worming its way past her denials was that the bolt had been poisoned. If that were the case Aysel doubted she had any chance of surviving. She was too far from the palace and the more sophisticated physicians who might be able to treat such a thing. Even then it would require knowledge of the poison, and since she had lost her quarry once they entered the city and she was overtaken with exhaustion, there was little hope for that.

She reached the corner of the inn where it sat on the intersection of the main north-to-south road that ran through the Merchant Pier district and the smaller lane that led to the water. Aysel paused to breathe, trying to summon the strength it would take to get to the door and inside and find Ela amongst whatever crowd filled the place. Hopefully Ela would take her in again. Harun had thought she was trying to steal from him. The sun was just a thin line at the edge of the water now, and once it set the inn would only get busier.

"Aysel?" a man's voice said. Aysel's mind had turned to thoughts of Bashir, how nice it would be to have him to carry her just then, and so that's who she heard. She turned toward the speaker and was confused to see Harun's willowy form.

"I'm surprised you came back. The palace lackies are looking for you." He clutched the pouch at his waist, the one with the silver medallion, his eyes narrowed at her. Aysel wanted to explain she wasn't a thief. She took a step and collapsed to her knees.

"What…"

There was blood on her salvar, she noticed. Had she bled that much? Shouldn't have. Harun's expression turned frantic when he crouched in front of her. "Come on."

He slung a long arm under hers and lifted her to her feet, helping her hobble toward the inn. He didn't ask what had happened, and even if he had she wasn't sure she could speak coherently enough to tell him.

Only a head or two turned when they entered the inn. The benefit of hiding in a place filled with thieves and violent types was that it was not so out of the ordinary for someone to show up bleeding. Harun led her into the kitchen and sat her down on the pallet, then helped her lie on her side. Ela came in shortly after. Or maybe it wasn't shortly at all. Aysel was having trouble holding her thoughts together, and her vision was starting to blur. Not good.

"What is going on here?" Ela demanded, kneeling in front of Aysel. Aysel felt her put a hand on her forehead, and even tug up her eyelids to look at her eyes. "Harun?" Ela asked, but if he responded Aysel didn't hear it. She felt hands touching her back, at least she felt their pressure on the muscles. The wound had gone numb. Also not good.

Aysel's one thought was slippery and difficult to make into words, especially since her mouth felt fuzzy.

"My brother," she managed, "at the palace. Mathei." Mathei knew more about poisons than anyone she'd ever known. She closed her eyes because she couldn't keep them open another moment.

As she sank into something that felt like sleep, and like death, she had the strangest sensation of reaching, tugging strings in the darkness, crying out to something that answered her plea with a thin trickle of power.

TWENTY

ASHIR KNELT IN FRONT of the Sultana, who had been silent, allowing Makram to pace and rant. Bashir maintained a facade of calm, but if they could not see the worry that was threatening to break him into pieces beneath its thin veneer, he would be amazed. It felt as if everything inside him was vibrating apart, his magic rolling and erupting in little quakes of power that flashed across his skin and certainly on his face, which he kept downturned.

"I have been patient with this absurd need you have to deal with the Vizier in an aboveboard manner, and I am finished." Makram looked from the Sultana to Bashir. "Did she tell you she found something in Kadir's house? Did she warn you?"

"She tried," Bashir ground out, trying to keep the rumble of his magic from erupting in his voice and failing.

Makram paused, and his black eyes narrowed. "Control yourself," the prince commanded.

The Sultana sighed. "Makram. Enough." She rose to stand before Bashir. Her air magic, which was awake and irritating his, did not feel anything like Aysel's. One was still winter, the other unchecked tempest. "Commander Ayan, tell me the truth."

At the patience in her tone, Bashir's control snapped, and he shattered apart, his magic bursting gold and harsh across his skin, shining through his clothes and coloring the stone beneath him with warm light.

"Forgive me, Sultana. I should have listened to her. I knew I could trust her, I knew it, and I did not, because I wanted to do what you asked me to. It put you in danger, and now her. She saved me from an attack and now she's out there, Wheel knows where, chasing a killer. She is wounded." The stones under him rolled. "And I am here doing *nothing*." He didn't shout the word but he might as well have, the way the room echoed his temper back at him. "Punish me, Efendim, if that is your wish. But send someone to help her."

"I told you not to interfere with her. I told you she could take care of herself," Makram said, fury in each word.

"I know!" Bashir shouted, and the building shook. Plaster rained down around them.

"Bashir." The Sultana used his name as an order for obedience. "What did she find at Kadir's estate?"

"I don't know." He didn't understand why they weren't listening to him. Did they not care that she was hurt? "She gave me a gold medallion, but it did not have any markings. She said it had something to do with the katil's swords."

The Sultana looked at Makram, who shook his head. Then his eyes closed and he tipped his head back with a quiet curse.

"How big was it?" he asked, and Bashir formed a ring with his fingers to approximate its size. "That's about the size of the seal they have on their swords," the prince said.

"She said they aren't after her family, she did not think they were katil." All of which was obvious now, since they had attacked the Sultana.

"So," Makram said, "she found this blank medallion in one of Kadir's estates. She thought the katil were not truly katil, just assassins. She must have seen something else to make her believe Kadir had anything to do with this. An unmarked medallion proves nothing." He addressed the Sultana, "We need her here."

Bashir wanted, needed to crumble something to rubble. These were all revelations they would not have to guess at if they allowed him to leave and find Aysel. She was hurt somewhere. He couldn't bear it. "Please. Efendim. Let me go find her."

"Bashir, you haven't been able to find her all this time. What makes you think you will be able to now?"

"Please," he said again, because he didn't have the words to explain that if she was badly hurt, if she was alone and dying somewhere, he did not think he could live with himself.

The Sultana's expression, normally as unreadable as polished marble, softened, her gaze searching his face, her lips parted as she drew a long breath and looked sidelong at Makram, who frowned.

"Go," she said.

"No," Makram protested. "He failed to do the one thing he is supposed to do and if it were not for Aysel—"

"Then do not allow her to be out there in the city alone, injured and facing another opponent. Besides"—she turned her back on Bashir and faced Makram—"it is not your decision to make. I have known Bashir to be loyal and trustworthy since the first time I met him and I would have no one else as Commander of my guard. You can trust that he will not fail so again. Bashir"—the Sultana looked at him again—"when you find her, please return with her to the palace."

"Yes, Efendim." He got to his feet and hurried through the doors of the receiving hall and through the hall. Erol met him in the courtyard and shook his head.

"Nothing. I've set the City Watch on her too. Someone reported to them that they saw a woman matching Aysel's description running through the north end of the city, but they didn't see much else."

If she was injured, she might be bleeding enough magic that he could find her. But he'd need to expend a great deal of power to do so. He turned and headed for the arena. Erol followed but stopped at the edge of the sand when Bashir kept going, walking to the center of the oval field and kneeling.

Bashir closed his eyes and pictured her, building the feeling of her with every detail he had ever stowed away. The storm grey and earth hazel of her eyes, the quirk of her mouth when she teased him, the way she bit her lip when she was thinking. He flexed his hands as he remembered the way her hair felt coiled around his fingers, and the flat, smooth plane of her stomach beneath his touch. The sound of her giggling, the way her footsteps didn't feel like anyone else's on the earth around him, the strength and gentleness of her hands, the shape of her as she moved.

He slid his hands into the sand and released his power, directing it toward the city, commanding it all the way to the sea. It felt as if it only crept away from him, gaining distance more slowly than it ever had. He had to sort through and dismiss so many vibrations, so many senses, making them all disappear except the one he wanted. The barest touch of quiet feet, magic that felt like storms.

The rhythm of the city felt like endless heartbeats in his mind, against his magic, so he lost himself to it, to the earth through which his awareness traveled.

"Sir," Erol said. Bashir's grasp on the spell shattered. He turned to Erol, temper bursting upward like magma. He knew better than to interrupt—

A woman stood beside Erol.

"Ela." Bashir staggered to his feet, then nearly dropped to his knees. He hadn't felt the drain of his spell until just now. His head spun as he crossed toward them. "Why are you here?" He grabbed one of the pillars that framed the arched entrance to the arena for balance. It had grown dark while he was casting. How long had he been kneeling in the sand?

"Your girl is back," she said. The resigned look on her face told him the rest of her news was bad. Weakness spread through his body so that it was all he could do to stay standing. "She won't be on the Wheel much longer, I'd say. Poison, if I were to guess. She sent me for her brother."

"Is she at the inn?" She was still alive, at least. Ela nodded. "Erol, get Mathei, take him to my mother's house."

"Yes." Erol ran for the palace.

"Ride with me," Bashir said. Ela put a steadying hand on his arm when he stepped away from the pillar and wove in place.

"You'll need me to keep you in the saddle," Ela said dryly. "What were you doing? That's too much to put into a single spell, even for you."

"I've been looking for her." He led Ela into the stables. The guard there retrieved Huzur, and saddled him, an effort that felt as though it dragged for a lifetime. Bashir's pulse beat harshly through his entire body, so that by the time his guardsman handed him his reins he was ready to fly apart again. Instead, he forced himself to mount, then helped Ela up behind him when the guard gave her a boost into the saddle.

"She must have done something bad, for you to be after her with so much force," Ela said as Bashir spurred Huzur to a trot. He wanted to send him at a full gallop, but that was too difficult with two people in the saddle and with his balance and strength upset by his expenditure. Ela didn't have the strength in her hands to hold on tightly enough to stay seated either.

"Not really, no," Bashir mumbled, the truth of it settling over him heavily. What a disastrous mess.

"I see. Complicated is it?" Ela said, patting him on the back. "For now, I'd just worry about the one thing," she suggested, and Bashir nodded. There wasn't a possibility of him thinking of anything else but Aysel, dying of poison. Poison that would have taken him, if the bolt hadn't done the job. Poison probably meant for the Sultana.

He ran a hand over his face, his legs tightening around Huzur, who responded with a toss of his head and a snort. Bashir forced himself to relax and tried to wrench his thoughts away from the idea that he might arrive too late. How long had it taken Ela to hike from the pier?

The foot traffic around the pier was beginning to pick up as darkness grew deeper and people were heading to or from their work shifts. Bashir had to slow Huzur, making tension roll beneath his skin. The gelding fidgeted with nerves, sidestepping and shaking his head because of Bashir's anxiety, his need to go faster. All he could think of was finding her…gone. Her lifeless…Bashir shook his head. He shouted at the people in front of him to move. It worked only moderately, clearing a few paces of space in front of him. A spell would work, a ripple of earth to clear the path in front, but he had drained the vast majority of his reserves with his tracking in the arena, without realizing it. Fool that he was.

"Steady now," Ela said, patting his shoulder. "Harun's with her, he'd have sent word if she took a turn."

Bashir didn't find that comforting in any way, but he did feel a flicker of relief when he saw the inn's roofline over the buildings around it. He turned, and Ela slid her arm through his and he bent to let her slide down, then followed, collecting his reins and walking the rest of the way. Ela took the reins from him when they reached the inn, and Huzur sidestepped, eyes rolling. He'd never cared much for fire mages. Ela clucked at him as she lashed Huzur to the post outside.

Bashir shouldered through the door. People looked up and conversations died as he appeared, disheveled and wild-eyed, he imagined. He'd washed Aysel's blood from his hands, but it still stained his sleeve, standing out against the pale caftan fabric. Two young women, servers he'd seen sometimes when he visited Ela, looked up from the counter where they were pouring drinks and began whispering to each other.

"Kitchen," Ela said behind him, and Bashir strode through the central hall and into the kitchen, where Harun was just standing up from the pallet in the back corner. Bashir hurried through, nearly colliding with the dish washtub then the spit over the fire, before dropping to his knees beside where Aysel lay.

"What is he doing here?" Harun said to his mother.

"Aysel?" Bashir leaned over her. He cupped her face in one hand. It was pale, washed of color and life. She lay unnaturally still, and cold, and her limbs were limp and heavy as he tried take her hand in his.

Ela sat on the pallet near Aysel's head and hovered a hand above her mouth and nose. She clicked her tongue. "She's breathing. Just barely. Get her to Havva, boy."

Bashir slid an arm under her legs and the other under her shoulders to lift her. He wanted her to wake up, to look at him, to smile like it was all a joke, but her head lolled against his chest and shoulder, and Ela had to tuck her arms in against him to keep them from hanging limply.

"Harun," Bashir said, "help me get her onto my horse."

Ela and Harun followed him out of the inn, and when they reached his horse Bashir lifted Aysel into Harun's arms. He mounted, then pulled Aysel up as Harun boosted her, sitting her sideways in front of him and wrapping his arms around her to grasp his reins.

"You send word, one way or the other," Ela demanded. Bashir nodded, turned his horse, and urged it to a canter. He avoided the cobbled roads, choosing the dirt streets to give his gelding purchase. Aysel kept slipping, the dead weight of her unbalanced and precarious in the saddle, and he eventually had to slow and readjust her to keep her from sliding off completely.

The Earth District butted up against the Merchant Pier, and so the ride was much shorter between the two than from the palace to the pier. He slid down when he reached his mother's house and lowered Aysel, slinging her up into his arms again to carry her into the house.

Havva looked up from where she sat in the center of the house, mending something. Her eyes widened, and she stood as Bashir carried Aysel in.

"Well," she said, "this is new."

Bashir carried Aysel to the back of the house, elbowing his way through the cloth hung to hide the beds, and laid her in his.

"What's happened?" Havva asked, already rolling the sleeves of her caftan to her elbows and moving into the kitchen to collect her supplies.

"She took a bolt for me, and I think it was poisoned." Bashir unbuckled Aysel's sword harness, rolled her gently onto her belly, and worked her arms free of it. He set it and the swords on the floor, out of the way.

"Sit her up." Havva sat on the edge of the bed. Bashir pulled Aysel into his lap, leaning her shoulder against him and holding her upright as Havva lifted her caftan to look at her back and the wound there. "This needs to come off. I can't see."

She tugged up on the caftan and Bashir helped maneuver Aysel's torso and limbs to pull it over her head. Havva drew a small knife from the basket of materials she kept and sliced it through the fabric that bound Aysel's chest, then pushed the fabric away. She hissed, setting her hands in her lap. Red, angry lines laced away from the wound, and the wound itself oozed red-tinged, oily foulness.

"I…" She looked up at him with hopelessness that sent fissures of agony through him. She'd been treating the women of the city's brothels, the poor of the city, anybody who didn't have access to a physician since she had left the brothels when he was a teen. Havva knew what she could treat and what she could not.

"Anne. Please," he begged, his voice cracking around the lump in his throat, and his eyes burning like he was staring straight at a fire. "You have to try." His arms tightened around Aysel, and her head fell into the crook of his neck, like she was just asleep, just resting in his embrace.

"That is not a poison I know, baby. She is too far taken by it," Havva said, gently, petting Aysel's braids. "I can treat the wound, but that is not what is killing her."

"I did this," Bashir choked, lifting his hands to cup Aysel's head and rotate her into his arms. "I did this to her." He couldn't bear the feeling of how cold her skin was beneath his hands, and he fumbled for one of the blankets on the bed, pulling it around her shoulders and wrapping his arms around her again.

"I'm so sorry." Havva touched her fingers to his cheek, the sadness in her eyes only turning his into consuming misery. She stood, heading for the kitchen. To make tea. She always made tea when she had to tell anyone that the person they cared about was dying.

Bashir couldn't breathe. His throat closed around the lump there, his breath was stale in his lungs, and his hands shook as he ran them down Aysel's back. "Don't do this to me," he whispered. "Don't run this time. Stay." He only barely heard the knock on the front door, and it did not sink past the numbness settling over him.

"Erol," his mother said. "And?"

"Where is my sister?" Mathei's voice, sharp with fear masked as anger, broke Bashir out of his stupor.

"Here," he said.

Mathei stalked to him. "Why isn't she at the palace, being tended by a physician?" he demanded, and when he saw Aysel, wrapped in Bashir's arms, outrage transformed his entire countenance, and Bashir felt magic stir across his own.

"Havva is better than any palace physician," Erol said. "She's treated more ills than all of those academic windbags combined."

"You get your hands off her," Mathei said to Bashir, "and if you're such a good healer"—he turned on Havva as she approached—"then why aren't you treating her?"

Bashir's mother was more than accustomed to being the focus of people's anger and fear. She merely raised an eyebrow.

"Your sister has been poisoned. Even if she had come to me immediately, I've never seen this poison before. I cannot treat her." Havva took a deep breath and shook her head. "I'm very sorry, but your sister is dying."

"When the Fifth House freezes into solid ice and the Wheel snaps in half." Mathei turned to Bashir and fully unleashed his magic, its dark shadow invisible but akin to the feel of Makram's. Not Aysel's. Not air. Destruction. "You did this to her, and if she dies, I will turn your corpse into a tomb for your desiccated organs."

At the threat, Havva dropped the ceramic dish she had in her hands, and it shattered on the floor. Bashir stared at Mathei. If Aysel died because of him he didn't know what would be left of him anyway. He was supposed to protect people, not be the cause of their death.

"Fine," Bashir said.

Mathei ignored Havva as she backed away, grabbing for Erol's arm. "Get that blanket off her and let me see. You"—he turned to face Havva and Erol—"I need something to write with."

Bashir nodded to his mother as he gingerly pulled the blanket from around Aysel, baring her back and her wound to Mathei. Mathei knelt in front of Bashir, touching his fingers to Aysel's skin as he looked at the wound and the evidence of the poison.

"I know what this is." He sat back on his heels. "I don't know how they even got their hands on it. It is rare and forbidden in both Sarkum and here, as far as I know."

Havva approached him and held out a pot of ink and a quill from too far away for Mathei to reach. He raised an eyebrow. "Afraid? Maybe you should be afraid of him." Mathei turned an accusing look on Bashir. "Of the two of us, I am not the one who has done his best to get my sister killed."

"I didn't…" Bashir looked away from Mathei. "He won't hurt you, Anne."

"Is she a death mage too?" Havva set the ink and quill on the floor beside Mathei, then backed away again, looking in suspicion from Mathei to Aysel.

"No," Bashir said. If her family was Sixth House, then his questions were answered. Aysel was a Charah. He could not care about that now, with her lying near the edge of the void, likely to tip into oblivion at any moment.

"What are you going to do?" Bashir asked Mathei, who had picked up the ink pot and turned it over to spill some across his fingers.

"If we're lucky, I'm going to destroy the poison." Mathei began to draw black sigils down Aysel's spine.

"Have you done that before?" Bashir had never heard of such a spell and he didn't care for the sound of it. But he knew very little about the capabilities of the Sixth House.

"Not on a person." Mathei's frown turned to a scowl. "So, if you would kindly shut your mouth and let me concentrate, I would appreciate it." Mathei drew more sigils around Aysel's wound. "Lay her on her stomach and get these off her." He plucked at her salvar.

Bashir turned, laying Aysel on her belly. Mathei pulled her boots off, then tugged her salvar off and tossed them on the floor. If he wasn't consumed with grief and guilt, Bashir might have cared that Aysel was naked but for her small clothes, which covered nothing more than her backside. But even then, the flayed flesh across her lower back drew all his attention. It should have been a minor wound. It was barely deep enough to need stitches. Instead it was killing her.

Mathei continued drawing on her skin, over her legs and arms, and one on the back of her neck. Then he stood beside Bashir, at the side of the bed, and put his ink-stained hand over Aysel's wound and began to chant his spell. Something tickled the back of Bashir's neck, and the hair on his arms and his head stood on end. With a snap, a jagged line of lightning shot down Aysel's back, turning the ink across her skin to smoke.

Mathei cursed, yanking his hand back and shaking it as if burnt. Her magic continued to swirl across her skin, little flashes of lightning-like streaks of blue-white fire.

"Her magic is fighting me," Mathei growled, and grabbed the ink to redo his work. "Can you null it?" He looked at Bashir.

"You want me to null a Charah?" He almost laughed but raised his eyebrows instead.

"You should be able to," Mathei said. "Even a weaker mage can null a mage in opposition on the Wheel. Here, get up there and hold her." He pointed, and Bashir obeyed, crawling onto the bed near Aysel's head. "Lift her up."

Mathei waved to Erol to help. The three of them lifted Aysel and Bashir sat, folding his legs in front of him, as they positioned her as if she were hugging him, her head against his shoulder and her arms over his. Bashir held her up with his hands on her waist to avoid disturbing the drawings on her skin. She had never felt as small and breakable as she did now, too small. Too fragile. Bashir squeezed his eyes shut then opened them again.

"You hold her magic while I cast. I don't know how long it will take me, but you can't let go until I've finished. All right?" Mathei watched him with a hard stare until Bashir nodded. His magic was not recovered from casting his tracking spell, but even if it killed him, he was going to do this to save Aysel.

"Now." Mathei put his hands over Aysel's wound again. Bashir closed his eyes and released his hold on his own magic, threading it around Aysel and toward the pulse of her power. When Mathei began speaking his spell, her magic billowed up like a summer storm cloud, and Bashir grit his teeth and pushed, containing it within her, commanding it to silence.

It was not a working he would have thought himself capable of, holding the magic of another. Especially a Charah. But the only alternative was unthinkable, and so he fed all his energy into it, into building a tighter and tighter grip. Her magic was like an entity itself, avoiding the touch of his power, swirling and darting for holes in his hold, crackling with sharp bursts of energy like lightning that hammered pain through his entire body.

He could feel when his reserves of power were emptied, when he started drawing on his life force to hold her magic in check. He could feel the strength bleeding out of him, and his hold on her raging magic slipping. Distantly, he felt his physical hold on her, his hands, loosening. A lash of lightning slammed against the wall of magic he'd built, and he felt it crack, thunder reverberating in his head and knocking loose his hold on her magic. The severing of it caused a backlash of his own power, like a tensioned rope snapping at one end and flying back, and knocked him into blackness.

Twenty-One

AYSEL WOKE, BUT DIDN'T open her eyes, trying to understand why whatever she was lying on was moving. Up and down. That didn't make any sense, but nothing was coming to mind to help her orient. Everything seemed far away, like a memory of turns, nothing sooner, that would have explained the oddness. She opened her eyes, blinking.

There was a wall in front of her, and the room was dark, lit by the pale, oddly frantic light of an oil lamp somewhere behind her. Not her shelter in the camp, there would be no lamp. Not the palace or the inn, that would be lit by magelight.

She realized the steady, thrumming rhythm against her ear was a heartbeat. Aysel jerked, lifting her head to look down. The person beneath her stirred, and in the light that flickered she recognized Bashir's face. Confused, Aysel relaxed, then realized she was naked, sandwiched between him and a soft blanket thrown over her back. He wasn't naked, why was she naked? He had one arm slung across her back. The last thing she remembered of Bashir…her eyes narrowed. Was too long ago. She remembered arguing with him, fighting with him in the arena and running. Everything after that was dreamlike and fuzzy. She'd been shot…no, someone had tried to shoot him, and she'd knocked him out of the way. Poison. She'd been poisoned. But hadn't she gone to the inn?

"Ox?" she whispered, because the darkness seemed to require she be quiet. She patted her fingers against his stubbled cheek. "Ox?" He shifted again, turning his face toward the wall. His eyes opened. He blinked, his brow furrowed, and he frowned, surveying the wall before turning his head so he was looking up at her. "Hello."

He stared at her, and the light showed the muscles in his jaw jump as he clenched his teeth. Bashir squeezed his eyes shut and released his breath slowly as he tipped his head back against the blankets. Aysel folded her hands over his chest and set her chin on them. She realized she felt weak and nauseous and holding her head up was making her back muscles cramp and twitch.

"Would you happen to know why I'm naked and lying on top of you?" She caressed his cheek with her fingers. Did this mean they were friends again? "I'm not complaining, necessarily."

He let out a soft laugh and lifted his head, moving his hands to cup her face. He traced her cheeks with his thumbs. The tender touch and the grave look on his face silenced her instinct to tease him. What exactly had happened between her getting shot and this moment to make him act in such a way?

"You"—his voice was rough and hoarse—"are not allowed to die. Ever."

"Oh?" Perhaps she had been closer to death than she realized.

"I recently discovered I could not bear it." His voice shook, and he swallowed, blinking rapidly as he laid his head back.

Warmth filled her with tender fondness, and she relaxed against him. "All right." She traced the line of his cheekbone, happy to be touching him again. "I'll consider it. But you'll have to keep me company."

One corner of his mouth lifted and he let go of her with one hand to prop himself on his elbow, curving the other hand behind her neck and urging her to him. Aysel grabbed his shoulders and slid higher, meeting his kiss. His hand on her neck tightened, his kiss harsh. Aysel tugged back to catch her breath. "Wait. I'm still angry with you." He hadn't listened to her, and everything had gone wrong because of it.

"You are," he agreed, "and I am angry that you ran from me. But"—his fingers skimmed her neck—"just let me have you here, with me, for a few more moments."

"Hmm." She pretended to consider. Bashir watched her, his expression still too serious. Aysel scooched higher, and Bashir laid his head back. She traced her fingers over his mouth, soft lips made for secret smiles. "Why am I angry, again?" she wondered, and he tensed beneath her, lifting his head toward hers.

A shadow moved over them and Aysel turned her head to look up.

"You're angry with him because he almost got you killed," Mathei said, standing over them with a look like he might drive a sword through them both. Behind him came a woman's voice.

"Are they awake?"

"Mat? You're here?" Aysel asked. Mathei glared at her. Bashir sat up, taking her with him, and pulled the blanket that lay over her back around her to keep her covered. He tugged it up to her chin, frowning.

"Why didn't you move her? You just left her…" He gestured at her and glared at Mathei.

"You were in mage sleep," Mathei said, tersely.

"And so were you," the woman said to Mathei. "Bashir collapsed, and you shortly after. It was all I could do to move this one to the floor." She gestured at Mathei. "And it is best not to move an injured mage in the sleep."

Aysel turned, sliding off Bashir to sit beside him. The woman stood behind Mathei, pinning errant strands of light brown hair touched with grey into a coil at the back of her head. Aysel hugged the blanket around her, noticing a black stain on her hand. She stuck an arm out of the blankets. Sigils drawn in black ink marched up her arm.

Her breath caught in her throat and she looked at her brother, her heartbeat seeming to speed and harshen. "Did you?"

"You were nearly gone," Mathei said, trying to look angry to cover the haunted look in his eyes. "I'm sorry, I had to." He'd revealed her. Revealed she was a Charah.

"You should be grateful. I would not have been able to save you." The woman knelt in front of Aysel.

Aysel glanced at Bashir. What was he going to do? He looked back at her with the same expression he had worn since he woke, too serious, and unreadable.

"Bashir, if you're recovered, why don't you and Mathei go to the kitchen and eat. I made tabbouleh. I'm going to look at her wound."

Bashir rose, weaving a bit in place, then walked away. Mathei followed. A cloth hung from the ceiling that obscured where they went, and across from her another bed lay hidden behind a second cloth. "Where are we?"

"This is my home. Bashir's as well. I am Havva, his mother." She motioned for Aysel to lie down with all the confidence of someone accustomed to giving such direction. Aysel stretched out on her belly. She felt nauseated, and shaky, and lying down felt better than sitting.

"Aysel." She closed her eyes against a wave of vertigo.

"Aysel. This wound isn't terrible. It is very shallow. I'd still like to stitch it for you, it will heal faster." Havva poked around the wound, and Aysel nodded in response to her suggestion, though a thin sheen of sweat broke over her face at the prodding.

"Where did your brother learn such a spell?" Havva said as she set a basket of supplies on the bed beside Aysel and sorted through it. Aysel didn't watch. She'd had stitches before, and the sight of the needles made her want to vomit.

"In the Academy in Sarkum they teach Sixth House mages how to clean wounds of fragments, like bone, or dirt, with their magic.

He thought he could adapt it to cleanse the blood of poison. It seems he was right," Aysel said, flinching as she saw the needle glint in her peripheral as Havva threaded it.

"I'd never have thought a death mage to be a healer." Havva pinched Aysel's wound closed and drew the first stitch. Aysel buried her face against the blankets, grabbing fistfuls of fabric. Havva sewed several more before she paused to give Aysel a moment to catch her breath.

"Do you know any?" Aysel wiped the moisture from her eyes and nose. She wasn't going to call them tears.

"No." Havva sewed five more stitches, and Aysel considered kicking her in protest, but crossed her ankles instead, flexing her toes against the bed.

"Death is another spoke on the Wheel," Aysel said. "As necessary as winter."

"And there is a difference between *death* and *destruction*," Mathei called from the kitchen, repeating a line he had used countless times throughout their lives. Being born in the House of destruction did not make one a death mage.

Havva made a sound in her throat but said nothing else as she finished the stitches and cut the thread, then got up. "I'll put a poultice on this for a bit, then you can dress. I've a caftan you can wear."

Aysel eyed her. She was tall, and sturdily built. The female version of her son. Aysel's face must have reflected her doubt, because Havva smiled, and Aysel saw Bashir's face in hers. Their eyes crinkled at the edges the same way, her mouth curved up more on one side than the other, like Bashir's.

"I have treated all shapes and sizes of women," Havva said. "Many of their things end up left behind." The words reminded Aysel that Bashir had revealed he was the son of a prostitute. But Havva stood straight-backed and proud, and seemed at peace with herself and her life. Not what Aysel had pictured at all. "Are you hungry?"

"Not yet." The thought of food stirred her nausea.

Havva nodded as she pulled a blanket over Aysel's back and took her basket in the direction Mathei and Bashir had gone. Aysel could hear them talking in hushed tones, the lower hum of Bashir's voice, and the quicker pace of Mat's. There appeared to be a sitting area beyond the hanging fabric that separated the beds from the rest of the house.

Well, Bashir hadn't gone running to the palace to announce Aysel's status to the Sultana. Yet. What was going to happen to her now? And what had happened to the Sultana and Makram, and the two assassins?

"Bashir?" Aysel called. She heard a thud and rattle.

"You really are an ox," Mathei complained. "Could you leave the table here at least, some of us chew our food and it takes longer to eat."

Bashir muttered something in response and slapped aside the fabric. The home must not be very big, if it took him only a beat to stride from one end to the other. His mother walked close on his heels, with a bowl of steaming water laced with herbs and a cloth hung over her arm.

"Step over there." She bumped him with a hip. He shuffled closer to Aysel's head and sat on the floor, wrapping his arms loosely around his bent knees.

"Are Makram and the Sultana all right? Did you find the other assassin?" Aysel asked.

Bashir nodded. He took a moment to watch his mother, who dipped the cloth into the water then rolled the blanket down to Aysel's hips to expose her back. Bashir straightened, craning his neck to see.

"Anne sews the finest stitches in Narfour, so you won't have to worry about scarring too badly," he said, leaning back against the wall. Havva made a shushing noise and laid the soaked cloth over Aysel's back, then pulled the blanket back over her. The warmth felt good, though the wound stung.

"Well, that's a relief," Aysel said. "I wouldn't want a scar to spoil my otherwise ballad-worthy beauty." She raised an eyebrow. "Especially not on a place that so many people see on a daily basis."

Bashir laughed a little, though she could tell he was still brooding. Havva collected the bowl of water and cleared her throat. Aysel and Bashir both looked at her.

"I'll leave that on for a bit. You should rest," Havva said with a pointed look at Bashir.

He frowned at her. "She saved the Sultana's life, Anne. And mine. Let me answer her questions."

"You cannot sit around chatting with her while she's naked."

"She has a blanket, and since when have you cared about naked women? I saw more bared breasts and backsides—"

"Ba—shir!" Havva stamped her foot. Aysel winced at the way she broke Bashir's name in half. It was never good when a mother did that. "She is a noble."

Aysel propped her head in her hand, watching the two of them in silence while she tried not to laugh.

"If you're worried about her virtue you needn't be." He reached beneath the bed and lifted up Aysel's harness and swords. "She doesn't carry these around for decoration. She's practically a palace guard at this point." He dropped the swords at his side.

Havva wrinkled her nose.

"False," Mathei called from the far end of the house. "Wouldn't that require her to be tall enough to see over the battlements?"

Bashir laughed. Aysel was warmed by the sight, even if it was at her expense.

"I am certain I could find something to stand on," Aysel called back.

Mathei ducked beneath the curtain behind Havva. "Yes. All right. 'I'll be there to join you in defending the palace momentarily, my friends. I seem to have misplaced my stool.'"

Bashir snorted, then hung his head into the circle created by his arms, shaking as he laughed so hard, he made no sound. Aysel stuck her tongue out at Mathei.

"You are a fine cook, Mistress, thank you for the meal. And do not concern yourself with these two. I shall chaperon," Mathei said to Havva, who regarded him and her son with disgruntled bewilderment. Aysel felt sorry for her, a bit. She suspected Bashir was a dutiful and respectful son, and not many people were prepared for the effect Mathei had on others.

"She really should rest," Havva said.

Mathei nodded as he pushed aside the other curtain to reveal the second bed and sat on it.

"I'm certain the commander has no intention of overtaxing her." Mat smiled but gave Bashir a frosty look. Havva sighed and moved out of the small space.

"Mathei, did you send word to Anne?" Aysel asked.

"Lieutenant Terzi went this morning after we woke. When you and the commander are done with your chat, I'll return as well." He looked at her in pointed reminder. He would need to warn their parents Aysel's secret was no longer a secret. If Erol wasn't already informing the Sultana.

What would Makram do? Would he be angry? Would he force her to join the Sultana's Circle?

"In answer to your question," Bashir said, wiping a hand over his face and taking a deep breath, "both the prince and the Sultana are fine. The prince…dispatched one assassin. The Sultana wishes you to return to the palace, when you're well. She'll want to know what you discovered at Kadir's estate that made you suspect they weren't katil. Did you catch the man you ran after?"

Aysel shook her head. "I cast something I never had before, and the poison slowed me down. I lost him in the city."

"You mean how you moved? How fast you were. Like lightning," Bashir said.

Aysel blinked at him. "What?"

"You moved like lightning. All I saw was a streak, then there you were, with the Sultana. You did the same thing to push me out of the way of that crossbow bolt." His brow furrowed as he looked at her, clearly confused by her lack of knowledge of her own power.

Aysel grimaced, looking sidelong at Mathei for rescue.

"I heard that the Sultana is most displeased with your utter failure to predict the attack," Mathei said, crossing one leg over the other and propping an elbow on his knee. He set his chin in his hand and looked at Bashir with raised eyebrows. Aysel glared at him.

"The Sultana was generous with me. The prince was not. I don't know what he'll wish to do with me after this. I begged them to let me come find you. I should return to the palace soon and face whatever punishment he's devised." Bashir shoved his fingers into his hair and gripped a handful as he stared at the floor.

Aysel laced her fingers together under her cheek. It was not entirely his fault that things had gone the way they had. She should go with him to the palace. She should help him. But what if they forced her to stay, to be a Charah? What if they locked her up? What if the secret got back to Kinus? He might send real katil this time.

"Bashir," Havva called from the front of the house, "I'm going to the market to get herbs and run my medicine rounds. Make her rest."

"Yes," Bashir called back. The door closed, and the three of them sat in brooding silence for a long time. Aysel did feel tired, exhausted, in fact. She rubbed her eyes.

"I believe that is my cue to leave," Mathei said, standing. "I'll be back in the morning and see when Havva thinks we can move you to the palace."

"You're leaving?" Aysel said. "I can go with you." She didn't want to be alone with her thoughts and her worries. If they both left her, she'd go mad.

"Don't be daft. Go to sleep. I'll try to convince them not to come running down here."

"Yes, please," Aysel said. The last thing she wanted was for her mother to see her as she was. Or have to admit to them she had managed to give away the most important secret they had to keep. Perhaps staying wasn't such a bad idea.

"Let me take care of her poultice, then you can ride up with me." Bashir got to his feet. Mathei nodded and crossed between the two beds to crouch near Aysel's head. Bashir folded the blanket back and rolled the poultice up, then pulled the blanket back into place.

"Do not scare me like that ever again," Mathei said, after Bashir left the little space, and put a hand on her hair.

"Sorry," she muttered.

"I hate you." He frowned.

Aysel grinned. "I hate you too." He nodded, then stood, rolling his shoulders. "Mat"—Aysel propped herself on her elbows—"thank you." He'd revealed his power in front of strangers to save her, risked his life to use a spell he had only examined in theories. Magic was dangerous to toy with. Mages lost their lives casting spells they did not know the cost of, drained to the bone of magic and energy.

"Go to sleep," he ordered, and passed Bashir as he stepped back through the curtains. Bashir watched Mat's back for a moment, then dropped to a knee beside Aysel's bed.

"Do you need anything?" he asked.

Aysel traced his face with her gaze. They had things to discuss. She wanted to tell him she regretted running from him after he found out about Kadir's estate, she wanted to tell him a number of things. And she wanted to know where they stood, now. What was he going to do about her being a Charah?

And of course, what would happen to Kadir? She realized she still hadn't told him.

"The Grand Vizier spelled a lock, or someone did. It exploded when I tried to pick it."

The warmth disappeared from Bashir's face, then anger hardened the lines of his expression. "Enchanting is outlawed. No wonder he wouldn't let me come to his estate." He added a curse under his breath.

"I also saw a medallion like the one I gave you on his desk, stamped with the Rahal insignia, but didn't realize it until later. I tried to go back, but there were too many guards. I doubt he's left it lying around, now that his men have made their move."

"I'll tell the Sultana."

Aysel could see his regret, his anger at himself for the missed opportunity. She laid her head on her bent arm and reached the other to him, tapping a finger against his temple.

"I will find something else." She tried to grin, but couldn't. He frowned at the floor. "Oh. Someone saw me, he was—"

"Cemil. The Grand Vizier's son. Did he say anything to you?" His voice revealed exactly how he felt about the man. It was not a tone Aysel would ever want Bashir to use to say her name.

"He offered to let me out the front door, then tried to incinerate me," she said.

Bashir's jaw twitched, his eyes narrowed, then the expression was gone. He touched her hair, circling a thumb over her temple.

"Are you coming back?" she asked, softly.

"Will you be here if I do?"

She wasn't certain he was teasing. Aysel nodded gravely.

"Then I will, as long as they don't put me in the Cliffs for failure to protect the Sultana." He dug his fingers into her hair, sending little sizzles of awareness over her skin.

"You didn't fail. And if they do, I will break you out," Aysel promised. Something fierce lit in his eyes and he leaned toward her. Aysel lifted her head in anticipation of another kiss.

"I hope you aren't doing anything that will prove to your dear mother I am absolutely the worst choice for chaperon," Mat said in sing-song from somewhere on the other side of the curtains. Bashir's eyes narrowed, and Aysel smiled a little. Mathei was a poor choice for chaperon. As long as he had a book or something to entertain himself, he didn't give half a spin about what went on around him.

"I'll be back." Bashir stood.

Aysel laid her head on the pillow, listening as they shuffled about. The door closed and silence buzzed in her ears. She hadn't slept in silence since they'd escaped the estate in Sarkum. There was always noise, people talking, moving about, a bit of chaos to lull her to sleep. How could she rest when there was so much to do, so many questions to answer?

The most important of those was what to do about the Sultana and her Circle, but all Aysel could think about was Bashir, and what to do about him.

Twenty-Two

After Bashir parted ways from Mathei in the courtyard, he went to the armory room. There, he retrieved the katil's sword. It had been stored there after the night he'd shot the assassin chasing Aysel. He took a moment to examine the gold medallion on its hilt. It should have been inset, one solid piece. But it wasn't. The top part, with the Rahal crest, did not sit flush with the hilt. Bashir drew his knife from its place on his belt and pried at the medallion with its tip. It popped off, held in place only by five little spots of soft metal someone had used to secure it in place. He retrieved the stamped medallion from the floor and took it and the sword with him as he headed for the palace.

What a complete, ox-headed fool he had been.

They could have had Kadir, with evidence. If he'd listened to Aysel, he could have taken guards to Kadir's house the next day to retrieve the stamped medallion that proved the link between Kadir and the assassins. But she had run from him and he'd been hardheaded and set on doing his duty.

"Bashir," Samira called to him when he was halfway to the Sultana's rooms. He turned. She strode down the carpeted hall behind him with a tray of coffee. Behind her, two more women carried trays of what appeared to be breakfast. He tried to smile. He owed her an apology as well. Samira returned it, with warmth to spare. "How is your friend?" she asked as they walked together toward the Sultana's rooms.

"I found her in time. I don't know what poison it was, but it nearly killed her."

"I'm glad she's all right." She looked at him sidelong with the same halfway-curious, halfway-knowing look he saw on his mother's face every time he mentioned a woman in more than passing. Bashir frowned at her, which was apparently enough to confirm her suspicion. Samira's face lit like a mage orb. "I've never met her. I only saw her that first day with the Sultana. She sounds very brave."

"Reckless," Bashir corrected. Reckless like her master, Makram. Aysel *was* brave. Brave and fierce and foolish. He didn't want to be away from her. He chaffed under the weight of the requirements he needed to fulfill when all he wanted was to lie next to her and watch her breathing. Every time he closed his eyes he could feel the limp, cold, lifeless weight of her in his arms.

"I think I would have expected someone softer," Samira said. "A quiet, proper, well-behaved herb wife."

Bashir raised an eyebrow at her. "I have no idea what you're talking about."

Samira made a sound in the back of her throat. "No?"

"It seems a bit late for breakfast."

Samira suppressed a smile. "I believe the Sultana and Charah Rahal were up late discussing matters. They've only just called for food," she said. Bashir scowled and blinked hard to try and clear away the images that brought to mind. "I also believe they've made up, as it concerns your fate."

"Should I be relieved?" Concern replaced his discomfort. What if the Sultana bowed to Makram's wishes? What if they relieved him of his position? He didn't know what he would do if he wasn't a guard at the palace. It was all he knew. Samira gave him an apologetic look to indicate she didn't know.

Two of Bashir's men saluted to him from either side of the door when he and Samira arrived at the Sultana's rooms. He knocked to save Samira the trouble of shifting her tray. The door opened, and Tareck looked from Samira to Bashir, then stepped back, opening the door wide.

"You have impeccable timing," Tareck said dryly, to Bashir.

"I heard they were up all night deliberating on my fate," Bashir returned, just as dryly. Tareck grimaced.

"We'll go with that." He shut the doors. Samira tsked as she swept past them and toward the table near the windows. Bashir tried to discern some hint of their decision from the look on Tareck's face, but was denied.

"How is our Kit?" Tareck asked, as they both stood near the door and watched Samira and the other two arrange the trays of food and coffee. She selected several items from the tray and put them on a little plate, which she brought to Tareck. He winked at her and she smiled, before returning to the table. "Ooo!" Tareck said under his breath when he saw a fig on the plate.

"Resting. How much have you heard?" Bashir raised his eyebrows as Tareck all but inhaled the food. He glanced at Samira in question, but she only smiled, then pointed to the array of breakfast. Bashir shook his head.

"Your lieutenant gave a thorough report this morning," Tareck said after finishing. "I knew Mathei had been experimenting with destruction spells to cure poison but was not certain how far he had gotten with it." Tareck scratched his jaw and set the plate aside on a little table against the wall. "I think I'll owe him an apology now for all those times I suggested his time studying was wasted."

"What else did Erol say?" Had Erol passed the news of what Aysel was to the Sultana yet? Surely Makram knew? Surely Tareck? They seemed nearly as close as family. Bashir did not know why their family kept the secret of Aysel's magic, but he did not wish to divulge it until he understood. Erol would be unlikely to think in a similar vein.

"That you found Aysel and took her to the Earth District for treatment, to your mother. Why didn't you bring her here?" Tareck asked.

The Sultana had made her appearance, striding into the room, fully dressed and put-together. There was not even a hair out of place to suggest she had spent her night doing anything but "discussing." Heat crawled up Bashir's neck, and he couldn't quite look at her.

"My mother was a midwife for many Turns, and began treating other ills when neighbors came to her. She's served the poor of Narfour for two decades and seen more fight wounds, diseases, maladies, and accidental injuries than your palace physicians will likely see in the rest of their lives. I couldn't trust Aysel's care to anybody but her." She had been an apprentice midwife when she met his father and had only had to take position in the brothel because she could not feed herself and a baby with an apprentice's pay.

"What have you there?" Tareck indicated the sword in Bashir's hand. Bashir handed it to him, then the medallion he'd broken off. "This is what Aysel discovered."

Tareck frowned, studying them, putting the medallion back in place and turning it over to look at the back.

"Commander," the Sultana said.

Bashir retrieved the items from Tareck and crossed the room toward her. He bowed and set the sword and seal on the table near the food. "This is fake. Aysel saw a stamped seal in the Grand Vizier's estate, but we agree he would not have left it there to be taken were I to conduct a search."

"No, he wouldn't." She picked up the counterfeit and examined it. "And he will make certain no one in the Council will take her word about what she saw. What a disaster." She tossed the medallion on the table and pressed her fingers to her forehead, hugging her other arm around herself as she rubbed the spot between her eyebrows.

Frustration. He could have helped in solving the problem of the Grand Vizier for her, and instead he'd only made things worse.

"Sultana. Forgive me. This is my fault."

"Not entirely, no. There were better ways to go about integrating Mistress Attiyeh into our planning, and you were following my orders." She turned to look toward her bedroom as she said it, a bit of accusation in her voice. Makram emerged just as she looked, buttoning the top of his caftan. He surveyed the room, his gaze going from Tareck, to Samira and her subordinates, to Bashir, then he said something under his breath about a moment's peace.

"I see you decided to throw a fête in the three heartbeats it took me to dress. Is that necessary?" He sauntered toward them, giving Bashir a look of irritation. "How is she?" He grabbed the pitcher of juice that sat on one of the trays and poured a glass, which he handed to the Sultana.

"You wouldn't know she was a breath away from death last night." Bashir said it without thinking, then felt the despair and aching desire to be near her roll through him again. He shook it off, lowering his gaze from them both. "She is under my mother's care. The wound itself was minor, and with the poison dealt with, I believe she will be on her feet in a day or so."

Makram poured himself a glass of juice and looked at Bashir as he drank it, slowly, his eyes narrowed over the glass. Bashir shifted, clasping his hands behind his back. He felt just as he had when he first met the Sultana and she had looked at him in that particular way that she could, as though everything inside someone was laid bare to her assessment. Apparently, she was rubbing off on her betrothed, because his gaze looked the same. Though much more frightening magic stirred in his eyes.

Makram finished his glass and set it on the table. The Sultana watched him with a raised eyebrow.

"Because Aysel Attiyeh so bravely risked her life to save both the Sultana and our commander of the guard, and because it seems her family is not in danger, you will pull your guardsmen from their watch on them. Her family will be allowed to settle in the city so that Elder Attiyeh may continue his service to me. I have informed him already. You will inform Aysel that when she is well enough, she is to report to the Sultana for assignment."

Would Aysel be pleased with that? What about her magic? He kept his face from reflecting his questions.

"And you," Makram said, "will see to it that you and your men get more rest, and that you request additional forces when you need them. I do not believe things would have happened as they had if you had been honest about your force's capability to keep up with the Sultana's demand, instead of trying to shoulder a burden you and they could not bear."

"Yes, Efendim." Bashir grit his teeth. He might have preferred a harsh punishment, to feel absolved from his mistakes and failures. Instead he was left to come to terms with them himself. That had to be the Sultana's doing, she favored forced introspection to something more physical and easily dealt with, like a caning.

"As for Kadir, pull your guards from his estates. Did Aysel manage to deal with the other assassin?"

Bashir shook his head. Makram rubbed his fingers across his forehead. "Fine. You and Aysel come up with a plan to find the bastard, and I want him alive. Perhaps I can convince him to give up his master. For the time being, I want the guards that were dedicated to the Attiyehs bulking up those assigned to the Sultana."

"Yes, Efendim." Bashir hesitated. "She did say something troubling." Makram and the Sultana both looked at him in expectation. "When she was in Kadir's estate, there was a lock on an interior door that had been…enchanted. It exploded when she tried to open the door."

Makram glanced at the Sultana, whose expression wavered between anger and disbelief. She sat on the sofa, touching her fingers to her temple. Bashir glanced furtively at Samira, whose face had washed of some of its color, her folded hands clenching together.

"I will need proof of this," the Sultana said, in a quiet, dangerous voice. Bashir nodded once. That she had not specified how he was to obtain proof spoke to how dire she considered the accusation. Aysel would likely be pleased at the opportunity to try again, though Bashir despised the idea of her going anywhere near Kadir. And his son. He glanced at Samira again. Color had returned to her cheeks in earnest. A flush of anger.

"I believe that is all," Makram said.

Bashir bowed, glancing back to the Sultana as he rose. She gave her head a tiny nod in agreement. He turned to go.

"Bashir," Makram said when Bashir grasped the handle of the door. He turned back. "Never again." No magic showed in his eyes or on his skin, but it was there, darkening his voice and making the two simple words into a violent threat.

"No, Efendim," Bashir agreed. He bowed again and stepped out, closing the door.

Bashir strode down the hall toward the guest quarters, where his men still stood watch outside the Attiyehs' suite. Weight lifted from his shoulders. He would not lose his position, at the very least. They had been too easy on him. But he would not waste this chance to redeem himself.

There was an entire day to fill before he could return to Aysel. There was also a bitter place, a dark spot, still angry, or hurt, that she had chosen to run from him rather than try to explain. He could not help but wonder if she would even stay at his mother's. She did not sit still well, and with the other assassin out there, it would not surprise him if he returned to find her gone, even with her injuries and all the questions between them.

He stopped in front of the Attiyeh suite and his men. "You are reassigned, for the time being, to the Sultana. There is at least one assassin who we believe participated in the attack at the refugee camp. Be on the lookout for distance attacks, especially. Be aware that they use poison." The two men saluted and left to obey.

Bashir knocked on the suite doors. They were answered by Adem, the steward, who did a fine job of hiding his accusatory look behind a mask of deference as he bowed.

"Commander." He stepped aside and Bashir strode past him, then excused himself to one of the bedrooms.

Mathei sat in almost the same position and place he had been the last time Bashir had entered the rooms. The light of day filtered brightly through the glass windows. Mathei's face was drawn, his skin pallid. His spell had drained him more than he had let on. Overextension seemed to be a family trait. Mathei eyed him as he entered the room.

"My parents have gone to the receiving room to discuss our sudden change in fortune. I assume you're here to collect your guardsmen?"

"I am," Bashir said. Mathei nodded, turning his attention back to his book. Bashir walked past the couch to the garden door and opened it. The two guards stationed there looked up as he stepped outside. He repeated his instructions to them, and they headed through the garden toward the main palace. Bashir went back inside and shut the door. He hesitated, staring at the back of Mathei's head, pondering whether to ask about Aysel's magic.

Mathei sighed and closed his book with a thump, tossing it on the table. "I find your breathing vexing. Say what you have to say."

Bashir stepped around the couch so they could look each other in the eyes.

"Why have you kept Aysel's magic a secret?"

"Because the man who rules Al-Nimas has a problem with being unendowed. Magically." Mathei waved a hand. "And presumably in other ways as well. Mages disappeared for less nefarious crimes than being a Charah. The man would rather go to war with his own brother than accept mages more powerful than himself. Why do you think we kept it a secret?"

"But the Sultana—"

"One does not waltz into a new land, after fleeing attempted murder in their own, particularly one who has been at odds with one's own for generations, and announce they are powerful enough to contest its current ruler." Mathei sniffed. "It is generally bad for one's health. I don't care how perfectly perfect everyone thinks your Sultana is, she is certainly imperfect enough to think twice before allowing a mage that could obliterate her to take up residence in her city."

"She is going to marry a destruction Charah," Bashir said. "I think he would be more threat to her than Aysel."

"Don't count on it. Aysel doesn't have a penis, or a weakness to luxurious eyelashes."

Bashir cleared his throat. "I'm glad to hear she doesn't have a…"

Before he could conceive of anything witty Mathei continued. "Aren't you though." Mathei met Bashir's gaze until Bashir flushed and had to look away. "Are you going to inform your Sultana, like a good commander? Or have you already?"

Bashir tamped down his rolling temper enough to maintain a polite tone. "You seemed interested in the Sultana restoring the Circle of Chara'a. I thought Aysel might wish to be part of that."

"I cannot speak for my sister. I did try to convince her, but you cannot undo a lifetime of hiding in one conversation. Perhaps you will have more luck, since Aysel does appear to have a weakness for big, broad shoulders, and a lust for unbearable broodiness. I've always said she had poor taste."

"How has no one ever run you through with a blade?" The man was just as maddening as Aysel, without any of the charm.

Mathei reached for his book, opening it in front of his face. "It is hard to impale someone who can reduce your weapon to rusted scraps before you've even finished the thrust." Mathei slowly turned a page. "Although I've been thinking about trying the eyes next time. It's just a change in phrasing and"—he snapped his fingers—"blind. A more lasting impression, I think. Though admittedly messier."

"Is that a threat?"

Mathei chuckled, setting the book against his stomach. "No. A threat would be something more along the lines of 'if you ever cause harm to my sister again, I'll rot your spoke and stones right off your body.'"

"We've moved on from my corpse as a tomb, have we?" Bashir said dryly.

"I've downgraded, yes." Mathei lifted the book. "Creativity is the exercise of a finely tuned mind."

"You and your sister are going to send me off the Wheel."

"We must all embrace our gifts, Commander," he said. "Feel free to see yourself out."

<hr>

Bashir and Erol sat at his desk, reviewing the day's events and the roster.

"There have been two more attacks on the refugee camp. Last night another fire attack, probably that same mage we couldn't catch yesterday," Erol said. "And this morning an angry mob trying to get past the guards. The mob can be handled, but the fire…it spreads quickly. All the oiled canvas and trash are perfect fuel. I think you should consider assigning all my Fifth House group to that rotation."

Bashir frowned as he studied his rosters. He did not need the lives of innocents on his conscience as well as a failure to protect his ruler. "Do it."

Erol nodded and they moved on from the camp to the other areas. As they worked, Bashir made a list of the areas he could augment with the City Watch or whoever the Sultana chose to help ease the palace guard's burden. It took him and Erol the rest of the day to re-work rosters for the Sultana, the refugee camp, and the palace.

"One of these days they'll give us some time off," Erol said at one point as he rubbed his eyes. "We should go hunt boar in the valley."

"They aren't out in the winter, Stone-Brains." Bashir laughed as he made a notation. "And they'd never let us both go." Boar hunting had been a summer tradition for the boys who grew up together in the neighborhood. Even Harun joined in, and when they were successful all the families got together to roast and eat it. Erol and Bashir hadn't been once since graduating from the University and joining the guard force. Bashir scowled. That was probably his fault.

"Good point. If we both left then Kasim would appoint himself in charge and declare a two-turn holiday." Erol laughed at his own joke but Bashir just shook his head. Most of his guards were good, solid men. He'd taken command at the beginning of spring, and had since weeded out those who were corrupt, known for taking bribes or slacking off. He'd paid special mind to those with ties to the Grand Vizier. That left him with a sadly depleted guard force, and a handful of men he'd like to be rid of and couldn't just for the sake of numbers. Kasim, for instance. One of the few remaining of the old guard who preferred the previous commander and his more relaxed standards.

The work and conversation kept Bashir's mind off Aysel but only barely. When they had completed the rosters and hung them in the barracks, Bashir turned to Erol.

"Did you speak to the Sultana about Aysel's magic?"

"You mean that she's a Charah?" Erol asked, as they walked toward the stables. He shook his head. "I assumed she knew, or that it was too big for a lieutenant to be reporting about. Why?"

"No reason," Bashir said with a forced casual tone. "She didn't mention it, so I wasn't certain if you had."

"Are you headed back to Havva's?" Erol asked. As a boy Erol had spent at least half his nights camped out on their living-room floor among the sitting cushions. The deviant was always hoping to catch a glimpse of one of Havva's brothel acquaintances. Or at least parts of them.

"Probably. The Sultana wants to know when Aysel will be well enough to return to the palace."

"Tell Aysel if she needs someone to comfort her, I am available." Erol grinned.

Bashir resisted the urge to slug his friend in the shoulder hard enough to knock him over. "I think you should look for someone else to comfort."

"The Wheel turns, he admits it." Erol laughed. "You think I'm a simpleton? You've never been so useless in your life," he said, and Bashir did punch him then. Erol stumbled sideways with a shout of pain. "Grumpy bastard," he said. "I'm only poking fun."

Bashir swiped his hand through his hair. "You and Samira have lost your minds." How was everyone else so certain something was going on between Aysel and him when he didn't know what to do with her?

Erol rubbed his shoulder, then rolled his eyes. "It doesn't surprise me," he said.

"What?"

"Aysel. I always knew you'd end up with someone who drove you crazy. You were always too good and respectful. You were the one standing up for everybody else when we were kids. Balance, my friend. You need a little crazy in your life." Erol slapped him on the back. "Though I personally wouldn't want someone so capable of stealing my purse whenever she wanted, but to each their own."

"Wouldn't you be more worried about the fact she wields a blade as well as you do?"

Erol chuckled. "I don't know, most of the women I've known are pretty handy with a kitchen knife at the very least. And my anne is well known for her prowess with a wooden spoon." He winced. Oh yes, Bashir had been at the wrong end of that spoon after the barley wine incident.

"If you're finished with your lecture? I still need to get down to the pier to update Ela."

"Just go." Erol pointed toward the stables. "Get it out of your system one way or the other, would you? We could use you back with your full faculties sooner rather than later."

Bashir shifted his foot across the gravel, initiating a push of his power that knocked Erol off his feet.

"And a good evening to you too," he rasped from his back as Bashir strode away.

Twenty-three

IT WAS WELL PAST time for sleep when Bashir made it from the pier to his mother's house. He spent a bit of time unsaddling his horse and switching his bridle for a rope halter, to smooth his thoughts. There were so many things in his head, he didn't even know what he was going to do. They would be asleep, and there were no beds besides his mother's and his, which Aysel had taken up. He could just look at her, reassure himself that she had kept her promise to stay, that she was still whole and healing, then he could return to his room in the barracks.

The house was dark but for the amber glass lamp his mother left lit, so people would know they were welcome if they needed her. He opened the door quietly and slipped in, then eased it shut behind him. The house was still, and he navigated carefully through the kitchen and living area to avoid disturbing it with clomping boots or over-turned furniture. He'd been less careful in his teens and paid for it in extra chores and withering looks.

The curtain that sectioned off the sleeping area was pulled closed, as was his mother's, suggesting she was sleeping, and not out sewing up a drunk after a fight.

Aysel's curtain was open, revealing her curled into a tight ball beneath a mound of blankets, her face buried against the pillow and obscured by her hair. He didn't want to disturb her, neither did he want to leave. She was charming when she slept, and he could almost imagine her as she might have been as a girl.

"It is dangerous for a man to loom over a woman's bed in the dark like that," Aysel mumbled, and pulled her hand from under her pillow, brandishing one of her knives at him. "Don't make me leave this glorious pillow to correct you."

"I don't know that I've ever thought that pillow was glorious." Bashir willed a minor dampening into place around them so they would not wake his mother.

"Then you have never slept for several small turns without one." She slipped the knife beneath the pillow again and brushed the tangle of curls out of her face, tilting her head to look up at him. "I hope you weren't standing there long, drooling over me."

"I'm certain I've never drooled over a woman." He sat on the edge of the bed. Aysel propped her head in her hand.

"Did you come to make certain I hadn't run off to hunt down an assassin?" She lifted her other hand, and ran her thumb across the embroidered tiraz that circled his upper arm.

"I think so," he said, his thoughts stuttering as she closed her hand around his arm and squeezed, then gave a soft sound of pleasure and a wicked grin. His body and mind were tired, but not so tired that the greedy look on her face didn't make him want to put her beneath him this instant.

She sat up, scooping her hair over one shoulder. "It would be very difficult to go running about the city in half my clothes, and this great billowing tent of a caftan." She plucked at it, and he saw that it hung half off her, baring the slope of her neck, her collarbone, and one shoulder nearly to the elbow. His thoughts fell more off track, a slow pulse of heat beginning in his groin. He concentrated on his dampening spell.

"But I had hoped you might start to trust me when I promise you something." Her eyes found his, her expression grave, though she did push her bottom lip out in a mock pout that nearly knocked his breath from his lungs.

"You choose to run instead of explain. You choose to sneak instead of address things head on. You'd rather be by yourself than have help. You hide who you are, what you are," he said. "I don't know what to do with you."

"You had your orders, and I had mine. Some of those things are because of what I do, Bashir. And I knew you wouldn't listen to me." She held his gaze. "Would you have?"

"No," he said. "Forgive me. I should have listened to you. I should have listened to my instincts, just as you and the prince said. If I had…" He reached toward her back, but stopped.

"I'd like a chance for you and me to be on the same side. Am I off the Sultana's list of criminals?" She stopped as if listening, then glanced up and around, and frowned, and he felt her exploratory swipe of air magic across his dampening spell. She raised an eyebrow.

"Anne can be a bit of a bear if you wake her for no reason."

"She isn't here," Aysel said. "A frantic child burst in a few candle-marks ago and announced that his mother was in labor."

Bashir released his dampening spell, and considered that without his mother there, even asleep, it was one less thing to hold him back from Aysel. Whether that was a good thing or a bad thing…

"To your question, you are off the list of criminals, in fact I think she intends to give you my position." He watched her horror turn to realization that he was teasing, then she scrunched her face at him in mocking reprimand. "I'm thinking of taking up a cart as a sweets vendor." He wanted to touch her, especially after reminding himself of watching her with that infernal piece of candy.

Aysel laughed, softly, giving him a knowing look that held the heat of her own memories.

"The prince said to tell you that you would be reporting to the Sultana for assignment. I assume that means you are now a sanctioned spy."

"Oh. Spies outrank guardsmen, don't they?" She slipped behind him, kneeling, and hooked her chin over his shoulder, her hands closing in the back of his caftan. The slow pulse of heat deepened, becoming an ache, and he gripped the edge of the mattress in his fists to prevent himself turning to grab for her. "Will you have to follow my orders?"

"I will never follow the orders of a woman who is not even tall enough to look me in the eye."

"I think you are forgetting"—Aysel shifted behind him, her hands slipping to his shoulders—"that I can, and have, looked you in the eye." She twined her legs around his waist from behind, laying her feet against his thighs. Her legs were bare, her honeyed skin taunting him with his desire to touch her. "Remember?" she whispered, and her hands slid down his back, then made their way back up, slowly, her fingers digging into the muscles along his spine.

"I remember." He barely recognized his own voice. The memory of her wrapped around him, her hips against his, her soft, unbearable mouth. She rubbed the heel of her palms into the broad muscles between his shoulder blades and Bashir felt he might melt to the floor. How was she so adept at finding ways to torture him into oblivion? They hardly knew each other. Yet she had always felt familiar, things between them easy, even if they were complicated, as if it all fit together.

That had never happened to him before, and he had not even realized it was happening until he was threatened with the absence of her. She pressed her thumbs in small circles at the base of his neck, and one of her feet slid up and down his thigh, between his knee and his hip.

"What are you doing?" He released his grip on the mattress and wrapped his hands around her ankles. She felt so small in his grip.

So breakable. But she wasn't, and he wanted her all the more for her strength.

"I am thanking you for coming to find me and saving my life. I am also apologizing for breaking your trust. I…" Her hands stopped, then slipped down and under his arms and around him. She clasped her wrists, laying her head against his back. "I wanted to tell you, to explain. Makram forbade me. I think I hurt you, and I don't…" She sighed. "I found the idea made me unhappy."

All his uncertainty melted away, replaced with wild desire that consumed him instantly, burning everything in him down to nothing except the primal want of her. "You're making it difficult for me to leave," he said. In fact she was making it impossible. His self-control was eroded to the barest of threads, his exhaustion overtaking what small part of his mind was not consumed with lust.

"Then stay." She nuzzled her face against his back. "I'm cold."

"You are also injured." He was not cold. He was burning up from the inside out. "You should rest."

"Stay," she said. "I'll behave if that's what you want. But stay."

"No." Bashir carefully unwound her legs from his waist, gently urged her hands apart, and stood. He turned to face her, fully aware his magic was unleashed, making it obvious the effect she had on him. She sat with her arms around her shins, the caftan pulled down over them for modesty, her chin resting on her knees. Disappointment furrowed her brow. Her toes peeked out from beneath the hem of the caftan, and what was left of his control was utterly undone.

"I meant, no, I don't want you to behave." He unbuckled his sword belt, slinging it on the floor beside her weapons, then unwound the cloth at his waist. Aysel watched him without speaking, her gaze following each movement but the rest of her was completely still. He turned to pull the curtain closed at his back, then unbuttoned his caftan and shrugged out of it, tossing it with the other things. He toed out of his boots as he pulled the second, lighter-weight caftan over his head and threw it on the pile of clothes, leaving only his salvar. Aysel uncoiled, moving as effortlessly as a dancer as she lowered one slim leg over the edge of the mattress, then stood and moved to him in one flowing movement.

"Oh, Wheel," she said, the breathless awe in her voice stoking his ego and his lust. "Let me touch you."

"I want your hands on me more than I want breath," he said, catching her wrists and lifting her hands to his torso. Aysel ran her palms across his chest, down his ribs, cold heat rippling through him at her touch.

"What I want requires breathing," Aysel replied, and tipped her head to look up at him. Bashir lifted his hand, grazing his fingers and thumb up the slender column of her throat, then traced the curve of her jaw with his thumb. Her lips parted as she inhaled, then came the barest flash of lightning in the depths of her eyes. Magic.

"Your brother asked me to null your magic while he cast his spell on you," Bashir said. Aysel lowered her chin. "You are lightning and storm. Did you know that?" He was beginning to suspect Aysel did not know her power the way other mages knew theirs. If she had spent her life in hiding, it would explain her ability to disguise it completely within herself so that even he could not sense it. He had never heard of an air mage who could control lightning, but he had never known a First House Charah, either.

"No," she said. She was the stuff of legends. Old stories, proof the Sultana was right about the Wheel. And Bashir did not care a wit.

"Let me see you." He needed to know he affected her the way she did him, until her control was threadbare, and her magic unleashed in her passion. The languor disappeared from her demeanor, replaced with tension.

"I don't know if I can…" She shook her head. "If I let go, I don't know if I can control it. I've never tried."

"All right," he said. He had all night to convince her she was safe with him, or as many nights as it took. He longed for that, for nights that belonged to them. He'd wanted only one night, to cool the fire stoked between them, but now…he wasn't certain it would be enough. "You should know you never have to hide yourself from me."

Her expression softened, and she searched his face. Then she stood on tiptoe and caught his face between her hands, pulling him to her for a kiss. Her mouth was soft, gentle, taking slow, lingering strokes over his that numbed him to everything but her, where she touched him, where the heat of her reached him in the space between them, the suggestion of her naked body beneath the too-big caftan.

"And you should know I'm growing very fond of you," she whispered as she withdrew enough to lift her eyes to his.

Something inside him cracked open, something fragile, and hopeful, and he stared at her, at the pale, fleeting flicker of lightning in her eyes and knew, down to his marrow, that she could break him open if she chose to.

"Good. Are you finished torturing me?"

"Who's being tortured? Do you have any idea how breathtaking you are?" She lowered her hand from his face to trace a jagged, glowing line of his unleashed magic where it zigzagged across his chest and down his abdomen. "It's been all I could do to keep my hands off you." Even her slightest touch commanded his body to attention.

"You shouldn't have." Bashir gripped her hips and urged her backwards toward the bed.

"You were so very serious. It's hard to pet someone when they are threatening to put you in prison. But I thought about it." She slid both hands down his chest. "A great deal."

"And I have wanted you"—he tugged at the caftan, lifting it up her body—"until I am a useless wreck."

Aysel raised her arms, and he pulled the caftan off her completely. There was nothing underneath. No cloth binding her chest, no small clothes, not even a chemise. Bashir nearly picked her up and threw her on the bed, but he wasn't certain she could lie on her back because of her wound, and it would not be a pleasant start to things to cause her pain.

He traced the shape of her with his hands instead, the small swell of her breasts, the dip of her waist, the slight curve of her hips. She was not a woman built of soft, padded places. Everywhere he touched was lean strength, a body honed to its craft. Beautiful. He pulled her against him, easing the ache of his arousal against the taut sweep of her belly. Aysel leaned into him, her bared breasts moving against him as she clasped her arms around his neck.

She pressed a series of soft kisses against his chest, within the circle of her arms. Bright bursts opened over his skin with each of her kisses. He shivered and she released her grip on his neck, trailing her fingers down his torso, and hooking them into the top of his salvar. She lifted one leg onto the bed behind her, then the other, so she was kneeling, and continued shifting backwards as she urged him to follow. Bashir knelt in front of her, and shoved his hands into her hair, closing handfuls of it in his fists and tilting her head back as he pressed himself as close to her as he could.

"Aysel," he breathed, and kissed her. Her arms went around him, and she dragged her nails down his back, sending fire and lightning straight between his legs. Without thinking, he kissed her harder, bending his body over hers with intention of laying her back, sliding one hand free of her hair to skate down her body to her thigh. He lifted it to his hip, and remembered her wounds.

"Can I lay you down?" he asked, guiding her leg as she circled it around his hips.

"Just no dragging me about." She smiled a little, and nipped a line along his jaw. "The stitches catch on the sheet."

Bashir closed his eyes as she continued her nips, and they became warm, sucking kisses across his throat. He slid his hand up the back of her thigh and dug his fingers against the flesh of her backside. Her muscles tensed and flexed beneath his hand as she slung her arms around his neck and lifted her other leg off the mattress to wrap around his hips. Bashir felt his magic begin to unwind, the wall he kept it behind cracking like a dam under pressure.

"I like how you climb me." He laughed softly into her hair as he let her fall slowly back against the bed and held himself over her on all fours. Her eyes were half-closed as she looked up at him, and lightning snapped between her lashes. Bashir nuzzled his face against her neck to hide his smile.

"Any woman who sees you and claims not to want to climb you like a tree is a damned liar," Aysel said.

Bashir grinned, and kissed her again, running his hands up her arms, tracing them above her head, and pinning her wrists together with one of his hands. Aysel tipped her head back against the mattress to see, then lowered her chin and tilted her head to look down the length of him.

"I thought you wanted me to touch you," she cajoled, and unwound one leg from his hips, pulling down with the other to urge him toward her. Bashir obeyed, stretching his legs out along hers, and regretted leaving his salvar on, because he wanted her naked legs on his, the soft skin of her thighs cradling and torturing his aching erection.

"Me first," Bashir said, smoothing a hand up the curve of her waist. Her lithe body, whipcord and strong, shifted restlessly beneath him. He traced the outline of her left breast, small and perfect as he cupped it against his palm. Aysel's breath slipped out in a gasp, and she arched against his touch, her eyes closing as she bit her bottom lip. "You destroy me when you do that." He touched his fingers to her mouth as she slid her lip between her teeth. She kissed his fingertips, then nipped them as she opened her eyes to look at him.

"I'll remember that." Half promise, half threat in her tone.

Bashir kissed her throat, then a circle around one breast, and the other. Aysel arched into him, her leg cinching around his hips, pressing the apex of her thighs to him, her arms flexing against his grip. He took one tightened nipple into his mouth, circling it with his tongue, and Aysel bucked, her skin prickling under his touch. A low, soft moan issued from her throat. He closed his eyes, wrestling his body's surge of impatience.

Bashir lifted his hips enough from hers to slide himself against the warm, silken skin of her inner thigh. He wanted her now, but he also wanted all the touches and caresses he could possibly manage in one night. He turned his attention to her other breast, replacing his mouth with his hand on the first. As he did, he slid his erection against the wet heat between her thighs that he could feel even through the fabric of his salvar, and Aysel's body tightened beneath him like a bowstring. Her breath rushed out; her hips tilted up in silent request for more. Her hands twisted in his grip. Bashir bit her nipple, in gentle reprimand, drawing it between his teeth, and she shook, her other leg lifting around his hips, his name leaving her mouth as a breath.

Heat stroked through him, hearing her say his name like he had always wanted her to. He wanted her. He wanted inside her, he wanted his magic and hands all over her skin. He needed the storm and wildness of her, he needed the way she broke him apart.

"I want to touch you," Aysel pleaded, flexing her hands against his grip again. He loosened his hold on her wrists and she jerked them free, tangling her fingers into his hair and pulling his mouth to hers. Bashir laughed softly, falling to his elbows over her, and returned her breathless kisses. Her fingers slid from his hair, her blunt nails trailing down his neck and back, then raking up his sides to urge him up. She was too short and he too tall for them to fit perfectly together. He could not kiss her and nestle his hips against her. When he shifted as she demanded, her legs tightened around his hips and drove them against hers, her nails raking down his back. Bashir reared back with a gasp, a nip of pain from her nails with a wash of pleasure after threatening to break his battered control and send him over the edge.

"Careful," he warned, as she looked up at him with storm and desire in her eyes, "I have been on the edge because of you for too long."

"We can forgive each other if things do not go perfectly this time, can't we?" She traced light fingertips in the wake of her scratches, sending shivers across his body. "I have never shied away from practice."

She smiled her teasing smile, this one made smoldering by her lowered lashes and her fingers slipping beneath the waistband of his salvar, her nails scratching lightly and slowly near his tailbone. It had the effect of sending pulses of pleasure and need through his hips and thighs, and he had to blink and take slow, deep breaths to think of anything but plunging into her.

"I respect your dedication a great deal." Bashir raised up on his knees, and Aysel immediately reached for the waist tie of his salvar, her little fingers quick and deft as she untied them.

"You have too much sense and control left," Bashir accused as she pushed against the fabric. "I'm not doing something right."

"I must be good with my hands even under pressure," she purred, and tried to shift to get better leverage to push his salvar down. "You're doing everything right."

Bashir shifted and dropped to his back beside her, and the bed bucked, bouncing her a little. Aysel giggled, and he shoved the salvar over his hips. She sat up, crawling down to tug the fabric off his legs and toss it to the floor. The view of her, on her hands and knees, the backs of her thighs, the perfect curve of her backside, the glimpse of her sex just before she turned to crawl up his body, turned his grip on his magic to dust.

"You're trying to kill me," he croaked, reaching for her as she knelt over his hips. Aysel shook her head, and her hair swept back and forth across her breasts. Bashir grabbed her hips, adjusting her against him, and the damp heat of her slipping along the length of his erection made him grit his teeth against a rolling wave of desire. He closed his eyes and held still beneath her, breathing, as magic swirled inside of him and broke over his skin.

"Look at you," Aysel breathed, sliding her hands over his stomach, and chest, and down his arms. Her fingers traced the jagged, pulsing lines of his magic as it fractured over his skin, her touch igniting fire and lightning, until there wasn't a thought left in his head but need. She retraced her touches, her palms flat against his skin as she slid them up toward his throat, pausing to rub the pads of her thumbs over his nipples. Bashir moaned a coarse word, sliding his hands from her hips to her breasts, then around to her shoulders, to pull her down on top of him, tangling his hands in her hair and gathering it into one fist to pull her head to the side and bite her neck.

"Oh." Aysel curled against him, shuddering, as he bit her again, not hard, just enough to redden her skin. "Oh," she moaned, and he rolled her onto her side, kissing where he had bitten, half covering her with his own body and marveling again at how small she was. But then she undulated against him, her breasts nudging his chest, her legs tangling with his, one little hand circling his erection and gripping him in demand.

"Aysel," he growled, as she stroked her fingers over his length. He buried his face against her neck as shudders of relief and pleasure tightened his muscles.

"Nothing about you is small, is it?" she whispered in his ear, her breath slipping across his neck and sending another shiver rippling through him. Her thumb traced exquisite circles around the head, along the unbearably sensitive tip, bringing him to an edge he needed and did not want, not yet, and not like this.

"You are small," he muttered, nonsensically.

Aysel laughed, tracing his jaw with kisses, releasing her grip on his cock to slide her hand up his side and over his chest, letting it rest upon the other side of his jaw, her fingertips tracing his ear and the sensitive skin below it.

"I am," she said. "Shall we see if we fit together?" Aysel touched her mouth to his, and he caught her lower lip in his teeth, pressing her onto her back. He reached between them to return the favor of her intimate touches, to give himself time to relax, and to make certain she was ready for him. He slid his fingers across the soft skin of her mound, tracing the warm, wet evidence of her arousal up her inner thighs. Her legs shifted apart in invitation that, for a moment, made him forget what he was doing.

"You don't know what you do to me." He rubbed slow circles across the small, sensitive nub at the center of her pleasure. Aysel gasped, arching her head back, then bending her knees up and squeezing them together, forcing him to stop until she relaxed and freed his hand. Bashir began again, slipping a finger between her folds, and tipping his head to hers as he relished the feel of her. Her leg that was nearest him hooked over his and rubbed up and down with the rhythm of his touches. Aysel opened her eyes and met his gaze, her hands clasping the back of his neck. Streaks of lightning shattered the stormy colors of her irises, and he became aware that the hair on his arms was standing on end. Bashir bared his teeth at her in pride. He liked that she was coming undone at his hands. "There you are."

Her fingers dug into his neck, and her body molded to his as he slid on top of her. She spread her legs as he fit himself to her and moved in a slow rhythm, teasing and torturing them both. He paused to kiss her, suggesting with his mouth what he would like to do with his body. Aysel gave a plaintive mewl, pressing her calves down the backs of his thighs, and her nails down his spine, nipping his neck. When he could bear it no longer, he lifted up enough to slide an arm beneath her hips, and Aysel reached down to help guide him to her.

He planned to tease her more, to torture her like she did him, to take an age sliding into her. He pressed into the slick, burning heat of her, just a fraction, and forgot who he was, and where he was, and anything else as her magic flashed in streaks across her skin. Shimmering lightning like stripes painted her in blue and white, dazzling his vision and sparking against his own. She said his name, gripping handfuls of the sheets as her legs tightened around his hips and drove him fully into her. Ecstasy, the heat and grip of her across the painfully hard length of him nearly finished him, and he gathered her in his arms and lifted her up as he sat back on his heels to take a moment.

"You're beautiful," he breathed, gripping the back of her neck in one hand and tracing his other across the paths of white fire on her skin. "I need you."

"I'm here." Aysel touched her nose to his. "And we fit very well." She took a breath, and he rejoiced in the deep flush across her chest and cheeks. She put her hands on his chest and pushed, and he lay back, sliding his hands down her arms, then twining his fingers with hers. She lifted herself off him while he stretched his legs out, and his body raged at the separation. He thought she'd fit them together immediately, but instead she slid back, down his legs, tugging her fingers free of his. He knew what she intended, and he'd imagined it dozens of times. Her mouth…

Bashir grabbed her by the elbows. "Next time," he said. She paused, looking at him, wild lightning flashing like a summer storm over the sea in her eyes, and wrapped her hand around the base of him. She drew her lips across the tip of his erection, from one corner of her mouth to the other, and everything in him clenched, and shuddered, and he grit his teeth. "I've changed my mind," he gasped.

"Hmm." Aysel slid back up, her breasts like silk against his chest, her belly gliding against the now-painful ache of his arousal. "Next time."

"You love that," he accused, taking handfuls of her backside and coaxing her knees up against his ribs, wanting her so badly he could hardly see straight. "You love torturing me and leading me around by the nose. Are you always like this?" He wanted more of it, of everything she offered him, the gorgeous, unbearable, joyful pain of what she could do to him.

"I like to play with you, Ox." Aysel's voice whispered wind and storms, magic echoing her words, its spark and flash dancing in electric opposition against his own power and making his skin feel almost too sensitive. "But only if you like to play too."

"I do," he said, pushing her back, guiding her hips to his and reaching between them again to fit them together. "I love what you do to me."

She lifted her chest from his, her hands on his arms, and sank against him, and he was enveloped in the blazing, silken heat of her again and it felt like the only thing he had ever wanted in his life. She folded her legs beneath her, to either side of his hips, and he gripped her hands again, pulling them up and holding them near his shoulders, so she leaned over him. Her hair fell around her face, chestnut curls made wild by the electric pulse of her power. With each rock of her body against him, nips of lightning zipped across his skin, skimming the edges of his power, which flared in protective response, and he wondered what it would do to him if he were not an earth mage.

Moving with her was like nothing he had ever experienced. He had never been with an air mage. Her magic and his seemed to dance together one moment and battle the next, so that the edge they rode shifted from pleasure that he thought might end him, then moments of too much, almost to the edge of pain, like being plunged into a river of ice. Aysel occasionally whispered a quiet spell to contain her magic, but she also said his name, pressing her forehead to his throat.

Because she was on top of him, she controlled the pace, and apparently in this she preferred slow, measured torture, that was the best and worst thing that had ever happened to him. And when Bashir was certain if he did not release his hold on himself soon he was simply going to stop existing, he could feel the change in her, the tightening of her core around him, the strength of her legs around his hips, and her whispered spell became choked.

Aysel's fingers squeezed his, her breath catching, her body tensing.

"Bashir." She was not saying his name in pleasure, but in fear, and he released her hands and pulled her flat on top of him, wrapping his arms across her back. "I can't hold it and keep doing this with you." She sounded bewildered and ashamed. She was afraid of her magic.

"I have you, I can hold it, you don't have to." He ran his hand down her back, lifting it over her wound, to settle on her hip. He did the same with the other. "Trust me?"

"If I hurt you…" She met his gaze.

"I am stone and earth, Little Storm. You can't hurt me."

"Big Storm," she said. Then Aysel closed her eyes, her brow furrowing, and magic flared across her skin once more, striping down her brow and through her eyes like warpaint. When she opened them to look at him, her steel and hazel eyes were lit with skyfire. "I trust you."

When he tipped her hips against his, settling deeper in her, she let out a throaty sound and buried her head against his chest, her fingers digging into his shoulders. He closed his eyes, helping her move, slower than he wanted, but they both needed the pace so he could tangle his power around hers, confining it to the small space around them, tamping back the sheer force of it with the opposition of his. She was wild storms and fast lightning. He was steady earth and slow change. Some said mages in opposition could not be together, and it was rare to see them so. But Bashir thought, as the joyful pleasure of her overtook him, that in this case, they were perfectly matched.

Aysel's hands tightened against his shoulders, then swept down his arms to grip his wrists where he held her hips, her nails biting against his pulse, and her legs squeezed around him. He felt her magic building toward an outpouring as if in mirror to his own, and Aysel arched her back, lifting her head and letting out a long, shallow cry. Her climax forced his, dragging him deeper into her, sending waves like after-shocks through every muscle in his body. Everything in him locked for an instant and all the tension he'd been carrying broke across him, and he cried out, holding her hips hard to his as he tumbled through crash after crash of pleasure and release and his power erupted out of his hold. Aysel's opened around them at the same moment, and it was as if he'd been tossed into the heart of a thunderstorm as he scrambled in his mind for control of himself and the unbelievable surge of electric power that burst out of Aysel.

Bashir let go of his own magic to hold hers, the greater threat of the two, and arcs of lightning coursed over her, and him, and across the shield of his magic he threw around them. His unleashed power rolled through the house, and it shook, and Aysel squealed when a section of cracked plaster fell from the ceiling into her hair, releasing her grip on his wrists and throwing her arms over her head.

"Ow!" she said. "Spokes," she swore. Then she started laughing in between gulps of air and collapsed against him as he lay in a wrung-out stupor. He felt her pull her magic back under her own control and he released his hold on it with relief. Another aftershock of pleasure rolled through him at the release, and the house creaked as his magical grip eased and the stones settled. Something in the kitchen smashed. Bashir didn't even have the energy to wince.

"Somebody once told me that earth mages are boring lovers," Aysel breathed in his ear as he stared up at the ceiling. She nipped his ear-lobe and bent her legs up, crossing them at the ankles. Then she gave a deep, satisfied sigh that was all the praise he needed. "Maybe we should be boring in a sturdier building next time. Or…outside?" She lifted her head to look at him.

He laughed, a little, because he didn't have the energy for a full laugh. Her hair was a complete, tangled mess, sticking out in every direction, with bits of plaster scattered in it. But there was a pretty streak of red across her cheeks and throat, and a look in her eyes he hoped he could put there countless more times.

Bashir lifted his hands and smoothed her hair back from her face, coaxing it into as much order as he could get without taming it, as she did, into some kind of braid. Aysel closed her eyes and rested her chin on her hands, which were folded over his chest. He picked at the plaster flecks, tossing them away.

"Was it horrible?" she asked. He frowned. "I mean holding my magic. Was it so horrible that you wouldn't"—her gaze flicked away and her voice faded—"want to again?"

Bashir slid his hands down her back and slapped one against the perfect, slim curve of her buttock. She jumped in surprise, her eyes wide as she looked down at him.

"Daft girl. I think I did an admirable job. Are you accusing me otherwise?" he said, massaging her offended flesh.

"But if you are concentrating on holding my magic, is it even enjoyable for you?"

Bashir laughed in disbelief. "I would have sworn you were with me just now, when I almost collapsed the house. I thought I was going to die. A good death." He was completely and utterly stripped of anything that resembled energy or vigor.

She let out a whisper of a laugh as she kissed a line down his chin and throat, her fingers sliding to trace the skin just below the swell of his chest. He'd believed she'd wrung him out completely, but a sluggish thread of heat twisted in his belly as her touch raised gooseflesh across his body. She sprang up, propping herself on her elbows on his chest. "I have never"—she looked innocently surprised—"not been able to hold my own magic."

"Never," he echoed. He was not certain whether he felt impressed with her control, or immensely prideful that he had been the first to affect her so. He settled on the last and grinned at her.

"Oh, he is proud of himself." She smiled, drawing a slow circle on his chest with a fingertip. "Bet you can't do it again."

"Is this you trying to assassinate me?" He closed his eyes. "There are worse ways to die, I suppose." He sat up, centering her over his lap. It would take some coaxing, but he could manage a second round, if it weren't for her power. "Let's sleep," he said, tipping her head back so he could graze his lips over the hollow of her throat. "Otherwise I don't think I'll be up to the task of holding you a second time."

"Pity." Aysel wrapped herself around him, her legs around his waist, her arms around his neck, and didn't say anything else for a few moments, while he caressed her body and pressed his forehead against hers. "Bashir?" she eventually whispered. He took a moment before he answered, relishing the sound of his name the way she inflected it, the way it felt to finally have this freedom between them.

"Hmm?"

"Did you tell the Sultana about me?"

He opened his eyes and lifted his head from hers so he could look at her. "No."

She searched his face, then lowered her gaze.

"Mathei told me why you hide."

"He didn't tell you I'm not even a good mage. I can control my magic, but I don't command it. That's why I needed your help with that katil, and just now. What good is a Charah who doesn't even know her own power? I'm only good at being a spy. And I don't think I want to be anything else."

"It's your choice. You are not the only Charah that has refused. She will not force you, but please don't ask me to keep secrets from her," Bashir said.

Aysel looked at him again, cocking her head and trailing her nails lightly against the nape of his neck. He liked how comfortable she was in her own skin, happy to sit naked with him and discuss something that mattered to her.

"You are very loyal to her."

"She has made a place for herself among people who do not want her, and has helped me do the same. When I took the exams to enter the University, I did it because I was mad at my mother. We couldn't afford it. But the Sultana saw how highly I scored and paid my way. And she gave me, a fatherless lowborn, a position in her guard because she saw potential when any other noble would just see a stable boy. I admire and respect her, and I owe her a great deal."

"Do you love her?" Aysel asked, gently, and without any hint that she would be offended by his honest answer.

Bashir tried not to laugh. He shook his head.

"She is beautiful." Aysel did not say it the way he'd heard some women say it, like it was bait for him to jump upon. Aysel said it the way one might say the grass was green or that the sun shone in the day. If she was jealous, it did not show in the least.

"She is. And you are beautiful," he said.

Aysel snorted and rolled her eyes. "Oh, of course. Is this the 'she mentioned another woman so I have to say it' compliment, or the 'she let me tumble her so I should say it' compliment?" Aysel flicked his earlobe. "I am not a sad, lost little refugee girl who needs obligatory compliments for her to suddenly realize she is a princess. Please don't insult my intelligence. I know what I am, and what I am not."

"I know." Bashir dug his fingers into her hair again. "You wear yourself well, whether you are dressed as a noblewoman, or a thief, or a Sarkum refugee, or in nothing at all." He slid a knuckle from her throat to her navel. "And I think you are the most maddeningly attractive, formidable woman I have ever met." He flicked her earlobe in retribution. "Your strength is beautiful. Your confidence is. Your mind." He searched her face with his gaze. "Many earth mages see beauty differently, did you know that?"

"I thought you were just a big dumb ox." Aysel pursed her lips. "Don't disabuse me of that, or I really will be in trouble."

"Poor Aysel," he teased.

"None of this matters anyway, because I would despise being like the Sultana, no matter which way I looked seeing some man making cow eyes at me." Aysel frowned in distaste.

Bashir laughed, sliding an arm under her backside and rising up on his knees, then he laid her down and settled on top of her. He wound a curl around his finger. "What if I don't want you to think I'm a big dumb ox?" He didn't look at her eyes as he spoke. It had been a long time since he had been nervous at the prospect of telling a woman he wanted to be with her, for more than trysting.

But Aysel…what if it scared her? Those who lived in the Fourth House, like him, were steady, and serious, and dependable. Most chose a partner young, and stayed faithful. The First House was notoriously detached or flighty, rarely known for their interest in romance or stability. And Aysel was storms. She ran. She could not sit still. His throat tightened. And she was a noble.

There could not be a worse match for him in the world. But Wheel help him, he wanted her, he couldn't pretend it wasn't so. If she wanted something different than that, he had to know now, he couldn't survive on pieces and scraps.

"I don't do casual very well," Bashir warned, his voice uneven.

The smile on her face tightened and she raised her hand toward his face, then hesitated before brushing his hair away from his brow. It was a tender touch, and Bashir felt buoyed by it, but Aysel only looked worried. "I have never done anything that wasn't," she said. It felt like an avalanche of stones dropped into his belly. "When you're trying to hide the very essence of who and what you are, it is impossible to have anything else."

"Is that how you prefer things?" Bashir tried to stay relaxed, tried not to let his thoughts travel through possible scenarios that would leave him a shredded mess.

"I don't know how to do anything else."

His breath left him in a slow stream. Better to get it out of the way now, than later, if his heart was completely in it. He should have said something sooner, before they lay together, but he was so exhausted, so stretched thin he knew he would never have had the presence of mind to do so.

She shifted beneath him and he rolled to his side to give her space. Aysel faced him, pressing the length of her body against his.

"There are a number of reasons it would be difficult for us to be together. Does that not bother you?" she asked.

Besides that she was air and he earth? That she was an ambiguous entity in the palace? Or perhaps because she was a noble. He brushed a hand down his face, growing irritable at the thought of her brother and his threats. He forgot sometimes that she was a noble. Perhaps she never forgot that he wasn't.

"Your parents would be ashamed if you were associated with the son of a whore?" Bashir rolled onto his back, away from her touch. Let it be any reason but that. He'd allowed himself to believe she wasn't like that.

Aysel sat up. "My parents have a son who loves men, and a daughter who acts like one. They are quite over being shocked," she said. "And you? Have you considered what it would be like to care for me, when you know I am doing dangerous things and you can do nothing to help, or to stop me?"

"I know your capabilities. I could handle it," Bashir bit out, and slung an arm over his eyes.

"Could you? You are a shield, Bashir."

He lifted his arm enough to peer at her from beneath it. "Pardon?"

"You are a shield. You have been standing in front of other people all your life in some misguided attempt to pay homage to the one person you couldn't protect. Your mother," Aysel said. "Imagine, if you will, lying alone some night. You know that I am out sneaking into the Grand Vizier's house. You will be lying there in the dark, imagining all the things that could happen to me if I am caught. I could be burned alive. I could be caught by a roving guard and shot down off a roof. I could mistime a landing and break all the bones in my legs, or even my neck—"

He surged, grabbing her wrists as he sat up, and gave her a hard shake. Aysel slid him a knowing, patient look.

"Stop," he said. He clutched her neck, touching his brow to hers. "Stop." His heart pounded, and his mouth was dry, and he needed her, desperately needed her so he could feel her heat and her power and banish the visceral memory of how cold and lifeless she had been after the poison.

"Bashir," she cajoled. "I would happily let you teach me how to be yours." She touched his face. "But I think you would die a thousand tiny deaths over time, unable to shield me."

Before he could respond, or even think of a response, the front door opened, signaling his mother's return. He wrapped Aysel in his arms and lay down, kicking the covers down and away. She was soft and malleable in his embrace and tucked her face into the space between his jaw and neck, tracing his skin with soft brushes of her lips. He hooked the blankets with one foot and managed to pull them up over both Aysel and himself.

From the kitchen came his mother's exasperated sigh, and he remembered the sound of something smashing to pieces as his unbound power shook the house. Bashir rubbed a hand down his face. She was going to shout him into the next district in the morning.

Aysel gave a breathy giggle against his throat, and his heart leapt up, lodging somewhere near where her lips touched his skin. She wasn't wrong, and it made the inside of him rage in impotent fury. What was the Wheel's purpose in torturing him with her? Had he not been dealt enough broken turns in his life?

"When you hold me…" Aysel breathed, "it feels good to hold still."

Bashir squeezed his eyes shut and hugged her harder. Aysel shifted, pushing her hands against his chest, and he rolled to his back. She draped herself over him. Her hair blanketed his chest, and one hand drew little circles on his shoulder, her thigh across his belly and her foot nestled against his thigh. She fit like that, against him, as if she'd been made to, and even his magic settled with a kind of slow rumble down his spine.

"Stay," he sighed. If she was gone when he woke up…

She slipped a hand down his arm and found his. He laced his fingers with hers, and she squeezed. It was promise enough.

TWENTY-FOUR

AYSEL WOKE BENEATH THE weight of a mountain. She was halfway onto her belly, one leg cocked up toward her chest, as though she had attempted to roll away from Bashir in the night and he had pinned her before she completed the move. His chest was against her back, his arm, as big around as her thigh, slung across her shoulder and his elbow bent, his hand curled around a handful of her hair. His leg lay across both of hers. She was utterly trapped. There would be no sneaking out the morning-after with this man. Not that she could imagine ever having that desire. She closed her eyes again as she slipped her hand beneath his where it gripped her hair. His hand tightened over hers, his fingers lacing in between her own, and he nuzzled his face into the crook of her neck.

"Are you here?" he mumbled.

Aysel opened her eyes. "I think so?" she whispered back.

"Just checking," he said in a sleepy rumble. "That you were real." He didn't sound entirely awake.

"Do you dream of me often that you would need to ask?" She pulled his hand to her lips and kissed his knuckles, one at a time. His hand dwarfed her own.

"Mmf."

Warm affection filled her and she wanted to turn and kiss him, but couldn't move. "That's very sw—"

"Nightmares of fuzzy little foxes stealing my money and my food and all my weapons."

She heard the grin in his voice, and when she shifted to roll toward him, he let her, meeting her scowl with laughing eyes and a happy grin. She shoved her hands against his chest, despite that he held her too close for any leverage, and he caught her wrists, lifting his head so he could guide her arms around his neck. Then he kissed her, silencing her irritation.

"Good morning, Little Storm," he said against her neck after he released her mouth, then he pressed his lips to her throat.

"Big Storm." Aysel nipped the tip of his nose in reprimand.

"I'm the big one. You're the little one." He slid a hand down her waist and grabbed a handful of her backside, urging her hips against him. The hard length of his arousal pressed against her leg. "So, you are my *little* storm." He curved his hand down her leg, coaxing it over his hip.

Wheel and spokes. She was in trouble. Her body warmed to even his simplest touches, the heat in his expression, the possessive way his gaze traveled her nakedness. What he'd done to her in the night had ruined her for any but him, his hands and mouth and voice and the steady thrum of his magic butting stubbornly against hers.

But...

He had admitted he couldn't separate caring from coupling, and she didn't want to hurt him. And in truth, she wasn't certain she could keep her affection from growing at the wild pace it already was. This would hurt them both. But Aysel didn't want to have to be the strong one and walk away. She didn't want to walk away. She wanted him.

Whatever of her thoughts showed on her face shuttered his, and the easiness with which he touched her disappeared. Bashir kissed her, roughly this time, pinning her beneath him and branding her with a kiss that was desperate, and angry, and hurt. This could not be what shaped the rest of their day. Aysel cupped his face in her hands and pulled him back a fraction. He resisted her, frowning.

"Shh." Aysel slipped her fingers through his hair, her eyes open so she could meet his gaze, and brushed her mouth softly over his. She told him in gentle, lingering touches of her lips that she did care, and he was not alone.

His big body relaxed onto her, and Aysel's breath came short under his weight. He hiked a knee up to lift his weight off her and took over the kiss, his thumbs stroking along her temples in slow measure.

The curtain on the side that faced the second bed flew open, and Aysel jerked in surprise, but Bashir only moaned, dropping his face into the pillow beside Aysel's head. She blinked up at Bashir's mother. In her healing and the few other interactions between them, Aysel would have described her expression as gentle but matter of fact, warm, and practical. Right now, it was hard as granite and warm as pack ice at the mountain pass.

"Anne," Bashir protested into the pillow. Beneath the blanket, Aysel gripped his shoulders, not certain if she was embarrassed, or amused, or concerned.

"Get up," Havva snapped. "Not in my house you won't."

Bashir propped himself on his elbows and turned his head just enough to look up at her, shielding Aysel from the woman's stony glare as he did so. "What—"

"I said get up. Go back to the palace and take her with you. If she is well enough to bewitch you into doing something this foolish, then she is well enough to leave." Havva set something on the little table beside the bed. "And she *will* drink this, where I can watch her, before you leave."

"Bewitch me?" Bashir sounded as though he might laugh, but Havva turned, shoving the curtain the rest of the way open as she stalked back toward the kitchen.

"Oh dear," Aysel breathed. "And you were worried about my parents." She was not hurt, especially. She didn't think she was any mother's dream woman for her son. But she was surprised at the ferocity of Havva's reaction.

"Anne." Bashir lunged up, his sharp tone, the set of his jaw, the flash in his eyes telling Aysel he was furious. The bed bucked and swayed as he shoved off it. Aysel watched him wide-eyed as he yanked on his salvar and followed after his mother.

She sighed and sat up. Havva had rounded up better-fitting clothes, which were piled beside the table, where a cup of steaming tea sat. Aysel suspected she knew what the brew was for, and if the situation had been a bit…friendlier, would have thanked Havva for the consideration. Babies were not in her near-term plan.

From the kitchen she could hear them furiously whispering at each other, though Bashir's voice was not made for whispering, and many of his words broke through into full volume. Aysel dressed. Havva had provided an extra length of fabric that Aysel used to bind her chest, and the rest of the dull brown clothes fit reasonably well. Her own boots were on the pile, and she tugged them on.

"…don't know anything about her," Bashir argued.

Aysel scrubbed her hands over her face, trying not to listen, and not to care. Perhaps it stung a little more than she had initially thought. She wasn't certain anyone had ever hated her on first sight. She had also never been in the position to meet someone's mother before. Aysel worried her thumbnail. It would be best if she started for the palace without him. Or at least went outside.

"She is a noble, and doesn't want anything from you but fun." Havva gave that statement at full volume, and Aysel halfway rolled her eyes. She fixed her knife sheaths against her wrists and pulled her sleeves down, then shrugged into her sword harness. When she was ready, she took the cup of tea and did her best nonchalant saunter into the kitchen.

Bashir and Havva both looked at her, twin expressions of anger directed at her, one with gold eyes, one with brown. Aysel stood facing them and drank the tea in one long pull, then bent to set the cup carefully on the low-slung table. She straightened, and Havva's gaze followed her movements like she was a snake the woman wanted to behead with a spade.

"Well," Aysel said in mock cheer, "thank you for your care, Mistress. I am indebted to you." Holding back something more sharply worded was difficult. She would not apologize, but she knew this particular fire did not need the fan of sarcasm. "I hope never to trouble you again."

"No. See that you don't, and to your debt, you can repay it by staying away from my son." She spat the words out.

Aysel held Havva's glare for a moment, and heat crept slowly up her own throat and cheeks. Her gaze flicked to Bashir's, whose entire expression transformed from anger to pleading. Aysel sucked in a deep breath and looked away from him to Havva. She inclined her head in acknowledgment, and strode for the door.

"No," Bashir said as Aysel swung the door shut, then she heard him say it again, in an explosion of temper she suspected he directed at his mother. "No!"

As soon as she was outside she broke into a run. It didn't last long, her magic was erratic and sluggish, her body overtaxed. It also hurt her back, tugging at the stitches, and she slowed to a walk at the edge of the Earth District. She didn't know exactly where she was, but if she headed generally uphill and kept the ocean at her left, then she knew she was pointed in the right direction. She considered hiding, dodging between buildings and taking a long route, but she felt the ripple of his tracking spell sweep past her and decided it wasn't worth it.

He caught up with her shortly after, his horse's hooves striking sharply against the stones behind her. He wheeled the gelding in front of her and glared down at her.

"Never again," he said. Aysel folded her arms and looked up at him. He was so angry that she could feel his temper in the earth around her as a slow, threatening rumble. "I don't care what you and I decide to do with each other. And it will be you and I who decide, no one else. But do not ever run from me again."

She took a deep breath to settle her own temper, which was not at him, but at the rest of the world, then held her hand up toward him. He took it and pulled, and Aysel used his foot in the stirrup as her step as she swung up behind him on the horse.

"I promise," she said. "I'm sorry." It was too much. Wondering what to do with Bashir, with herself and her magic, with her new identity in a place she didn't know, everything. And his mother hated her. Too much. "Is everyone in the city like that about nobles? They hate them?"

"Resentment isn't unusual when someone has more than you do and there isn't a good reason why," Bashir said, temper still unsettled in his voice.

She did not have an answer to that.

The horse had a smooth, easy walk, even over the cobbles, but still it swayed, and Aysel tucked her hands into the fabric at his waist to keep her seat. Bashir reached around and took one of her hands, pulling her arm around his middle. She followed suit with the other, and clasped handfuls of his caftan as she laid her head against his back. He took a deep breath and let it out slowly.

"He hurt her. Whoever my father was, he was noble born, and he made promises he didn't keep."

"And left her with a baby and no hope," Aysel said. "I don't know that I can blame her. I was just surprised."

"I cannot promise she will change her mind."

Aysel could tell that wounded him. They must be close, a son and his single mother. More reasons why she should not allow things to grow between them. Aysel did not care for the idea of Bashir having to choose between her and his mother.

She straightened. The silence stretched, the only sounds those of the city waking around them and the steady beat of his horse's hooves against the stones. A dog barked somewhere close, and someone shouted reprimand in response.

When they began to climb the hill of the palace road, Bashir shifted, his back straightening a fraction more, his posture tightening. Aysel imagined she could feel his guard commander mantle settling into place. She slipped her arms from around him and set her hands against her thighs.

"All done with the affection now that people can see?" he said grumpily.

"You can sheath your prickles," Aysel said. "Consider this professional courtesy. Or are you suggesting I am so pathetically in need of a tossing that I would allow a man who I am ashamed of to bed me?"

"No," he said.

Aysel gave the fabric at his waist a little tug. They were at the Morning Gate, and the guards at either side gave him nods and salutes, fists pressed to hearts, then looked at Aysel with curiosity.

"Shall I climb you again? So everyone can see?" Aysel offered as they passed under the stone wall.

His shoulders rose with a quiet laugh. "Can you manage while I sit my horse?"

"You'd be pleasantly surprised what I can manage. Shall I show you?" She grabbed his shoulders.

"No." He laughed. "You've made your point."

"Have I? Good. How steady is your horse? I suppose I'd say steady, considering he was quite polite to me when I snuck into the stables through his window."

"What?" Bashir turned to look at her, but Aysel had already slid backwards off the horse, sliding over his rump and sidestepping in case he gave an irritated kick. But he only flicked his ears. Bashir reined him around, looking down at her with raised eyebrow and irritated amusement. "My own horse betrayed me?"

"He did." Aysel gave the beast an affectionate pat on his broad cheek. He flicked one ear back. She suspected if horses could roll their eyes in exasperation, he might have at that moment. A guardsman came to lead the horse away, and Aysel became aware that many of the guards were either turned to look or were gathering at the barracks door to do so.

"What is it?" she asked Bashir as he moved to her side.

"You're a bit of a legend now, between sneaking past every one of my men, and me, and saving the Sultana. Being famous is bad for spies, isn't it?" he mused. "I suppose you'll have to become a guard after all, and all that nonsense about me worrying about you will be a moot point, because I can simply assign you to guard the rose garden for the rest of your days."

"You wouldn't dare."

"I would," he said. "In a heartbeat."

"And here she is," Erol announced as he strode from the barracks, elbowing his way through the crowd of men. He turned and gave them an order to find something better to do. They scattered, a bit, but drifted back together as he crossed toward them. "Looking well." He smiled at her as he gave a bow.

"Hello, Lieutenant Terzi. I've brought you back your commander. He was wandering alone in the Earth District."

"Ah." He grinned, with a bit too much sparkle. "We have been looking everywhere for him. There's been an impostor posing in his place for, well…" He glanced at her then away and when he would have finished Bashir put a hand on the hilt of his sword and glared.

Erol laughed at him, giving him a little shove. "The Sultana wishes to see you, Commander. Shall I escort Mistress Attiyeh to her family?"

"Do you think she'd see me now?" Aysel asked Bashir. There was no sense in pretending her secret wasn't out. She could make no decisions until she had spoken with the Sultana, and Makram. Bashir nodded once, though his expression was neutral and shuttered.

"She's in her rooms, I believe," Erol said.

"Anything else?" Bashir asked, in his commander voice. Aysel decided she liked that voice, the serious, stony tone that hid all the little veins of sweetness she'd been privileged to see. It allowed her to keep those for herself, just something between him and her. Had she given him anything like that? Little secrets of herself? Besides her magic. That was hardly a little secret.

She wandered away from them, toward the palace steps, as Erol ran down a list of dry, boring details about what the various guards had seen or not seen the previous night.

She had made it halfway up the stairs when Bashir trotted to catch up with her. "I think your job is going to be very boring now that we're on the same side. No deep-night wakeups to chase fire mages, no city-wide searches." Aysel gave him a sympathetic look.

"We'll manage." He almost smiled, but not quite. "We should both clean up before we go to the Sultana. I'll take you to your family, then we can meet again there when you're ready."

"I know the way," Aysel said. Bashir raised an eyebrow. "Well, don't you live there?" She pointed at the barracks. "Your things are there, don't waste your time escorting me."

"I have a room and an office in the palace, I just choose to stay with my men." He nodded toward the palace.

"A room all by yourself?" she mused. "How lonely. Would you like to show it to me sometime?" She couldn't help thinking she wouldn't mind having him alone this very moment. There was tension and distance between them. Some of the commander shifted away, and she saw eagerness steel into his expression.

"Now?" Bashir's eyes shifted, dark lines cutting fissures through the jasper. She did like how aligned their thoughts were.

"In Sarkum it might be considered"—she held her thumb and forefinger a fraction apart—"this rude to keep a ruler waiting while two of their subjects rutted, but perhaps it is different here?"

Bashir's eyes widened and he laughed. "Rutted?" He swept a hand through his hair. "Yes. It isn't a good idea. So why did you put it in my mind?"

"Well, it was in my mind, and I thought we were sharing," she teased. "Perhaps we can discuss it later. "

"Later," he agreed, and turned back toward the barracks. Aysel watched him for a moment, enjoying the view of his broad back and confident, easy stride. She rubbed her fingers over her brow and turned, heading for her family's rooms.

❧❦❧

THERE WAS NO BATH available in her family's suite, and she doubted she had time for a trip to the palace baths, so she made do with a cloth and a washbasin, though she did use almost the entire extra bucket of water to wash her hair, because there were still bits of plaster in it, as well as salve and other unpleasant things. Aysel braided it and looked at the clothes that had been waiting for her when she arrived. Apparently Tareck had dropped them off. She suspected he was hiding away somewhere, laughing to himself. She dressed, vowing she'd pay him back.

Aysel paused in the doorway of the bathroom, watching the scene she'd stumbled upon as she headed in to wait for Bashir. He was already there. Mathei had been the only one in the rooms when she returned. But he'd been reading when she entered the bathroom. Now he was standing, facing one of the two couches that sat near the door to the garden. Bashir was seated in the middle of the couch Mathei was glaring at, his arms stretched nearly from one end to the other along the back of the couch, his long legs outstretched between him and Mat, and crossed at the ankles. She couldn't see Bashir's face, his back was to her, but every bit of him radiated dominance. His posture practically screamed, *I am the biggest bull in the room.* Aysel raised an eyebrow and crossed toward them.

Mathei noticed the movement and looked at her, then gestured at Bashir with one hand as if to say, *look at this nonsense.* Aysel winked at him. Bashir tipped his head back against the couch to look at her and Aysel kissed him, upside down, and slid her hands over his chest to link her arms around his neck as she whispered to him.

"He isn't sizing you up for brotherly revenge, Ox. He's storing you away under fantasy fodder."

Bashir lunged to his feet. "No. He hates me."

"He is only cross because I saw you first." Aysel sat on the couch.

"I saw him first," Mathei said. "You stole him. But more to the point, I do hate him, because he almost got you killed. And because he is constantly interrupting my reading." He gestured at the book lying on the other couch.

Bashir collapsed next to Aysel. "To be fair, Mat, it is impossible not to interrupt your reading."

"He threatened to rot my stones off," Bashir said, as if tattling on a sibling. "After he threatened to rot my organs. I think."

"Mathei, you know the rules," Aysel warned.

"No fun bits." Mathei sat on the other couch and picked up his book. "I was only attempting to get my point across."

"He makes these threats often?" Bashir asked.

"He feels he is honor-bound to seem overprotective. Don't listen to him, it's mostly smoke."

"I believe the commander knows what was smoke, and what was not," Mathei said, with a dark thread in his voice, though he did not look up from his reading.

"It was made very clear." Bashir glanced at her sidelong. Then his tawny eyebrows rose and he gave a slow, slow grin. "Is that a guardsman's uniform?"

Aysel scowled at him. "Don't get any ideas. Tareck brought this. I assume so I look less like an outsider when I'm working with you. I don't think it will fool any of your men into forgetting I have breasts though."

"They'll forget about your breasts," Bashir said as his eyebrows snapped together, "or I'll have five score of new stable boys."

Aysel let herself enjoy the little flare of jealousy for just a moment before she frowned at him harder. He frowned back. From the corner of her eye Aysel saw Mathei pretend to vomit into his book. She twisted up her mouth to prevent a smile and stood.

"Ready?"

"No, please stay and force me to watch you mouth each other like carp at mossy pond stone," Mathei said.

Aysel grabbed Bashir's hand and pulled him to his feet because she thought if she didn't, he might remain there, stunned into silence, until nightfall. "Later, perhaps," she said to Mat.

"I shall wait with bated breath," Mat said as Aysel pulled the door closed.

"I always thought I would have liked to have a brother or sister," Bashir said. "But..."

Aysel laughed. "He warms up, after some time."

"Time." Bashir gave her a broody look that took her mood down with it. The distance from the Sultana's wing of the palace and the guest quarters was long enough for the silence between them to stretch painfully. Aysel was almost relieved to arrive at the Sultana's quarters, though a new nervousness twisted in her belly for the unknown of the Sultana's impending reaction. Four guards, two to each side, surrounded the ornately carved wooden doors, one of whom she recognized.

"Ali." She grinned. He blushed. His comrades laughed. She felt sorry for him, having to bear the burden of her tricking him and also getting stuck on a roof trying to retrieve her. "Since I am no longer considered a dangerous criminal, I thought you and I could make amends. Would you like me to show you a trick I know for heights?"

He was air, she could sense it around him whenever he was near. No more than a Deval, but that was all he needed to do what she was suggesting. His face lit up, but then his gaze slid sideways and up, to where Bashir loomed over her shoulder. Bashir dipped his head in permission.

"Yes, Mistress Attiyeh."

"You can teach the other First House section," Bashir said. Ali nodded, and his three companions had traded laughter for envious looks.

Bashir knocked, his gaze slicing quickly across hers as he did so, though the expression in it was unreadable. "You are a good person, Aysel Attiyeh," he said under his breath. She smiled a little. The Sultana's handmaiden opened the doors, standing between them with one hand on each as she looked at Bashir, then at Aysel. The handmaiden bowed, then stepped back to allow them in.

"They are in the garden. It would be best if you waited here." She gestured to a grouping of chairs and a settee in the center of the sprawling sitting room. "May I offer you coffee, or something to eat?"

"No, Samira, thank you," Bashir said at the same moment Aysel pleaded the word coffee. Samira's mouth quivered as she bowed again. "Fine. For me as well. If it isn't a bother," Bashir said, sitting in one of the chairs.

"It isn't." Samira turned to Aysel. "I hope I am afforded the chance to speak with you soon. I am very grateful to you for saving the Sultana and Bashir."

Aysel nodded. The woman was a fire mage, Aysel would have known even without the trio of three sigils that decorated her red and gold tiraz. She was the most subdued, controlled fire mage Aysel had ever seen, but fire mages were utterly incapable of hiding what they were. It showed in the warmth in her eyes and the sinuous shape of her body, the way temper sat just at the edge of her smile. It showed in the fierce beauty of her, though hers was less obvious than many that Aysel had met. She hid it or disassociated from it. How interesting. A puzzle Mat would enjoy picking apart.

"She seems pleasant," Aysel said when Samira had left the room to obtain the promised coffee. The tone she used was the same she would have for her brother, a tone which belied her words. Bashir, to whom deception seemed anathema, did not notice at all.

"She is."

Grinning in amusement at his blunt assessment, Aysel paced to the glass door and looked out into the garden. Makram and the Sultana stood outside, deeper into the garden, toward another set of rooms farther along. The garden was not completely dead, the winters in Narfour were too mild for that. But it was subdued and added to the melancholy mood of the scene. A few evergreen vines trailed from pots that lined a gravel walk, interspersed with bushes, and Aysel thought she saw the tell-tale brown streak of a mongoose slithering amongst the foliage. She shuddered. If there were snakes in the palace, she was sleeping on the roof. She checked in on Makram again.

The Sultana stood with her head bowed, one hand pressed over her mouth. She was not close enough for Aysel to see the details of it, but Aysel recognized the posture of a woman trying not to cry. Her brow furrowed. Makram faced her, his hands on her shoulders, speaking to her with a look on his face Aysel had never seen there before.

"What are you looking at?" Bashir moved to stand behind her. Makram gently moved the Sultana's hand and cupped her face, wiping his thumbs across her cheeks. She shook her head, and he pulled her against him, and Aysel's heart filled.

"Oh," she murmured, "he loves her."

"What? Don't stare at them." Bashir tugged her away from the window.

"I didn't know. I thought it was political, I thought he only did it for the alliance." She shook her head. "You don't understand." She felt like she might cry, and turned her back on him, tipping her head against the glass again. "He is like a brother to me. And he was never happy. He was so loyal and steadfast and deferent and his brother treated him like horse dung. It was unbearable, and I thought when he came here it would be the same. A destruction mage in Tamar, beholden to a princess who only meant to use him."

Makram continued to hold the Sultana, his cheek against her hair, and there was such a peaceful, calm look on his face. "He's happy. He loves her." Her heart squeezed. If the Sultana was a woman Makram could love, then perhaps she was a woman Aysel could serve. Not like Kinus.

"Of course he loves her. Anyone with eyes can see that. Are you"—Bashir turned her toward him and peered at her face in suspicion—"are you crying?"

"No." She shoved him away and flopped into one of the chairs.

"Does that bother you? That he loves her?" Bashir seemed puzzled. Poor Bashir.

"No, Ox. It makes me happy for him. He deserves that."

Samira entered again, bearing a silver tray with a matching set of ibrik and cups. She set it up on the table and poured coffee into the little cups. "I also brought some things for you to eat," she said.

"Why is the Sultana upset?" Bashir asked.

Samira stopped mid-pour. She steadied her grip and resumed, and without looking at Bashir, said, "She had been with her father. Were you spying on them?" She leveled him with a look that revealed a bit more of her fire. Why would being with her father upset her?

"I was," Aysel admitted.

"Please do not," Samira said. "They have little enough privacy as it is."

Aysel liked her more for being protective, and nodded. "Thank you for the coffee."

Samira dipped her head. Aysel dosed her cup with sugar and cream then took a deep inhale of the cardamom-perfumed steam. Bashir didn't sit back down, but picked up his cup, which looked comically small in his large hands, and downed it in one drink, then set the cup back. He watched Aysel savor hers, a smile pulling at the corner of his mouth, and Aysel saw Samira watching him with the same look.

"I have not had a chance to speak with Erol, recently. Is he doing well?" Samira asked, conversationally, to Bashir, though her gaze flitted between them. Aysel did her best to hide a flush.

"He is Erol," Bashir said. "He wants to go boar hunting."

Aysel's interest piqued. She'd never been boar hunting. Samira's expression pinched.

"He has forgotten the last time, when the beast almost gored him to death."

"Ooo," Aysel breathed. "I want to go."

Bashir laughed and Samira's honey-brown eyes widened with incredulity. "You are as reckless as your prince," she said. Aysel grinned.

"We'll take you, if we go. But not until summer." Bashir tugged Aysel's braid. She narrowly managed to subdue the urge to jump out of her chair with excitement. Mathei would doubtless have a grand time teasing her about pigsties and her affinity for them. "And no magic is the rule," he added as an afterthought.

The glass doors were at her back, and the latch gave a snap as they opened, then Samira and Bashir bowed in unison. Aysel set her cup down and turned, dropping to her knees as she slid out of her chair.

"Aysel," Makram said in a displeased, sharp tone. He grabbed her by the arm, hoisting her to her feet and wrapping her in a fierce hug.

She coughed, blushing because she felt odd having just witnessed him comforting the Sultana and now being hugged by him.

"Little sister," he said, one hand tugging sharply on her braids. "How many times have I told you that you are not allowed to bleed for me?"

"It was not my intent," Aysel protested.

He set her down and looked her over from head to toe. "We have more work for you."

"She isn't recovered," Bashir began, "from the…"

Aysel looked at him, her throat tightening. Even at such a simple test, he failed. Bashir clenched his teeth at her look of accusation, dropping his gaze as Makram glanced at him as well.

"I'm ready. But, first," she said as she stepped back and turned to the Sultana, who stood near Samira. Aysel's pulse sped, an uneasy knot writhing in her belly and causing her skin to feel tight. The Sultana did not look like a woman who had just been falling apart in her lover's arms. She appeared composed and controlled, a study in the First House's ability to hide their minds. Aysel could distract and misdirect, but the Sultana was like polished marble. Unreadable, devoid of even the smallest expression to grasp.

"You have something to tell me," the Sultana said in a voice like winter wind. Aysel's breath hitched halfway out as they looked at each other. It should have been easy to say the words. But a secret kept for a lifetime apparently imbedded itself in every pore, so that when she opened her mouth to speak, the words did not come, could not.

The Sultana's composed expression softened. "Do you wish to speak to me in private?"

Aysel chewed her lower lip, glancing over her shoulder at Makram. He looked from her to the Sultana and back. A notch appeared between his brows.

"No." She owed him the truth as well. "I am a Charah." The words came quickly, tumbling over each other, as if she were a child admitting to a theft. "I am a First House Charah."

"*The*," the Sultana corrected. "The only First House Charah."

If Aysel had expected the chains of the lie to loosen, or that she might feel free, she would have been disappointed. Instead they seemed to tighten around her. The only. This Circle they all wanted, it required a Charah of every House.

"What?" Makram almost laughed. Aysel turned to him and went to her knees again, prostrating herself on the floor.

"Forgive me," she said, her voice weak. There were so many times she almost told him. So many times she felt unworthy of his loyalty for the lie that gaped between them. "My family hid my power because they feared your brother's retribution if he were to find out. I did not wish to lie to you, but we had no choice."

"You knew?" Makram accused the Sultana.

"I suspected it because she escaped Bashir. I could only imagine an air mage could do so. And after the poison, I was certain." A thread of winter returned to the Sultana's voice, and Aysel's skin prickled.

"Aysel," Makram said. She sat back on her heels. The corners of his eyes pinched, his mouth tightening, and she swallowed back her guilt at the hurt in his eyes. "You didn't trust me?"

"We did not trust the Mirza. And did not wish to ask you to bear my secret when you were already burdened with so much. He went to war with you, what would he do to me? He has always hated our family. Before he sent Firestormers after us, we heard rumors that he had taken a half dozen Sival prisoner and tortured them. I confirmed it." Aysel pushed the vile memory away. "But not in time to help them. I found their bodies staked at the Wadi, at the crossing."

Makram cursed under his breath, lifting a hand to cover his eyes.

Aysel remained kneeling as she turned to face the Sultana again. The Sultana regarded her in silence for moments that felt endless. Yet, in the stillness that reigned while the Sultana considered her, Aysel felt a tickle of something against her magic. A subtle tug. Nothing she'd ever felt before, but a draw toward the woman before her. Aysel frowned. If the Sultana felt anything, she did not show it.

"Your brother, Mathei, told me about the poison used on the bolt. He called it Black Sleep. Have you heard of it?" the Sultana asked. Revulsion turned Aysel's stomach.

"Yes." A remnant of the Sundering War, poison used to silence unwanted mages. It had since been outlawed, not because it killed. But because to make it required blood from a mage in flux. One of the many brutal things done to destruction mages, or any mage who defied the Old Sultanate's edict to banish the Sixth House. Destruction mages were exceptionally difficult to kill, able to destroy most weapons before they could get near enough to do harm. But poison that could kill with just a scratch, or secreted into food and drink…it was invaluable to a tyrant driven to murder.

"Do you know why it didn't kill you instantly as it would have anyone else?" the Sultana asked. Aysel shook her head. The Sultana lifted a hand when Bashir made to protest. "Many people forget that Chara'a are not just mages capable of greater works than the rest of us. They are capable of greater works because the energy they use to power their spells is not their own. They can pull from every mage of their House to feed spells of enormous magnitude."

Weight settled in Aysel's belly, making her want to tip forward and press her forehead to the pale stone tiles once more.

The Sultana continued, "You instinctively reached out and pulled from people who were unaware of it, to keep yourself alive."

The sinking turned into nausea.

"Can you imagine what that would have done if you were not in a city, surrounded by hundreds of air mages to bear the burden? What if you were alone? The first person to come to your aid could have been drained of life by your power." The Sultana had not raised her voice, or changed her even tone, but Aysel felt stripped and diminished. And she felt like a monster. What if she had hurt someone, or they had paid the balance price for her life?

"I didn't know."

"Ignorance is a child's excuse. I give you a choice. You will remain to join the Circle of Chara'a and train to control your power. Or you will leave Tamar."

"Naime, you said you would not force anyone to the Circle," Makram said, but she lifted her fingers to silence him.

Aysel stared up at the other woman. Beautiful and cold. Responsible for more than Aysel had ever been, as leashed to her palace and her role as Aysel was to her secrets. She did not want that, to be chained, to be responsible for so many. She was only one person, cursed with magic that was almost an entity unto itself, a burden she carried, not a power to be used as they would have her do.

"She is untrained and uncontrolled. A danger to herself and the people around her. It is unacceptable." That cool, crisp voice, the matter-of-fact tone. Not meant to hurt, simply the truth unvarnished, unsoftened. Aysel didn't mind that. At least she knew she would never misunderstand her new mistress. "I am not forcing her, I am giving her a choice."

Aysel met the woman's gaze and one corner of her mouth lifted in respect. The Sultana folded her hands in front of her pale entari and raised one slim, dark eyebrow.

"Am I to be imprisoned until I decide?" Aysel asked. How could she make such a choice? Leave her family, or give up what little freedom she had left?

"No. You are temporarily under the command of the palace guard. You and Bashir are to find the other assassin. That is your only focus until it is done, do you understand, Bashir?"

Aysel closed her hands into fists on her thighs, staring at the patterned tiles and trying to breathe away the melee in her mind. Her magic, her family, assassins, Bashir, Makram, no home, a slave to magic that had always been more prison as it was an aid.

"Yes, Efendim." Bashir's earthen voice calmed Aysel enough to lift her head and look at them, to follow the conversation, to understand her orders. Because she wasn't a great mage to stand in a Circle to advise a ruler. She was a spy. A hunter. That was what she was good at. What she was made for.

"Do you feel you are capable of leashing her power, if it becomes necessary?" the Sultana asked. Aysel stared hard at the floor, willing away the bit of heat that touched her cheeks. Bashir must have chosen to nod instead of speaking, perhaps to prevent his voice from betraying them, because Aysel only heard silence in answer to the Sultana's question.

"Then begin now," the Sultana said. "You are both dismissed."

Aysel gave Makram a quick glance, and he returned it with an encouraging nod. She all but ran from the room, surprising the guards outside the door. If they could hear what went on, they showed a great deal of discipline in not revealing it to her in the few heartbeats of awkward silence between when she exited and when Bashir did.

He held something wrapped in a white napkin out to her. Aysel took it and they walked down the hall, toward the palace entrance. He'd given her a pastry, something flaky and rolled around a filling of dried dates. She ate it in silence, studying the pristine whiteness of the napkin it had come in. No, she did not belong here. Noble daughter, yes. Certainly more accustomed to fine things than most of the people languishing in the refugee camp at that moment, but not this. Not wandering the palace endlessly and attending Councils and reading books on magic like Mathei.

She had always served Makram, but it had been a kind of freedom, and she an outsider to all the machinations of the palace in Al-Nimas. She did not want to be a slave to white napkins and high walls.

"Thank you." Aysel brushed the crumbs from her hands off on her salvar. It hadn't done much to put the fire of her hunger out. She hadn't eaten since before the incident at the camp, and had expended quite a lot of energy in…other pursuits.

"She can be harsh, sometimes," Bashir said in the softest voice he could manage, which was to say it was barely soft at all.

"She tells the truth as she sees it," Aysel said. "I cannot fault her for that. There are enough lies in the world."

"Says a spy." Bashir tried to smile in teasing, but it was reluctant, and Aysel knew he was wondering what she would choose. To stay. Or to run. To serve, or to be free.

"Yes. A very good spy." Aysel forced cheer into her voice. "Shall we get to work?"

TWENTY-FIVE

BASHIR STARED AT THE city map he'd pinned to his desk, trying to decipher the scribbles Aysel had made on it. She'd covered twice the ground of anyone else, and in less time, though he could barely read her notes. He thought nobles were born able to write calligraphy. This looked like flyspeck. The sun sat low in the sky by the time he'd returned from talking with the City Watch, and now it was hovering just above the ocean. He hadn't seen Aysel since he parted ways with her that morning, but he'd been doing his best to leave her handling to Erol. The last thing he needed were rumors. The men were already unsettled by having her working with them. They would adjust, but it would be best if they didn't have too many things to adjust to at once.

"Time for drills," Erol announced as he strode by Bashir's office. "Lieutenant Attiyeh said she wants to do them too." She wasn't an actual lieutenant, but they needed to call her something, and so that was what they'd decided on.

"No. She's not healed yet," Bashir called after him.

"Tell her that," Erol called back.

Bashir darted around his desk, trotting to catch up to Erol. "You outrank her, you tell her. Just because she's noble born doesn't mean she isn't subject to the rules everyone else is. No one trains injured." He'd tell her, if Erol was going to wilt over confronting her.

Erol raised an eyebrow. "I recall an inductee failing to tell the section leader he'd twisted his knee. Nearly lamed himself faking it."

Bashir cut his gaze away from his friend as heat suffused his neck. "Nothing from your men?"

Erol snorted, but grew serious immediately afterward. "No. I don't think he's in the city. He's in the outskirts, or worse"—Erol grimaced—"the palace."

His words echoed Bashir's thoughts, fears. He was going to have to put Aysel on a night watch. If she could do what the Sultana could, and expand her hearing, then she could cover more of the palace than any of his men. It shouldn't be a hardship for her, considering how many nights she had spent prowling the city under everyone's noses.

They passed through the stables and into the walkway below the arena seats. The men were gathering out on the sand, broken into their House squads to form up for drills. They only broke this way for magic drills, four groups for the four Houses. Otherwise Bashir scattered them evenly between six-man squads. Each had mages from all four Houses. It was possible he would live long enough to see the day when the Sultana restored the Circle and there were Sixth and Third House mages among his ranks. That would be remarkable. Though he wasn't entirely certain what a Third House mage was capable of.

The First House squad, of which there were fifteen men, stood in a circle at the far end of the oblong arena, peering up at the roof of the walkway. Three men were on the tiled roof, and Aysel stood below them with her hands on her hips. Bashir smiled. Aysel was keeping her promise to Ali. The other three groups were scattered around them, milling. His smile disappeared. He could blame her for the disorder as well.

Normally, they would have begun their drills already, even without Erol or him there. He liked to think it was his insistence on discipline, but more likely it was Erol's love of sneaking up on slacking guards and super-heating their boots.

"Troublemaker." Erol sounded too pleased. One of the air mages on the roof jumped. Aysel shoved her hands toward him to break his fall with her power. Barely break his fall. The man griped and staggered to his feet, rubbing his backside as he turned to climb back up. If that was how she had learned, with no one to teach her, then it shouldn't surprise him to find her a hard taskmaster.

"They can work with her on that," Bashir said. "You handle the Fifth, and I'll take the Second and Fourth." Water and earth. He wished he had a Second House Sival to work with them, but he had no water workers greater than a Deval in the guard. None powerful enough to divine any great distance, which would save him valuable time spent running messengers to and from the Engeli Gate.

"There goes Kasim," Erol said, as the burly, dark-haired guard broke away from the loose grouping of earth mages and headed straight for Aysel. Kasim was an older guard who had served longer under the previous commander than Bashir had, and who was forever testing Bashir's authority. Not a bad soldier, he simply preferred the "old way" of doing things. That did not include women serving in the guard. "Want me to head over?" Erol asked.

"She'll handle him," Bashir said, proud at how steady his voice sounded, despite the rumbling monster which stirred inside him, one that would happily bury Kasim in a pile of rock and earth so deep they would not find his bones before they'd turned to stone themselves. He could not interfere, not unless one of them was in danger of losing life or limb. Because Aysel had to prove herself for his men to trust her. And because he wanted to prove to her that he could do exactly what she believed he could not.

He could let her be in danger, he could let her take care of herself.

Bashir kept walking, pretending not to notice the impending confrontation. The men parted around him, watching him apprehensively.

Bashir ordered them with gestures to form up for drills but they lingered, too distracted to obey.

"What's this?" Kasim said, as he stopped beside Aysel. "We've no need for a thief's tricks. We're guards. We don't hide on rooftops."

All the Houses had positive aspects and their mirror. Steadfastness and surety could become stubbornness and a propensity for bullying. When you could be as strong as earth and stone, you could be tricked into thinking you had a right to push others around. That was the case with Kasim, who often mistook oppression for leadership.

Aysel glanced sideways at Kasim, her gaze lifting to his face, then down to his boots, taking in their significant height and size difference and that most of his size was not muscle. "The commander gave orders for this training. You can take it up with him."

"You're teaching them women's tricks. Just because the Sultana saw fit to put you in the guard doesn't mean you *are* fit."

Several of the men close enough to hear snorted laughter.

"Is there something you want?" Aysel continued to direct the air mages with gestures and nods of her head, controlling three to four of them at once with her magic while half-engaged with Kasim. That alone spoke to her talent and power. Kasim was a good guard, but not always the fastest on the uptake. Erol elbowed Bashir, grinning.

"What I want is you out of the guard. You'll cause us nothing but trouble and reduced discipline."

"Yes, I can see that," Aysel said in a voice as dry as the arena sand. "You're still speaking to the wrong person. I'm just following my orders."

"The rest of us had to prove we belong here, you know," Kasim continued, growing more irritated with each moment that passed in which Aysel continued to half ignore him.

Bashir drew breath to call everyone into formation, *again*, but Aysel turned abruptly toward Kasim.

"I'm going to ask you a question, and if you cannot answer, then I win and you'll crawl back into your mud mage hole." She made a scurrying motion with her fingers and Kasim's bronze skin turned scarlet with temper.

"What?"

"No," Aysel corrected. "I'm going to ask *you* a question. Try to keep up." More snickers, and Bashir fought back his own smile. "Do you think," Aysel said each word slowly and carefully, "that Commander Ayan"—her eyes widened—"would put someone who looks like me"—she indicated her height and size with her hands—"in a guard uniform and set her amongst a pack of ruffians and handsy half-wits if she could not take care of herself?"

"What?" Kasim repeated, this time in disbelief. Now real laughter broke out amongst the men.

Aysel sighed. "Fine. No battle of wits. What brave and heroic feats did you have to accomplish to make you eligible to stand for days outside the gate? Did you want to lock arms, or measure cocks, or was there some other contest of strength you think I won't pass?"

Kasim advanced on her. Aysel stood her ground, and Kasim pushed his body up against hers and grabbed her shoulders. The ground at Bashir's feet shuddered, and Erol eyed him, eyebrows raised, words half ready to be spoken. Bashir released his breath in a short exhale, wrestling himself under control and avoiding Erol's gaze.

She had lived a lifetime without him. She did not need him now.

"You should have chosen to measure cocks," Aysel said, standing still and glaring up at him. "You might just have barely won."

The men made low, heckling sounds, and Kasim's lips peeled back in a sneer.

"Get your hands *off,* if you do not want me to give them back to you one finger at a time."

"Make me, little air mage," Kasim baited.

Aysel's hands moved, a flash Bashir barely saw, and Kasim's sword belt fell from his hips, slashed by one of her knives. Kasim made for it as it fell, but she gave it a vicious kick and a thread of power and it sailed up onto the roof of the stadium walkway. When he grabbed for her, Aysel ducked, drawing a sword and lunging at his midsection, driving the hilt of it into the soft flesh just below his breastbone. Several of his earth mage cronies gave sounds of sympathy as he toppled like a pile of bricks, landing on all fours with a hoarse gasp.

"If you want your sword back, you're going to have to climb up onto the roof. Let me know if you want me to teach you how." She kicked sand at him as she sheathed her sword. Then she turned back to the group of air mages, every single one of them grinning like idiots. "Again," she ordered the three men still on the roof.

"Good girl," Erol breathed. "If you get tired of her—"

"Shut up," Bashir said.

Erol snickered as he turned and headed across the sand to the gathered fire mages.

"If everyone is done exchanging pleasantries, you're late for drills," Bashir ordered, and sent the barest thread of power into the ground and forward, so the sand beneath Aysel's feet shifted. She didn't turn around, but she did cock her head enough to glance at him from the corners of her eyes. Bashir crossed to where Kasim was getting to his feet and helped him up.

"Kasim," he said. Kasim brushed himself off, then looked up to where his sword belt and weapon lay, and cursed. He glared at Aysel, who ignored him, watching the air mages as they practiced whatever it was that helped Aysel drop from such unbelievable heights. "You can't really mean to have her as a guard?"

"She works directly for the Sultana," Bashir said. "So, unless you want to explain to her why you're harassing her people, I suggest you find something else to occupy your time."

"My sword," Kasim griped.

Bashir squinted at the roof. "You better make a First House friend."

"I'm not taking orders from some woman."

Bashir shuttered his expression the best he could. The problem was that Kasim might have been the only one to openly approach Aysel, so far, but he was not alone in his opinion. Aysel would have to work three times as hard as any of his male guards to earn their respect. He was certain she could do it. He was not certain how many times he'd be able to force himself to stand back.

"Then you are without your weapon, which is against standing orders. A small turn spent cleaning the pits at the refugee camp."

Kasim stared in shock for a moment, then glanced over his shoulder at Aysel. "I see."

"You can start now." Bashir and Kasim had butted heads before and would continue to do so even if Aysel was not always part of the guard. Bashir hooked a thumb toward the stables. Kasim stalked away. Bashir rubbed a hand over his face, then strode to Aysel.

She did not look at him, watching the men as they stepped or jumped off the roof, and he saw her whispering under her breath, her gaze tracking each man as they fell.

"What is this spell?" he asked.

"You can wrap your power around you, and it creates a change in the air, so you're lighter, and land more softly. Shall I stop for now?" she asked.

He shook his head. It was a useful skill, if they could show her prowess in using it.

"I like teaching." She beamed up at him. He forced himself not to stare at her, turning his gaze to his men. Ali seemed to be getting the hang of it, Aysel didn't whisper when he jumped, but he also appeared to be the only one.

"Do you want to spar with me sometime?" Aysel asked. "I haven't practiced in such a long time."

"Yes."

Aysel gave a soft huff of a laugh at the speed of Bashir's answer, looking up at him from the corners of her eyes.

Unfortunately, some of the men waiting their turn heard, and turned to look at them both.

"You're going to spar?" one of them said, too loudly, and it carried because of the damned acoustics in the arena, then half the men stopped what they were doing to look.

"The commander is going to spar!" someone else yelled out.

"No." Bashir frowned. "I am not interrupting drills. Another time."

"Scared?" Aysel's face scrunched to hide her smile.

He scowled at her. "You are still wounded."

She grinned, but said nothing. Bashir sighed in exasperation. His soldiers had barely begun their drills. "Fine. But don't whine to me when all your stitches tear."

"And don't whine to me when I embarrass you in front of all your men," Aysel said, bouncing on the balls of her feet. Bashir's men moved for the seats—no one was allowed in the pit when earth mages were sparring. Bashir walked beside her to the center of the pit and gave her a once-over as the rest of the men hurried for the relative safety of the walkway and the stone bleachers, their frenzy evident in the volume of their shouts and jeers. They loved an excuse not to exercise.

"They like to watch you spar," Aysel said.

"I do not do it often," he said. "Because it is rarely challenging." Perhaps if he were fighting on a boat, where there was no earth for him, but certainly not in the arena.

"Not even Erol?" she asked.

"Sometimes. And the prince"—he tossed her an accusatory glance—"but we have been busy lately, chasing criminals."

Aysel skipped a few steps ahead and whirled to face him, grinning. Energy shot through his limbs at the look in her eyes, and he smiled back.

"I've wanted to face you again, since the first time we met here," Aysel said.

Bashir surveyed the pit to make certain everyone was out of it. "Ready?"

Aysel nodded.

Bashir shoved a blade of power into the ground around him and it buckled, opening up beneath Aysel and swallowing her. He rolled one shoulder then the other to loosen his muscles and some disappointed calls of derision came from the stadium seats. Her power swelled, filling the air with crackling and the distinctive smell of ozone. Her magic sliced through his and sand exploded around him, blinding him to her movement. He grabbed the sand in his power and shoved it to the ground, just in time to see Aysel halfway through an aerial somersault aimed at him.

He turned sideways and threw an arm up as a block, and she unfolded in the air, her hands closing on his arm and the rest of her body continuing its arc over him. She dropped her legs, and the weight and momentum of her was enough leverage for her to halfway flip him over her, and he landed in a heap at her feet. Cheers erupted from the section where his First House mages were seated. At least she had made some friends.

Aysel danced away from him through the sand, avoiding the ripples of ground he tried to send under her feet as he got to his. She drew both her swords, rounding on him. She didn't look troubled, nor did she bear the intense look of concentration so many of his men wore when they sparred. Aysel was smiling at him, goading. When he looked at her face, she mocked a kiss, and Bashir bared his teeth, drawing his sword.

She didn't wait for him, but came at him with a series of quick, slicing swipes, one sword always darting in, harrying, so he did not have time or room to take a proper swing. When he did see an opening—she had jabbed in with one blade, her body turned sideways, the other arm and blade slung out to the opposite side for balance as she leaned in to go for his ribs—he swung at her neck. Aysel bent backwards, underneath the swing, and kicked her legs up and over, flipping and landing on her feet. She spun to drive both swords at his midsection.

Bashir drove a thin shield of stone up from the earth in front of him. Aysel's swords pierced it and stuck, and he dropped the shield, taking her weapons with it. His men roared in encouragement, and Aysel stumbled back as Bashir advanced, stepping over her swords and swinging his lazily in a circle. Still, she looked unfazed, her stormy gaze darting, examining him for an opening.

"Don't crouch like that, Aysel, you'll tire your legs!" A shout came from the entrance. Bashir glanced and saw Tareck standing with the prince. Tareck was just lowering his hands from his mouth, and Bashir wondered what they wanted when Aysel's foot connected with his ribs. She swung and knocked his sword out of his hand, then sent it flying across the arena the same way she had Kasim's. Aysel continued her spin and stepped onto the leg he had braced on, using it as a boost to climb onto his back.

There were shouts and cheers and laughter, as her arm came around his neck, the same way she had done the last time he had chased her in the arena, her legs twining around his torso, and locking. "Hello, lover," she whispered in his ear, cinching her arm closed on his throat. This time he fell back immediately to try and break her loose.

Aysel laughed, and her power wrapped around them, cushioning her from the blow. Bashir rolled to his hands and knees and grabbed at her arm as his thoughts tumbled across themselves and his wits grew fuzzy. He had more muscle than her, and he managed to dig his fingers in around her wrist, one at a time, and loosen her hold enough to suck in a breath and allow the blood to circulate.

When he had loosened her hold halfway, she released him, planting her feet against his back and vaulting backwards, landing in the sand behind him. She made a dash for her swords. Bashir shifted his foot, and turned his palms up, and another wall of earth erupted in front of her.

Aysel ran up its face.

Bashir marveled for one moment as she took three running steps up the wall and used it as a springboard to launch herself higher and clutch the jagged edge at the top. She hung for a moment, then swung, pushing off with her feet to then scramble over, and slide down the other side.

Wheel and spokes she was incredible.

The men howled, some jumping to their feet. Bashir shook his head, turning in a jog to the other end of the arena, and retrieved his own sword. When he turned back, he collapsed the earth wall and Aysel stood on the other side, watching him with her head tipped at a slight angle and one hip cocked, her swords held down and slightly away from her legs.

Bashir wiped the sweat from his eyes. She was his new favorite pastime, whether it was this or more intimate exchanges, and it was impossible not to think of those latter pursuits now, looking at her.

"Tired?" she called. Her own chest rose and fell at a rapid pace.

Bashir gave his head a slow shake. "I am not the one wasting my energy hopping around like a crazed rabbit."

Aysel smiled. "Can oxen hop?" She paced toward him, careful and alert like the fox they sometimes called her, and half his wits fell into his groin, a problem he had never had to deal with before when sparring. What an unfair advantage. He wasn't prepared when she moved. As had happened when she saved the Sultana, when she had saved him. One moment she was walking toward him, the next there was a flash and a sound like thunder, then he felt an impact like a cannonball, sending him flying onto his back. His sword was knocked from his grasp when he landed, the air rushed out of his lungs, and lights swung through his vision, decorating the darkened evening sky.

Aysel pounced on his chest. She crouched over him, crossing her swords over his throat and pinning him to the sand. Lightning danced in her stormy eyes, and a fierce grin bared her teeth. Bashir groaned as all his men roared with shouts and cheers.

"Hmm." Aysel tipped her head to one side again, and surveyed him underneath her, her grin easing into a teasing smile. "This feels a bit familiar."

"Perhaps without the swords." Bashir's desire grew more insistent with every moment that passed, and he resisted his instinct to grab her hips. "Next time we fight…no audience," he said, controlling his magic so the entire arena was not witness to his lust.

"Agreed." She stood, her feet planted to either side of his ribs. Aysel sheathed her swords. She held her hands down to him and took steps back to give him room to get to his feet, leaning back as she tugged to get leverage enough to pull him up. Bashir grinned and pulled, hard, sending her toppling into the sand beside him.

"Poor loser," Aysel sniffed, pushing to her feet. She walked past him to retrieve his sword and handed it to him as he stood. Bashir put a hand on her shoulder and willed the sand off of her. It showered to the ground. "Aren't you useful to have around."

She looked up at him, storm in her eyes, and the edge of her power raised the hair across his arms. He was pleased to know he was not alone in his desire to be somewhere private with her.

Tareck and the prince crossed toward them, and Aysel went to meet them. The match with Aysel had eaten up all Bashir's time to run drills. He caught Erol's eye and lifted his hand to signal him the men were released to their shift change. Erol called orders, and the men shuffled about, moving out of the seats and towards the barracks.

"This means all those times I beat you that you were holding back." Tareck sounded scandalized as he stopped in front of Aysel. She twisted her mouth.

"If I had used magic, I might have won. I can't beat you in a straight sword fight," Aysel said. Tareck frowned, then looked past her to Bashir. He sheathed his sword and joined them, bowing to the prince.

"It is an honor that you've come to observe, Efendim," Bashir said.

"Spare me," Makram said. "I've told you before to save that formality for the Sultana."

Aysel met Bashir's gaze from the corner of hers, a little smile touching her mouth. The easy camaraderie of standing at her side, after just being soundly beaten, made him fill with a mix of need and melancholy longing. He just wanted…there were no other words. He just wanted. Her.

"Are you bleeding?" Makram pointed at her. Aysel tried to look over her own shoulder at her back. Bashir took her arm and turned her. She was indeed bleeding.

"I told you—"

"It's fine." She batted his hand away. "It's likely only one or two stitches."

"Get it seen to, Aysel." Makram only turned his attention from her when she nodded. "I came to see what you've found in your search," he said to Bashir.

"Nothing that pleases me. I do not believe he's in the city. He's camped outside it, or worse." Bashir closed his hand around the hilt of his sword.

"He's in the palace," Tareck said.

Bashir nodded. "I'll have Aysel on a night watch rotation, and I'll be on day. I'm also going to augment the Sultana's guard with more men, and request she limit her movements until I can apprehend this bastard."

"Good. I have also come to tell you that Elder Attiyeh and I are returning to Sarkum for the time being."

Bashir glanced at Aysel, and her expression was stiff with surprise.

"Why?" she asked, softly. Bashir was certain there was fear in her voice.

"I must prepare my forces, and I cannot do that from here. I also intend to investigate the Blight," he said. The troubled look on Makram's face stirred Bashir's curiosity.

"What do you mean?" Aysel asked.

"The Sehzade, who is Vizier of Agriculture, has a team of mages studying the Blight. They are beginning to believe it is a construct, of magic or something else."

"Something else?" Bashir asked. How could someone *construct* a malady without the aid of magic?

"If I continue, you will need to cast a dampening," Makram said.

Bashir obliged. He noticed Aysel glance at him, and something warm passed across her expression and woke an answering heat in his belly. "The Sehzade believes it is possible that the Corsan Republic is involved with it, their science or their machines. We will be collecting samples to bring back, as well, though I do not know how long I will be away."

Bashir didn't know what sort of machine could make plants sicken and die, or what exactly science entailed. He'd heard the Corsans worshiped many deities. Perhaps one of them could grant deadly boons.

"Makram." Aysel's voice hitched.

The prince smiled his dark smile, the one that reminded Bashir that he bore the burden of seeing life and death in a way other mages did not. "It is necessary. The world does not change because we sit back and wish it to. It changes because we do the things we must, make decisions we do not wish to make, to move it forward. Yes?"

"Yes," Aysel said in resignation. Was she thinking about herself, and her magic, and the Circle? "When are you leaving?" She seemed to shake herself free of it. Something in her tone, some thread of resolution, made Bashir tighten his hands into fists. Did she wish to go with them?

"Tomorrow evening. I had hoped to put it off until you captured the assassin, but things have progressed too quickly." He raised an eyebrow at Bashir. "I have no doubt you'll catch this assassin, but I also want you to promise me that you will never leave the Sultana alone with Behram Kadir, even after you do. I do not care how cross she is with you."

Bashir ducked his head.

"Good." Makram seemed to shrug the subject away before he grinned, looking at Aysel. "Well done, by the way. And when I return, I think it is time you and I had a similar match."

Eagerness stole over her expression as she nodded.

Makram's smile slipped a little as he looked at her. "Unless you decide to refuse the Sultana's offer. I would prefer you stay here and join the Circle. But if you choose not to, come to Sarkum with me. You would be invaluable."

Bashir did not care for the thoughtful expression on her face. He hadn't, until this moment, truly thought about what would happen if Aysel did not accept a place in the Circle. She'd be gone. He'd never see her again. She considered it, he could see it in the way she looked at Makram. Leaving. Running, even though she promised.

The tension in his hands spread up his arms to his shoulders as irritation transformed to temper.

"Please relay whatever you need for escort to the Engeli Gate, Efendim"—Bashir forced his voice to be level, untouched by his hurt and his anger—"but, unless there is anything else, I should oversee the shift change."

"Of course."

Bashir bowed and headed for the arena entrance. He didn't want Aysel near him just now. Because he wanted to shout at her, to be angry at her for making him care for her and then to consider leaving, as if it would not affect him at all. Did she care? He thought she had, he thought…

What was he even doing? Every choice involving Aysel ended in his misery. If she stayed, she was right, it would torture him to watch like he did today. It would break him to send her into danger. And if she left…if he never saw her again…his throat closed.

He reached the stables and strode down the main aisle.

"Bashir," Aysel called from behind him. He wanted to ignore her but stopped anyway. He couldn't bring himself to turn and look at her, afraid he'd fall off the edge of temper and say something he didn't wish to. There was no claim between them, no promises that gave him any leave at all to be angry with her for living her life as she saw fit. He knew that. It did not soothe his ire or the aching loneliness that overtook him at the thought of her absence.

"Do not call me by name around the men."

Aysel stopped. "Of course," she said, obediently, not rising at all to the bait.

He turned, and she looked at him with reluctance. Come to tell him she was leaving with Makram, perhaps? The inside of him turned to stone, and his skin washed with cold. He rolled his neck in a circle, and it cracked. He looked down at her, coasting on a rumbling fissure of aimless fury that was going to break beneath him at her slightest provocation.

One corner of her mouth curved up.

"Look at you," she said, breathlessly. "Even when you're angry I want you."

He ground his teeth, his jaw tightening as he tore his gaze away from the heat in her eyes.

Aysel closed the distance between them and grabbed fistfuls of his caftan. "Can we speak to each other? Instead of…this?"

"I do not think I want to hear what you have to say." He took hold of her wrists and pulled her hands off of him, then released her.

"I don't understand." The edge in her voice was enough to slice through his hold on his anger. "What happened?"

"You have a little over a candlemark to rest before you take the night shift on the palace. I suggest you do so." He managed to keep his voice smooth, instead of rocky, but still her face twisted with anger.

"And I suggest you take your childish temper tantrum and go jump off a bridge." Aysel shoved past him, stalking to the end of the aisle past the stalls, and turned into the barracks. He lunged after her, storming in her wake, so that every soldier he passed on the way flattened themselves to the wall and pressed their lips together to avoid making a sound.

"Stop!" Bashir barked as Aysel neared the door on the other end of the barracks.

Aysel spun around to face him. Her gaze raked the hall, taking in the heads poking out of doors and the few men in the hall who had paused to watch, stopping on Bashir's face. She raised one eyebrow. "Yes, Commander?"

"Go to the palace and see a physician about your stitches." He tried to level his voice, to exact some damage control over the mess he was creating. He didn't need the men to see him obviously infuriated at her, so that they could guess he cared, and use it as leverage to take liberties in their discipline or behavior.

"Where do I report for night watch?" she asked, and managed a far better approximation of her normal tone of voice than he did of his.

"To me or Lieutenant Terzi," he said.

Aysel whirled and left, and Bashir went to his office and closed his door. He sat at his desk and scrubbed his hands through his hair, staring at the map. His temper waned and he felt like an utter fool for losing it at all. It was her. Them. The way they fit together. Sparring with her was not so different from making love, the way their magic danced and clashed. Was that how it had to be with them in everything?

He didn't know if he should tell her why he was angry. Because if he told her, and she left anyway…it would rend him more. Loneliness for her, for her teasing and her smile, washed over him. He jerked to his feet.

Twenty-Six

"THERE WE ARE," THE physician said, a man of middle Turns, whose hair was already completely silver, in that way that made some men look distinguished and sophisticated, instead of older. He'd introduced himself as Ceylik, the head physician at the palace. "Those stitches look like Havva's work," he said, carefully replacing his tools on a tray as Aysel settled her caftan back into place and began winding the cloth around her waist.

"Yes. Do you know her?"

"I do," he said, attempting to sound as if that were unimportant, but Aysel got the distinct impression it was. "How is she?"

"Uhm." Aysel reached for her swords. "Opinionated."

Ceylik chuckled, nodding. "The same as always, then."

"I wouldn't know." Aysel lifted the harness over her shoulders. She watched him as he moved about the little room that served as hospital, putting things away, trying to appear uninterested. She stifled a loud, gusty sigh. "Is that all I need?"

"Unless you want a salve for pain?" He turned, his eyebrows rising in question. Aysel shook her head. The pain wasn't bad enough to warrant dealing with oily salve that stained her hands and clothes and made her stink.

"I'll take it." Bashir's graveled voice came from the doorway. The sigh escaped Aysel's control, and she added a little groan at the end for emphasis.

"I don't want it, I said." Aysel glared at him. He ignored her, and Ceylik looked from one to the other, as he reached above his head on a shelf and retrieved a small jar topped with a square of burlap and tied with string. He set it into Bashir's outstretched hand.

"Thank you."

Aysel hopped off the table he'd made her sit on, striding for the door. Cursing her short stride as Bashir easily caught up with her, she sped her pace and headed for the entrance to the palace. "If you're here to tell me I'm late, it isn't my fault. He was mining me for information about your mother."

"He does that." Bashir slipped his big hand underneath her elbow and tugged her in a different direction. "This way. The garden connects with every room and would be an easier place to gain access to than the Sultan's hall." He did not let go of her arm and Aysel yanked at it.

"Please do not drag me about like a stray dog," she ordered.

Bashir released his grip on her, but whether because she had asked or because they had arrived at whatever appeared to be his destination was unclear. He opened a door into a darkened room and put his hand on the back of her neck, steering her inside.

"I said, stop that." Aysel whirled, and he caught her by both arms, kicking the door closed behind him and backing her across the room. She couldn't see in the darkness, and she backed into something that stood at hip level. He lifted her onto it and leaned over her, his hands to either side of her hips.

"I chose to ignore your request that I jump off a bridge," he said. The ceramic jar he carried made a soft echo in the darkness as he set it on the surface somewhere to her left. "Do you have any other, more reasonable requests?" His voice was devoid of the quaking anger she'd heard in the stables, but held an edge she wasn't sure she liked.

"Why am I sitting in the dark alone with you when I should be hunting an assassin?"

"Because I want you to," he said.

No. She definitely did not care for his tone.

"Well I don't want to. Does that matter?"

He straightened, and even in the dimness she could see the motion as he swept a hand through his hair. "Of course it matters." Some of the edge left his voice, and he sounded a bit remorseful.

"Are you going to tell me why you were angry with me? Why you manhandled me into this closet?"

"No."

"Then I'm leaving." Aysel slid off the surface, which she judged to be a table or desk, but Bashir blocked her.

"Or you could stay, and I could make you forget about the rest," he said warmly, but still there was that sharp pitch that irritated her.

"No. I don't find myself aroused by a man who loses his temper with me and will not even tell me why."

"Why should I tell you anything, if all you're going to do is use me until you return to Sarkum with your prince? Like my mother said you would do."

Aysel put her hands on her hips and glared at him in the dark, despite that he couldn't see it. "He isn't my prince, he is very clearly the Sultana's prince. And who said I was leaving with him?"

"I saw your face when he spoke of it. And I know you don't want what the Sultana offered."

"You saw my face and made an assumption about what I was thinking. And you also know what I want, despite that even I am not certain. But you'll lower yourself to tumble me, despite that you apparently think I'm a monster?" Aysel shouldered past him. "This is absurd. Get out of my way."

"Aysel," Bashir said, his voice falling on her name, telling her he knew he was wrong, that he wanted to make up. She opened the door and slammed it closed behind her. She pressed her back to the wall beside the door, and closed her eyes, pulling her magic around her in threads and wraps, commanding herself to fade, to go unnoticed against the geometric lattice of lace and poppies that decorated the wallpaper.

The door opened and he stepped out, and stopped, looking around the foyer. He wouldn't look at the wall behind him, and unless he cast a spell that pitted his magic against hers, he wouldn't see her. There was the back of his neck, lit by the mage orbs captured in the colored glass cages that hung above them, and the faint glow of his magic. Angry, or hurt, or lusting. She wished she didn't care which one. His words, his assumptions, stung more than she wanted them to. Why didn't he believe she cared about him? Why couldn't he be patient with her? Fourth House mages were supposed to be patient.

Aysel closed her eyes and tipped her head back against the wall, trying to swallow back tears and anger. This couldn't distract her from the assassin. It couldn't distract her from the choice she had to make. But it was all she could think about. He was all she could think about. Why didn't he feel that?

When he moved away from her, she felt it, felt the heavy press of his magic easing, felt the absence of that pressure the way she missed the weight of his body against hers. She opened her eyes and watched him walk toward the hall that led to the courtyard, the heels of his hands pressed over his eyes, his posture burdened. He dropped his hands, and cursed, loudly, then he turned down the hall and out of sight.

Aysel stepped away from the wall, but held her fading spell around her as she walked in the opposite direction, toward the Sultan's hall. There were two turns and three long hallways, and when she reached the hall where the Sultana's rooms were she felt a rush of power sweep away her spell.

She turned, and the Sultana was walking toward her, lowering her hand to her side. Behind her a veritable circus of people trailed, three attendants, six guards, Makram, and Tareck. Aysel dropped to her knees.

"That is a fascinating spell," the Sultana said, stopping before her and folding her hands, one over the other, in front of her caftan. Aysel bowed her head. "Did you devise it yourself?"

"Yes, Sultana. I did not attend the Academy in Sarkum. Everything I do is from instinct and trial and error."

The Sultana tipped her head to the side. "I must apologize. Yesterday I said you were uncontrolled, but I see, and am told"—she looked over her shoulder at Makram, who winked at Aysel—"I was mistaken."

"How did you see me?" Aysel looked up at her. Her eyes were a mesmerizing shade of cinnamon brown, and despite her cool expression, revealed there was warmth to the woman Aysel hadn't realized was there. Aysel did not have any female friends, her work isolated her too much for it, and she had so little in common with most women of her station. The Sultana was, by all reports, a powerful air mage. Thinking she might be friends with the heir to the Tamar Sultanate was reaching a bit, though.

"I saw your footprints on the carpet." The Sultana pointed as amusement lit her eyes, and Aysel grinned sheepishly. She usually lightened her steps as well, but had been distracted by thoughts of Bashir.

"I was coming to speak with you."

"He mentioned I would be welcome in his forces. I did not come to discuss the choice, I came because I was hoping you might be willing to teach me a spell." Aysel shifted. Her muscles were tired from sparring with Bashir, and they were starting to cramp from kneeling.

"Come with me then," the Sultana said.

Aysel obeyed, rising and allowing the Sultana to move past her, falling into step beside Tareck.

"I just saw Bashir," Tareck said. Aysel made a non-committal noise. "I think he's vexed about you besting him in the ring—he was storming out of the palace like he meant to crumble something to rubble. Perhaps you should go easier on him, next time." Tareck sounded both proud and amused.

"I went easy on him this time," Aysel said. Tareck laughed. Inside she crumpled. She'd never had to think about someone else's feelings before, not this way, and even though she wanted to, and she cared about him, she hadn't thought about what Makram's offer would mean to Bashir. It would not have killed her to offer him reassurance, instead of worrying about her hurt pride. How could he possibly know what she was thinking or feeling if she didn't tell him out loud?

Aysel wanted to run back to find him, but that would require explanations she wasn't prepared to give. Besides, he would not likely be interested in talking to her right now.

Samira hurried ahead, two other attendants in tow, and opened the Sultana's rooms, stepping aside as the Sultana and Makram entered, followed by Aysel and Tareck. Tareck nudged Samira with his elbow on his way past, and Samira responded with a wrinkled nose. That was Tareck, making friends of everyone.

Four of the soldiers followed them all inside and made their way through the rooms and into the gardens, and the other two posted in the hall outside the door. Samira shut it and stood quietly to the side, though she did offer Aysel a quick smile.

Aysel enjoyed the pale colors that dominated the palace. Blues, silvers, and white. They were soothing, different than the dark, warm colors her mother had always preferred in their own home.

The Sultana sat on one of the couches. "What is this spell you wish me to teach you?"

"Commander Ayan mentioned to me that you could hear any part of the palace you wished to," Aysel said.

The Sultana made a thoughtful sound as she swept a glance from the top of Aysel's head to her toes. "Not every mage in a House shares the same advanced abilities. You and I, for example, are very different though we were both born in the First House. Makram tells me you have incredible acrobatic skill. I assume this is augmented by your magic, and the speed with which you moved the day of the attack at the camp suggests to me you use your magic to alter yourself, instead of your surroundings. You may not be capable of the same spell."

"I would like to try. It is Commander Ayan's intent that I oversee the night watch, and I believe this spell would help me cover more of the palace." Aysel shifted from one foot to the other, restless under the gazes of so many.

The Sultana's mouth kicked up at the corner, and she held a hand toward the couch opposite her in invitation. "To begin, it is best to silence your other senses." She looked at Aysel in cool expectation.

Aysel closed her eyes.

AFTER TWO MARKS OF practice with the Sultana and an entire night fighting back exhaustion, Aysel was ready to fall asleep face first in the gravel of the courtyard. She had located an ideal perch on the copper cupola of a tower on the west end of the palace, from which she could see the entirety of the garden and she was only a moment away from the Sultana's room by rooftop. Still, she had spent most of the night pacing back and forth across it in an effort to keep her eyes open, when she was not practicing casting the hearing spell, or kicking herself over her disagreement with Bashir.

She did, however, have what she considered to be a halfway decent idea of how to apologize to him, and it had required an early morning trip to the Grand Market. After her many trips there while observing the Grand Vizier's estate, she had become familiar with its layout and most of its vendors. There had been a trinket vendor who caught her eye because she sold charms meant to be worn to repel misfortunes cast by the Wheel. Obvious hoaxes, all of them, yet there had always been people lined up to buy them.

Despite Aysel's arrival right when the sun came up, the woman was happy to sell Aysel one of her charms and now she clutched it in her hand, tying a length of leather cord around it. The shift change was not for another two marks, and she hoped she could find Bashir before he was out of bed. While she had not seen nearly enough of Sleepy Bashir for her liking, she had seen enough to know he was far more open to suggestion before he'd fully recovered from sleep.

It was unlikely he had gone all the way to his mother's house to sleep. He would want to be close if someone found the assassin in the palace. So she tried his room in the barracks first. There were only two guards assigned to barracks watch, one leaning against the wall outside the entrance, looking half asleep, the other pacing the hall in an attempt to stay awake until his shift change.

"I'm looking for the commander. Is he here?"

The guard yawned and pointed to Bashir's room, where Aysel had first encountered him when she stole her swords back. "You can look, he never locks his door."

"He doesn't sleep naked, does he?" she asked, giving him a wide-eyed look of innocence.

The man chuckled. "Never had occasion to check, but I doubt it. The way he always appears out of there ready to go we all just assume he sleeps in full uniform. Or he doesn't sleep at all." He grinned, and Aysel returned it. Bashir had managed to dress pretty quickly at his mother's house to pursue her.

She didn't knock, because she didn't want to give him extra time to remember he was cross with her, she just opened the door. The room was empty. She frowned. The hall guard peered over her shoulder.

"Might be in his office." He walked down the hall to the first room and swung the door open, then shook his head. "He could be in the palace. He has a room there too."

"Where are his rooms in the palace?" She'd seen what she suspected was his office, but not whatever room they'd given him for sleeping. The guard explained, and Aysel thanked him before jogging across the courtyard and up the palace steps. She followed his directions, retracing her steps to the office Bashir had herded her into the night before, around a corner and down a short hall to a compact wing with three rooms. According to the guard, Bashir's was the center room.

She glanced behind her as she walked down the hall to the middle of the round foyer to which all three doors opened. Aysel touched her fingers to the latch handle, watching the hall as she gave it a gentle test. Not locked. That made sense. He wouldn't want to fumble with a lock if he was trying to leave the room quickly, or prevent a soldier from getting in to wake him up. She pressed it down all the way, and the door opened.

Aysel slipped inside and shut it behind her, allowing a moment for her eyes to adjust.

The room was very much like the one he kept in the barracks, only more ornate. In the barracks he had a simple platform topped with a straw-stuffed mattress against the far wall, and a cabinet for his clothes. In here the stone floor had thick woven carpets for comfort, a large window to the right of the bed, though the heavy velvet drapes were almost completely drawn, letting in only a sliver of dawn light. The bed itself was two or three times the size of the one in the barracks, with four towering posts draped with gauzy fabric. She couldn't tell colors of anything in the dim light, but she could see Bashir.

She tiptoed over the carpet to the foot of the bed. He lay sprawled on his back, one knee bent up and falling open to the side, one arm over his eyes, the other stretched out to the side. Unfortunately he was not naked but almost, he wore only his salvar, and they were not tied. They lay especially low on his hips, revealing the jut of his hip bones and the muscles that sat just above them, the beautiful span of his flat, muscled stomach, and the broader expanse of his chest and shoulders.

A scant smattering of tawny hair covered his chest and thinned to a delicious line of slightly darker hair that led from his navel and into his salvar.

Aysel could have stared at him for the rest of the day. She had not had nearly her fill of his body and had promised herself she'd coax him into allowing her all the time she wanted to touch and kiss and revel in every bit of him. But for now, she only hoped he didn't kick her out the moment he woke.

"Out," he said, without moving.

Aysel rolled her eyes toward the ceiling. It had always been her secret belief that the Wheel found itself amusing. She rounded to the side of the bed, kicked off her boots, and crawled over it to kneel at his side.

"I can see why you prefer the barracks. This looks terribly uncomfortable. Is this a feather-stuffed mattress?" She bounced a little.

"I am certain I just told you to leave." His voice was sleepy hoarse and alluring. Had she ever been so physically attracted to anyone in her life? She didn't think so.

"Hmm," she agreed.

He slid his arm off his eyes and let it curve above his head, glaring up at the fabric that crisscrossed the frame of the bed above them. Aysel admired the flex of his arm, the bulk of muscle there, and bit her lip. Bashir lifted his arm and slapped around on the bed until he found a pillow, which he shoved over her face. Aysel grinned, tugging the pillow out of his grip and hitting him with it. He batted the pillow away with one arm and snaked the other around her waist. He tugged her sideways on top of him, then jerked and groaned, cursing.

"Take your cursed swords off," he said, shoving her away again.

Aysel winced, and unbuckled the harness, then pulled her arms free and dropped it over the side of the bed. "I'm sorry," she said, stretching out on top of him.

"The knives as well, you madwoman," he growled, lifting his head to try and look at his ribs, but Aysel was in the way. "You probably snuggle those damn things when you sleep alone."

"I will not admit to anything." She pulled her sleeves back and offered him one arm. He unbuckled the sheath from her forearm, and tossed it away, then did the same when she offered the other.

"Is this how I can expect you to report to me every morning?" He reached above his head to grab a pillow and stuff it behind him to prop himself up.

"Only if you promise to look exactly like you did when I came in here," she replied. "I've never seen anything so magnificent in all my life."

His lids half-closed over his eyes, and he closed his hand over her two braids. "Flattery," he said, "is acceptable."

Aysel smiled, filling up with fondness for him until she thought it would overflow from her and she'd drown in it. "And apologies?"

Bashir's expression turned grim, but he nodded.

"I shouldn't have left. I should have stayed and talked." She swept her fingertips over the light wash of coarse hair on his chest. "But please don't keep things from me." She kissed his chest, as an apology, and his breath shuddered out.

"Aysel." He grabbed her wrists in his hands to stop her petting. "If you leave, it will hurt me," he said, bluntly, like he were slicing through something. "And I am afraid you don't care." He took a deep breath. "I think I want more from you than I should. Or that you want for me too. And I don't know how to feel but angry."

Aysel blinked, her throat tight and her eyes stinging. "Oh," she said, stupidly. He could make his words count, her ox, and they pierced straight through her heart.

Silence sat between them, as she cast about for her wits and tried to gather them into some kind of formation to produce thoughts. Finally, she managed a coherent sentence. "Why couldn't you say that earlier?"

"It is best to give me time to rein in my own temper," he said, "or you will find yourself wrestling with something that does not budge. I thought you saw a chance to run again, and you were going to take it, and what I might want didn't matter to you."

Aysel sat up, gently twisting her arms free of his grip. He held her hips instead, his brow furrowed. She reached a hand into the front of her caftan, feeling about with her fingers for the purchase she'd made that morning.

It was wrapped in a bit of canvas to protect it. She retrieved it and held it out to Bashir. He searched her face as he shifted higher on the pillow and took it from her. "What is this?"

Aysel nodded for him to unwrap it. He did, revealing a glass vial approximately the size of her pinky finger. It was filled with sand, though when she had bought it there were tiny dried flowers in it. Supposedly the flowers protected against pox, which Aysel was less worried about than helping Bashir understand how much she cared for him. He turned it around in his fingers. He stretched out the cord she'd tied around the top, below the cork, clearly confused.

"No matter what I choose, I may have to leave. I serve Makram, and I always will. If he needs me in Sarkum, then I will go, just as you would go wherever the Sultana asked you to."

Bashir's expression darkened, then relaxed into something like gloomy stoicism. Aysel stretched the cord out and ducked her head into it, though she didn't take the vial from him.

"You told me once that you could always find your earth." The heat rising in her cheeks irritated her. Her throat tightened more, down to her chest, and her voice wavered. "I thought…" She cleared her throat, and Bashir's hand closed slowly over the glass, his eyebrows rising at the same pace.

"I thought if I put some of the arena sand in it and kept it with me"—she struggled to finish, because she suddenly felt foolish—"that you would always be able to find me."

He stared at the vial clutched in his fist, silent. Did he not like it? She'd been so sure.

"That would work, wouldn't it? The glass wouldn't interfere, you could—"

"Yes," he said. "Yes. It would work." His voice did not sound better than hers, and he was as still as stone. Then the muscles in his jaw jumped and he grit his teeth, his gaze sliding to hers, unleashed magic glowing from his eyes in the dim light. He liked it. Her held breath eased out of her.

"Dumb Ox." She tried to smile. "All you see is that I run." A tear slipped down her cheek. She swiped it away. "Why haven't you realized I always come back?"

His breath left him in a short, stunned laugh. He pulled gently on the leather cord, so that she leaned into him. He rolled on top of her.

"Be careful," he said, one hand against the side of her face, his thumb sliding across her cheek. "I might be tricked into thinking you care about me."

"I care about you," Aysel said. "It isn't a trick."

She watched realization paint subdued surprise over his face, then resignation. He moved as if he would kiss her but stopped halfway into dipping his head. "Aysel, I…"

Her pulse became a roar in her ears, pounding through her body like little drumbeats of thunder. She knew what he wanted to say, and she wasn't ready. Maybe her fear showed on her face, or perhaps her stiffened body gave her away, but Bashir swallowed back the declaration, snapping his gaze away from hers. The sense of him pulling away was tangible, she felt his magic retract behind mental walls, and his weight against her lessened as he prepared to get up.

She wasn't ready for him to love her. She didn't think she could bear the full weight of another person's heart. But neither could she bear his absence. "Don't go," she pleaded.

Bashir turned his face back toward hers. After a long moment, he shifted his elbows higher so he could trace the lines of her face with his fingers, his gaze roving like he was memorizing her.

"Where did you go last night?" He closed his eyes and tucked his face into the slope of her neck, resting his head there while his thumb drew a line up the side of her throat.

"To ask the Sultana to teach me her listening spell."

His lips brushed the skin below her ear and Aysel closed her eyes, her body relaxing beneath his.

"Did she?" He coaxed her arm out to her side, smoothing his hand over it, then doing the same with the other. Aysel wrapped them around his back and ran her fingertips over his skin. She traced the curve of his shoulder blades and the rise of muscle to either side of his spine, then rubbed her fingers lightly over the dip in his lower back.

"She tried. I practiced all night, but it does not come easily to me. I can't seem to direct it, it just, does what it wants." She slid her nails lightly up his back, and smiled a little. His skin prickled beneath her hands.

He lifted his head. "Her strength has always been in spells centering around the mind. Yours is different. I've never seen an air mage do what you can." The way he looked at her, with pride and greed, made her warm and senseless.

She circled her arms around his neck. "Do you want to sleep a little more?"

He shook his head and lowered it, grazing her mouth with his. The contact stoked an ember that had not gone out since their first time together. After a few more slow caresses of her mouth with his, he kissed her deeply, and Aysel arched beneath him, stymied by the weight of him.

He pushed up on all fours and released the kiss, moving down so he could untie her salvar and pull them off. Then he did the same with his, pushing them off his hips and kicking out of them before he grabbed her hands and tugged her so she was sitting. He unwound the fabric at her waist, then pulled the short-sleeved guard caftan off. The one beneath it was thin, lightweight, and long-sleeved, and he cocked his head, looking at her. The space between her legs was already demanding, and the way he looked at her only made her want to beg him to hurry up. She bent her knees up, first together, then slid her feet apart and leaned back on her hands in invitation.

Bashir made a sound very much like a growl and fell forward onto his hands, walking them over her legs, so his face was in front of hers and his hands beside her hips, her knees resting against his ribs.

"I think about you, and this, until it feels I'll crawl out of my skin if I cannot have you," he said.

"Me too." She leaned forward, pressing her lips to the point where his collarbone met his shoulder, and bit him, lifting her hands to his neck and pressing gently, urging him onto his back. There was something she wanted to do to him, and she doubted she'd be coherent enough if she let him have his way. He obeyed her urging, dropping to an elbow and rolling onto his back. Aysel straddled his chest, and he grabbed fistfuls of the caftan she still wore, pushing it slowly up to reveal her stomach, then the fabric wound around her breasts, the tiny vial of sand hanging between them. Bashir tugged and Aysel leaned forward, stretching her arms out so he could pull it off. He gripped the vial in his fingers, and magic burst all over his skin, jagged lines shooting down his body.

"It is happy in its new home." His magic swirled through the vial, lighting the sand so it glowed like it was molten. He released it and gave the cloth hiding her breasts a tug. Aysel smiled, and unwound the fabric, tossing it off the bed. Bashir skated his hands up her waist and over her breasts, and the warmth of his touch felt so good after the constricting pressure of the binding that Aysel whimpered.

He pulled her flat on his chest, letting out a pleased rumble. "You like my hands on you," he said in her ear, petting one hand after the other down her back, avoiding the line of stitches that bisected her lower back.

"I would like it if you touched me all the time," Aysel agreed. She was so small in comparison to him that his hands were almost big enough to span her entire back, and she adored it. She scooted down the length of his torso, pausing to kiss a line from his throat and down his chest. When her kisses brought her lower, tracing the transition of chest hair to the narrow line pointing downward, Bashir's breath stopped. He spread his legs enough to accommodate her, and she settled between them, her hands spread on his lower belly.

His erection greeted her with a pulse, and she pressed the flat of her hand from the base to the tip.

Bashir's head fell back against the bed with a shakily indrawn breath. "You don't have to do that."

"What if I want to?" she said, more to his arousal than to him, examining the gorgeous length of him. Bashir threw an arm over his eyes and lifted the other hand just enough to wave her on. Aysel laughed, then rose up, kissing a slow line from base to tip. Bashir whispered something too softly for her to hear, casting about for a pillow, which he slammed over his face.

She held him in one hand, drawing circles at the sensitive point where the base joined the head, and his entire body went taut. He bent one knee, and Aysel slid her hand up his inner thigh, the coarse hair tickling her palm, as she licked a trail up his erection. His hips followed as she moved up, and she stroked her hand in the wake of her tongue. He groaned, his stomach flexing, his hand curling into a handful of the bedsheet.

Watching his pleasure was perhaps the most erotic thing she'd ever seen. She considered ceasing her teasing and simply mounting him. But that hadn't been her original plan, and there was time for that when she was finished torturing him to the edge and back down. Aysel pet him again, once up and slowly down, then took him in her mouth. The hot, silky skin of him was pleasure enough, but the deep, rumbling moan that issued from his throat and was muffled into the pillow almost undid her.

Aysel played, in sucks and strokes and licks, some slow, and others fast, teasing him with flicks of her tongue around the tip, and deep sucking kisses. He threw the pillow aside and his hands came to her head, and she could tell it took all his willpower not to take over control of her movements. She sucked the length of him into her mouth as far as she could then retreated, slowly, grazing the length of him ever so lightly with her teeth as she did. His magic thrummed, his body tightening and every muscle jumping into relief, his breath catching and his fingers digging against her braids.

She released him and waited, dragging her fingers over his hips. His breath left him in a rush and his body relaxed. When his breathing evened out, Aysel began again, coaxing and teasing him to the edge of release, then stopping. She gripped him in her hand and kissed the tip of him as he lay panting.

"Shall I continue?" she asked.

"Only if you want me to bring the palace down around us," he warned. She kissed a trail back up the way she had come down, but she only made it halfway when he caught her shoulders and flipped her on her back, kissing her savagely.

"You are evil, and breathtaking, and all I've ever wanted," he whispered in her ear, and before Aysel could fully assimilate the words, he had slid down the length of her, slung her legs over his shoulders, and kissed the molten, empty place between her thighs. Aysel would have liked to mention that no one had ever done that to her before, but Bashir's warm hands closed on her thighs and he kissed the sensitive nub that sent slow pulses of pleasure through her hips and she forgot how to speak.

His tongue stroked up one side of her then the other. She went limp with a soft cry, reaching down to tangle her fingers in his hair.

His tongue was like warm, wet silk, coaxing her body to a height of wild arousal she didn't know was possible, so she felt like the emptiness between her thighs would kill her if he didn't fill it. And still he kept on, trading slow licks for soft, sucking kisses that made her body shimmer and quake, her muscles utterly out of her control, and her thighs quivered with her denial of their need to tighten together as he teased her to the edge of a climax that might break her into a million shards. When she knew she was going to fall, he stopped, and returned to her, hovering over her on all fours and gazing down at her with magic bright in his eyes.

"Was that revenge or foreplay?" Aysel croaked, her body tightly strung.

"Both," he said. "Do you feel remorseful?"

"Not in the least." She grinned, and he reached down to hook his hand beneath her knee, pulling her leg up against her body as he fit his hips over her. He slid into her with one long, perfect push, and Aysel cried out as her body shook, ready to burst apart at the next stroke. Bashir paused as she caught her breath and relaxed. She felt his magic twine around her, the weight of it bearing down on her own flashing, thundering power. He began again in steady rhythm that had both their magic spilling out, pushing against the boundaries of each other's, twining together and apart. Sometimes her magic struck at his, but his was like stone, patient and imperturbable, like its master could be.

He pushed her leg higher, and when he drove into her it was deep and hard and Aysel's body trembled and shimmered apart, her breath stolen as she said his name, and her power left her in streaks and storm as release and relief arced through her. He fell against her, burying her beneath the weight and breadth of him, and she felt his body overtaken by his magic, his hold on her slipping, as he shuddered and moaned. She knew the feel of it now, could separate it from the slow roll of his, how it behaved, how she could hold it. Aysel took hold of her power and wrapped her arms around his back, kissing and nipping at his skin as he relaxed against her.

He slid down, settling his shoulders between her thighs and pillowing his head on her abdomen, because if he stretched out fully on top of her she'd be buried beneath him head to toe. She slid her fingers through his hair and closed her eyes. Their breathing slowly synchronized, his magic waning back under his control, and hers settling inside her like a perturbed cat, curling into a flashing but subdued storm cloud inside her.

His words played inside her thoughts, toying with her emotions, making her feel bubbly and happy then sending her sinking into melancholy. She wasn't good for him. He needed steadiness and dependability. He needed things to be black and white. She was the antithesis of that down to the very power that coursed in her blood. If she truly cared about him, she should walk away.

"When all of this is over, I'm going to make love to you until there is nothing left of either of us, then I'm going to sleep with you for two days," he mumbled into her belly.

Aysel brushed a hand over his head. She didn't have the words to tell him how glorious that sounded.

He pushed himself to all fours. "But today, I have to go."

"I know."

He slid off the bed then bent over her and picked her up as if she weighed nothing at all, depositing her at the top of the bed and stuffing pillows around her, then pulling the blankets up over her. Aysel nearly melted into a sloppy puddle of adoration at his care.

"Do you want me to wake you…" Darkness cascaded across his face, but he seemed to shove it aside. "Makram said he was leaving today, with your father."

"Yes, wake me." That same darkness passed across his face again at her words. "So I can say goodbye."

He sat beside her and leaned over her, frowning. "If you do not go with them today, you may not have the chance again."

"If I choose to join them, I can find them. Mathei and I have been beside our father through all of the time he has been in command of Makram's army. I know where his camps are, and what his plans are. He wanted us to be able to take up his mantle if something happened to him." She tried to play. "I could potentially be the shortest general in history."

"You are incredible," Bashir said, the intensity in his gaze and fierceness in his voice silencing anything she might have said in return. "Do you know that?"

She allowed the opportunity for teasing to pass, squirmy and uncomfortable under his praise.

"The more I know you, the more I cannot bear the idea of you…" He trailed off and looked away. Then he picked up the vial from where it lay between her breasts. It glowed under his touch, the same earthy, golden light that shone on his body in flux, and when he laid it back against her skin, it was warm. The light faded from it slowly, and when it was gone, Bashir stood and dressed.

"Go to sleep," he said as he left.

TWENTY-SEVEN

AYSEL SLEPT THROUGH BASHIR returning, climbing onto the bed and staring at her for what he later reported to be half a mark. She woke because he kissed her. Not her mouth, but the point of her shoulder where it peeked out of the covers. It was, she decided, the second-best way to wake up. The first had been waking up nearly suffocated by the weight of him and his affection when they'd slept at his mother's house.

"Your brother is waiting outside, so I don't have the time to show you exactly what looking at you like this does to me," Bashir spoke into the curve of her neck. "Wear this exact thing again the next time I'm alone with you."

"I'm not wearing anything," Aysel said sleepily. He tapped a finger against the vial of sand, then stood.

"I'll see you in the courtyard."

"Mmhmm." Aysel closed her eyes again.

"On your feet, or you won't be able to tell your father goodbye," Bashir ordered as he swung the door shut behind him. It shut with a bang, startling her completely awake. Aysel forced herself out of bed and dressed, sluggish and tired. She was still fighting her way into her sword harness when she staggered out of the room.

Mathei stood in the middle of the round foyer, arms folded, face clouded with impatience. He unfolded his arms and helped her into the leather straps then buckled it for her.

"Perhaps you should sleep more, and spend less time admiring the view," he said.

"Would you?" Aysel asked.

"No, I would not," Mathei agreed. "It's probably spectacular."

"Mmm." Aysel rubbed her hands over her face and eyes, then smoothed them down her hair. Mathei offered her his arm and she slung hers through it as he led her toward the entrance and the courtyard.

"I halfway believed you would go with Makram and Father," he said as they passed into the courtyard. Aysel had to stop, squeezing her eyes shut against the pale glare of the sun.

"You and Bashir both, it seems." She rubbed away the sting in her eyes and took Mathei's arm again. "I don't know what I should do. "

"You know exactly what you should do, you just don't want to," he scoffed.

"You only say that because it's what you would do. Join the Sultana's Circle."

"Don't be ridiculous. That sounds like far too much work. You, however, love work. A good portion of my life was wasted watching you throw yourself fruitlessly at walls until you learned to climb them. Why are you so different about your magic?"

"It's so much bigger than me," she said, quietly, and Mathei stopped at the bottom of the steps, before they crossed the courtyard to join the others. "This power, this potential. If I'm part of the first Circle of Chara'a since the Sundering, people will expect enormous things from me. I was happy with the way things were."

"You were? With mages being persecuted? With hiding everything that you are? You were happy with that?"

"I understood where I fit in. I am nothing like Makram. He's tall and dark and you can tell he comes from old Eastern blood where they lop your head off and tie it to their horses as ornaments. He looks every bit a powerful mage that can help reshape the world. I can barely hold his gaze. Have you ever tried? It's as if you can feel your heart start to slow down, your body begin to stop."

"So?" Mathei asked.

"So. Have you looked at me?" Aysel said in exasperation. "Nobody is going to rally to battle for me. For all the reasons I make a good spy, I will not make a good Circle mage. I am not inspirational."

"I'm not certain I've ever seen you underestimate yourself quite so spectacularly," Mathei said in a flat tone. "I also don't believe this is only about the Circle."

"What is it about?" she asked.

Mathei tipped his head to indicate something he was looking at. Aysel followed his gaze to a spot past where Makram stood speaking with their mother. Nearby, Bashir stood in front of three of his guards, his face set with stony irritation as he slapped the back of his hand against one of their chests, indicating the sloppy placement of the guard's sword with his other.

"I think he loves me," Aysel said in answer to Mathei's wordless accusation. Her throat closed around the words and the rest of her filled with too much emotion.

"Of course he does. The man isn't a complete imbecile," Mathei said. "Why say that as though it makes you sad?"

"I couldn't be a worse match for him."

"Well. You are short. That does not seem to have deterred him," Mathei said, thoughtfully. Aysel glared at him and he rolled his eyes.

"He likes to protect people, Mat. He cannot stop himself. Yesterday one of his guardsmen grabbed me and I thought Bashir was going to bring the entire Kalspire and all its foothills down around us."

"It appears he contained himself." He squinted at the peak of the snowcapped mountain.

"I suppose," Aysel said.

"Is it fair to expect him not to care if someone mistreats you?" Mathei glanced at her.

She sighed, tipping her head back. "If he nearly has a magic-induced heart attack because some dung heap of a man tries to throw his weight around, how will he survive if I have to go to war with Makram? Or hunt down evidence against dangerous people?" She waved her hand instead of saying the Grand Vizier's name or title.

"Is he less capable of bearing the burden of worry than you are? Would you not worry if the roles were reversed? His shoulders seem… sturdy," Mat said. "Very sturdy."

"You've made your point." Aysel gave his shoulder a little shove. Mathei reached up to pluck at the vial of sand that hung around her neck. Aysel yanked it away from him and tucked it into her caftan, beneath the cloth that bound her chest.

"Do you love him?" he asked, all the teasing gone from his voice.

"I care about him. I do not want to hurt him."

"He's a warrior, Aysel, not a pampered noble son that can barely stand the sight of his own shadow. Why would he not want you? Want someone who is kindred? Who is fully capable of facing all of the worst of what he might experience, not as someone who stands by and pats his back to comfort him, but who can stand beside him through it? And why would you want anything other than someone who can do the same for you?"

"I don't think I do," Aysel admitted.

"Of course not." Mathei nodded. "I'm glad we could have this chat. Shall we go say goodbye to father?"

"Mat"—Aysel grabbed his elbow, forcing him to turn back toward her—"when did you know you loved Reis?" She had never loved anyone but her family. But Mathei had. Fiercely.

"When I realized he was written into every breath I took," Mat said, the darkness of his magic slipping into his voice. "You will know. It will just overtake you, and you will know." He nodded toward their father, who had caught sight of them. Aysel touched Mathei's hand in apology for stirring up his pain, and Mathei shook his head in dismissal.

"Thank you for deigning to make time to say goodbye to me," Thoman said, glowering at Aysel as she and Mat joined him, their mother, and Adem.

She glowered back. "Some of us have important work to do, Baba, and I was catching up on my sleep so I could singlehandedly protect the Sultana."

His eyebrows rose, and her mother sighed in exasperation. "Some respect for the gravity of the situation, Aysel," Dilara scolded.

"When has Aysel ever cared about the gravity of a situation?" Mathei said under his breath. Dilara fixed him with a murderous stare, and Mat pursed his lips. "Father, I bid you safe journeys and hope you return soon," he said, quickly. Thoman enveloped him in a hug, which Mathei accepted with all the pleasure of a cat plunged into a bucket.

"And I, the same," Aysel said, but she jumped up, catching her arms around Thoman's neck, and he chuckled and hugged her hard. His arms hit her too low, pain shot through her back at the pressure along her wound, but she remained silent. Asking Mathei about Reis reminded her that one never knew when they were hugging someone they loved for the last time. And if her father and Makram were preparing to make a move on Kinus, then the situation was as grave as her mother claimed. "You know I will come if you send for me."

"What the Sultana is doing is vitally important, Kit," Thoman said. He looked at her as though he had more to say, but she also recognized when he decided not to say it, smiling instead. Perhaps he wanted to suggest what she should do.

Aysel turned, looking for Makram. He stood with the Sultana, with Tareck nearby, and another man Aysel had never seen before.

"Mat," she asked, "who is that?"

"Ihsan Sabri," he said, clasping his hands behind his back and regarding the man with a look of interest. "Until a season ago, he was next in line to the throne, but I understand it was recently revealed that his mother was a maid, or some such drama. I believe he is referred to as Sehzade Sabri, or was. I've been pondering how very attractive he is, and I have come to the conclusion that the Sultana has had all the unattractive people in the palace murdered or sent away."

"That cannot be right," Aysel said, "because you're still here."

Mathei made a face at her, and she elbowed him in the ribs. The trio of royalty made their way across the courtyard to join Thoman, and Aysel and Mathei dropped to their knees in the gravel.

"Aysel," Makram said, "shouldn't you be sleeping?"

"I wanted to wish you a safe journey, my prince," she said. His jet brows rose at her lofty emphasis of his title.

"I will be sending regular word to the Sultana, and it will include news of your father," Makram said. With so many people around, his tone and posture were formal.

Aysel nodded. What she wanted to do was hug him. Just because he was powerful did not mean he was invincible, and unease at the idea of them leaving to battle without her made her restless.

"On your feet then," he said. Aysel and Mathei obeyed, and Makram wrapped an arm around her shoulders. "Take care, hmm?" He tugged one of her braids. "And Mathei." Makram released Aysel's shoulders and reached for Mathei's hand. The two men clasped forearms, and Makram put his other hand on Mathei's shoulder. "The Sultana has an offer for you that I would like you to consider."

"Of course, Efendim," Mathei said, awkwardly suppressed glee manifesting as reddened cheeks. Aysel grinned. Makram winked.

"Oh. I've forgotten." Makram released Mathei's arm and turned. "The Sultana's cousin, Sehzade Ihsan Sabri. Ihsan, this is Aysel and Mathei Attiyeh."

"The spy," he said as he looked at Aysel, in a rich voice that immediately identified him as a Second House mage. Aysel had never met a water mage who didn't have a voice that made the hair on her neck stand on end in the best of ways. She flicked her gaze to his arm, where turquoise tiraz confirmed her suspicion, and labeled him a Sival. She smiled. He did not return it, but gave her a lingering look of amused incredulity. "You are…not exactly what I pictured."

"She is entirely unnoticeable, which is why she's a good spy," Mathei said. Aysel elbowed him in the ribs, and Ihsan gave a small smile. He was handsome, though more to Mathei's taste than hers. As tall as Makram, with a lean build and hard lines defining a face that bordered almost on beautiful instead of rugged or handsome. He kept his hair a bit longer than most of the men she'd seen in Narfour, it hung to his chin, but was secured back away from his face, and he sported a goatee and beard that confined itself to outlining the line of his jaw.

She also saw, when he glanced sideways at the Sultana, a broad, puckered scar running up the side and back of his neck, jagged in shape. Fire. It was a feat to burn a Sival of the Second House. Free fire could not do so. Had someone done that to him? Aysel's belly churned.

"We should speak, at some point," Ihsan said to Aysel.

"That would require that you show your face in the palace again," the Sultana said, as if in warning.

The Sehzade made a face. "Yes, thank you. I'll manage."

Makram chuckled, placing one hand on Aysel's shoulder and the other on Mat's. "Ihsan is a bit of a recluse. We have trouble finding him where he's supposed to be, instead of hiding in his home and tending to roses or shuffling about a garden plot."

The Sehzade rubbed a finger up the bridge of his nose, narrowing pale eyes at Makram. "I am the Vizier of Agriculture. I believe that requires some time spent in garden plots, as does my research of your Blight." His rich voice pushed and pulled like a tide, directing everyone's eyes to him involuntarily, despite that it was laced with irritation.

Aysel felt Bashir's approach at her back, the pressure of his magic, like a big bull putting its head against a fence and leaning into it. Her magic swirled in irritation, zipping through her blood and over her skin. Makram hissed, snapping his hand away from her and giving her a look like she'd pinched him.

"Sorry"—Aysel glanced over her shoulder—"your magic," she said to Bashir, frowning. He blinked in surprise, and she felt him pull it back, so that its edge only teased the boundary of her own. What had him so irritated that he was bleeding magic everywhere like that? Erol walked with him, looking more serious than she'd ever seen him.

"Sultana Efendim." They both bowed, and tapped their fists over their hearts, though it was Erol who spoke. "My men are prepared when the prince and Elder Attiyeh wish to leave."

"We are ready." Makram looked over his shoulder at Thoman, who nodded. Aysel gave her father one more hug, and he pet a hand over her hair as though she were five Turns instead of nearly four Cycles. "Be safe." He looked over her head at Mathei. "Both of you."

He turned to Dilara, and because he was tall and she was short, he went to a knee instead of bending himself halfway over so he could take her face between his hands. "I will return, I swear it."

Aysel's mother nodded, doing her best to hold back tears though her face was red and her eyes shimmering. She gripped Thoman's hands where they touched her cheeks and kissed him. Aysel turned her gaze away to allow them some semblance of privacy. Might she ever have occasion to kiss Bashir publicly? She didn't like the idea of him having to kneel to kiss her when they were standing, she much preferred jumping into his arms. But someday she would be old, and maybe then she'd let him kneel.

Aysel realized what she'd been thinking, and her gaze swung to Bashir. He was looking at her, and she knew, with heart-rending certainty, he was thinking of forever at the same moment she was. She knew because of the way he watched her, with resolve and sadness in his earthen eyes, and a small, wry smile on his mouth. Aysel wanted to kiss him right then, as an apology for the sadness she'd put inside him, and because she didn't know how else to show him her heart.

"Aysel," Makram said. She looked at him. "I have a favor to ask."

"Ask and I am commanded." She grinned. He raised an eyebrow and put a hand on Erol's shoulder. Erol looked grim.

"I am taking every Sival available from the guard force. That's four powerful mages that Commander Ayan will no longer have at his disposal. One of them is his second in command." Makram glanced at Erol, who acknowledged the look with a nod. Aysel's grin faded, and she looked to Bashir, whose jaw was set and expression unreadable, his own gaze trained on the Sultana.

"I would like to offer you an official position in my guard," the Sultana said to Aysel, but turned to Samira, who approached at her back and handed her something. The Sultana held it out to Aysel. Twin gold braids, like the ones Bashir wore on his uniform. "As second to Commander Ayan."

"I had nothing to do with this." Bashir held his hands up when Aysel turned a look on him. "And I told her you were as likely to take orders from me as you were to eat sand."

"Less likely," Aysel muttered, and Bashir halfway smiled.

"As a favor, Aysel," Makram said. "It does not commit you to the Circle, only to protecting what matters most to me." He looked at his betrothed and away as oblivion flashed then disappeared from his eyes. "Until I return."

"The men will not be pleased to have a woman they barely know promoted over them so suddenly," Aysel said, taking the braids reluctantly in her grip.

The Sultana smiled, her eyes sparking in amusement. "I'm certain a woman who can thoroughly humble her commander in the arena is also capable of gaining their trust."

"Thoroughly is an exaggeration," Bashir said under his breath. The Sultana's amusement broke into a true smile, and Aysel stood dazzled by the woman's breathtaking beauty, moving her hand slowly toward Bashir so he could pin the braids on her. He stepped in front of her, taking the braids from her hand and blocking her view of everything in front of her. Aysel tipped her head back and narrowed her eyes as she looked up at him. He pinned one braid in place near her left shoulder, and she could tell how hard he was trying to stifle a grin.

"Not so big and dumb, hmm, Sister?" Mathei purred in her ear. "I do believe you've been outmaneuvered."

"Thoroughly," Bashir agreed.

"Thoroughly is an exaggeration," Aysel mimicked Bashir's words as he pinned the other braid in place.

"Thank you," Makram said when Bashir turned to stand beside her.

Aysel frowned at him, picking at the braids. "Only while you're away." She looked at Erol. "And you absolutely *will* return, because I refuse to be his nursemaid indefinitely."

"He's not so hard to deal with, once you get used to him." Erol grinned at her.

"Nursemaid?" Bashir scoffed.

"I've stalled enough." Makram turned to the Sultana, taking her by the shoulders and tugging her toward him. Samira's eyes widened in surprise, but the Sultana did not protest or pull away.

"If you allow anything to happen while I am gone, if you let your pride put you in a situation where you are in danger, there is nowhere in the world or the void you can hide from me."

"I know," she said, gently.

Aysel turned away from them and slid one arm through Bashir's and one arm through Mat's, tugging them a respectable distance away.

Erol and Tareck joined them. Aysel released her grip on Bashir and her brother and hugged Tareck.

"I'll see you soon, Kit. And maybe you can put the commander's guards in order, hmm?" He laughed a little when she drew back and they both looked at Bashir, who wore a dark scowl on his face. Tareck slapped him on the back, then tipped his head to them in farewell as Makram strode past. Erol saluted Bashir, who grabbed him, hauling him into a brief embrace in which he slapped him hard on the back and Erol let out a pained gasp.

"Wheel keep you, my friend," Bashir said as he released him, and Erol nodded.

"And you," Erol said. Samira came up beside Bashir, and smiled at Erol, holding her arms out to him. He lifted her up in a hug, and whispered something to her that made her laugh as he set her down. Then he jogged across the courtyard to where the other three guards waited for him. The guards joined Makram and her father, and Makram raised a hand in farewell.

Aysel's magic sizzled inside her, stirred by another's freed power. It was a familiar touch, the same magic she had felt the day she first kissed Bashir and the Sultana had summoned him with a spell. She glanced over her shoulder, and saw pale light in the Sultana's eyes, wisps of wind stirring at her coffee-colored hair. The Sultana turned abruptly away when Makram and the others disappeared through the gate, and strode for the palace.

Samira gave a quick curtsy and hurried away after her mistress. Mathei went to Dilara, and put an arm across her shoulders, leading her back toward the palace.

Aysel drew a shaky breath. Until this moment, war had felt like a problem that would happen sometime in the hazy future. But now it was a certainty, and people she cared for were deeply involved. She stared at the great arch over the Morning Gate, at the empty space where her father had been only a moment before, where Makram had smiled as he waved goodbye. She thought about the men and women in the refugee camp, whose lives had been uprooted, and the families she knew in Sarkum that had not been as lucky as hers, for escaping Kinus. Like the murdered mages she found just after Makram left.

She lifted her hands, flexing them open, palms toward the sky. A storm was coming. In the form of war. In the form of a Blight, if what Makram had said was true and it was a construct, a weapon. It was coming. The Sultana was trying to prepare, despite those who stood against her, despite the Grand Vizier.

Aysel dug her fingernails against her palms. What was she doing? Nothing but thinking about herself. Thinking about what she wanted instead of her duty. The Wheel expected recompense for all its gifts, and it was time she paid hers.

"You're all right?" Bashir asked, moving to her side. He folded his arms across his chest. She couldn't tell if he was trying to appear nonchalant, or if he wanted to touch her but resisted. She decided it was the second, because the thought made her happy.

"Only thinking," Aysel said.

"You should get more sleep." He squinted up at the sun. "Before the shift change."

"I'll try. Is this going to be all right, me as your lieutenant?" She tapped the shiny new braids on her shoulders.

"Between you and me, yes," he said. "Though I expect a great deal more discipline from my men than you may be accustomed to, and I will expect it from you as well." He relaxed his arms to his sides. "You were right though, for the men it will take time. And more encounters like Kasim, yesterday."

"Thank you for allowing me to deal with him on my own. You did very well." She laughed when he narrowed his eyes at her.

"As did you. Are you prepared for more of the same?"

"I am small, and female, and plain. I've been proving myself to people all my life." She looked up at him. "Are you prepared for more of the same? Or worse?"

Bashir looked at the ground. He kicked up a small mound of gravel then bent to retrieve a stone. "Do you want the truth, or do you want me to tell you something flattering about how I have the utmost faith in you and my men?"

"Hmm." Aysel tapped her lips with a finger, and watched as Bashir threw the little stone he'd retrieved and it knocked a fist-sized divot out of the palace wall. The gate guard nearest it flinched then looked toward Bashir and her in bewilderment. Earth mage strength was something to marvel at. "The truth."

He picked up another stone and tossed it. Another divot, a hand span from the first. The gate guard moved to the opposite side of the Morning Gate's arch. Bashir crouched, picked up a rock the size of a lemon, and rose again. He bounced the rock in his hand, testing its weight.

"The truth," he agreed as he half turned, raising the rock level with his shoulder and cocking his elbow. His eyes narrowed, and he threw it. The motion looked easy, casual, like it lacked any effort at all. The rock sailed over the wall, which was at least two hundred paces away and as tall as four men, and smashed into the cliff face that Aysel had climbed when she broke into the barracks. A sheet of stone the size of a horse broke off and slid down, smashing to pieces against the top of the wall and raining down shards into the courtyard.

The gate guardsmen looked at each other, at Bashir, then away.

"I told the Sultana I didn't want you as a lieutenant." He turned his back on the destruction he'd caused. "I told her"—he gripped the hilt of his sword—"that you are a loner from spoke to spoke, and you would ruin the discipline of my guard force."

Aysel folded her arms over her chest. "I do appreciate your honesty, Ox. But I'll admit this time it stings a bit."

"I told her that because I could not bring myself to tell her that I love you, and that having you beside me every day and not being able to tell you or anyone else that you are mine, will probably kill me." He rolled his neck from side to side, not looking at her. "So." He shoved his hand through his hair and turned his back on her. "Prove me wrong."

He strode toward the barracks. "I'll wake you at shift change," he called.

Aysel tried to swallow her heart back into her chest, but it seemed to stay stubbornly lodged in her throat.

Twenty-Eight

Something woke her, but she lay as she was, on her belly, her head buried beneath a pillow, for long moments trying to understand what it was. A noise. It had been a noise. She sat up, and her ears filled with it again. Screams. The snap and crackle of flames. She scrambled off the bed and pulled on her boots, then ran from the room.

The foyer was quiet, as was the main hall. Aysel slowed to a walk, confused. She didn't smell smoke, and no one was about. She jogged to the palace entrance and stopped outside on the steps. Quiet. Aysel took the stairs slowly, scanning the courtyard. The sun had already sunk halfway into the ocean, the light waning quickly. The gate guards chatted with each other under the arch of the Morning Gate, and the barracks and arena were quiet. Bashir would have been coming to wake her soon…had it been a dream?

The sounds came again, and she realized that, like the night before, the listening spell was behaving of its own volition. Aysel's throat went dry. She was hearing something that was happening somewhere else.

Her gaze slid sideways, up the slope of the mountain, to where the refugee camp perched high above the palace. The blood and shadow of flames danced, reflected against the hill behind the camp. It looked so much like her final view of her home as they fled that Aysel felt she might be sick. They still hadn't caught the fire mage from the mob that had marched on the camp. This time, he had succeeded.

"Fire!" she shrieked, running toward the barracks. "Fire at the camp!"

The two guards at the gate turned toward her, bewildered, and Aysel pointed as she ran. Bashir appeared in the barracks door and she slammed into him. "Fire. The refugee camp is burning," she gasped. He took her by the shoulders and pulled her inside.

"Everybody up!" he bellowed, and when the two gate guards followed them inside, he sent them down the aisle of the barracks, pounding their fists against the doors to the rooms. "Form up in the courtyard," Bashir ordered, and took Aysel's arm, leading her back out of the barracks so he could look up at the hill. He breathed a curse.

Men stumbled out of the barracks, still pulling on clothes or arranging weapons. They formed up into a shuffling, grousing mass of irritation and confusion. Aysel watched the growing light on the hill with rising tension. All the Sival from the guard were gone except for Bashir, and she would be next to useless unless they wanted the fire to be bigger.

"Are there any other Fifth House Sival?" she asked Bashir. A Sival would be able to control the course of the fire while it was put out.

"Samira," Bashir said. "Go get her. And the two Second House guards that are part of the Sultana's watch."

Aysel turned and ran, darting up the stairs and through the halls toward the Sultana's rooms. As she passed her family's suite, the door opened and Mathei stuck his head out. "What is going on?" he said in sleepy protest.

"The camp is on fire," Aysel said, turning backwards to speak to him, then spinning around to jog the rest of the way through the halls. The two guards at the Sultana's door greeted her with nods. Neither of them were water mages, so those two must be in the garden. Aysel knocked on the door. When the answer didn't come quickly enough, according to her racing heart and anxious mind, she knocked again. The door opened after the third knock, and while Samira's face had been the picture of serenity as the door opened, when she saw Aysel it flickered to irritation, then to concern.

"The camp is on fire. We need you."

Samira's expression turned grim, and she nodded. Aysel followed her into the room. The Sultana rose from where she sat on a couch, across from Ihsan, who did not rise, but flicked his gaze across Aysel in assessment.

"Forgive me, Sultana. The camp is on fire, we need Samira's help, and the two water mages in the garden."

"Of course." The Sultana turned, opening the glass doors and calling to her guards as Samira shrugged out of her brocade entari and stepped into the hall. As the two guards came into the room and hurried into the hall, the Sultana turned to Ihsan, who had risen to his feet. His face had washed of warmth, his magic flashing in his eyes and across his face, cool blue whorls of swirling ice.

"San," the Sultana said, softly.

He shook his head. "I'll be all right. I can at least help with anyone who's"—he closed his eyes and the magic faded but did not dissipate—"hurt." He joined the others in the hall.

The Sultana faced Aysel. "If you can, keep an eye on him. He's… The fire may overwhelm him."

Aysel bowed and returned to the hall, leading the group of them back into the courtyard, where Bashir had divided his men into groups and was calling orders. A handful of other guards had brought horses from the stables and were saddling them. Bashir glanced back at the group when Aysel moved to his side, then gave a second, wide-eyed look when he saw Ihsan. He looked at Aysel, and nodded.

"Let's go," he said. Ali Macar brought him his horse, and he swung up. "One of you take Samira," Bashir ordered the two guards Aysel had brought, "and someone saddle the Sehzade's horse."

One of the guards working with the horses darted back into the stable.

"If you're mounted, go," Bashir said, wheeling his horse in place because it was beginning to chomp and paw with all the tension in the air. "Aysel," he said when he came around, and held out a hand.

Aysel jogged to him, catching his arm and swinging up behind him. He watched as half the riders made their way out of the gate at a trot, then surveyed the remaining ones.

"Hold on." He urged his horse to a trot.

Aysel's gaze stayed on the camp as they rode down the palace road and made the tight switchback before climbing the road to the hill. When they were on the dirt, Bashir's horse broke into a gallop. She tried not to think of the people she knew, the farmer's two little girls, and what might be happening in the panic. How could someone hate so much that they would murder innocents? Strangers? She pressed her forehead against Bashir's back, her hands tightening in his caftan.

When they reached the top of the hill, Aysel slid off his horse before it had fully stopped. She had imagined it would be chaos, but the immensity of it crushed her. In the thick of it, the screams she had heard through her spell were amplified and blood-curdling, some of them the fast, panicked screams of fear, some of them shrieks of pain that sliced down her spine and brought tears burning into her eyes. The smoke choked her, even though the fire was on the far side of camp. The heat of it burned her skin, even from that distance, and she broke out in sweat. Ash fell around them like snow.

People ran in every direction, so confused and maddened by the smoke and fear that some were running into the camp instead of away from it, tricked by the labyrinth of shelters and detritus. Aysel looked for the shelter she and her family had given up to the farmer and his family.

"Wait." Bashir grabbed her arm when she moved to run into the camp. "It will not help anyone if you get lost in there."

Aysel stood in his grasp instead of running, but her heart continued to beat so hard and so fast that she feared it would break apart into pieces.

"Samira," Bashir said as the soldier she had ridden with helped her down. "You go with them." He pointed to a group heading into the center of camp, toward the northern edge where the fire's flames danced upwards. She nodded briskly, rolling her caftan sleeves to her elbows before she trudged into the fray. "The rest of you start there." He drew an imaginary line across the south end of camp starting at the road. "And sweep the camp. I want all these people on the road. Separate the injured, you two"—he pointed to the two guards Aysel had retrieved from the palace—"are on burns."

Bashir turned to the Sehzade. The fire reflected in Ihsan's pale eyes, and Aysel watched his magic flicker and die, flicker and die, as cold and frost rose up from the ground at his feet. She was not sensitive to other people, not the way water mages could be, sensing feelings. But his fear was as tangible as his magic.

"Sehzade," Bashir said, gripping his arm, hard. Ihsan jerked, looked at Bashir, and snapped his mouth closed, though his chest rose and fell at a frantic pace. "Will you oversee the triage for the wounded?" Bashir pointed to the guard house near the road, farther away from the fire.

Ihsan spun and strode without a word or gesture.

A great burst of flame billowed up and over the northern edge of camp, accompanied by more screams, and a frenzy of people running into the midst of the guards. Bashir turned as a group broke through and made the road, and raised his hand, flattened like a blade, and stabbed it upward. A shelf of rock and stone broke upward halfway down the road toward the city, a wall of rock.

"What are you doing?" Aysel cried, lunging toward the road, but Bashir caught her arm and swung her back toward him.

"You four"—Bashir pointed to his guards—"no one goes past that." He looked at Aysel as the four guards sprinted for the stone barrier. "If these people run into the city, I will not be able to account for them, or find them, or treat their injuries. They may be attacked in the city." He raised his eyebrows as Aysel nodded, her shoulders sinking. She didn't know why she doubted him at all. He was obviously thinking more clearly than she was.

"What do you want me to do?" she asked.

"Get up the hill, see if you can find where it started, or who started it."

"You don't think it's the same mage from the mob when the Sultana visited?"

"It's too big to be an accident," Bashir said, as something collapsed to the north of them, accompanied by shouts and a cloud of sparks and smoke. "That mage has cost me too many candlemarks already. These men should be guarding the palace, not…" Bashir spun to face the cliff, and the palace beyond.

Dread like ice turned Aysel cold then hot. They'd taken Samira. And the Sehzade, and two of the Sultana's guards. Makram was gone. All the Sival in the guard force were gone. Nearly all the guards were now embroiled at the camp. She looked up at Bashir and saw the same realization in his eyes. His expression darkened with fury and helplessness, because there was no way to return in time. Not for him, anyway. But she was lightning.

Aysel eyed a clear path between her and the cliff, and ran. She heard Bashir shout her name, but it was distant, because she pushed her power into herself, so the entire camp passed her in a blink, and she was over the edge of the cliff and in open air, falling.

She readjusted the direction of her power, wrapping it around her body, creating a cushion of air and reducing her speed and weight, so that when she hit the sloping hill at the bottom of the cliff she rolled, came up on her feet, and kept running. Down the hill, on light feet, toward the palace road, on almost exactly the same route she had taken the night the fire mage had chased her toward the palace. Aysel pushed her power again at the palace gate, flashing past the two guards left in the courtyard and toward the garden. If there was an assassin planning an attack, he'd go that way, not through the halls.

The garden, like the palace it wound through, was a maze, and Aysel did not know it well enough to navigate it. She made a leap to the roof of one of the long halls, pulling herself up and continuing her path in the general direction of the Sultana's rooms. The rooftops she did know fairly well, she'd mentally mapped them the night before during her watch. There were two more roofs between her and where she felt fairly certain the garden outside the Sultan's hall lay. Just as she started in that direction, she saw a dark shape slip across the skyline of a roof then slide down into the garden. Aysel pushed, flashing across one roof, then the next, and hurling herself into a flip as she reached the spot she'd seen the figure.

She landed in the garden behind him and drew her swords. The two palace guards that had remained behind, positioned to either side of the glass doors and windows into the Sultana's rooms, were already dead. One had just fallen backwards against the wall, his face frozen in a rictus of shock. Aysel lunged at the assassin's back as he lowered his arm from whatever spell he had cast. He spun away from her, swinging his own sword and knocking hers aside.

"Attack!" Aysel cried in warning, hoping the guards inside could hear her. The man she faced smiled. He might have been twin for the fire mage that Bashir had shot, average height, average build, dark hair, arrogant grin. But it was not fire magic that swept in black, inky tendrils around his hand. She immediately regretted calling the guards. Even a Deval of the Sixth House was capable of stopping a heart at a distance, if his magic touched a person.

"Hello, Aysel," he said. "I wondered if we might meet. You are a quick little rabbit, aren't you? I saw you leave to head up to the camps, and yet…here you are." He lifted his sword, resting the edge against his shoulder as he looked at her, frowning in apology. "This isn't going to go well for you."

"Who are you?" She kept her distance, because she didn't want him to touch her or her blades. He had a crossbow slung against his back, likely the same that had fired the poison-tipped bolts at the camp.

"Rifat." He stepped casually toward her, drawing a knife from the cloth that wrapped around his waist and almost to his chest. There were several knives tucked into it, and Aysel did not care for her odds in the face of a sword-, knife-, and crossbow-wielding death mage. "Do you know we've crossed paths before? At the palace in Al-Nimas." He drew the knife across his palm, carving a sigil. That he used sigils meant he was a Deval, and not a much less powerful Aval, snapping her last remaining thread of hope.

The glass doors to the Sultana's rooms slammed open.

"No!"

But Rifat raised his bleeding hand, and dark magic coalesced around it, shooting from his palm and against the guard who stood in the doorway. The man dropped to his knees.

"Inside!" Aysel cried to the second guard who almost stumbled over his comrade's body. "Keep the Sultana inside." Aysel leapt at Rifat, swinging a sword at his neck and one at his belly, pulling up her power and driving it into a cyclone around her, pushing him back, slinging the next bolt of his magic sideways.

Rifat laughed, dodging backward, agile and at ease. Aysel pulled her magic back, facing him with her swords, preparing to flash at him in the hopes she could drive a blade straight through his belly before he touched her.

"I've upset you." He smirked.

"And me." Mathei spoke from behind her. Aysel did not look, it would be all the opportunity Rifat needed to end her.

"Big brother to the rescue?" Rifat squeezed his hand into a fist, drawing more blood from the carved sigil, and tossing another bolt of magic at Mathei. This time Aysel did look, in panic. But Mathei sidestepped, so quickly he nearly fell over. When he recovered he moved to Aysel's side.

"Rifat," Mathei said. "I wouldn't have believed there was anyone left in Sarkum who would hire you."

"No one in Sarkum did." He smiled, and magic wrapped his arm, a coiling snake of the darkness of the void.

"I'd really rather you weren't here, Mathei," Aysel hissed. He was just one more factor to consider in an already too-complicated situation. "Do you know him?"

"He's dog shit. A sword people hire for the ugliest jobs. Now would be an excellent time for you to tap into that vast Charah power of yours and come up with something useful against a death mage." Mathei moved past her, drawing his sword, and Aysel followed.

Rifat swung when Mathei lunged, and their swords clashed together, and both men reached for the other's sword in order to use power to erode it away. They shoved apart, and Rifat tried throwing another bolt of magic, but his wound was closing, and the sigil losing its power. Mathei swung, aiming for Rifat's midsection, but the man was quick as a mink, and spun halfway around, avoiding most of the swing. It opened a line along his shoulders, and he laughed, reaching back to swipe at the blood. He gave a series of quick, sharp whistles.

Then, two men materialized out of the darkness. Rifat moved backward away from Mathei's advance and drew a new sigil against the back of his hand. He gave a quick gesture to the two men, and they ran for Mathei.

"Mat!" Aysel cried, when Rifat opened his hand again. Aysel rushed, shoving all her power into the speed, and flashed past Mat, knocking him sideways, and crashed into Rifat. They tumbled over each other, landing in a tangled heap. Aysel rolled, grabbing for his wrists before he could grab for her, and he kicked his legs against the ground to get out from under her, wrestling his arms away from her grabbing hands to try and keep his own free to cast.

Aysel drove her knee into his groin, and when he grunted and curled in on himself briefly, Aysel got hold of his wrists and pinned them to the ground with her hands. She ground the sigil he had drawn on the back of his hand across the mud, ruining it. He cursed then started to chant a spell, black swirling against his palms as he sneered up at her and rolled, pinning her beneath him. A huge disadvantage of being short and lightweight was that if she didn't get control of the fight initially, by distance, speed, or disabling her opponent, she could rarely get it at all. He bore down on his arms, his hands reaching for her face. The spoken spell did not work at a distance, but he only had to touch her with his fingers, where the magic was beginning to twine and swirl. She braced her elbows against the ground, trying to hold against his strength, but his hands crept closer, and his sneer became a nasty smile.

Aysel grunted with the effort of resisting his heavier weight, and it turned into a shout of rage as she curled her shoulders upward and slammed her forehead against his nose. He jerked back, and the pressure he was exerting downward ceased for a moment. She shoved him sideways, scrambling out from under him and casting about for her swords, which she had dropped when she ran into him. They were, unfortunately, on the far side of Rifat, who was getting to his feet, clutching his face in one hand.

Mat had already killed one man, driving his own sword through his chest, so Aysel turned her attention back to Rifat. He swiped blood from where it had poured from his broken nose, looking at her with narrowed eyes. "Thank you." He smiled. The blood had poured over his mouth and stained his teeth, and in the last light of day he looked like every nightmare story of death mages Aysel had ever heard. He carefully drew a sigil on one hand, then the other.

One bolt after the other raced toward her, like he was throwing stones instead of death spells, and Aysel dodged, ducking and spinning between them, trying to get closer. If she could dive past him for her swords, she might have a chance. Even using sigils a Deval's power was limited. There was a slim chance she could outlast his reserve of power as well. Or, she could take Mathei's suggestion and do something useful with her magic. That had better odds.

Unbinding her power was not unlike unbinding her chest. Peeling away layers of mental tension that kept her magic compressed inside her. Though she had never had to unwrap her chest while also dodging magic. Rifat paused to redraw the sigils with more blood.

Her magic spun through her, storm clouds of power filling her until they burst outward, drawing raw lines of lightning across her skin, and the air around her grew charged. She did not know what to do with it. She did not know what the storm inside of her was capable of, because she had never fully unbound it. The hair on her body lifted, and shocks tickled across her scalp.

Whatever she looked like, it surprised Rifat. He stopped, one hand lifted, shadowed magic twining restlessly around his arm, as he stared at her.

"Storm mage." He started to lower his hand, then he hurled a bolt at her instead. Aysel dodged, her freed magic responding to the barest of thoughts, and she zipped sideways, then at him. Another bolt of black magic left his hand, and she dove into a roll, coming up in front of him and flicking one of her knives into her hand. But he was fast, and his hand closed on her throat, the other on her wrist.

"Foolish." And he was right. She could feel his hand tighten on her throat, cutting off air and blood, and Aysel clawed at Rifat's fingers, frantic to get away before he could say his spell and send her spiraling into the void. She kicked at his shins. He forced her hand, still gripping her dagger, around and slammed it against her thigh, driving the knife into her leg. Pain like fire shot up her spine and she let out a strangled cry.

"Aysel!"

She recognized Bashir's voice, and tried to look for him, but could only see him out of the corner of her eye, where he stood framed in the glass doors of the Sultana's room. Her momentary distraction was just enough for Rifat. He hissed the words of his spell. Some spells were beautiful to listen to, like the call of a fire mage to their element, or the singing of a water mage to a river. This was opposition to that. Death and decay whispered within his words, and the darkness in his pupils captured her, holding her gaze, calling her quietly into their depths so that her body stilled in his grasp, despite her mind's frantic demand that she fight.

His magic coalesced around his grip on her throat, filling her with death, and cold, and nothingness. But it wasn't so bad. It felt like peace, and calm, and rest. Her heart slowed, and her pulse weakened, and her breath stopped. Her limbs became heavy, her muscles weak. Her heart gave one last, slow beat that echoed through her body and her thoughts. The dark of his eyes swallowed her.

Aysel floated, or felt as if she were, and pieces of who she was began to flit away, memories, the things she cared about. None of it mattered, at the end. She was tired. Distantly she felt a rumble—quaking that struck her magic, demanded that it fight. Aysel ignored it, sinking deeper into the darkness, and an eternity passed in which there was nothing. She was stripped of desire, of care, of anything.

And…another presence manifested in her solitary darkness, and she turned her attention to it. Oh. It was her. Or rather, it was her power, outfitted in Aysel's reflection. Her power, the power of every Air Charah who had ever come before, the Wheel's own Storm. It smiled at her, and she saw, in its eyes and its grin—magic. Magic unconstrained, the heart of a storm, the oppressive roll of thunder, the pulse-pounding flash of jagged, dazzling lightning across a night sky. The limitless potential of air.

"I don't want to die," Aysel told it, coming to the realization as the sounds of her words were swallowed by the void.

"Not yet," the Storm agreed.

It flared, streaks of bright, sharp lightning shooting through her veins, shocking her heart into rhythm again, and exploding outward from her, pushing the tendrils of Rifat's power away. Because he touched her, the lightning arced through Rifat, and she felt it tracing his power, following it back to the core of him, attacking that which had attacked her, and he lit like a mage orb for a heartbeat, then he dropped to his knees, his hands releasing her throat and the dagger he'd shoved into her thigh.

As he dropped, he raised his hand, and the last sigil flared black, sending a final, weak bolt away from him. It missed Aysel by a wide margin and she sneered as she punched him, a quick, sharp jab, and he fell, and lay still.

To her left, Mat dispatched Rifat's second man with a hand to his face. The man started to scream at the touch of Mat's magic, but it cut off sharply and he dropped.

Aysel stared at Rifat, gasping for breath, the beat of her heart painful in her chest from the terror of realizing how easily she'd given in to his spell. She grabbed for the knife in her thigh and yanked it out with a grunt of pain and effort, then wove in place as light swam across her vision and dizziness threatened to send her to her knees.

The Sultana's voice broke through her shock, and though Aysel did not comprehend the words, she heard the sorrow in them. The pleading.

The feverish pace of her heart seemed to slow, and a loud, dull roar filled her ears as winter's cold bled the heat from her from scalp to heel. She knew before she turned. She knew. Rifat had not been aiming for her with that last bolt. He'd been aiming for the Sultana.

"No," Aysel choked, spinning around. What she saw made her wish she had stayed in the void, stripped of care and concern. The Sultana on her knees, trying to hold Bashir's too-large frame from falling over and failing, as he slumped in slow motion out of her grip.

He'd turned into the bolt to save her.

Aysel ran toward them, tripping and falling to her hands and knees, scrambling to her feet then falling to her knees again beside Bashir. "Don't you dare." She threw her arms around him and fell onto her haunches as he collapsed backwards against her, his body heavy, dead weight. The Sultana released her grip on him and sat on her heels, tears in her eyes. Aysel couldn't even look at her. She should have stayed inside, away from the doors. It was her fault.

He was stone. He was unbreakable. He was *not* dead.

But he was falling, sliding away from Aysel's grip, until only his shoulders and head were supported across her lap and chest. She stroked a hand over his face. "You're all right," Aysel sobbed. "Please, please don't do this."

His magic was silent, unresponsive to even the antagonism of hers, his body stripped of the warmth and pulse of life. Aysel sucked in a strangled breath that wanted to escape as a scream.

"No. No. No." She could barely see Bashir through her tears. "You can't," she begged. "You *stupid* Ox."

"Aysel." Mathei crouched at her back and put his hands on her shoulders.

"No!" Her power filled her voice and her body and Mat jerked away from the lightning touch of her. "Get away," she snapped. At Mathei. At the Sultana. At the single remaining guard who stood dumbstruck and infuriatingly alive.

"Please, Aysel," the Sultana said, her voice gentle. Aysel's power burst across her skin in streaks, unleashed by her anger and showing in the glare she leveled at the Sultana. Aysel wanted to do to her what she had done to Rifat. Her life for Bashir's seemed only fair. The Sultana dropped her gaze, and got to her feet, backing away.

Aysel hugged her arms around him, burying her head into the slope of his neck.

She hadn't even been allowed to say goodbye. In one breath he was there, and gone. He hadn't even given her time to tell him that she loved him too. He'd walked away, he'd said it and walked away and she hadn't been able to tell him the truth. Her chest squeezed so hard around her heart she was certain it would stop again.

Aysel drew a short breath. Her heart had stopped. She had died, even if it was only for an instant. It was beating now. It had…

She tugged herself out from under Bashir, laying his head against the stones and kneeling beside him. Her power had started her heart again. Could she do that for someone else?

She looked at her palms, flexing her fingers apart, then curled them into fists and whispered to her magic, closing her eyes and calling to the Storm. It answered, swelling up inside her, storms, and thunder, and lightning. She only wanted the lightning, but it was too difficult to hold, or summon, or direct. It whipped and swelled, and trying to hold it in her mental grasp was like trying to wrestle a writhing, clawing cat.

"Aysel?" Mathei's voice was muffled by her concentration, by the storm that filled every one of her senses.

"I can save him," she said, but she didn't know if Mat heard her. She continued speaking to her magic, learning the rhythm of the words she needed as she went, like feeling out the tumblers of a lock, collecting the storm inside her into a contained space within her mind, holding it around her, calling to it again and again until it felt strong enough, as strong as it had when it arced through her of its own accord.

"Aysel, that is enough. You need to come away from him," Mathei said, less patiently.

Something wet struck her face. But she kept her eyes closed. She reached into the storm of magic inside her, and fastened control over the lightning, collecting it into her mental and magical grasp.

She opened her eyes. Rain had begun to fall in fat, slow drops. Aysel looked up to see an enormous storm gathered above them. She looked at her fists and flexed them open. Lightning flashed across her palms, over and between her fingers, and up her arms.

"Step away." A storm of magic filled her voice. Her magic had killed Rifat because he'd been touching her when it shocked her. The Sultana moved back, as did the remaining guard.

Mathei reached to touch her, watching the lightning, but then drew his hand back.

"This is not a good idea," he said. She glared at him. His face was set with sorrow, and worry. She couldn't think of that, or she would doubt herself. She looked away. At best, this would work, and at worst…she was desecrating the dead. Aysel swallowed the lump that rose in her throat and blinked away tears.

She leaned over Bashir and placed her hands over his heart. She closed her eyes, sucked in a breath, and faltered. This was madness. Her magic had brought her back to life. It knew what to do. She didn't.

The power crackled around her hands as she hovered them over his chest. The air reverberated with the lightning that twined and curled around her hands and arms. It wasn't going to hurt him, she chanted mentally. He couldn't feel it.

"Do it, or step back," Mathei ordered.

Aysel slapped her palms to Bashir's still chest and tensed, releasing a hiccup of power, and the lightning snapped at him like a biting dog. He jerked, then lay still. She bit her lip, holding back her fury, and sorrow, but not her desperate tears. Not enough. She was too afraid. But Mathei was right. If she was going to do it, she had to commit to it.

She pulled more power, winding lightning around her arms like a sailor with tie lines. Her body obeyed, dolling out energy in the form of magic. Her head grew muzzy, her arms heavy, her pulse slowed, her lungs filled with breaths that tasted of lightning. The air around her was fuzzy with the charge, and the pulsing glow of the lightning nearly blinding. Did she even have enough energy to generate what she needed to save him? Blood trickled from the wound in her thigh, her body turning all its assets to her command for power.

It began to rain harder, soaking her and everyone else.

"Aysel," Mathei warned, but came no closer. The Sultana had her hands clasped tightly together.

"I can," Aysel said it for herself more than them. "Forgive me," she whispered to Bashir. Then she braced mentally, as she would just before swinging a punch. Two quick breaths, and then she did exactly that, swung both arms up and over her head and slammed them down on Bashir's chest, shoving all the collected lightning out in the same moment.

His body bowed upward and then relaxed.

Aysel collapsed over his chest, trying to breathe and only managing little gulps of air. There was nothing left in her. She could have run all day and night and had more energy than she did in that moment. And she had failed. Everything inside her began to fracture, her hope crumbling.

"Please." Rain washed over them in cold, heavy drops. "Don't go."

Against her ear, Aysel felt Bashir's heart give a heavy, strained thump. His magic flickered to life and quaked against hers, the granite and loam smell of it filling her nostrils and making her sob in disbelief. She bolted up, staring down at him.

Bashir stiffened like he'd been stabbed, and cursed. Then he rolled to his side and vomited on the stones of the Sultana's patio. He groaned, propped on one elbow, his other hand outstretched to hold himself up, his head hanging.

"Who lit me on fire?" he croaked. "What happened?"

"Merciful Wheel," the Sultana breathed, pressing her fingers to her mouth as she met Aysel's wide-eyed stare.

"And we'll never hear the end of this," Mathei muttered, crouching near Aysel. "As if you weren't already arrogant."

She wanted to laugh, and couldn't. Couldn't believe she'd done it. She reached for Bashir's back. She needed to touch him, for him to look at her, she needed to see that he was real and alive, but stopped with her hands outstretched, hesitant. Bashir's head jerked up when Mat spoke, and he rolled to his belly, looking through the rain to where Rifat lay.

"Aysel?" He tried to get to his hands and knees. "*Aysel.*" His voice held the anguish that had been hers only moments before.

"I'm here." She put her hands on his back.

He turned, saw her, and collapsed onto his haunches, grabbing her arms and yanking her against his chest. "I told you. I told you that you are not allowed to die."

"Me?" She slapped her hands against his chest. "Me? I only died for a moment. Don't ever do that to me again!" She hit him again, and again, closing her hands into fists and slamming them against him. Tears streamed down her face, lost in the deluge from the storm, and he wrapped his arms around her, squeezing her against him.

He rested his chin on top of her head. "What did you do to me? I feel like I was run over by a team of shod carthorses."

"I struck you with lightning. And apparently called this storm." Aysel wiped water off her face—it was pooling in her eyelashes and blurring her vision. She looked up, into the swirling rain. "Oh." She gently extracted herself from Bashir, getting to her feet. Her legs trembled, and when she raised her hands toward the sky and the storm, her arms shook. Too much power expended in too short of a time.

But if she could just use a little more, she might move the storm into the camp.

Just a bit more, she coaxed herself, and her magic rose inside her, tracing a spiral of blue and white lightning in her mind's eye. A new power joined hers, glowing cold like winter sun, pulled into and plied with her own by her magic's demand. The Sultana. Another mental reach captured a thread of the guard's, a Deval's cool air. Her magic wrapped them together like spinning wool, and filled her up with strength.

The wet stones of the patio reflected the blue-white light of Aysel's power as it coiled around her. She focused upward, pushing the storm with her augmented power, commanding it east.

The rain falling around them slowed then stopped as the storm obeyed, and Aysel pushed harder with her will, until the dark sheets of rain enveloped the camp. When she released the storm her knees buckled. Bashir caught her.

She gripped his shoulders as nausea and exhaustion joined forces to remind her, again, that she was quite mortal. "I may have…done too much." Her head swam. She laid it on his shoulder because it was suddenly too heavy. "I hope it helps."

All she wanted was to close her eyes. In fact, her body demanded it, despite her effort to stay awake. Perhaps it was mage sleep descending on her. She had never needed it before and didn't know what it felt like. But there was one thing left, and it seemed important.

"Sultana," Aysel mumbled, "I think it would be best to begin my formal training sooner, rather than later."

"As you wish, Attiyeh Charah," the Sultana said. Was that… amusement…in the woman's voice?

Bashir's arms tightened around her and he pressed his cheek to hers. "My storm," he whispered. He lifted a hand to her hair. "I love you."

"I love you too." She closed her eyes and nuzzled her face against his neck. "Don't you ever die to get the last word again."

He laughed softly, and caressed her cheek with his thumb. "Promise."

TWENTY-NINE

BASHIR PULLED A STOOL up beside Aysel's bed and took her left hand in his. It was impossible to wake anyone from mage sleep. It was a completely involuntary reaction to expending more power than a mage's body could. It had been three full days since Aysel had killed Rifat and sent a storm to wash away the fire at the camp. He'd heard of mages sleeping as long as six days. Ceylik and Havva had looked at him afterward and pronounced him hale and whole, except for the shadowed lightning that marked his back, a dark burst of forked lines that mirrored the magic she had used to save his life. It was a burn—his mother had treated it with salve and declared it a small price to pay. Of course he agreed. Bearing Aysel's mark made him feel linked to her.

But he missed her, and there were still jagged pieces from watching her die in Rifat's grasp that could only be soothed by her voice and her hands and her blazing life.

"She isn't going to wake up if you keep her in this cave," Havva said to Ceylik. They stood on the far side of the infirmary, putting together supplies for Havva to take to the camp. There were many refugees who had been seriously burned or hurt in the ensuing melee. Havva and all the apprentice physicians from the palace went every day to treat them. Ceylik remained to monitor Aysel. Bashir had not had one moment alone with her. Ceylik, Mathei, her mother, and the Sultana had stopped by at least once a day to check in. Mathei often sat and read to Aysel. When Bashir had asked, Mathei claimed she despised it and would likely wake up just to throw the book at him.

Havva marched around the room and began pulling open the curtains.

"No, I think the light will only tax her," Ceylik said, following.

Havva snorted. "Light is good for all that ails us. We are not bats, Ceylik. Honestly, what do they teach you at that University?" Havva threw open the final curtains and looking toward Bashir. She gave him a frown to indicate she was not pleased he wasn't resting.

Bashir shook his head.

"I learned medicine," Ceylik said, firmly. This was a fight they'd been having since they met, before Bashir had entered the University. Havva had learned her medicine and healing in the trenches of the poor districts, and Ceylik, a competent physician, had learned his methods at the University.

"But not people. She needs sunshine." Havva crossed to Aysel. She shooed Bashir off his stool and took it when he moved to sit on the bed near Aysel's hip. Havva took Aysel's hand from his and pressed her fingers across the pulse in her wrist. She stared at Aysel's face as she counted the beats, her toe tapping softly against the floor. Bashir had watched her perform the little test countless times over his life, but now he watched her intently, looking for even the tiniest sign that something was wrong, or had changed.

"She's fine," Havva said. "She doesn't need you hovering over her like this. You should rest."

"No. I can't." He couldn't rest unless he was holding her, and the bed was too small and the place too public. Havva leaned to pat his cheek.

"Then talk to her at least. Mage sleep is a lonely place and can be full of twisted memories of what put a mage there," she said as she rose. "And tell her when she feels better, that you'll bring her to my house, and we'll start over. Yes?"

"Yes, Anne." Bashir grinned at her and she scoffed and rolled her eyes. He took Aysel's hand again.

"I'm going," Havva said. "Ceylik, make him rest." She turned to retrieve her freshly resupplied pack for the camp from the table in the center of the room.

"I've been trying," Ceylik said, following her to the door.

Aysel's fingers tightened against Bashir's, barely at all, just a twitch of her hand.

"Anne." Bashir leaned over Aysel, watching her face. Havva and Ceylik rushed to stand behind him. Aysel's brow furrowed, her eyebrows drawing down like she was in pain, and her hand locked tightly around his. She wailed.

Her power flared across her skin, and would have struck out, but Bashir contained it with his own. Barely. It was like a different entity than that which he had held during their trysting, something far more wild and willful.

"Aysel," he said. "Wake up." Sweat broke out over his brow as her power snapped and fought like an angry wildcat.

Her eyes opened and she gasped, her gaze feral and panicked. She saw him and bolted up, throwing her arms around his neck. He closed his arms around her, crushing her to him.

"It's all right. I'm here. We both are," he said quietly against her hair. Her power settled beneath his touch, and she gripped his neck and kissed him, her mouth salty with tears, the kiss ferocious.

Bashir eased her back down and nodded to indicate Ceylik and his mother behind him. Aysel looked up at them, then away, flushed, swiping at her cheeks with the back of her hand.

"How do you feel?" Havva asked.

"Out of sorts," Aysel said, her voice hoarse and weak.

"Mmm." Havva moved to Aysel's side and lifted her wrist to take note of her pulse again. "That's to be expected. It would be best if you rested another day or two." She sighed. "But you won't, will you?"

Aysel looked up at her, then at Bashir, one corner of her mouth lifting. "My commander promised me two days' of sleep."

Bashir glanced down to hide his grin.

"Take him up on it then, and when you are feeling well again, I've told him to bring you to the house, for dinner." Havva hitched her pack up higher and turned. She hesitated, then spun back around. "Thank you, Attiyeh Charah"—she blinked away tears— "for saving my son."

Aysel ducked her chin, weakly. "You will be pleased to know he has promised never to die again."

Havva gave a breathy laugh, lifting her hands to wipe her fingers beneath her eyes. "You take good care of her," Havva said in an accusing tone as she looked sharply at Ceylik.

"I'll escort you to the entrance," Ceylik said.

"Don't be daft. I know where I'm going." Havva marched out of the infirmary.

Ceylik turned to give Bashir a pointed look, and shut the door as he followed Havva.

Aysel grabbed handfuls of Bashir's caftan and tugged, pulling him down with her. "I like him," she murmured, just before she pressed her lips to his.

Bashir chuckled, adjusting so his forearms held his weight above her and he could hold her head in his hands. It soothed him to meet her soft, exploratory kisses, as though she were rediscovering him. Her eyes remained open, and lightning danced in the very depths of her pupils, like he could see a far-off storm.

He brushed a finger across her temple. "I've missed you."

"I woke up and couldn't remember anything, but that you had died." Aysel's eyes slid closed, moisture beading at the corners. Bashir wiped it with his thumbs. Behind him the door to the infirmary opened. Aysel shifted her head, her eyes open, to peer around him.

"Wheel and spokes," she breathed.

Bashir turned to look over his shoulder. Samira entered, followed by the Sultana, the Sehzade, the Sehzade's teenaged steward Kuhzey, and Aysel's mother and Mathei. The last time Bashir had seen the Sehzade and Samira had been right after everyone who had gone to fight the fire had returned to the palace. They'd been smoke-stained and exhausted.

Samira was back to her usual, composed self, and offered him a warm smile. The Sehzade also seemed none the worse for wear, though he had been even more reclusive than usual in the days since the fire.

"Aysel!" her mother said in a scandalized voice.

Bashir sat up, slowly, then stood and bowed. Aysel's mother gave him a quick appraisal then frowned more sternly at her daughter, who frowned back. Ceylik returned as Bashir straightened. The procession of people barely fit inside the cramped infirmary and Mathei made a face of distaste as he was forced to stand beside a shelf where Ceylik had an array of specimens in jars. He eyed a jar of sickly green-tinted liquid with a preserved frog floating in it, in a position as if it had been swimming for the surface.

Ceylik edged around them to stand near the central table.

"I felt you wake," the Sultana said to Aysel as though she found the idea fascinating. "My new Master of Libraries"—she smiled sideways at Mathei—"has informed me this is a good sign. That every First House mage in proximity to you should be aware of your presence. That a Charah should give and receive strength as a matter of course."

Bashir looked at Aysel, who looked back with wide eyes and an expression that read, *I haven't a clue.* He suppressed a smile. Even when things were so much bigger than she, Aysel was flexible and agile in the face of them. Not overwhelmed, just…Aysel. His storm.

"They have a great many books on the history of the Circle of Chara'a. You should come see me soon. For example, the Circle of Chara'a ruled the Old Sultanate for several generations before there was ever an appointed Sultan. And—"

"Mat," Aysel pleaded.

He pursed his lips and folded his arms, glowering.

"Your brother has learned a great deal in an impressively short amount of time," the Sultana said.

"He does that."

"It would not kill you to read a book, Aysel." Her mother sat on the bed next to her. Aysel pushed herself up, slowly, so she was sitting, and took her mother's hands in her own.

"It might." Aysel frowned. Someone snorted, and Bashir thought it might have been the Sehzade.

"I am glad you are awake, Attiyeh Charah. There is much work to do, and my High Council is howling like a pack of wolves caught in a thunderstorm." The Sultana smiled, as if she were proud of her analogy.

Bashir frowned. "She's only just woken."

"I'm all right," Aysel said, but she sounded tired and weak.

"Of course I will not risk your health, but binding her to the Circle will provide her and her family not only prestige, but political protection. My Council"—when she said *Council* she almost always meant the Grand Vizier—"is displeased with the refugee situation. Attiyeh Charah will act as ambassador. After the ceremony, I will excuse her to rest until she feels recovered. You, Commander Ayan"—the Sultana raised an eyebrow as a means of reprimand—"do not appear recovered either. May I assume you have not been resting?"

Bashir dropped his gaze. "She saved my life. I could not help but worry about her."

The Sultana spoke to Aysel. "I would like to leave you in place as Lieutenant Commander, in addition to your new role as First of the Circle. Your burden may be greater for the interim, while the prince is gone." Her voice gave the tiniest of wavers, and her lashes lowered and lifted once.

"Aysel is always happier when she has too much to do," her mother said, reaching to brush a bit of hair away from her daughter's face. Aysel frowned at her.

"That is good, because I do not see a time in her near future where she will not have too much to do." The Sultana looked to Aysel. "You will also, of course, study the history of the Circle with your brother, and with me, as well as instructors I select from the University, to better understand and command your power."

Aysel chewed her lower lip, her eyes slightly narrowed. "Will I have to attend Council meetings regularly?" she asked.

Bashir almost laughed, trying to imagine Aysel sitting through the endless, roundabout discussions in which ceaseless insults masked as politeness were thrown between the Viziers.

"I might prefer to be strapped to a board and drowned a single drop at a time," she said.

Her mother gasped, placing a hand over her heart and turning to give the Sultana an apologetic look. Naime suppressed a smile. Mathei laughed. Ihsan chuckled. The Sehzade had been a master at avoiding the council chamber.

"Not habitually," Naime said. "The entire point of the Circle of Chara'a is to be outside the influence of the nobility. However, the Council will be present for the ceremony to name you to the Circle. Which I would like to conduct tomorrow."

"Yes, Efendim." Aysel threw her blankets back and got to her feet, weaving a bit. Her mother reached for her, but stopped. Bashir caught Aysel's upper arm to steady her, and she batted his hands away, sliding a grumpy look at him. Then, she started lowering to her knees. "Speak, and I am commanded."

"Aysel." The Sultana touched her elbow to stop her descent. "You are a mage on the Council of Chara'a. We serve each other. You do not bow to me."

Aysel blinked. "But…"

Naime smiled. "You do not bow to anyone."

"Because the Wheel randomly chose to give me power?" Aysel said, dryly.

Bashir put his hands on her shoulders, pulling her backwards against him and looking down into her face when she tipped her head back and frowned at him. Still the storm danced in her eyes, not unleashed, not in flux, it was simply unveiled now, unhidden.

"Because you have served the prince in humility, without flaunting your power," he said. "Because you saved hundreds of lives with your storm. Because you almost sacrificed your life twice in service of the Sultana." Bashir mocked the same scowl Aysel bestowed on him. "Because she knows you are trustworthy."

He felt too full, pride and want and joy filling him as he looked at her, as though he might break apart from the pressure of it all inside of him.

"Exactly that." The Sultana ducked her head to Bashir. Mistress Attiyeh lifted her hands to her mouth, looking at Aysel through tear-brightened eyes. Mathei grinned, and Samira looked pleased.

Now if he could just get them to leave so he could congratulate her properly.

"Fine," Aysel said, "but I still have a score to settle. Rifat, the assassin, admitted he was not hired by someone in Sarkum." She flicked her gaze to the Sultana, whose smile faded. "And the things I found…" She hesitated, perhaps not trusting the number of ears.

"We will discuss that soon. For now, rest, and tomorrow morning I will present you to the Council."

"Yes, Efendim." Aysel started to bow again, but Bashir squeezed her shoulders, then stepped around her so he could bow, pressing his fist to his heart.

"Bashir," Naime said. When he straightened to look at her, he saw lingering sadness, or relief, in her gaze. They were friends, of the sort a Queen and her Commander could be. He grinned, and she smiled back, her breath leaving her in a soft huff. "I'm pleased you're all right. I could imagine no one else to lead my guard." Her words rarely held emotion, but now they did, echoes of whatever sorrow his death had caused her.

The Sultana turned, and everyone else went with her, except Samira, who hesitated, given permission with a nod from the Sultana. She crossed from where she stood near Ceylik and hugged Bashir. He grunted in surprise, embracing her in return.

"I think I understand a little better," he said softly as she pulled away, "what it feels like to care for someone you should not."

Samira tried to smile, but her mouth quivered, and she blinked, looking from him to Aysel. "I am eternally grateful to you…for saving two of the people most important to me," Samira said. "Not once, but twice. If you ever need anything that I can provide, you have only to name it." Aysel shifted, and Samira smiled. "I shall see you tomorrow at the Hall of Chara'a." She bowed to both Aysel and Bashir, before she hurried from the room.

Aysel looked up at Bashir, and a slow grin spread over her mouth. Her color was coming back, and she looked disheveled, but almost herself.

"I think it's safe to release you to your own quarters, but I would like to see you both tomorrow at your convenience," Ceylik said, watching as the door shut behind Samira. "Oh, and this is the salve for your burn." He crossed the room to the shelves and brought down a little pot, which he handed to Bashir when he returned. "Once a day should help, or anytime it's bothering you."

"Thank you," Bashir said. He put his arm around Aysel's shoulders before she could ask and urged her from the room. The hall was empty, except for the Sultana's retreating party. He took a deep breath to be free of the place. It felt good to stand on the soft carpet instead of the hard stone of the infirmary floor. The smell the ointments and whatever Ceylik preserved his specimens in gave Bashir a headache. It had been cramped and too quiet in there, as though the void waited in every shadow. This portion of the palace was entirely comprised of infirmary rooms, a surgery, and the housing for the medical apprentices.

"What burn?" Aysel leaned stubbornly backwards against his arm.

"Your lightning," he said. "If you're nice, and behave, perhaps I'll show you." He released his grip on her shoulders and headed in the direction of the main palace and his room.

"Race?" She darted past him. It took him a moment too long to understand, then he ran after her. She laughed when he grabbed for her, dodging away and turning down the next hall. Bashir collided with the wall when he tried to cut the corner, and Aysel giggled again as he recovered. But she had reached the door and fumbled it open, then slammed it in his face.

He lifted his hands to the doorframe on either side, listening, waiting. But she didn't open the door again.

"Aren't you lonely in there?" he called. He liked her games, but this one was hard to play, after being separated from her for so many days.

Aysel opened the door a crack, so he could see one eye and a sliver of her face as she peeked up at him.

"You owe me two days' of sleep. Your mother even ordered it."

"I believe I prefaced that with something else." The idea of having her alone, uninterrupted by anything, for a day and a night, made his body stir.

She threw the door wide and backed into the room, and he followed, shutting the door behind him. He tossed her the little jar of salve Ceylik had given him. Both he and Aysel were dressed only in salvar and the lightweight caftans generally worn under other clothes. He pulled his caftan over his head and tossed it away as he approached her. She watched him cross the floor to her with a look that made the stir in his body become a full rush of heat. Like she wanted him. Like she loved him.

He crouched enough to wrap his arms around her waist and lift her up against him. "Say it again."

Confusion passed across her face, then understanding. She smiled, tracing her fingertips over one of his brows then down his cheek.

"I love you, Bashir Ayan. My heart and shield. As long as you will have me, I am yours." She touched her mouth gently to his, and nibbled his lower lip.

Bashir set her down. "Earth mages can live a very long time, Storm. And I am certain I will love you for all the Turns that remain to me. Are you prepared?" He tugged one of her loose braids, then went to work unwinding it.

"I was not prepared for you, no." She beamed up at him. "But I think I've adjusted well."

He grinned back and started work on her other braid. "And the same," he said.

"Where is the burn?" Aysel held up the pot of salve.

Bashir turned so she could see the jagged lines that had bloomed across his left side.

"Oh," she breathed. "I'm so sorry." Her fingers traced down his spine, avoiding the actual marks, which were angry, red, and sensitive.

"For what? Bringing me back from the void?" he asked. "I am not angry or ashamed to bear your mark."

She laughed softly, and gently applied the salve across his back, then crossed to set the jar on a table by the bed. She climbed onto the bed and patted the blankets in invitation. Bashir crawled onto it and over her, forcing her to lie down beneath him.

He slid his hands up her body, pushing her caftan up as he did. Aysel writhed out of it, then lowered her hands to work at the cloth that wrapped her breasts. Bashir untied her salvar and tugged them off, and when he returned to her he ran his hands up her legs, the beautiful strong shape of them like a bellows on his building desire. The stitched wound where Rifat had stabbed her bloomed with an angry bruise.

"Doesn't it hurt?" Bashir said, to distract himself from the wrenching memory of seeing her in Rifat's grasp. He needed to connect to her, to erase any separation, to be whole and complete as he had only felt tangled with her. But if she was tired, or hurting, then he would hold her as they slept, and it would be enough.

"Not enough to matter right now." She pressed her fingers over his. The little vial of sand slipped against her skin to rest just below the hollow of her throat. Bashir lay down, his ribs cradled between her knees and thighs, as he lifted the vial. His breath left him in a soft sound of disbelief. Aysel lifted her head to look.

The sand in the vial had fused into a shard of glass.

"Your lightning must have." He turned the vial one way then the other.

"Hmm." Aysel gave him a sheepish look. "Perhaps we should go to the market and buy a supply of these vials."

"Some other time." Bashir shifted against her as he set the vial against her skin and kissed her throat. "For now, I know where you are."

He kissed her again, because there were no words to tell her how she made him feel. So, he showed her, breathing in her breath and her power, giving his in return, worshiping all that she was, and all that she made him. And when they lay quietly afterward, tangled together, her ear pressed to his chest as she listened to his heartbeat, Bashir understood she was a piece of him he had never realized was missing. Until she had made him whole.

THIRTY

T HE DOORS TO THE Hall of Chara'a stretched above them, ornate and golden. The wall around it, like many in the palace, bore intricately painted murals in vibrant color. These were the only ones Aysel had seen which depicted great acts of magic. In other places in the palace there had been battles, portraits, and agrarian scenes. To the left of the door a pictorial depiction of the raising of the Engeli stretched down the hall. Mathei examined it in dark amusement as Aysel tugged at her collar. The white brocade entari rose much higher against her throat than the caftans she normally wore. Dilara slapped at her hands.

"Stop it," her mother said. "You can manage to survive one day in formal clothes."

"Are you certain? I believe this is trying to choke me." Aysel gave her a mother a look of dismay. Dilara closed her eyes in exasperation. Beside her, Mathei adjusted his own clothes. They were charcoal, with silver embroidery of poppies. He was tall and handsome and perfectly composed, as though he could absolutely stand his ground in front of a score of Viziers.

Aysel looked down at her clothes, ones the Sultana had ordered made for her, apparently some time ago. The white overlaid with steely blue lattice represented the First House. Aysel had never worn blue, silver, or white, to stay as far away from hints of her power as possible. When she had looked in the mirror that morning, she had been surprised that the colors suited her. Her mother had wanted to braid her hair, but Aysel refused. So Dilara had worked oil through it instead, smoothing the frizzy mess into something like actual curls.

Although leaving her hair down was impractical in her day to day, doing so now felt like paying homage to the truth of herself, removing the mask fully. The storm inside her had not dissipated since the night she had fully unleashed it to save herself, Bashir, and the camp nearly five days before. And when she looked in the mirror it was there, in her eyes, waiting. Storms in her eyes the way death coiled in Makram's.

"This is quite revisionist." Mathei pointed to a painted figure with arms raised as he surveyed the newly birthed Engeli. "It is hard to look quite so triumphant when one is dead."

Before he could elaborate, the doors to the hall opened, revealing Samira. She bowed to them.

"The Sultana is ready for you," Samira said. Mathei linked his arm through Aysel's at the exact moment her stomach filled with nervous buzzing. Her apprehension must have shown on her face, because Samira gave her a warm smile. "You are not alone, Attiyeh Charah. Do not fear."

Aysel nodded. The Sultana was not feeding her to the wolves. She was not being exposed, as it would have been were she still in Sarkum. No. She was being freed, recognized. She was a Charah. Her power was to give and to receive. To protect. She was not subservient to the Council; they were subservient to her. Aysel nearly snorted trying to imagine herself barking orders to a gaggle of middle-aged men in frippery even she wouldn't wear. Soldiers who needed schooling? Yes. Politicians? Aysel would rather chew glass. Her mother would be better suited to taking this sort of men to task.

Her humor dissipated as they entered the chamber. Mathei led her behind Samira. The Hall of Chara'a was the most expansive room

Aysel had ever seen, large enough to swallow her family's entire estate in Al-Nimas. Round, with stone benches rising like stairs around the perimeter, currently occupied by thirty men. The Viziers of the Council. She recognized only the Sehzade, who sat near the floor, looking as uncomfortable in his finery as she did. As she looked at him he hooked a finger under the jade collar of his entari and frowned.

The entire floor depicted a sun that Aysel saw was in fact a stylized representation of the Wheel. Each ray was a spoke, the sandstone ending with a cap of semi-precious stone. The one nearest the Sehzade was turquoise, for the Second House. The First House bore white marble, for air. Aysel stared at it as Mathei led her toward the Sultana, where she stood at the center of the sun, a large, marble circle in the middle of the room.

Why was there an almost magnetic pull toward the Sultana? It was so minute, so subtle, toward this woman she barely knew. Perhaps because they were both mages of the First House? Was that what an air Charah's affinity felt like?

As she and Mathei stopped before the Sultana, Aysel became aware of the voices. Not physical voices, but ghosts and power, whispering from every direction at once. The sound of magic in flux. Only the strongest mages, only Chara'a, could speak with the voice of magic, created by the remembered power of all who had come before, and all who shared their House.

Aysel had never spoken in the flux of her power, and so never spoke with the voices of hundreds. Though she had heard Makram do so, and it had raised every hair on her skin. This room, apparently, held so much power that magic could speak here, though no one else did. Even Mathei, ever willing to shatter a somber moment, was silent.

Gloomy winter light barely bled through the windows that circled the room and a misty winter rain prevented her seeing any of the sights beyond them. The sheer scale of the chamber made Aysel feel too small, too insignificant for this, for the Circle.

"Welcome, Attiyeh Charah." The Sultana used a thread of power in her voice, so it echoed, and the magic that whispered all around them picked up the sound and sang the words to Aysel. Voices from long ago, from the magic they left behind, woven into the making of the chamber.

Aysel met the Sultana's gaze, and the Sultana gave her a cool smile. Beside her, sunken into the floor, a scepter had been placed, and in the claw-like grip of its wooden prongs sat a pale, milky stone that glowed faintly and gave off the distinct tinkling sound of faraway chimes or bells. Habit dictated she bow, but Mathei held her firmly as she was, upright, giving her a sidelong glance of disapproval.

"Honored members of the Council"—the Sultana gave Mathei a tiny nod of approval—"I would like to present Aysel Attiyeh, daughter of Elder Thoman Attiyeh of Al-Nimas, Lieutenant Commander of the Palace Guard, and Charah of the First House."

Continued silence greeted the Sultana's declaration. Aysel's heart beat a slow, thumping rhythm in her chest, so she could feel the pulse heavily in her neck. Someone cleared their throat, and it echoed against the stone benches and walls. Another shuffled their feet, their slippers scuffing against the stone.

"You may take your seat." The Sultana indicated the obsidian-tipped ray of the Wheel to Mathei. Dilara already sat on the lowest stone bench near it, enduring the glances of the men in the room with dignity and silence. All the benches near each spoke held at least two people, but Dilara was alone for the Sixth House. She shouldn't be alone. Thoman should be there. Aysel's throat clenched. He would be proud, to see this, to see her taking hold of her power. Just as he had been proud of Makram for choosing to go against Kinus, to rise to his own potential. He had always only wanted that for all of them…a chance to become the best they could be.

They both belonged there, next to Dilara and Mathei, children of the Sixth. A House reborn. Did Makram know Thoman thought of him as a son? That they all thought he belonged more to them than he ever had to Kinus? He would be sad he missed this.

Mathei squeezed Aysel's arm and crossed the room to join their mother.

As Mathei sat, a man stood from the bottom level, his crimson-red caftan and entari declaring him a fire mage, even if she couldn't make out his tiraz from where she stood. He looked directly at the Sultana with one salt-and-pepper eyebrow raised.

"What an interesting menagerie your Circle has attracted thus far, Sultana. A deposed prince of an enemy land and his pet spy." Gold and gems capped the staff he held, indicating station of some kind. This must be Behram Kadir, the Grand Vizier.

Aysel glanced out of the corners of her eyes at Mathei, who watched the Grand Vizier with interest. This was the first time she had ever seen the man, though she did not know if that was true of Mat. He sized up the Grand Vizier the same way she'd seen him study an opponent. Fire preceded destruction on the Wheel, so the Vizier was seated near to Mat and Dilara.

Kadir's son, the man who had seen Aysel at their estate, sat on the bench next to his father. When Aysel met his gaze, he cocked his head and mimed the action of whispering *shh*. Aysel raised an eyebrow and looked away. Bashir's reaction to Aysel meeting him indicated that Cemil Kadir was no friend. So his ambiguous response to finding her in their estate left her on edge with questions. Situations like that often led to blackmail, she'd seen it many times in Al-Nimas.

"Whatever they were before, Grand Vizier," the Sultana said, "they are mages of the Circle now. Their origins have no bearing on their Wheel-given power, and what that power is meant for." The Sultana looked at Aysel as she spoke, and Aysel knew the words were meant for her. Whatever she was before, had thought she was before, today she was something new. Her skin prickled, and her pulse sped, and her magic whispered.

"And what is their power meant for, Sultana? You are collecting a harem of powerful mages and have made it clear they will be under your control. The High Council is in place to balance the Sultan, and this Circle will only confuse the governing of Tamar."

"The High Council was created to stand in for the Circle of Chara'a when it failed after Omar Sabri the First erased an entire spoke of the Wheel, and in consequence its opposition."

The Sultana's voice was the coolest, and steadiest Aysel had ever heard it. The woman was unreadable before, but this new height of adamantine coldness made Aysel marvel.

"As his descendant, it is my duty to undo that injustice, and to balance the Wheel. The Circle has always served the people, Grand Vizier. This is obvious in the histories from the many, many times they defied orders by the Sultan. I would expect nothing less of this modern Circle."

Aysel did not direct her attention to the Grand Vizier, but watched him from the edge of her vision. His focus turned from the Sultana to her. Did he know she had stolen from him? Had his son told him? Surely he'd be fighting for her imprisonment if he did.

"And you, young lady, can you handle such responsibility? It is my understanding that you stole from the palace upon your arrival and led our esteemed guard commander on a merry chase around the city for days." Kadir's plastered-on smile was polite when Aysel looked at him, his gaze bland. "It is troubling to have a mage of the Circle that even our"—he paused to smile condescendingly—"ablest guards cannot control."

There were chuckles from several of the other Viziers. Aysel's temper and magic stirred, storm swirling higher into her awareness.

"I am a Charah of the First House, Grand Vizier. Even those with the most rudimentary understanding of magic should understand why that made it difficult for the guard commander, who you may not be aware is a Sival of the Fourth House, to subdue me." Aysel returned his bland smile. The Grand Vizier's eyebrow ticked upward, and his gaze hardened at the insult. "I believed my family was in danger, and I retrieved my weapons from the guard barracks, without harming anyone, so that I could protect them."

"So you could be a vigilante and pursue criminals through our city with no license? This is exactly what I feared. These powerful mages, unleashed on our city, with no governing body." He shook his head. "I am very concerned. We are all very concerned. I have heard you wield lightning. That is not even a power of the First House."

The other Viziers began to talk amongst themselves, unease disturbing the latent magic that coiled in the stones and air of the chamber. The Sultana glanced sidelong to Mathei, who stood.

"Forgive me, Grand Vizier, for interrupting. We have not met yet, but I have been appointed by the Sultana as Master of her Libraries in order to study the history of the Chara'a and the Circle," he said. Mat and his books, ever ready to come to her rescue. Aysel suppressed a smile.

"I see," the Grand Vizier said with a glance at the Sultana.

"The Sultana has ordered me to ensure that the Council is comfortable in their knowledge of the Circle, how it operates, and what each Charah is capable of," Mathei said. "Though much of this knowledge is lost to memory, it has been recorded, thankfully. From what I have researched, it seems that Chara'a belong to the House of their birth, but their powers have always manifested differently than other mages within that House because they bridge the gap between their House and the next."

Mathei continued, and the Grand Vizier's eyes glazed. "For example, every Charah born to the First House, in all of history, have been storm mages." That information was only a little surprising to Aysel. She had never heard of a storm mage until Rifat named her one. But in the moments of her death, she had seen all those who came before. Had seen her power manifested as storm and speed.

"Storm mage?" One of the other Viziers stood. He sat in the seats of the Fourth House hub, along with a handful of other Viziers. Aysel was disappointed that Bashir was absent, but they could not both be away from command.

"What does that mean?" Another rose from his seat a row above the Grand Vizier. The unease in the room tensed Aysel's muscles and made her want to reach for swords or knives that were not there. This would be over soon. It wasn't Al-Nimas, where she had been, in effect, shackled. Here, they were not a threat to her. Even the Grand Vizier, with fire so near the surface, could not touch her if she used her magic. She relaxed.

"You shall see her magic, as you saw it for Rahal Charah at his binding. Attiyeh Charah." The Sultana held her hand toward the First House spoke, indicating the wedge of white marble. Aysel hesitated, glanced to Mathei, who could not have looked more gleeful. She was his very own Charah experiment. The wry humor that inspired made her brave, and she moved to the spoke. The Sultana followed, bringing the scepter and stone with her. Aysel watched as she set the wooden end into a notch in the floor between the marble and the sandstone, then reseated the orb. The stone made Aysel restless, reminding her too strongly of Kadir's spelled lock.

"To be bound to the Circle, you must choose the manner in which you will serve it. Touch the stone."

Aysel bit her lip, staring at the pulsing orb. The Sultana put her hands against it. Aysel gingerly touched her fingers to it. It pulsed and swirled, like the faintest of mage orbs, but was cool to the touch, as a stone should be. It did, and didn't, feel as the lock had. She'd never felt anything like it, as though it pulsed with life. With magic. Was it enchanted?

"Do I just…say something?" Aysel whispered, but it carried, and someone snorted a laugh. The Sultana pressed her lips together against a smile and they met gazes as she lifted her hands to cover Aysel's and pressed them firmly against the moonstone.

At the contact, the Sultana's magic flared, sunlight that nearly blinded Aysel, spearing into her so that she gasped. The tiny twist in her own magic, that infinitesimal tug, uncoiled, wrapped Aysel in her power and the Sultana's and swept her into herself, away from the room and into the same void that had claimed her at her death. This time the darkness was not empty. Lights shone within it like a night sky lit with stars.

Each star was a pulse, power, magic. An air mage. Gossamer threads of glimmering magic ran from each point of light to Aysel, vibrating with energy given and received.

Lightning arced through the void and hundreds of her brethren glowed in answer.

First on the Wheel, youngest, and oldest. Speed, and thought. Calm, and yet, inside each bright twinkle of light, the spinning energy of the wind. Fuel to the storm. The twisting, savage heart of the First House, the end of the beginning, the lightning that fractures the darkness and wakes the world.

Aysel grinned into the nothingness and opened her eyes.

"I am the storm." The voices of the First House spoke with her, hundreds of hissing whispers, bolts of lightning, rumbles of thunder, her words repeated and echoed around the chamber. The proclamation unwrapped the cords of control from her power. The storm inside her billowed up, filling her with the electric, thundering feel of her magic. It cascaded over her skin, lighting her clothes with the lightning that scissored across her body. The Hall of Chara'a crackled with unleashed energy. Aysel's hair and the Sultana's wafted away from them. Blue traced across the floor around her, veining the marble with her power. Azure outlined the First House spoke and circled the center of the sun depicted behind the Sultana.

Her magic reached for the Sultana, arced through the moonstone, and latched. The Sultana's eyes narrowed, the muscles in her neck straining. Her bright power shone brighter, and she spoke in a voice like the hollow ring of a bell.

"Storm of the Circle. You are bound to its service, from this day, until your last."

Aysel's magic receded, though its touch in the air did not, the threat of lightning's heat keeping everyone else in the room still. And in her mind there lay a new place, a sense of the vast oblivion, within which lay a map lit with stars, every air mage that breathed. Font of the storm, brethren and kin.

The Sultana was one of them, though Aysel could not have pointed to which. The other woman's power felt different to Aysel now. Instead of something simply familiar and harmonious, it felt like a thread spun off from her, one that she could pull and use in the same way she might use her own magic.

"Attiyeh Charah, may I and my Council serve you, and through you our people, well." The Sultana bowed. Aysel saw how hard her hand gripped the scepter that held the orb. Did she imagine it glowed a degree more brightly now? The Viziers in the room stood, some more reluctantly than others, and took their cue from the Sultana, bowing.

Heat rose in Aysel's face. She had spent her life hiding. Now everyone in the room stared at her, focused on her. Saw her. It would be impossible to hide, ever again. She glanced at Mathei, and her mother. Mat winked at her, and Dilara blotted primly at the tears in her eyes.

"Unless the Council has any questions"—the Sultana pulled the scepter free of its place in the floor and returned it to the center of the room—"I would like to release Attiyeh Charah to her duties as Lieutenant Commander. She has an enemy to hunt." Her gaze rested firmly on Kadir, who, to his credit, remained utterly nonplussed. The man showed remarkable control for a fire mage. But then, that was to be expected from someone who was likely plotting the downfall of a Sultanate.

"Our questions can be directed at you, Efendim." The Grand Vizier turned slightly toward Aysel, revealing a hooked scar that marred his otherwise handsome face. "A pleasure to finally meet you, Attiyeh Charah. I am certain we will become better acquainted in the coming days." Even smiling, his gaze lit with fire and threat.

"I look forward to it, Grand Vizier."

When she looked to the doors, Bashir stood framed in them, his arms folded over his chest, his legs set slightly apart. A wall of granite and earth at her back the entire time. Aysel grinned at him. Mathei and their mother met Aysel at the doors, which Bashir opened for them.

"Your father would be so very proud," Dilara said, reaching to fluff Aysel's hair with one hand as she blotted at her own tears with a kerchief. Aysel guided her mother through the doors, and as Bashir shut them behind, the Hall of Chara'a erupted into chatter, barely muffled.

"Well," Mathei said, shaking his arms and rolling his shoulders as if preparing for a sparring match. "Won't this be fun?"

Dilara made a sound of disapproval.

Aysel grinned, and Bashir shook his head, putting one hand on her shoulder and one on Mathei's, urging them down the hall.

"You two are insane."

AYSEL TOOK A SIP from the wineskin before holding it out to Bashir. They'd brought the wine, but no cups. Bashir took the skin in turn before handing it back to Mathei. The three of them sat in a line on the hillside, watching the sun drop in unmeasurable increments toward the sea. Mathei passed the wineskin back to Bashir, who sat in the middle of them, so big Aysel had to lean all the way forward or back when she wanted to say something to Mat.

"Aysel tells me you hunt boar," Mathei said. A harrier circled above, giving a sharp keen as it banked away. The only sound besides their talking, and the distant hum of sea and city. Aysel liked it, it was just as she had imagined it would be.

"Just a summer tradition." Bashir stretched a leg out in front of him, kicking loose a rock that tumbled down the hill. "We started doing it in the fall, to put meat away for the winter for the neighborhood. But now it's just sport." Bashir tilted his chin up, watching the bird above them. "You can come if you want."

"No," Mathei said, "thank you."

"He only eats meat when he has to," Aysel supplied when Bashir appeared taken back by the speed of Mathei's answer. Bashir's eyebrows knit together as if he didn't understand. He probably didn't. Being picky about what one ate was certainly a privilege of the wealthy. Bashir had probably known much leaner times than Mathei could comprehend.

"I am steeped in death by the very nature of my power," Mathei tried to explain, but Bashir's expression clouded even more.

"The plants you eat are dead…aren't they?"

Aysel cupped a hand over her mouth to hide her smile at Bashir's bemusement.

"Quite less violently, I should think," Mathei said, taking another drink from the skin. "It doesn't matter. I can eat meat, I just choose not to when possible."

"Makram eats meat."

Mathei exhaled hard, his nostrils flaring, and gave Aysel a wide-eyed, beseeching look.

"This is nice, isn't it?" Aysel bumped into Bashir's side, and he reflexively draped a heavy arm around her, pulling her into his side.

His warmth was a relief from the damp chill in the air and on the ground.

"I haven't done this in…" He squinted. "Too long."

"In summer, I want to swim in the ocean," Aysel proclaimed.

"Some shark will think you're a minnow," Mathei said. Aysel frowned at him. Bashir shifted, his expression pinched. Mathei caught the look, and a slow grin narrowed his eyes.

"Not a swimmer?" he teased.

"I can swim," Bashir said, slowly. Aysel remembered this same conversation from one of their first meetings. "Just…I don't like the deep water."

"You *do* sink!" Aysel giggled. Bashir's arm looped around her neck and he dragged her into his lap, glaring fiercely at her. She continued laughing, and Mathei snorted.

"Do not laugh at his misfortune, Aysel. It isn't his fault he is more boulder than man."

"Why do all your helpful comments sound more like insults?" Bashir bellyached, flopping backwards onto the hillside. He spread his arms and closed his eyes.

"Because they are," Mathei said, helpfully. Bashir chuckled at that, and bent his legs up to offer Aysel a cozy place to nestle as she turned her attention back to the sea. The sun sat half submerged, casting indigo shadow and flame across the ocean. Cold crept in as the light waned, and the evening promised to be a chilly one. She closed her eyes, took a deep breath and let it go. When she opened them again, Mathei was looking at her, complex emotions hooding his eyes.

"This is nice," she said. They were not in the exact spot where she had observed the city that night, wondering what it would feel like to do just as she was at that moment. But it was the same hillside, the same view of Narfour, her new home, and the experience as settling as she had imagined it would be. "Next time we'll invite Samira. I've never seen her not attending the Sultana."

"You won't," Bashir said without opening his eyes.

"I thought not," Mathei mused to neither of them in particular. Aysel frowned at him. Scuffing his boot against the hillside, he set the wineskin in the spot he'd cleared. "That one is hiding in her work, I think."

"Mmm," Bashir agreed.

"What are you talking about?" Aysel looked from one to the other. Bashir's eyes opened, but he stared up at the sky, unmoving, for a long time. Mathei didn't offer anything either. "You can't just dangle bits like that and not tell me," she demanded.

"Our dear boulder appears to know more than me." Mathei paused when Bashir snapped an irritated look on him. "I will simply tell you that I once observed lovely Samira and the Grand Vizier's son in close proximity and cannot name a time I have seen more repressed heat between two people. And I am not even speaking of their magic."

"They were betrothed," Bashir said. Aysel could tell he hated it by his stony tone. She could understand that. Samira seemed to be a good person, and Cemil…did not.

"And, what happened?"

"The Grand Vizier happened," Bashir said. "When Samira accepted a place at the Sultana's side when we all left the University, he decided she was beneath Cemil, and nulled the betrothal."

"Cemil simply bowed to that?" Mathei scoffed. "How intriguingly spineless."

"He does whatever the Grand Vizier tells him to do."

"Why doesn't the Sultana get rid of her Grand Vizier?" Aysel asked. "She isn't Queen yet, but she is Regent."

"You know things are never that simple," Mathei said. "Regent is just a title. Until the Council aligns with her, she is in danger of them rising against her. They are, as Makram has told me, beginning to shift. She even has another in mind for Kadir's position." Mathei plucked a long blade of dead grass, eyeing Bashir's closed eyes. "But until the majority favors her, moving against the Grand Vizier risks starting a civil war." Mathei dangled the grass over Bashir's face, tickling his brow with it.

Without opening his eyes, Bashir shoved Mathei with one hand, nearly sending him bottom over top down the hill. Mathei cackled and Bashir swiped the blade of grass then threw it at him.

"I hate politics," Aysel said, smiling at the two of them. Already they were like brothers. Brothers who didn't like each other. But they would settle into it, she was certain.

"Who does she have in mind for Grand Vizier?" Bashir said after a moment of watching Mathei for a counterattack.

"Yavuz Pasha. He is the next most influential in the Council, but he enjoys the loyalty of the valley provinces, not the coastal, as Kadir does. It has always been the money and the merchants that control empires, and so Yavuz's influence with the more agrarian Viziers is less important than Kadir's ownership of commerce. She must make subtle shifts, not great leaps, or risk upsetting the balance."

"While also preparing for war," Aysel said, thinking of Makram and the others. Mathei inclined his head. "I'll find something to help her."

Mathei grimaced, and looked out to the sea.

Bashir sat up, slinging his arms around Aysel and resting his chin on top of her head. She had a sense she'd troubled him with her declaration, but she settled into the affection with relish.

"You two disgust me," Mathei muttered. Aysel felt the shift of Bashir's jaw as he grinned, and she knew he heard the same fondness in Mat's voice that she did.

THIRTY-ONE

YSEL SLID DOWN THE steep curve of the dome that capped the Sultan's receiving hall, landing on the main hallway roof. She followed it west, toward the Sultan's garden, where the Sultana had commanded she meet her.

Several servants, water mages working on a precariously high mountain of laundry that appeared to be bedlinens, spotted her. Aysel waved. One timidly returned it, looking to her comrades, whose expressions ranged from disbelief to disapproval. Most of those who lived and worked in the palace were used to Aysel's unconventional thoroughfare. She'd found, once she had mastered the layout, that the tops of the buildings were much easier and faster for her to traverse than the halls.

There were often so many people moving about the palace that attempting to go anywhere within its environs was like trying to swim upstream. Spring was many turns away, and though it had not snowed once, there was a deep, damp chill in the air that necessitated ferace, and in the mornings, mittens. Aysel had hers slung around her neck, now that the day, and her hands, had warmed.

Aysel found the Sultana standing in the Sultan's garden with her arm twined through that of an elderly man. The physician, Ceylik, and a steward were near at hand, chatting together, though both kept an eye on the man. The Sultana had summoned her, so she could only assume she was meant to come as quickly as possible, even if it meant interrupting the two of them.

Aysel dropped from the roof above them to the path they walked on, which seemed to both startle and delight the man.

"Sultanim," the Sultana said with a smile that said the man's chuckle pleased her, "I would like to introduce you to Attiyeh Charah, First of the Circle."

Aysel went to her knees, though she was not supposed to. It would feel too wrong to force a Sultan to bow to her. The ground was wet with mud, but she leaned forward to touch her hands and forehead to it anyway.

"Why is she kneeling?" he said, blinking in bemusement. "She'll soil her clothes."

"To pay you respect, Sultanim. Attiyeh Charah, please stand."

Aysel wiped her sleeve across her forehead and brushed her hands off on her salvar as she stood. "I am honored to meet you, Sultan Efendim."

"Ah, ah yes. You are the woman my daughter and her betrothed have told me about. He kneels too, you know."

Aysel slid her gaze to the Sultana, then back, smiling the best she could in the grip of her confusion. He did not appear extremely old—in fact, despite his unsteady posture and slightly hunched shoulders, he looked healthy. His gaze wandered to the random details of their surroundings. He did not seem possessed of all his faculties.

"Sultanim, I wish to speak with Attiyeh Charah. May I come see you after?" The Sultana glanced back at the steward, who hurried forward to grip the Sultan's other arm.

"I will check with my daughter, to see if I have time. She knows my schedule," he said over his shoulder with another chuckle as he shuffled away. The Sultana watched him for a moment, her brow hosting a single furrow. Then she turned back to Aysel.

"He does not know you?" Aysel asked. She could not imagine her father speaking of her as if she were not his daughter. Her chest ached at the thought.

The Sultana smoothed her fingers across her brow. "Some days. Makram is able to temporarily lift his confusion, but it grows harder for him and lasts for a shorter duration each time. Mathei cannot seem to perform the same working, his magic does not cross the divide between the Sixth and First House, into the mind, as Makram's does."

If it caused her sorrow, she did not let it show. Not as she had to Makram, that day Aysel saw them in this same spot. Aysel looked up into the branches of a tree above. It appeared dead.

"I am sorry." She gestured lamely in the direction the Sultan had gone.

"The Wheel turns, and gives and takes in equal measure."

Aysel studied the woman in silence for a moment. People were not her strength. They were Mathei's, but even she could see the Sultana tried to use pragmatism to cover up her pain. At least she seemed to allow herself to feel truthfully with Makram, if she did not think she could with anyone else.

"While I do not know what it is to rule in a man's place, I do know something of the difficulty of not quite fitting where you wish to be."

The Sultana smiled then, a conspiratorial expression that buoyed Aysel. "I am certain you do. I am also certain you understand, as I do, the occasional power in being underestimated."

"Yes," Aysel agreed. The glass vial that hung around her neck, newly filled with sand, warmed against her skin. Aysel turned to see Bashir striding toward them. He bowed to them both, and the Sultana tapped her ear. Bashir cast a dampening spell, though Aysel only knew that because of the change of pressure in her ears.

"Thank you," the Sultana said. "I summoned you here because I have a new assignment for our lieutenant commander."

"Not Kadir?" Aysel asked.

The Sultana shook her head. "He is too aware of your capabilities now for you to move against him. I want proof of the enchantment you found in his house, but he is too wary now. Give him time to relax, to think we are too busy elsewhere to notice what he is doing."

"How do you intend to do that, Sultana? You all but accused him in the hall when you said she has enemies to hunt." Bashir's rumbling voice made Aysel's skin warm in pleasure and she looked at him from the corners of her eyes. His mouth quivered in an attempt not to smile at her attention.

The Sultana looked at Aysel. "Your brother has been studying what records exist of the exodus of mages during and after the Sundering War, hoping to find some evidence that there may be enclaves of Third House mages outside of Tamar."

If she hadn't been so busy with her new role in the guard, or ever listened to Mathei when he was talking about books, this revelation might not be news to her. "Did he find any?"

"What he found is both troubling in its clarity and concerning for its vagueness," the Sultana said. Bashir frowned at Aysel. "It seems that some of the mages who fled Tamar continued on beyond Sarkum, and they may have scattered descendants."

"That is good, isn't it?" Aysel asked.

"If it is true. That is what you are going to find out for me."

Bashir tensed, his hand settling on Aysel's shoulder as if he meant to yank her toward him, to deny the Sultana whatever she wanted.

Aysel reached up to lay her fingers over his. She did not wish to be separated from him either. But they were linked, in heart and magic, and she would always return to him.

As if he knew her thoughts, he released a held breath.

The Sultana witnessed the touch and silent exchange, but did not comment. "This task is twofold. You will verify the existence of these possible mages, and it will take you away from Kadir's scrutiny for a time."

"Where is it you'd like me to go?"

The Sultana looked at Bashir for a moment, then settled her gaze back on Aysel. "Do you speak Republic Trade?" she asked flatly.

The Republic.

"Some," Aysel admitted, excited and frightened. Part of what Sarkum considered a classical education and that her mother demanded of her and Mathei, though his, of course, was better. Bashir's hand tightened on her shoulder. "I promised Makram I would not leave you alone," she said.

"I will not be alone," the Sultana said. "And too much hinges on this for either of us to sit around waiting for him to return. I cannot command a mage of the Circle, but I can implore you. Without a full Circle we stand little chance against the Republic and its machines. Go there. If there are creation mages, find them. Tell me what you can of the military and their capabilities."

"And if she finds them?" Bashir's hand flexed.

"Simply report to me what you find. Their recruitment is a job I have in mind for another." Her smile was enigmatic and once again, conspiratorial. Aysel returned it. Whatever plot the Sultana had up her sleeve, it seemed interesting.

"They murder mages there." Bashir's voice edged toward a snarl.

"But she has spent a lifetime hiding her magic. She is a spy by training and one of the most powerful mages in the world. She is uniquely suited to accomplish this undertaking as no one else is."

Aysel looked from the Sultana to Bashir. The Sultana glanced to her room, which was only a few paces away. "I will give you a moment to discuss it." She left them.

Bashir took Aysel by the shoulders. She could see in his eyes how badly he wanted to tell her not to go. Instead of speaking, he touched his fingers to the vial, which lay beneath her clothes.

"I do not want to go," Aysel said.

"But you must," he replied. "Run fast, Little Storm, and return to me."

"Big Storm." She smiled, her eyes stinging. "And I will run faster than I ever have."

Epilogue

Their horses shifted beneath them, snorted breath billowing white in the bitter air. The hill Makram and Tareck had climbed rose sharply over the rolling steppes. Below and about a league away, a herd of antelope searched through the snow for graze. Makram propped his arm and the falcon perched on it against his saddle. He reached between his horse and Tareck's to tug the hood from the cliff eagle perched on Tareck's arm. She blinked, and Tareck scratched the back of her neck with a gloved finger. Sabah, Makram's falcon, twisted her covered head this way and that, shifting her weight in eagerness.

"I'm simply saying I felt it," Makram continued the thread of their conversation. He didn't want to talk about dreams and portents with the men. They were already skittish. Tareck grunted acknowledgment as he shifted in the saddle to adjust his arm against its support crutch, humming softly to the eagle, Ece. She twisted her head to look at him, then out over the landscape. The smaller goshawks and falcons couldn't go after prey as big as antelope. But Ece, the only golden cliff eagle to survive Kinus' burning of the enclosures in Saa'ra, was well past the age when she should have been released back to the wild and was monstrous.

Ece leapt from Tareck's arm in uncanny quiet, the only sound the first brush of her wings through the air. Sabah gave a chirrup of discontent, crouching as though she might fly, but Makram soothed her with a low sound.

"Felt it how?" Tareck shook his arm to relax the muscles. They'd been discussing Makram waking in the middle of the night.

"Like I was on fire. All I saw was lightning."

The eagle circled high before moving over the herd. Tareck watched as he spoke. "What do you think it means?"

"I do not know. Perhaps that Aysel accepted the Circle." Makram tried not to let his more troubling thoughts surface, but Tareck spoke them out loud.

"You don't think something happened to her?"

It had been two small turns since Naime's last missive, an irregular gap in her correspondence. He didn't want to ponder all the things that could mean. He wanted this respite from the travel, and the worry, and the skirmishes. He wanted to hunt and offer the weary, dejected men something more appetizing than lentils, rice, and root vegetables. Even the vegetables would be gone soon. What stores had been put away before the Blight were dwindling, and even those farmers capable of growing sturdier roots in the winter were hardly able to harvest anything, and certainly didn't want to give it up to soldiers when they could barely feed themselves.

This Blight was going to end the war with his brother before it even began, and cripple them for the Republic to sweep up with a handful of men.

Ece continued to circle, patiently surveying the herd, almost too high to be seen.

"Did Erol have the Blight samples ready to be sent back?" Makram asked.

"Mmm," Tareck confirmed, wiping at his winter raw nose and cheeks. They were all miserable in the cold, but the Tamar mages suffered more. They were not accustomed to it. Erol was fairly good at fostering morale, but even his cheerful attitude was beginning to wane.

Ece suddenly dropped, knocking a smaller doe into a tumble. She pinned the beast with her weight. The rest of the herd bolted, and Tareck grinned, reining his horse around and urging it down the hillside toward Ece.

Makram unfastened his falcon's hood and she ruffled, cast him a judgmental glance, and then took flight. By the time she was circling above them, Tareck had finished off the doe with his dagger and loaded her over his horse's back.

Makram watched Sabah as she dove, striking like lightning. She plucked something from the sky and landed with it, too far away to see, and took off again a few moments later. Makram frowned, watching as she drew closer. Another bird. She landed on his uplifted arm, a mangled pigeon dangling from her talons.

"You shouldn't look so proud," Makram murmured, as she tugged the bird from her grasp. Something small fell away. Makram leaned over the side, peering at the item in the snow. It was the tiny harness and message pack used to outfit pigeons as messengers. Straps to fit over the wings and a small cloth slot for housing a single, tiny message. "That's my good girl," he said. Sabah trained one black eye on him then turned her head away in disdain. Or at least Makram imagined it was disdain. He dismounted and tossed the pigeon on the ground, letting her pick at it while he retrieved the miniscule harness.

Tareck arrived, glancing from Sabah to Makram. "Trying to outdo you again, my girl," he said to Ece.

Makram dug his pinkie into the pouch and withdrew a bit of paper. He unfolded it. This was not one of the pigeons they had brought to communicate with Narfour. And Naime couldn't send pigeons to them.

"Anything interesting?" Tareck asked.

"It's gibberish," Makram said. A cipher. Only carefully printed script and nothing else to identify the sender or intended recipient.

And he hadn't seen the pigeon flying, so had no idea which way it was headed. They were east of Jaramin, too far east for the pigeon to travel to or from Al-Nimas. Unless it had been blown off course by the storm the night before.

Makram tucked the missive into his ferace and turned his attention west, toward the Engeli. Scouts from the Dar Afir mountains had reported that the Republic did have camps north of the foothills. It appeared to be a border contingent, not an invading force, but it was growing, swiftly. Makram had no assets to spare to travel farther into the Republic to glean information beyond that. His most useful spies were in Narfour. He should have brought Mathei, at least.

If that pigeon was a message to or from the Republic, then they'd have to considerably speed their efforts to consolidate his supporters and their available troops. Makram scratched at the short beard that had grown from his neglect of shaving. Shaving a face raw from winter wind was not an endeavor he cared to waste time and energy on. He wondered what Naime would think of it, but turned his mind away immediately. He missed her too fiercely to concentrate on her now.

"Let's take this and Ece's prize back to camp. We'll see what Thoman can make of this." Makram mounted, resettling Sabah on his arm and replacing her hood. The camp, which grew and shrank as arrivals passed through on their way to Jaramin, was a candle-mark's ride away. They'd scared away most game any closer than that. Makram had chosen to stage his forces at Jaramin, and had a forward camp out in the wilderness that was easier to move as he conducted his recruitments. The number of supporters had been encouraging, at first. Then he realized the magnitude of the Blight's effects. Winter crops that would have replaced the summer and fall harvests when they dwindled had been almost completely decimated. Now he had thousands to feed and very little to feed them with.

The camp was set up in concentric circles, with his and Thoman's tents in the center, along with the larger tent they used as a command center. Makram turned his horse over to a soldier when he arrived and Tareck took Sabah and Ece back to their mews.

Makram ducked into the central tent. Thoman and Erol stood with a sipahi captain in a circle, chatting quietly. The Elder looked up when Makram entered, and his face registered Makram's unease. Thoman dismissed the sipahi, who paused to bow to Makram on his way out.

"We were just discussing sending these samples." Thoman gestured to the table designed to stand at. Maps and correspondence were spread across it, and two small, stoppered glass bottles. Beside them lay a pouch with leaves peeking out. "It'll have to be a rider."

"I have something else to send, unless you can decipher it." Makram handed the bit of paper to Thoman.

Erol looked in curiosity.

"Where did you get this?" Thoman unfolded the paper.

"Sabah, trying to outdo Ece." Makram folded his arms. Erol gave a low whistle.

"Smart bird," Thoman said.

"Don't let Tareck hear you say that," Erol snickered. "He'll defend Ece's honor to the death. She's practically his daughter."

Makram tried to grin, but it was hard to find his humor these days. They all found their peace in different ways. Tareck focused on Ece when he could, Makram devoted too many hours to planning, Thoman was constantly in a state of advising, him or the captains. Erol somehow maintained his mischievous humor.

Thoman drew his middle finger up and down the bridge of his nose as he reread the script. "These aren't Sultanate words, even if they are in code. Not an alphabet I know at all." He handed the paper to Erol, who examined it for a moment before folding it and setting it beside the Blight samples.

"So either a language we do not know, or something invented simply for this purpose." Makram would bet on the latter. "Will Mat be able to?"

"One of mine will, I think. Dilara is quite good with puzzles. It would be more helpful if we could find a second one to compare. Especially if we knew where it was sent from or to."

"As long as Sabah thinks it's a competition, she'll do her best," Makram said dryly.

Out in the camp, cheers went up, followed by laughs and exclamations. Tareck had apparently unveiled Ece's kill, and Makram could just imagine her preening at the cheers that she would certainly interpret as her due. She was not their only hunting bird, but she was the largest, and the only eagle. And didn't she know it. The camp was too large for one antelope doe to make a meal, but even a bit of meat would be good for morale.

"Go," Makram said. "I'll be there shortly."

When the tent was quiet and empty, Makram took a sheet from the stack of paper on the table, and picked up an ink bottle. Three braziers burned in the tent for warmth, but the ink was viscous anyway. He rolled it between his palms as he contemplated what to write. Writing his heart onto the page was what he wished to do, but could not, as he did not know who else would read the letter. So when the ink was warm enough to wet the quill, he wrote about the samples of Blight, the plan going forward in bare detail, leaving out locations and timing, and the weather.

At the end he wrote, "from dusk, to the dawn."

His dawn, his light.

THE END

Author's Note

THANK YOU FOR READING. We're picking up steam, but there is so much more to come. Stay with me! The Wheel spins to the Second House, water, where dark secrets hide and hard truths are reflected.

What's next?

Keep reading for a sneak peek of book three, *Siren & Scion*.

I would love it if you left a review on Amazon. Your honest review helps other readers know what to expect, and it gives my books visibility—which means I can keep writing them! That's good all around, right?

Want more?

Website
jdevansbooks.com

Facebook
https://www.facebook.com/jdevansauthor

Twitter
https://twitter.com/jdevansbooks

Instagram
https://www.instagram.com/jdevansbooks

Want to be first to know about upcoming releases, extras, and all the fun times? Sign up for the newsletter!

https://www.subscribepage.com/motw

Acknowledgements

THIS BOOK IS FINISHED and in your hands because my husband believed in me. He believed in me enough to say "of course" when I asked for day after day to sit in a coffee shop and write while he took care of our son. He said "of course" when he spent all week working his own job and I asked him on the weekend to take baby boy to the playground so I could have a few extra hours. He said "of course" when he started a new, big, complicated job, and we moved across the country and rented a tiny house and started house hunting and I still asked for more and more time. He believed I'd finally found what I wanted to do. What I was meant to do. And he wanted it for me almost more than I did. When I felt selfish for taking so much time, he believed. And when I finally let him read my first book…he gushed. So if you ever want to know why it is important to me to write men who are strong and supportive and generally wonderful…now you know my inspiration.

A book is not a book without words that make sense, and Michelle Morgan makes certain my tendency to ramble is kept in check. Somehow she just knows where I want these to be, and she has an incredibly deft touch at steering them in that direction without erasing me.

I truly believe that no one would notice these books without the art of Tatiana Anor on the cover. I knew I wanted black and white covers, and I have always loved ink drawings. But this woman…I cannot gush enough. So incredibly talented.

Eric C. Wilder works magic. I swear it. Of course the art is stunning. But it is not a book cover. And the man is genius. I am eternally grateful for his insight and keen eye.

Terry Roy took my ramblings about setting and made a book that transports you. The inside is as beautiful as the outside, it sings to my heart to look at her work, and I hope you appreciate the work she's done to the interior.

Siren & Scion

SNEAK PEEK

AMARA'S HEART TUMBLED IN her breast as they moved away from the platform and she slid her feet, shuffling more than walking, because the little gaps between the boards of the bridge made her feel they would snap beneath her. If she looked down she could see the ground, far, far below. He took another step backward, coaxing her forward, and her hands seized against his arms.

She let her gaze roam his face and down the smooth, bronzed column of his neck. He needed a shave, or a purposeful beard, to look less unkempt. Though the halfway point he was at now, with stubble just long enough to no longer be sharp from the razor, suited him.

"Dodging the law must grow tiresome." Amara could not bring herself to look to see how much farther they had to go. Instead she focused on him, the fine details of his face. She had always enjoyed those distinctions in men, the little things that made them unique, like works of art in her mind. Whether they were beautiful, or masculine, or something altogether different, there were always intricacies worth looking at.

Cassian had many. She could not help but compare him to Ihsan, who was handsome bordering on beautiful, a Sabri trait. But Ihsan was cold like his magic, isolated by his past, and Amara could see that beneath his swagger and despite his secrets, Cassian was a man of warmth and laughter.

She had never been so drawn to stare at Ihsan.

"Do you know you have a way of looking at a man that makes him feel he is the only one you've ever seen?" he said quietly, moving backward in steady steps. Of course she knew. The way one looked at another human defined their relationship from the moment it was formed, whether that look was anger, disdain, attraction, or fear. A water mage was infinitely capable of changing and adapting to the people around them, and that, coupled with what Amara had learned just to survive the harem, made her perfectly aware of even her minutest glance.

Except for this moment, when she had merely been looking.

"You are the only man I can see right now," she said, because they were so close and he dominated her vision.

"Yes, but you were looking." He grinned, the dimple deepening, and she lifted her gaze to his eyes again. The bruised one was uncomfortable to look at, but not the worst wound she had ever remained stoic in the face of.

"I did not mean to imply I wasn't," Amara said. There was no reason to pretend she hadn't been. She'd never felt there was reason to hide attraction from someone. Nothing but discontent came from hiding it, and if both parties were amenable, telling the truth resulted in pleasure for both. "I think you know you are handsome."

His slight smile suggested her candor amused him. "I think some women find me so, but you have not seemed impressed by me thus far."

"You are rude." They had made the halfway point, where the narrow wooden bridge hung lowest. Her heart thumped at the realization and she clung tighter to his arms. "And little more than a criminal. These are not generally traits I am impressed by."

"I am more than a criminal." He glanced behind himself as he stepped from the bridge onto the platform. "Though not much more."

"Yes. How does someone with your particularly uninspiring resume find themselves a shepherd of stolen lives?"

His answer was a smile and a tiny shrug. She might have dug more, but they reached the end of the bridge and the bigger platform. He did not protest her continued grip on him as he backed across it. He stopped when they were closer to the others.

She released her hands, and realized how tightly she'd been grasping him, and that it must have been uncomfortable for him.

Amara filled her lungs with air, something she had been unable to do before crossing the bridge. The others had all ascended, and were gathered near the center of the structure. The platform here was expansive, encircling dozens of trees, as big as parts of the pier in Haenna. She couldn't quite see over the edge without a pointed effort. Djar stood at the perimeter of the group, watching Cassian and her with narrowed eyes and folded arms.

"Could I trouble you to let your man know he doesn't need to decapitate me?" Cassian asked.

"Perhaps," she said. He frowned. "In trade for me doing so, you and I will never speak of this"—she gestured broadly toward the bridge—"again."

"Fair enough."

Amara lifted her hand to Djar, and he turned his attention back to the twins, Bek and Kiya.

"Thank you," she said, grudgingly.

"Are you all right now?" Cassian asked.

Amara nodded. This platform did not sway, and with some distance between her and the edge she was settled enough to move around. Was it because he was kind that he spent his time and money freeing slaves? She had never met anyone that kind. Doing good just for goodness' sake.

"Are we meant to sleep up here?" she asked as they moved toward the others. One of the Suloi worked at gathering the ladders, folding them on top of the platform to prevent anyone else coming up them, which explained why the ladders were not fixed.

If she hadn't been so consumed with panic she might have come up with that on her own.

"In those." Cassian pointed to a series of lean-tos, constructed of boards, away from the edge but with their backs to it. Bek and Kiya were busy setting bedding into four of them, and Amara took another calming breath. She could do that. With something at her back, much of her fear would be soothed.

"Since you are in such a benevolent mood," Amara said, "perhaps you might educate me on how to broach the topic of assistance with Danel and his men." She nodded toward the Pathfinder.

Peio, Cassian's Suloi friend, sat with two of the other men, tossing dice back and forth. Kiya joined, plopping herself between two of them and folding her legs in front of her. Danel sat in the center of the largest section of the platform, a great circle pierced through by half a dozen trees. He leaned against one, the leg Amara thought was the injured one stretched out in front of him, watching everyone with a keen eye. She could tell something troubled him, from the furrow in his brow and the tense set of his jaw and shoulders.

"They want something, or we would still be tied up in that clearing," Cassian said. She saw him watching Danel as well. "But I do not know from which of us they want it. Let him bring up what he wants first, and then perhaps you can bargain for what you wish." He paused, looking at her sidelong. "Which is?"

"I told you when we met." Amara met his eyes. "I want mages."

ABOUT THE AUTHOR

J. D. Evans writes fantasy and science fiction romance. After earning her degree in linguistics, J. D. served a decade as an army officer. She once spent her hours putting together briefings for helicopter pilots and generals. Now she writes stories, tends to a tiny human, knits, sews badly, gardens, and cultivates Pinterest Fails. After a stint in Beirut, J. D. fell in love with the Levant, which inspired the setting for her debut series, *Mages of the Wheel*.

Originally hailing from Montana, J. D. now resides in North Carolina with her husband, small human almost-clone, aging canine, and too many stories in her head.